THE HIDING

"On its face, *The Hiding* is an enthralling adventure of demons, spirits, witches and their hunters. Within its secret rooms, it's an examination of identity and community and the very real magic therein."
—Rae Knowles, author of *The Stradivarius* & *Merciless Waters*

"A delightful weave of supernatural mystery and family drama, balanced against a tale of found family and pain."
—Alexander James, author of *The Woodkin*

"A surreal supernatural murder mystery through the streets of an alternate York, woven with chilling prose, throat-rending creatures, and a found family to triumph over all."
—S. A. MacLean author of *The Phoenix Keeper*

THE HIDING

by Alethea Lyons

Copyright 2023 © Alethea Lyons

This book is a work of fiction. All of the characters, organizations, and events portrayed in this story are either products of the author's imagination or are used fictitiously. Any resemblance to actual events or locales or persons, living or dead, is entirely coincidental.

All rights reserved. No part of this publication may be reproduced in any form or by any means without the express written permission of the publisher, except in the case of brief excerpts in critical reviews or articles.

All opinions expressed by characters in relation to magic and religion are their personal opinions and are subject to the rules of their universe, which are different from the rules of ours. No characters are scholars in this area, and all are simply coming from a place of trying to do good.

Edited by: MJ Pankey
Proofed and formatted by: Stephanie Ellis
Cover illustration and design by: Elizabeth Leggett

First Edition: March 2024

ISBN (paperback): 978-1-957537-83-2
ISBN (ebook): 978-1-957537-82-5
Library of Congress Control Number: 2024932440

BRIGIDS GATE PRESS
Overland Park, Kansas

www.brigidsgatepress.com

Printed in the United States of America

*To my husband, Christopher.
Without your support and your faith in me,
this dream could never have become reality.*

Content warnings are provided at the end of this book

Never scream, never tell,
Never taste, never smell,
Ears stone deaf, eyes blind shut,
Fingers broken, heartstrings cut.

What is hidden from sense,
Will be hidden from mind,
Forgotten, unknowing,
Forever entwined.

Chapter One

York was famous for its ghosts, but Harper had seen too many demons to fear rumours and trickery. Yet, as mist trickled down the cobbled street of the Shambles, curled up the sides of wonky buildings and flowed over her feet, that certainty wavered. The hairs on her bare arms prickled despite the lingering summer warmth. She didn't believe in ghosts, but she did believe in human evil.

She rubbed the back of her neck, casting a sideways glance at two men in long overcoats who leant against the railing of Saint Crux Church. No badges, no uniforms, but an air of threat so thick it polluted the air more than the noxious fumes of passing cars.

Queen's Guard.

They were always there, guarding the entrance to the most haunted street in England, but it seemed recently, there had been more sullen strangers in long, tan coats prowling the ginnels of York. One of the men returned her look, his eyes narrowing. His thumb tapped against the end of a black baton hanging from his waist.

Harper turned away to study the window of the shop opposite. She rolled her shoulders, resisting the urge to check the reflection and see if he still watched her. Tourists and shoppers scurried around her. The old glass warped their reflections, lengthened faces, rippled bodies, as though Harper observed them through water. The crowd hurried past the two men and didn't slow until they were under the twisted eaves of the Shambles shops.

Squaring her shoulders, Harper turned away from the Guardsmen and entered the Shambles. The uneven paving made each footstep unique as she wove through the milling crowds. Her sneakers curved over the cobbles in the centre of the row and each crack in the flagstone pavement grabbed at her toes. It was tempting to close her eyes, to walk it blind and see if her soles would recognise the well-worn path.

The further she progressed down the Shambles, the further back in time she fell. Buildings arched over the path like lovers leaning in to kiss. Hanging baskets of flowers brightened the monochrome Tudor architecture. Warped wooden signs adorned the walls. Harper stooped to see through panes barely larger than her head. Each shop dazzled, selling everything from jewellery to paper, from antiques to modern art.

The twisting ginnels and alleyways branching from the street promised portals to dark adventures in other realms. Magic seemed to fizz like static in the air. Shoppers disappeared around corners, or possibly were whisked off to faraway queendoms.

Harper could almost hear Grace's sceptical disapproval. York city centre was night-safe. The Veil was strong, and the Queen's Guard lurked at either end of the supposedly 'magical' street. There was nothing special about it being the autumnal equinox. She wouldn't meet anything supernatural in the Shambles. The arcane atmosphere was merely a ruse to bring in tourists. *Then again, I'm here …*

Harper's head twitched with the urge to look back at the two Guardsmen, even though she wouldn't be able to see them so far up the street.

The constant tinkle of shop bells reminded Harper of fairy laughter, high-pitched and secretive, almost drowned out by the chatter of tourists and the rustle of bags. Harper paused outside a shop of glittering figurines. She tugged her braid over her shoulder, worrying loose hairs, as she watched the door out of the corner of her eye. *Maybe if I catch the light right, I'll see them.* The thought brought a smile to her face. She flicked her hair away again, its red ribbon fluttering in the breeze.

The scent of sugar wafted down from the sweet shop: on the edge of saccharine, cut through with hibiscus and bergamot from the tea shop. Their windows stood open, inviting passers-by to sample the fragrant delights. Signs in Gothic fonts advertised wares from forbidden lands: green tea from Japan and American candy. Harper rubbed her hands together, remembering why she came to the Shambles.

She was here for a purpose, one even Grace couldn't object to. With a frisson of glee stirring deep in her chest, Harper dodged a family with sugar-hyped children to head into the fudge shop.

Intent on keeping the bright blues and sunny yellows of her patchwork jacket away from sticky-fingered kids, Harper didn't notice the rise in the pavement. Her foot twisted beneath her. She half-turned, half-stumbled, books scattering from her satchel. A strong hand gripped her elbow, an arm secured her waist. Harper looked up into concerned eyes, green as fir trees and as deep as the forest. The wind blew hair the colour of bark across them.

"Got your balance now?" the stranger asked.

When Harper nodded, the man released her and took a step back. He held his arms toward her as though waiting for her to fall again or shielding her from the flow of people.

She gave him a shy smile as she held out her hand. "I'm Harper Ashbury, she/her. Thanks for catching me."

"Theodore Edwards, he/him, at your service, Ms. Ashbury." The warmth of his hand sent tingles up her arm. As she took a step toward him, pain lanced up her leg and she inhaled sharply.

His narrowed eyes flicked up and down. "Sit on this step for a sec. Let me take a look at your ankle."

"It's fine. Really. I stepped funny—"

"It'll only take a moment. Don't worry, I'm a nurse."

Hand on her elbow, he guided her to the uneven stone steps of a shop entrance, seeming not to care about the patrons clattering in and out. The heat rose in Harper's cheeks as he pushed back the hem of her skirt and probed her right ankle with gentle fingers.

"Honestly, Mr. Edwards. I'm fine." A twisted ankle was nothing. Pain took her mind back to family holidays hunting el mohán, mula retinta, and other supernaturals. Even training with Grace's two older brothers carried the risk of greater injury than this. Fingers lingered on her ankle, warm, delicate. The flush in her face deepened and Harper wiggled her foot away, tugging her ankle-length skirt back down.

The young man started, then gave a small shrug. "Please, call me Theo. I don't think you've done any serious damage, but you should probably stay off it for a while. Are you going far? I've got a little time to spare if you need help."

"Thanks. You've been more than helpful already." Harper leant toward the fallen book closest to her, hoping he wouldn't see how red her cheeks were. He beat her to it. Their fingers brushed, and heat surged through her again. She yanked her hand back, too flustered to stop him from retrieving her other fallen tomes.

"*The Woman at the Well. Exorcisms and Other Evictions. The Divination of John Dee.*" As he read each title, the frown on his face deepened. Harper snatched the books out of his hands and stuffed them back in her satchel. She fumbled the buckle as she cinched it shut. Out of the corner of her eye, she watched Theo, certain he'd run. People came to the Shambles for a small thrill of the otherworldly, not to discuss exorcisms and illegal magic, despite the uptick in rumours of supernatural incursions. Upon discovering her job and Grace's family's notoriety as demonhunters, most people fled.

If he bolted for the safety of the Queen's Guard, she could justify having the books but probably not without a trip to the police precinct and a call to the archbishop. The Guard weren't always willing to accept the credentials of those who worked for the Council of Faiths.

Theo's eyes glazed over, shifting back and forth, but he made no move to leave. As he leant closer, eyes focused on hers, Harper wasn't sure if her heart throbbed from fear or because of the tingle in her lips.

"I can explain." She grabbed his arm. Muscle quivered through the thin cotton.

"Explain?" There was an edge of panic to his voice. Familiar. Harper's stomach sank. It always went like this.

"I work at the cathedral. I'm an archivist there. I help them keep dangerous books out of the public eye and research ways to protect people from the supernatural." Harper pulled a business card out of her bag and tucked it into his hand. On one side it showed the arms of the Archbishop of York, two keys forming an 'X' under a golden cross. On the other side was Grace's family crest, a blooming orchid with a halo.

Her rescuer studied it, flipping it between his fingers. "De Santos? I thought you said your name was Ashbury."

Harper winced at his accusatory tone. So much for asking if she could buy him a drink. "They're my foster family. They took me in after an accident," she explained. It was close enough to the truth. Reality would have sent him scurrying to the Guard for sure. "Grace, my foster sister that is, she and I don't fight supernaturals like the rest of the family. We're very safe, I promise. She's a vet. I research books and stuff. I was here to buy her some fudge. It's been a tough week. A normal tough week. Not a demon tough week." Harper was still clinging to his shirt, rambling. She let go and twisted her fingers through her hair instead. "I better be going. I'm going to be late for work. Thanks again for your help."

She retreated up the Shambles, teeth gritted against the pain in her ankle. She wanted to get away. The fudge could wait. Theo still wore the dazed expression Harper had seen too frequently in her life.

"Mind where you're walking."

The voice thudded in her ears, cold and unyielding as a tombstone.

Cold cascaded over Harper like she'd stepped through a waterfall. She spun and was confronted with a Dickensian apparition. A tall, black hat; a gaunt face; a swirling cloak; skin with the pallor of a corpse. It was the most vivid vision to afflict her in years. She gasped and icy water poured into her mouth, flooded her lungs, stopped her heart. Clutching her chest, she doubled over, fighting for air. The world seemed to tip and slide. Lack of oxygen scattered her thoughts as they fought the visceral omen. The soft flesh inside her throat was so cold it burned. Airways closed. Panic swelled in her chest, tight and unforgiving.

"Never scream…"

A tangled medley of disembodied whispers, all saying the same two words, over and over.

"Never scream…"

This time there was no one to save her as she lurched backwards. She clawed at her throat, desperate for air. A stolen scream needled like a thousand millipedes crawling under her skin. Harper fell against the stone wall behind her, the impact knocking the last breath from her body. It shook loose the ice blocking her throat, and she could inhale again. She gulped down air. As the cold trickled from her body, the spectre solidified into a real man, his back to her as he posed for tourists and hawked his ghost tours. His funereal appearance was nothing more than a costume.

"Just a ghostwalker," she muttered. A normal man, making a living. Not a ghost. Not a spirit.

Despite the reassuring thought, Harper couldn't quite believe it. The pent-up scream set her teeth on edge, static at the base of her skull. It had been years since she'd experienced anything stronger than the odd flicker of a vision during her waking hours. Not since the exorcism. There was screaming then too. Her own and someone else's; she never worked out whose. She scrunched her eyes closed, burying the memory deep. The banished screams of the exorcism mingled with the waiting scream in her head. Their soundwaves clashed, then cancelled each other out. The remnants of the exorcism still worked within her, cleansing, scorching.

Harper wrapped her trembling fingers around the strap of her bag, grasped to her chest like a shield. If it was a vision, a particularly visceral vision, she had no idea what it meant. As she shuffled out of the

Shambles, Harper cast a last look back down the street. The young man who helped her was nowhere to be seen. The ghostwalkers menaced a teenage girl who squeaked in fake terror. At the end of the street were two men who could have been clones of the ones at the other end of the Shambles by Saint Crux. Harper hurried on before she drew their attention, headed for the safety of the cathedral.

As she limped away, a breeze wafted out from the Shambles.

"Never scream …"

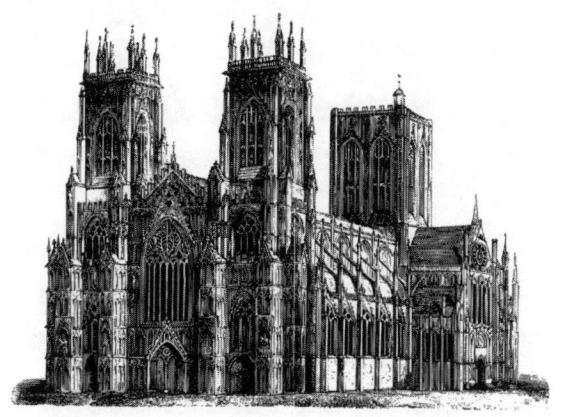

Chapter Two

As the sun set, Usa watched a crowd of humans gather at the foot of Lendal Bridge. A medieval watchtower loomed over them, blanketing them in shadow. Its twin on the opposite bank could barely be seen through the mist. Usa had already been old when the towers were built, hauled up the river, brick by brick. A chain had been strung between them, black and glistening as it dipped into the water. It had caused her people such anguish as they dashed against it, denied entry to the city by human spite and technology.

Even now, hundreds of years later, humans patrolled the great wall surrounding York, always vigilant against incursion from those they called 'supernatural.' They came armed with fire and iron, dill and mint, silver crucifixes and blood red hamsa. The core materials changed little over the centuries, honed by each generation to destroy.

In her head, a cacophony of voices urged her on.

Usa, hide us.

Usa, protect us.

Usa, save us.

The pleas of her people echoed through her like the patter of rain wearing down stone. It was time. Mabon. The quarter day. The autumnal equinox. A time when light and dark balanced. A time when the Veil was so thin, the faerie realm lapped at the shores of the human world. A time of power.

Usa ... Usa ...

Usa feared no human. She had been there long before they walked this land, and she would remain when their civilisation was no more than dust on the wind. The same could not be said for those she was sworn to protect.

It wasn't bullets or protective herbs Usa's kin feared. It wasn't the religious symbols of loving gods. They feared hearts hardened by prejudice, unwilling to accept that what was different was not necessarily evil. They feared the eyes, always watching atop those towers, which forced them into hiding. They feared the whispered stories teaching subsequent generations of humans to hate.

One such human spoke now. He led the pack who congregated in the shadow of Lendal Tower. In a small pool of light, hounded by darkness all around, he stood without fear.

He was tall, over a head taller than anyone else in the group, his stovepipe hat making him like a giant of old. He was as lean and pale as the crescent moon, his garments black as the river. Humans called his kind 'ghostwalkers,' and Usa often observed them leading groups of frightened sheep like these.

The ghostwalkers told the history of York, of the many deaths that plagued it and the myriad ghosts said to haunt it still. Their compelling tone and fanciful language dragged many a gasp and scream from the throats of the humans who followed them. The ghostwalkers spread terror and ensured humans rarely went out after sunset or ventured into the mists. Their tales kept humans vigilant and quick to turn on anything deemed 'abnormal.'

Tonight, he told a tale Usa hadn't heard before. His voice filled her mind with images, and she could almost remember the ill-fated day he described. It was the tale of a witch. To humans, these aberrant people were as much to be despised as any of Usa's kin. She had seen many of them during the Purge, strung out in a line from the cathedral down to the river. Hanged by the minions of the human queen just as she commanded the slaughter of Usa's kin.

The ghostwalker's voice was crackling and low, a smouldering ember in the dark night, and the humans huddled close to him. "The witch stood before him, her bloody wand pointed unerringly toward his heart, and the lord knew he was about to die. In fear of his eternal soul, he snatched the wand from her hand. Snapping it in twain, he threw it in the river and her spell was broken.

"She screamed, a roar of no true maiden but the demonic beast she really was. Her nails stretched into claws, her teeth like fangs as she lunged for him. He tried to draw his sword, but it was too late. Both witch and lord tumbled into the river, locked together in a deathly parody of their lovemaking the night before.

"Hours later, in that fleeting time 'twixt night and day, a fisherman rowed out hoping for an early catch. He saw a bedraggled young man standing under the bridge, searching the ground forlornly. Up close, the fisherman noted the richness of the young man's clothes and the bejewelled sword at his hip.

"'Have you lost something?' the fisherman called.

"'I have lost that which was most dear to me,' the young man replied, his voice full of mourning. 'All I was is gone; a piece of my soul lost to the devil.'

"Then the young man looked up. Where once his eyes had been, now rested only pools of darkness. Then the sun hit his face and he vanished. The fisherman went home as fast as he was able and told all he knew of the horror he had witnessed.

"As to the witch, she was never seen in York again. Did her demonic master preserve her to serve him anew in some other ill-fated town? Did the river swallow her whole, never to see daylight again? I cannot say.

"Many have seen the lord's ghost, although he has spoken to none since the fisherman. The doomed young man still walks the banks of the Ouse, forever searching for the piece of his soul stolen by the devil and by a witch."

A chill hung in the air as the ghostwalker finished his tale, and the mist thickened. Usa lingered in its embrace, hidden from human sight, had any looked. But their wide eyes remained riveted on the ghostwalker, their mouths agape.

The ghostwalker removed his hat and bowed low. "Do not linger," he cautioned his audience. "The night draws close and the mists rise. Death still walks the streets of York. Ghosts, witches, and demons watch from the shadows. No matter how many lies those in power tell, nowhere is truly night-safe. Be careful it is not your tale I tell on future nights. The bridge here is the fastest way back to your cars. Do not stray from the path, for where the ghosts do not walk, the Queen's Guard surely will, and innocence is harder to prove than guilt." His eyes flicked to the tower where a solitary light bobbed in the darkness as its owner paced. Always watching.

With a final bow, the ghostwalker stepped back, his dark cloak swirling around him as he left the sanctuary of the streetlight. The crowd dispersed like leaves falling on water. Most entwined together, swept away in clumps. Soon, they would clog into metal contraptions and disappear beyond Usa's ken.

When the other humans vanished, the sounds of their voices muffled by stone and fog, the ghostwalker left the sanctuary of the shadow and headed downstream. His head turned, back and forth like an oar, but he did not see her. For millennia, Usa lived among the people of York and none ever truly saw her. Her brethren, less powerful than she, were not so fortunate. Hunted, tortured, killed by humans. Humans who listened to stories like this one and believed all the Folk evil.

Usa studied the ghostwalker as he passed. For many years, she watched him wander this same path home. Different stories on different nights, but always the same off-key tune grated in his throat. The mists parted before him, and Usa trailed in his wake.

The calls of her kin grew more insistent with every step.

Usa, hide us.

Usa, protect us.

Usa, save us.

Their plaintive cries drove her on. They were hers. She ruled them. She served them. The duty of the Hiding fell to her. The honour. The shame.

Usa, hide us.

She followed the ghostwalker into the deepening night, her eyes hard and clear as diamonds. Frost filled her. She was a harpoon, a knife, nothing more. A small piece of a ritual more powerful than the ocean.

As Usa approached him, the ghostwalker's steps faltered and he turned to look behind. The world was silent save for his humming and the soft lap of waves against the shore. His gaze swept over her without perceiving. He tugged his cloak tighter around him as he resumed his walk, his pace quickened, head bowed. When he reached the end of the path, he paused again to search the surrounding trees. His eyes passed through Usa as though she were glass.

Usa, protect us.

She stretched out her hand to touch him, then hesitated. The voices cascaded through her, but she stopped, centimetres from his trembling throat. This wasn't natural.

He hurried on again, not taking the bridge to safety as she expected. Instead, he descended the few steps to stand at the edge of the path, where the Foss paid its tribute and flowed into the Ouse. As he watched the twin rivers, he was one with the night, as though he became less human, more of her Folk.

Usa, save us.

But he was not of the Folk. He was a threat. Usa hardened herself, cold and unfeeling as Morimaru, mockingly called 'the North Sea' by irreverent humans. She would do her duty.

The moment she touched him, he froze as though ice bloomed. Reality bent to her will and her hand phased through his skin, his spine, the cartilage of his neck. His larynx and vocal cords vibrated as he struggled to speak. The life drained out of him and into her. A scream died in his throat.

Usa, save us.

She wrenched her hand free and his lifeless husk fell to the ground.

The Hiding's first victim. Her first victim.

Usa stood over him, eyes dark as the new moon, face still as a doll's. The only colour was the bloody mess of cartilage and muscle dripping from her closed fist.

The crumpled body at her feet held no more value. Taking his organs had been like fishing, the skin as undisturbed as water closing over a sinking hook. She had done what was demanded of her.

Yet she could not leave.

She crouched next to him to arrange his body as she had seen humans arranged before, their corpses laid along this same path, row by row by row, driven into the water to drown, rejected and pushed back to the shore in death.

For a while, she observed the soulless form, still as a prayer. Then she washed her hands in the river and released the stolen vocal cords into the dark water.

She stayed by his side until the sun rose, then forsook her human form and retreated as the bells rang and humans stirred. When they found his shell, they screamed and water leaked down their faces. Then more shouting, sirens wailing, more humans. Other humans shied away from the newcomers, whose auras buzzed with dark energy. They took him away, the man she killed.

None who came saw her for what she truly was.

As the sun rose high, she withdrew, until all that remained was the lapping of the river against the shore and a whisper dissipating on the autumn breeze.

"Never scream ..."

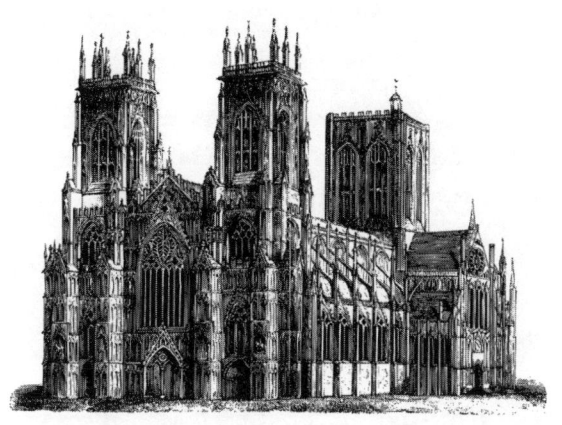

Chapter Three

The bells of Saint Peter's Cathedral resonated through the streets of York, destroying the stillness and scattering the mists. The sun peeked over the buildings; its feeble autumn rays cool yet bright enough to give the Ouse a dress of golden sequins.

Harper leant against the railing on Lendal Bridge to watch the spectacle and listen to the bells. Her breath hung on the air and faint patches of ice glistened on the river's surface. She liked being out as the sun came up. It always gave her a strange sense of déjà vu, as if it were important she watch the sunrise. Harper put it down to her general fear of the dark: it was a relief to witness the sunrise first-hand.

She glanced up at Lendal Tower but couldn't see the Guards lurking there. Curfew was only a suggestion, a recommendation on how to stay safe. It wasn't actually illegal to be out before dawn, just ill-advised, even with the tightened security of the last couple of days. With a ghostwalker's corpse, vocal cords gone but no trauma and no cause of death, most people paid heed. Through the ginnels and snickelways of York, one word echoed: witchcraft. Harper had recognised the dead man's photo splashed across the front page of the *Yorkshire Post*. The same ghostwalker she bumped into in the Shambles. Dead. Killed by some arcane mystery.

She raised a hand to her throat. The burning cold still haunted her dreams. Guilt settled in her chest, heavy and prickling. Such precise visions happened so rarely since the exorcism. Usually, they stayed confined to her dreams, surreal and vague. She'd been sure it was nothing; a panic attack or a remembrance brought on by his ghostly craft. Though the tabloids had printed increasingly outlandish stories over the last six months, she hadn't believed a supernatural attack was possible. If the rumours were true, the archbishop of York would've known, would've told her and Grace. Wouldn't he?

"Could I have saved him?"

Myriad voices answered her whispered question, none of them human: wind through trees, waves on the shore, the patter of rain, the scurrying of tiny, clawed feet.

"Never scream ..."

Harper clapped her hands over her ears. The voices roiled within her: nauseating, angry, yet full of sorrow. Panting, bent over the railing, she fought the voices until they diminished. One last, intimate whisper in her ear remained, then dissipated like mist on a summer's morning.

"Never scream ..."

She was left shaking, her eyes wet and burning, her mouth dry. Her ears strained, but everything was silent save for her shuddering breaths and the throbbing drumbeat of her heart. She rested her elbows on the bridge as she rubbed her temples.

The voice had been haunting her for days. Most nights she woke from dreams, trying to scream, hands clawing at her throat, yet all that came out was a raspy moan. A blessing, in a way. Grace deserved to sleep peacefully.

In the distance, the lingering music of a muezzin reciting the adhan called Muslims to prayer just as Great Peter, the largest bell in the cathedral, called their sister Christians. The beauty of the two melodies exorcised the voices and calmed her. The twin calls, proclaiming the end of night and the safety of dawn, had been heard each morning at sunrise for longer than living memory.

Harper turned her back on the river and followed the toll of Great Peter the last couple of blocks to the cathedral. Its ancient walls had offered solace and sanctuary for centuries. She paused for a moment, breathless before a majesty which never dimmed.

Saint Peter's Cathedral towered over her, yellow sandstone glowing like the sunrise. Saints and grotesques alike peered down from lofty perches. Each statue was protected from the rain by arches of delicate stone spindles. Twin towers overlooked an open square to the west, their crowns almost pierced the clouds. An arched window, three stories tall, was held in place by curving leaves of stone filigree. Intricate as lace, eternally enduring, mysterious yet comforting, the iconic cathedral was a microcosm of the resplendent city of York.

Harper nodded a greeting to Deacon Paul as he let her in the south transept door. Although there were laypeople who guarded the cathedral during the night and who guided visitors during the day, only a member of the clergy could declare the streets safe. Once they had, they unlocked the great oak doors that kept the darkness at bay. Inside, candles still glittered, filling the air with stars.

"You are out very early, Ms. Ashbury," the deacon intoned, his jaw set as he inspected her with beady eyes.

"The archbishop's work is never done." Harper gave him a bright smile, her statement true but not strictly relevant.

Deacon Paul's eyebrow raised from its usual high arch. Grace always joked he would one day ratchet it up so high it would become part of his bowl-cut hair. He left the door open and retreated into the church's safe embrace. As she followed, Harper dipped her hand in the Holy Water font without looking and made the sign of the cross. The deacon resumed his duties: preparing the building for the day, snuffing candles as he walked the same circuit he walked every morning. He sang a low, sonorous chant. Coming from a commoner, the Latin words and mystic tone might have meant witchcraft. Coming from a priest, they meant safety and reverence.

Despite the small whisper of cynicism, Harper was caught up in the ritual. It was a joy to watch the cathedral transform and sunlight pour through stained glass to chase away the shadows of night. There was comfort in the repetition, in practices older than any human, observed by Saint Peter's through the generations.

The deacon finished extinguishing the candles in the south transept, then disappeared around the corner into the nave. In his wake, Harper trailed a hand through the beam of coloured light streaming down from the rose window, imagining the women of many eras who had done so before her. The brightness, coupled with the smoke of snuffed out candles, made her eyes sting.

An inexplicable chill prickled her skin as she rounded the corner, shattering the meditative calm of a moment before. Though light flooded the cathedral, colour bled away to leave only the grey of gloom and mist. Shadows lurked behind the deacon. They crawled up the walls and slithered over the flagstones to clutch at his robes. The wet, earthy scent of a forest filled the air. Harper's breath caught in her throat, half a choke, half a sob.

She pinched her arm, hard enough to elicit a gasp and make her eyes water. In the seconds it took her to wipe them clear, the shadows disappeared. Streams of stained-glass sunrays danced around him. The scent of myrrh hung heavy in the air, warm and bitter. *Funereal.*

Trying to dispel her apprehension, Harper took a deep breath. The woody scent evoked memories: Father De Santos's stirring sermons on sleepy Sunday mornings, the joyous hymns of Easter, standing vigil for Grace on her eighteenth birthday.

Unable to fully shake her disquiet, Harper approached the main altar, its candles flickering a welcome. She stood in silence for a moment, her hands clasped in front of her as she stared at the flame; its heat so close caused a frisson of ice to run through her. The back of her neck itched like someone was watching, but when she glanced around, no one was nearby. She gazed up at the towering gold cross, in pride of place on the altar.

"I don't know if my presence here means You accept what I am, or if it just means You're not real," she said in a rush. "If You *are* real, are You hiding me? Did You bring me here to save the ghostwalker? Is that why You took me from my family? I don't know what to do. Something is changing. I can feel it smouldering in my bones. My nightmares are getting worse and I wasn't even asleep in the Shambles the other day. Why send me these torments when I can't do anything to help?"

The Great East Window soared over her, the top pane almost invisible from this angle—the figure of God. During the last restoration, she'd scaled the scaffolding to look Him in the eyes. She'd traced the scrolling words accompanying the image: *'Ego sum Alpha et Omega.'* For the parishioners, the words gave comfort. To a witch, they could be taken as a warning: no matter where they fled, He would always be there at the end.

Her eyes travelled downwards, searching for a more concrete answer in the window's bright majesty. After years of working at the cathedral, each scene was intimately familiar. The saints and heavenly company. Below them, scenes from the Old Testament. Creation. The fall of Babylon. David and Goliath. At the bottom, the apocalypse. A multi-headed beast warred with the saints, sharp teeth raked their flesh as it attempted to devour them, their bodies crushed under its long-clawed paws. Next to it, an angel poured blood into a river. Dead fish rose to its darkening surface. Another angel poured out fire upon the earth and people writhed on the ground as they burned. If God was answering her prayer, the window made His answer no clearer to her.

Turning away from the images, she tried to overcome her lingering unease as she made her way down into the crypt. Goosebumps covered her skin as she descended underground. Stone closed over her head, the only illumination flickering candle flame. The light shone through a cobalt glass cross to stretch the image across the floor of the vault and over the tomb of Saint William.

As she hurried past the tomb, Harper drew an ornate, iron key from her satchel. The tiny teeth formed a pattern far more complex than any house key. The scrollwork at the other end twisted around a bleeding book. It turned easily in the lock on the spindly gates at the north corner of the crypt.

Harper relished the mystery and the privilege of having access to hidden areas. When she first came to work there, fresh out of university, many resented her presence. Cathedral archivist was not an easy job to obtain. There were no set numbers, no 'one in, one out,' attending interviews and supplying CVs. It was invitation only. Most of the archivists were members of the clergy, or laity with an active history in the church and some significant achievement to bring them to the archbishop's attention. Harper's request for the position was seen as an affront by those who waited years for the opportunity. More astounding to them was the fact the archbishop granted it.

She'd not gone far before her path was blocked by another door, this one solid iron without decoration or keyhole. She placed her hand over a scanner beside it, then inserted a thin card into a slot below. It looked like a delicate bookmark of filigree gold, not dissimilar to the ones sold in the cathedral gift shop, but far more intricate. At one end was an image of the cathedral, at the other a cross.

After a moment, the card slid back out and there was a faint click as the catch released. Beyond the open door, a black well of nothing threatened to consume her. Each day the test to pass into the archives was different. Usually, it was a simple knowledge test or proving one was a normal human by drinking something said to poison supernaturals. Sometimes it was trial by combat. Harper liked those days—the archives were always quieter, the older librarians keeping away, almost as if they did not trust faith alone to guarantee a win.

The darkness ahead of her did not bode well. Since the ghostwalker's death, security had heightened, the tests more complex than usual, the potential consequences more severe. Stories circulated amongst the archivists of the last time the cathedral was on high alert and of those sad souls who entered the Hall of Testing and were never heard from again.

Some archivists refused to come into the city centre at all, but rumours said the archbishop sent his own people to test those reluctant to come in. It was tempting to turn around and spend the day scouring the city for arcana instead of descending to the archives, but backing down would not be looked upon favourably. Especially not for someone trained by demonhunters.

The thought of the endless mockery pressured Harper to take the first step into the darkness. All light cut off as the door slid closed behind her.

Chapter Four

"Breathe, Harper, breathe." Her heart hammered against her sternum as her eyes strained against the darkness. Her hand crept to her pocket. She curled her fingers tight into the fabric of her panelled skirt instead. The torch on her phone wouldn't work here. This area was a test of faith. If she fumbled around blindly, she was likely to be pricked by a spike covered with tranquiliser. If she wandered forward without waiting for instruction, she was as likely to fall as to find solid ground. Or at least, so she had been told. Harper thought it prudent not to test. She held her nerve, teeth gritted painfully as she waited for the trial to be over.

After an eternal minute or so, a voice came over an invisible speaker. A tear trickled down her cheek. The voice was feminine, but unremarkable.

"Psalm 23 verse 4."

An easy start and a timely reminder.

"Even though I walk through the valley of the shadow of death, I will fear no evil, for You are with me; Your rod and Your staff, they comfort me," she quoted.

"Proceed in the name of the Trinity," the voice intoned. Harper took three steps forward then stopped to await the next instruction.

"Matthew 6 verse 9."

"Our Father in heaven, hallowed be Your name …" Another easy one but a common test for a witch. Her mind was wandering. Harper focused until she finished the prayer. Being a witch wouldn't make her say it wrong, but not paying attention could. *Maybe that's the point?*

"Proceed with the children of Israel," the voice instructed. Harper took twelve steps forward. Cold seeped into her toes as water lapped at her shoes. Cold as the grave. Cold as death.

"Matthew 14 verses 22 to 33."

Too long and complex for a quote. An action? When the answer did not immediately come to her, Harper trembled. *Stop it. These tests don't really check if you're a witch. You know that.* She thought back to long Sunday afternoons spent in study under Father De Santos's watchful eye, the astringent smell of myrrh still fresh in her memory. She was concentrating so hard, she didn't notice the water rising until it trickled into her shoes to wiggle over her feet like worms over a corpse. The wet hem of her skirt clutched at her ankles like frigid fingers dragging over her skin. Harper bit back a sob, her fists clenched so tight her nails left imprints in her palms. The water squelched as she rocked back on her heels.

Water. Of course. A test of faith. Walk on water. Jesus invited Peter to walk on water and he stepped out of the boat and did not sink, standing on the waves.

Eyes still closed, Harper took a confident step forward.

Her foot met something solid—ground or water, she had no idea and didn't care.

"Admittance granted, Harper Ashbury," the voice said. A door clicked open, allowing a thin stream of light into the chamber.

Harper hurried toward it, not looking down lest she see only water and sink like Saint Peter. She dragged the solid wooden door open. The bright light beyond hurt her eyes but she revelled in it.

She stumbled to an alcove nearby to fill a cup from the drinking fountain with shaking hands. When her breathing returned to normal, she sank to the floor and sipped the cold spring water. Although she did this most days, she never got used to the rare occasions when the trial was in the dark. The shadows following the deacon played on her mind and dripped a shiver down her back. When the shakes were mostly gone, she continued onwards.

There were doorways carved into the stone walls of the corridor, far enough apart to hold vast chambers beyond. Each arch was themed with a biblical story, from the fall of Adam to the resurrection of Christ. None of the rooms bore any sign or number and each was protected by a stout iron lock and an iris scanner.

The passage appeared to terminate only a few doorways down, but after half a mile, the end was no closer. An almost imperceptible curve clockwise and downwards hid the entrance far behind. Harper trailed her hand over sandstone walls and oaken doors, comfortingly real after the horror of the testing. As well as being bound by iron, each door was adorned with sage, dill, and mint. Harper never understood why superstition held spirits and supernaturals could be kept at bay by the fragrant bundles. Certainly, they never stopped her entering any of the shops or houses sporting similar deterrents.

Harper counted under her breath until she reached the seventeenth door. She ran a finger along iron bands, which flowed over the wood like ivy leaves reclaiming it. Iron studs bored through the door, a last protection should the cathedral fall and the Hall of Testing fail. Overkill, in Harper's opinion.

The light of the iris scanner pierced her retina and gave the illusion of veins and arteries floating around her, as if she stood in the centre of a plasma ball. A key thicker than her finger, etched with a cross, opened the mundane lock with a rasping clunk.

On the other side of the door were long rows of library desks. Most were empty, but a couple showed signs of work with books and artefacts left out overnight. Harper wrinkled her nose in irritation. *What if they were damaged? Or someone else needed them?*

This library was the first of seven vaults in the archives. Well, seven Harper knew about anyway. No doubt there were more. The First was the general reading and study area. The Second held books and artefacts nominally known to the Queen's Guard, although they were never allowed entry. The Third ... The Third contained things most people would prefer to believe never existed. Historical accounts of things commonly held to only be myth, photographs and drawings of supernatural creatures not seen in over one hundred years, stories of Queen's Guard actions so extreme they were never released to the public. Harper's clearance granted access up to the Fifth Vault, although she could have select contents from the Sixth and Seventh brought to her.

She passed through the first few vaults quickly, nodding a greeting to co-workers in yesterday's rumpled clothes. She didn't stop until she reached the Fourth Vault, the home of books and artefacts relating to rituals, spells, and other realms but without details on how to perform the magic. Those books were kept far deeper in the archives than Harper had access. As she passed through the Fourth Vault, she came across a familiar figure, half-barricaded behind a precarious pile of books. Harper wasn't surprised to see him there so early. She would be more surprised if he ever left.

"Good morning, Alfred." As usual, he'd forgotten to turn on the lights, his nose practically touching the book he was reading as he strained to see the page by the light of a single desk lamp. Harper flicked on the main lights and repeated her greeting louder.

He peered up at her, his eyes containing the confusion of being abruptly ripped from one world to another. He adjusted his glasses, his pupils contracting as he blinked up at her, the bright light of the room taking him by surprise.

"Good morning," Harper said a third time, wondering briefly why all her friends were so odd. Alfred was one of the few people Harper counted as a real friend, mostly because he didn't notice anything that wasn't in a book.

Alfred shook his head as he ran a hand through mousey brown hair. "I almost had it. I was so close," he muttered, almost to himself.

Harper, accustomed to her co-worker's lack of focus, cleared herself space to perch on the corner of the desk while he collected himself.

"What did you almost have?" she prompted when he didn't continue.

"The answer," he replied as if it were the most obvious thing in the world.

Harper resisted the urge to sigh loudly. That and eye-rolling were common side effects of conversations with Alfred. Although he appeared only a few years older than her estimated twenty-five years, he possessed the air of someone who was nearing a century. He never seemed to do anything other than work. This he did with the distracted grace of a man obsessed with books and with little regard for anything else.

"What was the question, Alfred?" Harper asked patiently.

"If Elizabeth Fitzhenry had not been executed but had instead gone into hiding, where would her crown now be laid to rest and what effect would this have had on the production of apples in southwest England?"

Harper ran the sentence through her head a couple of times. She had nothing.

"I'm sorry I interrupted," she said. "I'll let you get back to work. I just need to know if the volume I brought in last Friday has been categorised yet."

"Sixth Vault," Alfred replied, already back to thumbing through pages.

"Thanks."

He didn't reply, completely absorbed in his book. Harper wasn't entirely sure what Alfred's job at the cathedral was, or what it had to do with the second daughter of Henry the Eighth, or apples.

With a shrug, she turned to the door leading to the Fifth Vault. There was a whir from deep within the stone walls as the door processed her card. A panel slid back and Harper leant forward to let it scan her eyes.

Access granted, Fifth Vault, Harper Ashbury.

The script hurried across the screen, then the panel slid back into place. Harper opened the door and entered her normal 'office' as she thought of it, for it was rare for anyone else to hang around the Fifth Vault. It was more of an in-between place than a real vault, being only used for studying select redacted materials from the vaults beyond and not housing any itself.

This room was much smaller than the previous rooms. Where they were lined with never-ending bookcases and glass cabinets of artefacts and relics, the Fifth Vault was a single room, barely five metres across. The stone slabs of the floor were set in a spiral, flowing outward from a mosaic of a Celtic cross set in the centre of the circular room. Harper skirted the cross and dropped her bag on the sole desk as she passed. A small computer screen sat atop an index card cabinet on the far side of the room. Harper tapped in her login code followed by the details of the book she wanted.

The screen glowed green and one of the drawers silently slid open. It contained a tablet, its screen displaying the cover of Lang's *Red Fairy Book*. When it was safe to do so, all new books were scanned. It ensured the texts were preserved and meant junior staff could view heavily redacted versions.

Harper placed the tablet on the workbenches, took out her writing pad and pencil, and settled down to read. It was a rare edition, one said to possess a twist to one of the tales. She'd brought a common copy of the book from home, and she began the laborious task of comparing each of the thirty-seven stories, but she couldn't focus. The whispers still stirred in the back of her mind and her thoughts kept returning to the dead ghostwalker.

After rereading the same paragraph several times, Harper slammed her book closed and returned the tablet to the index cabinet. There were plenty of documented accounts of supernaturals mimicking human voices. However, she couldn't recall any tales of a creature having to steal those screams from a human.

She skimmed the index cards, requested anything associated with sound, and staggered back to her desk carrying the books. One turned out to be an obscure book of death omens that featured fetches; creatures with the ability to copy a specific human's form and voice. It also had banshees, or bean sidhe, wailing women whose cries were only heard by those about to die. Unless they got their screams by stealing others', Harper doubted it helped.

She flicked through a book on Greek mythology, barely looking at the well-known tales, until a heading jumped out at her. *'Hesychia, daimona of silence and rest. Handmaiden of Hypnos, god of sleep.'*

The pairing of silence and sleep would certainly explain her nightmares. Harper settled into her chair to read in earnest.

She was absorbed in the book when a loud whoosh disturbed her, and a cylinder shot out of the pneumatic tubes that connected the archives. They'd been installed in the late fifties and never replaced. Too many of the archivists worked without technology for e-mail to be a viable alternative. Apparently, phones had been tried for a while but were declared 'too loud and annoying' in the official feedback. The fingerprint and iris scanners were viewed with a cynicism normally reserved for the supernatural.

The cylinder contained a handwritten note.

You are invited to attend the Most Reverend Simon Marshall, Archbishop of York, at your earliest convenience.

It was a very polite order, but an order nonetheless. There was nothing a man as important as the archbishop could want with a junior archivist. There was only one reason he would summon her. To hunt something and kill it.

As Harper hurried back through the vaults, she could almost hear words whispering through the shelves. They followed her, disturbing no one else.

"*Never scream …*"

Chapter Five

Out was faster than in as the Hall of Testing was always empty, appearing as little more than a broom closet, so it didn't take Harper long to exit the restricted section and enter the undercroft of the cathedral. She ignored the curious whispers and gazes of tourists as she hastened past Saint William's tomb, up into the main body of the cathedral and on to the archbishop's office. He was there most mornings following the early service and she wasn't disappointed. His door stood slightly ajar, waiting. Harper raised her fist and knocked once.

"Come in, child."

Harper slipped through the door and pushed it closed behind her. The room was not so different from the archives she'd left behind; wooden panels with glass-fronted bookcases stretched from floor to ceiling. Aside from leather-bound tomes, the only luxuries in the room were sun-bleached velvet curtains—a remnant of the previous archbishop—and a small fire crackling in the grate. Archbishop Marshall sat behind an oak desk, a complicated page of numbers lying in front of him. Harper gave him a shallow bow as he looked up.

"Ah, Harper, thank you for coming so quickly." He removed his glasses, placed them atop a teetering pile of paperwork, then rubbed his eyes.

"I'm not interrupting?" she asked.

"You are and I am grateful." The archbishop gestured to the chair opposite him. What his office lacked in authority, the archbishop himself more than made up for. A dazzling emerald cut gemstone on his finger reflected the dancing fire. A golden cross as long as Harper's hand gleamed against mauve vestments, settling against the archbishop's broad chest as he reclined in his chair.

As a teenager, Harper had punched him in the chest during a training mission. She flexed her fingers, remembering how her knuckles had crunched. Despite the grey at his temples, it was still muscle, not fat, which gave the archbishop his imposing stature.

"Church finance committee meeting today?" Harper asked as she took a seat. At least one course of any dinner she and Grace shared with the archbishop was taken up by him griping about the church finance committee.

"Tonight," he replied with a grimace. "But that is not why I requested you."

Harper nodded. "How may I be of assistance?"

"You heard of the death of Ghostwalker Adams?"

"Who hasn't? It's all anyone's talking about."

The archbishop folded his hands on the desk in front of him and leant forward. "We suspect the Queen's Guard wish it so."

Harper frowned. "Why? Surely all this talk of demons and witchcraft is against their policy of declaring England safe."

The Queen's Guard's official position was that no supernatural survived the Purge during the reign of the Bloody Queen. The Veil, the barrier between the human world and Faerie, was kept strong over England. Hadrian's Wall protected England to the north, Annwn's Trench stopped incursions from Wales, and the sea cut them off from Europe and Ireland. Armed guards patrolled the border to turn away unwanted humans and supernaturals alike.

If they were so sure of their official position, Harper wondered why they felt such a need to intimidate and interrogate people. Their desperate sniffing for even the faintest whiff of the arcane belied their confident policy. If they were so sure, why did people still disappear?

"One of the reasons people stay safe is because they obey the rules," the archbishop explained. "They obey the rules because they're scared. It serves the Queen's Guard's purpose to keep people afraid. A reminder now and again of why they're needed. The Council of Faiths would rather people were kept safe by love, but the secular authorities exert their control through terror. People are reporting anything even slightly suspicious."

"The Queen's Guard get a witch hunt," Harper said bitterly before she could stop herself.

"Most of those accused will be innocent, but history has shown us how these things can get out of hand. When neighbour accuses neighbour, it leads to lynchings and mobs. Already, people are disappearing. The Guard show no mercy. Most never return. Their families have reported them being bundled out of the house just after dawn, hands cuffed behind their backs, hoods over their heads. It is terrifying how quickly the Guard have mobilised."

People who went for questioning rarely came back. Their photos would vanish from window ledges, their names never spoken again, as if they never existed, no matter the paradox created. Of course, if asked, people would say how thankful they were the Guard protected them, but their eyes would dart to the side and their palms would slick with sweat. Awaking to see a plain, silver envelope embossed with the dreaded crown and halberds sitting on the doormat was an ominous sight for most of the citizenry of England.

"What is the Council going to do?" Harper asked. As the highest-ranking Christian clergyman in the North of England, the archbishop wielded a lot of influence within the Council of Faiths.

"Our petition for access to our imprisoned parishioners has been taken to the highest level. Her Majesty has taken the request under advisement." The archbishop's mouth twisted in pain as he added, "Parliament does nothing. It is York's problem to deal with, they said. The Veil has been strengthened, border patrols around the country doubled, and a Queen's Guard perimeter placed around Yorkshire. Parliament says the Queen is keeping us safe, that those the Guard arrest must be a threat to the city. They know any word against the Guard will cast aspersions on their own innocence. Once the Church held higher sway than sneaks and scoundrels but that changed with the Purge. That's why the Council was formed. We are stronger together."

Harper nodded. Her adolescent years had been full of the history of the Council and their silent war with the Guard. She'd heard the Queen's speech after the ghostwalker was found. It hadn't mentioned any faith by name, but the subtle aspersion had been there. Like most of the Queen's speeches, it cited a robust defence of England but remained vague on the details.

Harper often wondered about the Veil. Like the wall surrounding York city centre, the Veil was said to keep supernaturals at bay. Some said it was technological, like a shield in a sci-fi movie. Others said it was made of prayers. Whatever formed it, Harper doubted its efficacy. It might keep magic out, but it did nothing to stop magic within. A small cough drew her attention to the archbishop, who watched her over steepled fingers.

"Sorry," she mumbled. "If Parliament won't help and the Queen won't listen, what are we going to do?"

"Right now, the best thing we can do is to find the murderer quickly," Archbishop Marshall said. "Before the Queen's Guard interrogate too many innocents. All the Council's agents here in York are working on this, save those who are seeking the place where our people are being held for questioning. You and Grace must use your gifts to help. Your experiences in Colombia and the Scottish Highlands will be invaluable."

Harper shivered at his mention of questioning. Rumour stated the Queen's Guard hadn't altered their interrogation methods much since their inception during the reign of the Bloody Queen. It was the theme of many of her nightmares. *It's only a rumour.*

"Wait, you want Grace and me?" The archbishop's words finally sank in. "Most of the relevant books in the archives have already been requested and by archivists with higher clearance than I have. Surely your other investigators are more qualified."

"More qualified than a De Santos and her sister?" The archbishop smiled slightly. "I think not. You've been trained to recognise supernatural influence, have you not?"

"Well, yes, but—"

"The police are out of their depth. They have no cause of death and no suspects. The Queen's Guard may have more but they do not share what they know with the Council. Our other investigators have found nothing although Imam Muhammed has kindly offered the services of a young man in his community who has some forensic experience. In this matter, my faith in people is greater than my faith in science. You and Grace are uniquely placed to see the truth."

Harper clenched her fists in her lap. Although she was sure it was a coincidence, she didn't like the archbishop's choice of words. She didn't want to See things no one else could. That part of her was supposed to have vanished with the exorcism.

"Harper, you *will* do this. I cannot allow my fondness for my goddaughter or her sister to cloud my judgement in this case. You will find this killer. Alive, if possible. Or would you sit by and read books while more people are horrifically murdered? It is time to accept your duty."

His all-knowing, holier-than-thou tone grated. He had always protected them. He gave her a job, validated her. Without his patronage, his encouragement, she would never have been able to pursue her research. She should have known there would be a price.

"You know I don't want anyone else to be hurt, but Grace and I didn't sign up for the family job. We're not demonhunters, we just help now and then. I'm an academic. Grace is a vet."

"Grace cannot ignore her calling, Harper," the archbishop rebuked. "Nor can you. You cannot ignore God's will. Lives, *souls*, are in jeopardy."

Harper hung her head, her knuckles white. Reading about a demon of silence was one thing, trying to detect one was another. Usually, she and Grace only showed up for the fight, they didn't have to work out what was killing people or how to find it. She'd half-heartedly considered trying to force a vision, yet now that she was actually going to have to do it, acidic fear churned in her stomach.

Archbishop Marshall *had* always protected them, and she never asked him what price *he* paid for it. She couldn't stop trusting him now. Brushing away a tear, she gave a jerky nod, not meeting the archbishop's eyes. "We'll do what we can."

"The Holy Spirit will guide you," the archbishop replied confidently. He pulled two slips of paper out of his desk drawer. "These are for you and Grace. My authority should you have any entanglement with the Queen's Guard."

"Thank you, Archbishop." Harper's numb lips could barely form the words as she took the papers.

The archbishop's smile was a sharp contrast to Harper's pressed lips. "Your normal duties are suspended until such time as this case is finished; however, I expect you to exercise discretion in what you reveal to your co-workers and friends. This is not a matter to be gossiped over. Please give my goddaughter a hug for me and remind her to be on time for Mass this week unless the investigation prevents her from attending. You will both stop by for tea soon, I hope."

"Of course." The words sounded strangled. Harper cleared her throat and gave the archbishop a wan smile. "I look forward to it."

After leaving the archbishop's study, Harper found a quiet corner of the cathedral and sat down to examine the papers the archbishop gave her. Normally, they didn't get individual passes and worked as part of a taskforce on behalf of the Council.

This document is to signify Ms. Harper Ashbury of the De Santos family, researcher of Saint Peter's Cathedral, has the permission of the Church to be out after curfew if required for the execution of her duties in protecting the See of York and in service to God.

The second paper was the same save it bore Grace's name. After the name De Santos was a symbol: a crescent moon waxing over the dark slit of an inhuman iris. It was not the family seal Harper was familiar with, an orchid crowned with a halo. She traced the curve of the moon, wondering what it meant.

She tucked the sheets into her jacket pocket. Where to start? Those who worked for the archives always suspected the archbishop had his own agents, people not officially on the Church's payroll, so why had he asked her? Grace, she could understand. This was the De Santos's grand destiny, to protect the world from demons and the forces of evil. The only reason Grace wasn't out in the wilds with her brothers was so she could stay with Harper and make sure she was safe.

Aside from the occasional foray, the two women had avoided confrontations with supernaturals since they moved north to attend York University, but now fate was catching up with them. When Harper accepted the De Santos's offer of family, she hadn't realised she accepted so much more. She'd been warned: nightmares—visions maybe—gushing with arterial blood, panting breath, and screams in the air. She hadn't listened.

Harper patted her pocket. Could such a small thing as a piece of paper carry so much weight? If she did run into the police, or worse, the Queen's Guard, would it protect her? Going out into the pre-dawn greyness ahead of the bells was a minor infraction. It might lead to some uncomfortable questions if she were caught, but it wasn't enough to be arrested. The archbishop clearly expected her to be out late into the night.

Harper's chest tightened and her vision narrowed. Her breath hung crystalline in the air as the wet chill of snow seeped through her shoes. Darkness gushed in, disintegrating the warm sunlight infusing the cathedral.

Ink-black night, twinkling with diamond stars. Evergreens. A misnomer. No greens at night, only blacks and greys. The trees surrounded her: dense, consuming, dark as a black hole. Silhouettes of branches scooped up the stars and drowned their light in an abyss. The smell of pine. The crack of needles underfoot. Sharp, biting. Her heartbeat like thunder in her ears as she ran. *Don't look back. Don't look behind.* The trunks came faster and faster, cut her off, herded her.

"Are you alright, miss?"

A hand at her elbow caused Harper to jerk away, banging her arm against the wall of the cathedral. Biting back a curse, she closed her eyes and fought for control. The cold of the stone grounded her. The trees slipped from her vision to float in her memory like a bad dream. Too ephemeral to remember fully, yet enough to set her heart racing.

"Yes, thank you." She blinked rapidly until the dark lights obscuring her vision dissipated. "Just a little dizzy. I'll be fine."

"Can I get you some water?"

"No, no thank you. Just need some fresh air. Sunlight."

She stumbled away from the concerned onlooker, waving aside their proffered helping hand. The transept door was still open, and she staggered through it into the thin autumn sunlight.

Don't be a coward. It was ludicrous behaviour. She'd hunted at night with Grace's family. It was the nightmares that had her spooked. That and the test that morning. Her mouth set firm and she gave a decisive nod. If Archbishop Marshall thought she and Grace could help, then who was she to argue?

Chapter Six

"*Why* are we going on a ghost walk?"

Harper winced at her sister's sharp tone. Grace's stiletto heels clacked against the tiled kitchen floor as she paced. Glass-fronted cabinet doors rattled each time she stamped down a foot to turn.

"It's an honour walk, Grace." Harper shrank back as Grace pinned her to the kitchen chair with a glare. She swallowed and tried again. "If we follow in Adams' last footsteps, it might give us a clue as to who killed him. I've read about one or two possible supes it could be, but we need some evidence before we can plan how to vanquish them."

"Why are you dragging *me* into this?"

"It was an order from your godfather. Even you can't disobey the Archbishop of York."

"I don't like taking orders."

"Just giving them."

"What was that?" Grace stopped, hands on her hips as she scowled at Harper.

"Nothing, General." Harper changed tack. "A man was murdered, Grace. Don't you want to know why?"

"I don't see why I would. I didn't know him. I can't help him. We don't go chasing after every random criminal in York. If I wanted to chase killers, I would've joined the police."

"This is different. This is clearly supernatural. The police can't fight this. Your father—"

"I told Father I wasn't interested in following the family trade," Grace said.

"You only told him that because of me," Harper muttered.

Grace frowned, garnet-red lips a thin, hard line.

Harper ploughed on. "If I weren't around, you would've joined Gabriel in Venice. You would be out there, fighting side by side with your brother, not hiding here, pretending to enjoy—"

"Shut up." Coffee splashed Grace's hand as she thumped her mug down on the table. "Don't even think of finishing that sentence. You want to fight, then we'll fight. Properly. Go get that lump of metal you call a blade and meet me in the garden."

"Gray, do you really think it's a good idea to have a live blade practice in the garden? We do have neighbours, remember?" They all knew the De Santos name when Grace introduced herself. Everyone recognised it as soon as their landlady told prospective renters who they'd be living with. Somehow, no one found the idea of living with a demonhunter comforting. While Harper enjoyed not having to share the kitchen and lounge, their landlady's inability to find anyone willing to live with her and Grace was getting embarrassing. And expensive.

"Well, maybe we'll have fewer neighbours after we fight." Grace smirked at Harper's wide-eyed stare. "Because they'll run away, not because we'll kill them." Grace flicked Harper's forehead. "Dummy."

"All this because I'm making you go on a ghost walk?"

"Go get the weapon," Grace said in cold monotone.

Steeling herself for the gauntlet ahead, Harper dashed upstairs to retrieve her machete from the trunk at the end of her bed. It was an inelegant weapon, perfect for hacking hardened hides apart. It saved her life several times on the types of 'family holiday' Grace's father preferred. They usually involved dense jungles, campfire meals, and creatures with three heads and too many teeth.

She hadn't regularly carried a weapon since she moved to York. It hadn't been needed in the night-safe city except for the rare occasions when she and Grace were called to assist with the hunt and capture of a supernatural who breached the Veil. The last time had been a lone kelpie, and before that it had been almost six months since there'd been an incursion; a minor scuffle with a shapeshifting wirrikow that managed to slip past the northern border guard at Hadrian's Wall.

Harper rifled through piles of books, a medley of scented candles, old keys, and assorted weaponry she hadn't found time to unpack since they moved into the house three weeks ago. Under a stack of frayed material squares left over from a disastrous attempt to learn to sew, she found the other blade she was looking for. She strapped the sheath to her waist, the handle of the long hunting knife nestled against the small of her back, before tossing her detritus back in the trunk. She'd unpack at the weekend. Eventually.

By the time she clattered down the stairs into the kitchen, Grace was going through forms in the backyard. The sinking sun silhouetted the uneven terraced houses. A light mist glazed the lawn while buttery light oozed through the slits in the kitchen blinds to cast bumblebee stripes over the ground. Vines and weeds grew up the rickety wooden fence separating their garden from their neighbours'. The distant growl of car engines was the only sound as birdsong quieted and humans hurried to hide behind locked doors. Trees creaked in the wind and groped over the fence to litter their leaves over the backyard.

Grace avoided what little light there was, almost invisible in the shadow. She was dressed all in black, the tight clothing accentuating her lean fighter's build. Dark waves of hair framed her face, only secured by a pair of glittering pins. Harper tugged her plait. She'd never mastered the art of fighting with loose hair. Grace made it seem effortless, body and hair flowing like water. All Harper's hair did was blind her.

"There are other colours than black and red, you know." Harper pointed out when Grace deigned to notice her.

"Not once blood starts flowing there aren't. Stop trying to get me into your gaudy wardrobe."

"Are we seriously going to do this?" Harper raised an eyebrow.

"You've been skipping practice. We might not follow my family's trade, but we still have to stay prepared."

"For times like this."

"Whatever. If you're really going to do this idiotic thing, you cannot be sloppy in your training. If you get killed, I have to avenge you, and I have better things to do."

"Really, Gray, can't you say you're worr—" Harper ducked under Grace's blade. A kick caught her square in the midriff. She fell with an "oof," tucking her chin to avoid smacking her head on the fence. Grace held out a hand but Harper shook her head. She jumped up and raised her blade.

"I trained for this too," Harper protested. Metal rang against metal as Grace parried her thrust, blocking the follow-up kick with her thigh.

"Not enough." Grace's dark eyes glittered like her dagger. Harper aimed a low kick at her knees then sliced upwards as Grace danced out of the way. A second dagger appeared in her sister's off hand. Harper's machete squealed as the sharp edges scraped together.

Grace lashed out to bash Harper's elbow with the pommel of her blade. Harper bit back a cry as her fingers went numb. She switched hands, trying to shake the feeling back into her arm.

"You don't have to protect me." Harper sidestepped another kick. Her return attack was half-hearted, merely to keep Grace back rather than because she had any expectation of it connecting.

"You're holding back," Grace said. "You need to defend yourself better. You, you of all people, can't go investigating some supe murderer." She attacked fast and low, forcing Harper back.

"What—?"

Her distraction earned her a slap from the flat of Grace's blade.

"Pay attention," Grace snapped. "This is not a game."

"Why me of all people?" Harper dived under Grace's knife. Autumn leaves twirled through the air as she aimed a spinning kick at the back of her sister's knees. "Surely, I'm one of the best people to investigate a supernatural murder. This is what your father trained us for. Don't pretend you can leave all that behind. You'd be out there now, in Venice, in Colombia, with Miguel and Gabriel. You're only here because of me."

"What if I am?" Grace almost shouted. The clash of blades punctuated her words. "Why is it wrong for me to protect you? You're my sister. And you're—"

They both stopped, staring at each other. Grace clamped her lips shut, paling. Her eyes darted toward the house behind Harper. Following her look, Harper peeked over her shoulder. No one there.

The world tipped, pain lanced through her ribs, her ears ringing as her vision blurred. Her heart thrummed hard against her sternum as she gasped for breath.

"Don't drop your guard." Grace's voice floated down to her. "And don't be so gullible."

Harper scrambled to her feet; one hand pressed to her sore chest. "Now there's a boot print on my shirt."

A smile tugged at Grace's lips as she shrugged. "You gonna be serious, now?"

"Are *you*?" Harper took a quick step back as Grace raised her daggers. She balanced on the balls of her feet, ready for the attack. "C'mon. Admit it. You'd rather be out there, following the family occupation with your brothers. Admit you're worried about me, and I'll practice. No complaints. I don't exactly want to get skewered by some demon either."

"You remember in ethics class when we were given the problem of whether to save one family member or five strangers?" Grace asked. "Well, I'm sorry, Harp, but I choose one family member. If you do this, you could be killed. Your life is not a hypothetical."

"It's *my* life. I don't think it's worth more than anyone else's. I can do things other people can't. If I do nothing, then the next victim's blood will be on my hands. On both our hands. I had those dreams for a reason. I Saw him die. I'm meant to do something."

Grace pursed her lips, her knuckles white around the handles of her daggers. "You're wrong about one thing. I wouldn't rather be out demon hunting with my brothers. I'd rather be demon hunting with my sister."

Harper smiled. "Then you'll help me catch this murderer?"

Grace gave a curt nod. "On two conditions. One, you actually train, and two, you don't do anything that'll get you in trouble with the Queen's Guard. I meant it before. You get killed, by anyone, even our own government, and I *will* avenge you."

Harper swallowed. There was no humour in Grace's eyes. "Okay. Let's train then."

The sun dipped to the horizon as the ghost walk finished, diminishing with every passing minute. Clumps of people scurried away from Lendal Tower, huddled together as though the dead ghostwalker might appear in the last spot anyone saw him alive. As their shadows lengthened, they appeared like centipedes skittering across the paving slabs.

Rifles resting against their shoulder, two of the Queen's Guard watched from atop the tower. Normally, they looked outwards, vigilant against outside threats. Now they leant over the crenellations, faces masked by shadow as they focused their attention on seemingly guiltless humans. Seconds trickled away with the sunlight. Curfew was a recommendation backed by gleaming muzzles and bayonets sharp enough to cut your throat without interrupting your plea of innocence.

No one looked up. They hurried away, heads bent together, their fear no more than a susurration on the wind.

Harper shrank against the base of Lendal Tower. The Guard's gaze was like a hot poker shoved through her spine, like needles piercing her skin. But she didn't look up. Every second made it harder to step away from the protection of stone and shadow and walk into the full beam of their attention. They would watch her and Grace disappear under Lendal

Bridge, wait for them to emerge on the other side, observe every step down the riverbank.

"We learnt nothing on this ghost walk that we didn't already know." Grace scanned the area. Her knuckledusters gleamed in the last of the sunlight. She stood at the edge of the path and peered into the river below as she tapped her foot against the cobbles. Tall and straight, she wore her De Santos pride like a queen wore her crown.

"I didn't know about the ghost at the chocolate factory," Harper disagreed, shuffling closer to her sister. She kept her voice low, but her skin still prickled as she imagined her words wafting up to the Guard on the tower.

"We learnt nothing factual or useful," Grace qualified.

"This is the last place anyone saw Ghostwalker Adams alive. That's got to be helpful somehow. We know he was found by the river, even though the press hasn't reported where. It's an unusual path to take at night, but I guess he wasn't afraid of the dark. Probably doesn't believe in ghosts either. I reckon he would've gone down the steps here by the bridge and followed the river southeast."

"Why do you think that?" Grace asked with an amused smirk on her lips.

"Walking off with his customers would've been bad for the mystique." Harper glanced up at the tower. Nothing. Not even a glimmer of metal. She pictured the Guard hunkered down behind the crenellation, listening, and dropped her voice so low Grace had to lean closer to hear her. "Better to disappear into the night. West would've taken him out of the night-safe zone, but the Guildhall is to the south. He might've been heading there."

"Okay, fair enough. We follow the river. How will you know where he died? The police cordoned off over two miles precisely so people couldn't pinpoint it. Even if the police haven't cleaned up all the clues, the Queen's Guard definitely have."

"I'm hoping to See something," Harper confessed. Her ears strained for the scuff of metal on stone, of boots descending.

"Harper." Grace grabbed Harper by the arm and dragged her under the bridge. "They'll hear you."

"They aren't going to hear the capitalisation." Harper yanked her arm back. Agreeing with Grace would only make her more overbearing. "Do you really think they will take more from me 'seeing something' than from us discussing where a man was murdered? Or at least, do you think they would before you started making a scene? I'm being careful."

"You're supposed to try and *not* See things," Grace hissed. Harper had to step closer to hear her whispered admonition. "I know it's not your fault you have mag—that you See things, but it's not right, Harp. Besides, you can't See things like that."

The last was said with a hint of triumph. Harper shook her head. Since she had the idea, she'd been actively trying to See, working on subduing her own doubts and fears. It was difficult, but sometimes she felt as though she would have been able to See something others couldn't had there been anything around to be Seen. It was tempting to try it on some of the artefacts in the archives, but she was afraid of triggering some kind of mystical alarm.

After years of running from her abilities, there was an exhilaration in turning and confronting them. The adrenaline rush crackled through her veins. Magic, raw and powerful. It banished the fear of being caught, slew the threat of the Queen's Guard. It was terrifying. It was … fun?

This magic was part of her, part of the past she couldn't remember, part of the person she used to be. Sometimes it felt like her name and the magic were the only parts of her that were real. Everything else had been given to her. She was grateful, really, for everything Father De Santos did for her, but sometimes when she looked in the mirror, she saw a stranger. Deep in her gut, Harper knew if she could master her Sight, she could See the path home.

"I think I can do it," she said. "I want to try."

"But Harper—"

"Trust me, Gray. Please?"

Grace was the first to look away. "Let's get this over with."

As they walked beside the river, Harper concentrated on the strange shifting she'd experienced before. It was not dissimilar to daydreaming. Her eyes tingled. She resisted the urge to rub the itch away and focused on the growing burning sensation. It was a feeling of looking-beyond or seeing-past. The path flowed before her like a ribbon wafting on the breeze. Petrichor hung in the air, almost tangible as it coated her tongue. The gentle shush of water lapping at stone covered the last sounds of cars and human chatter.

"Harper!"

Harper stumbled backwards, almost falling into Grace.

"You were about to walk into the water, you idiot." Grace kept her voice low, her eyes dark as the night-clad river. "What the hell are you doing?"

Harper's shoulder clicked as she rubbed it. "Did you have to pull me so hard?" she snapped. "I was on the path. You broke my concentration. I could almost See." She glanced behind them, but Lendal Tower and the Guard watching from its roof, had faded into the shadows, obscured by the Ouse Bridge and the tall buildings beside it. There was no sign of human life, save for an out-of-tune operatic warbling from an unseen soul crossing the bridge.

"Fat lot of good it will do if you fall in the river," Grace said. "I'm the one who'd have to jump in after you, and I had my hair done this afternoon. Since I was supposed to be out with Antoinette for dinner, remember?"

Harper tried to hide a smirk, but a stifled giggle escaped. "Sorry, Gray. Guess I got my priorities wrong. I can swim, you know."

"Like a tortoise," Grace grumbled.

"You walk on the river side." Harper looped her arm through Grace's. "You can steer."

They set out again slowly, hips bumping as Harper meandered. The path narrowed as they left the safety of the city walls. Trees crowded on their left. The velvet abyss of the Ouse flowed on their right. Harper ignored Grace's muttered threats, trying to recapture the feeling. She faltered when the tingle itched her eye sockets, and the illusive sensation slipped away.

"It worked." Grace's eyes didn't meet Harper's. Instead, they darted up and down the riverbank, never still.

"Yeah, I think so, briefly." Awe and fear tinged Harper's whisper.

"No, I mean it definitely worked."

Harper's brow furrowed. "How do you know?"

"Your eyes change colour when you See things. When you wake up suddenly, if it's a bad dream your eyes are still brown—"

"Hazel."

"Whatever. If it's a vision your eyes are purplish for a moment when you first open them."

"Why didn't you tell me before?" Harper asked, aghast. "You could've told me which dreams were real. You could've told me there was a visible sign I was doing something supernatural. What if someone had seen? What if your father had seen?"

"Father is not really the kind to come comfort someone after a nightmare." Grace squeezed Harper's arm. "You weren't supposed to be Seeing things anyway. Telling you about the eyes would've made you nervous."

"Well yeah, probably, but—"

"The point is, whatever you were doing worked," Grace said. "So, if you must take this risk, do that again."

Harper wished it were that easy. She was struggling to slip into the in-between mindset. It was like trying to catch herself just before falling asleep, without waking up. Floating, falling, through a space between consciousness. Her body was heavy, yet distant, as though the aches belonged to someone else. She took a deep breath, then held it as time slowed. The image of a net formed in her mind. Streams of light flowed through it, caught on its threads, an aurora trapped in a spider's web.

She kept her eyes straight ahead. On the edges of her vision, something flickered. Trying to catch the movement, she twisted her head, feeling like a puppeteer manipulating her own body. As she looked out across the rippling surface of the river, a shadow materialised on the path to her left—a tall man in a top hat. His footsteps glowed lilac. He made his way along the riverbank until he neared the place where the River Foss flowed into the Ouse.

The path tapered to a point and a narrow footbridge crossed the Foss leading back to civilisation. Instead of hurrying on, the image of the ghostwalker stopped, the shadow cloak cutting swathes of black through the mist as he turned. Then he walked away from safety, headed down some steps to stand at the very end of the path and gaze out over the rivers. The air shimmered behind him, coalescing into a feminine form of moon- and starlight. She raised a hand toward the ghostwalker.

Pain, cold as ice, pierced Harper's spine. The sharp taste of iron and bile welled in her throat and she clutched at it, unable to breathe. A ghostly pattern traced the mist, then dissipated. The ghostly form of the man fell to the ground.

Chapter Seven

Harper's breath burst out of her, ragged and hot as she gasped for oxygen. Hand on her throat, she retched and fell to her knees as her stomach heaved. This was worse than in the Shambles. Cool hands pressed against the back of her neck, and she jerked away.

"Harper, it's okay. It's just me." Grace's voice chased away the last of the vision, and the pain subsided as the crumpled corpse faded from view. "What did you See?"

Harper allowed Grace to help her sit. Her trembling legs knocked her skirt askew. "The man ... who died ... I saw him ... walking ... by the ri ... the river," Harper panted. She closed her eyes and Grace wrapped an arm around her shoulders, holding her until the dizziness passed. As the last sliver of sun was swallowed by the horizon, mist rolled off the river to tease at Harper's shoelaces and fingers.

In other circumstances, Harper might have been amused at the accusatory glare Grace directed at the trees, or the way she flapped to drive the vapours back. Grace's knuckledusters dug into her arm where her sister gripped too hard. The solid reality of the weapon, coupled with Grace's big-sister attitude, eased the tightness in Harper's chest.

"I'm okay now, Gray." Harper used Grace's arm as a lever to pull herself up. She proceeded to describe her vision, concluding by saying, "It fits with my research and my dreams. I think it's Hesychia, or a hesychia anyway. Most old gods are actually based on a type of supernatural. We think Zeus was a compound character from stories of shapeshifters and electrical elemancers. Now the crossover where the actions of the same type of supes are attributed to Thor is interesting. A very different portrayal—"

"Enough with the lecture, academia. Why did this Hesychia do it?" Grace asked.

"I don't know. It's a theory. Do you have anything better? The only other clue was a rune of some kind, maybe dwarfish or Viking or something. It broke through the mist like someone stamped it there. It disappeared when—"

The snap of a twig behind her cut Harper off. Grace turned, poised on the balls of her feet. A man in a tan overcoat stepped forward, a revolver in his hand. Harper's throat went dry, and she raised her hands in the air like she'd seen people do in movies. The man didn't wear the Guard's coat of arms, but Harper didn't find its absence reassuring. Who else would carry a gun?

"You are under arrest for trespass and suspicion of murder," the Guardsman said, his tone devoid of any emotion. In the half-light from the streetlamp, his features were grey and hard to distinguish.

"No, we aren't." Grace smirked but didn't relax her stance. Harper wanted to kick her. "We have passes signed by the Archbishop of York and authorised by the Council of Faiths. You have no authority to arrest us."

Harper privately disagreed. Authority didn't come into it. If the Queen's Guard wanted them to disappear, no papers or law in the world could save them.

The man waved them toward a patch of light under a flickering streetlamp. "Show me."

"It's okay, John. They'll be the ones I told you about before." The excited tone of the newcomer was brighter than the electric lights. He waved from the other side of the Foss, a bulging bag slipping off his shoulder as he did so. He caught it with a laugh, shrugged it onto his back, then attempted to juggle three other cases and grab the tripod leaning against his beaten-up red car.

The Guardsman took a step back. When he made no attempt to help his companion, Harper automatically stepped forward and grabbed one of the cases out of the man's hand as he crossed the bridge over the Foss. She ignored the tap of Grace's toes against the concrete.

"As-Salaam Alaykum," he greeted her.

"Wa-Alaykum as-Salaam," Harper replied.

"Thanks for the help." He flashed her a sparkling grin, and Harper couldn't help but smile back. His walk had almost as much bounce as the curls in his hair. If it hadn't been too dangerous, Harper would have attempted to See his aura, just for the entertainment of watching it meet Grace's black-cloud mood. She wasn't even sure if auras existed, but excitement rolled off the newcomer in waves and banished the last of her chills from the dead ghostwalker.

He set the containers down by the edge of the river, then seized Harper's hand and shook it vigorously. "You must be Harper Ashbury. I'm so excited to meet you. I've been following your work for quite some time. Tell me, is it true you found—"

"Doctor Siddique. These women are trespassing in a restricted area." The Guardsman pinched the bridge of his nose. "You cannot assume they are the assistants your imam promised you. This is highly irregular."

Grace pulled their passes out of her pocket with a regal flourish Harper had never quite mastered. It seemed to be a genetic De Santos thing. The Guardsman examined the papers from a distance, revolver never wavering. The shadow of his high collar covered half his face. Harper couldn't tell if he was clean-shaven or whether his nose was large or small. At last, with a curt nod, he holstered the weapon, but his lips were pressed thin as he watched them, and his hand never strayed far from the gun.

"Great. All sorted. I was going to come by the cathedral and introduce myself. This saves me a trip. Have you found anything yet?" The doctor wasn't at all phased by being in the company of the Queen's Guard or by Grace's glares. He wasn't wearing the traditional long coat of the Guard nor was he in a police uniform. Instead, he wore jeans and a hoodie in navy blue with 'University of York' scrawled across the chest. The University's familiar coat of arms reassured Harper. Another academic she could handle.

"Who *are* you?" Grace pushed between him and Harper, knocking their hands apart. Behind her sister's back, Harper rolled her eyes. Like she couldn't take care of herself.

"Oh, I'm so sorry, I was so excited I clean forgot to introduce myself. Saqib Siddique, he/him, forensic supernaturalist." He held out his hand with a grin.

"Never heard of a forensic supernaturalist," Grace snapped, unbeguiled. "Sounds made up."

"I think I'm the only one." Saqib let his hand drop to his side.

"It sounds stupid," Grace said.

"And what is it you do?" Saqib raised an arm defensively as her eyes narrowed further.

"I'm a vet."

"Oh." He looked crestfallen, his smile slipping away. "That sounds—"

"Like a nice, perfectly sensible occupation," Grace finished.

"Did you have something you wanted to show us?" Harper stepped around her sister to steer the conversation to the less tense topic of murder.

Saqib's face lit up again. Even Grace's storm clouds couldn't keep away his sunshine. "Not yet, but I will. This time, I'll definitely find something."

"This time?" Grace raised an eyebrow.

"Yeah. Well. Not a hugely researched field, supernatural forensics. But I am certain there is a way we can track magic by science. The Council are really keen on it, and I've been working with the police." He cast a side glance over his shoulder at the Guardsman. "I thought if I came to the scene of the crime at the same time of day as he was murdered, I might be able to detect something."

"We'll leave you to it then." Harper grabbed Grace's hand, anxious to be away before Saqib asked her to help. If he did detect magic, she didn't want to be lit up like a Christmas tree. She was surprised to note Grace's hand was as clammy as her own. She shoved a business card into Saqib's hand. "Nice to meet you. Let us know if you find anything. Great. Goodnight."

The Guardsman scrutinised them, unblinking, as they hurried over the low bridge. It was the opposite direction to home but the fastest way to get out of the Guardsman's line of sight. The prickly sensation of being watched lingered even after they crossed the Foss and ducked behind a row of apartments. Harper collapsed against the wall of the nearest building.

"Too close." Grace peeked back around the corner. "They aren't watching anymore. Looks like they're taking samples of the plants and water. That so-called doctor must be the person Godfather said could help, but we can't work with the Queen's Guard. We can't, Harper. And he's been studying you? What the hell is that about? You have to be careful. If he does find a way to detect magic with that equipment of his, he'll turn you in for sure."

"I don't think he will." The knot of panic in Harper's chest eased. While she'd been wrongfooted by his job, she didn't sense any danger from Saqib. She looked down at her hand, flexing her fingers. His appearance was accompanied by the strangest sense of déjà vu.

Something clicked in the back of her mind, like a piece of a puzzle falling into place, but she couldn't see the full picture. "I don't think he'll turn me in. I think we'll need him."

Grace grabbed Harper's shoulders and shook her hard. "Have you forgotten what they do to ... to people like you?"

"Gray, let go of me." Harper's teeth rattled as her sister shook her again. She grabbed Grace's wrists, forcing her to stop. Grace glanced down at her hand, then her grip loosened.

"You can't keep on like this," Grace said. "Forcing visions, choosing a too-big house because it 'feels right,' talking about trusting people, scouring old bookshops for God knows what. You're going to get caught. One of these days, someone's going to report you to the Queen's Guard, and I won't be able to do a damn thing about it. Harp, please promise me you'll stop this."

"I can't, Gray. Something is happening, I can feel it. Like a part of me that was dormant is waking up. Ever since we helped out with slaying the kelpie up in Scarborough last month."

"Ever since you touched it you mean," Grace said sourly. "I told Father it was unfair to involve you in the family business. Why don't either of you listen to me?"

"Grace, being a ... what I am ... doesn't mean I condone supernaturals running around causing chaos and murdering people. But maybe it does mean they aren't all bad. Your father, the archbishop, the Queen's Guard, they could all be wrong about supernaturals. You don't think I'm inherently evil, do you?"

"Of course not." Grace stared up at the stars and, without looking, smacked Harper on the back of the head. "Why do I always give in to you?"

"Because I'm usually right about these things," Harper said with a hint of a smile. "I was right about the bogle, wasn't I? And the huldra? And ..."

"Okay, okay, your dreams are useful sometimes." Grace laughed, but Harper could still hear a tinge of bitterness. "My ancestors are rolling in their graves. A demonhunter doing something on the say-so of a wi ... Look. Stay away from him, okay? For me?"

"Sure. For you."

Arm in arm, they turned toward home, but Harper couldn't help but look back over her shoulder. The piercing gaze of the Guardsman still needled her back and deep in her chest something fizzled. As they left the river behind, the voice from her vision trickled through her skull.

"Never scream ..."

Chapter Eight

When they reached home, Grace started dinner. The thunk of knife through carrot became a steady beat. Harper chose not to mention dinner wasn't supposed to contain carrots. Interrupting Grace with a knife was an unwise thing to do if one liked their fingers. Harper dropped into a chair at the kitchen table, her limbs no longer supporting her, as though her strings were cut.

It never used to be this hard.

The stray thought niggled at her. It was true, she used to see little things out of the corners of her eyes when she was a teenager, unsure if they were real or not, but that stopped after the exorcism. Being honest with herself, she hadn't tried afterwards—the fear of what she Saw combined with her own wish to be normal.

Was normal really so desirable? She longed for home. How she came to this place, to Grace's family, was anything but normal—a girl wandering the mists alone, with no memory of how she came to be there, no record of her birth in any hospital database. Some feared she'd come through the Veil, but Father De Santos had assured his congregation that was impossible.

Then on top of that, she was plagued by demonic possession, or at least that was the explanation the Church gave for her visions. Letting them believe it kept her alive, painful as the exorcism to 'normalise' her had been. Harper wrapped her arms around her waist with a shiver. She swallowed the lump in her throat, blinking rapidly to clear the stinging in her eyes before Grace noticed.

If her arrival in Yorkshire was so abnormal, maybe the only way back was to embrace that. Maybe research would never be enough. She needed to learn to *do* something. Then she could find this killer before someone else died. Then she could find a way home.

Grace's cooking filled the air with pungent garlic and sweet, peppery basil. It masked the scent of the herb bundles their landlady had placed over the lounge and back doors to ward off demons and witches. Sometimes Harper stood in the doorway beneath them and waited for the lightning to strike.

Grace continued to bang around the kitchen, cursing under her breath when tomato sauce spat red juice on her black shirt. Harper rested her elbows on the pine dining table. She was so tired she could barely keep her head up. The stories were true: all magic did come at a price. She didn't move until Grace shoved a bowl of pasta under her nose and pushed a fork into her hand.

Harper gripped the utensil tightly as she ate, the solid reality of hot food failing to banish the chill inside. *I saw him die but what did that do? I learnt nothing and we almost got caught. If science can detect magic, I need to find a way to hide. Or use it. Maybe that's how I can find the way home. Maybe Saqib can help me, even if he doesn't know he's doing it.*

They ate in silence. Harper barely tasted her food. Grace sat opposite her, also lost in thought. The empty chairs around the table widened the gap between them with the unseen presence of strangers. Despite their lack of housemates, they always ate at the table. Grace's mother said it was uncouth to eat in front of the television.

Harper washed up on autopilot, then hugged Grace goodnight and left her to watch some crime drama. Before she headed upstairs, Harper creaked the door of the downstairs bedroom open, those invisible presences still strong in her mind. The scent of mint lingered in the air, a remnant of the last occupant. The brass doorknob pulsed under her hand. Curtains wafted in the draft of the open door, casting a shadow over the desk. For a moment, it looked like a man leaning over writing something. Harper's eyes burned.

She slammed the door closed, ran up the stairs, and jumped into the middle of her bed. Her nightlight glowed in the corner, moonlight velvet in the sky out of her open window. Too dark. Harper switched on the bedside lamp, but it was too late, adrenaline had chased off her earlier weariness.

The Victorian hardwood floor creaked as she crossed the room. She lifted her violin case from its resting place and laid it across her desk. Her nails caught on the strings as she reverently ran her fingers over the aged wood. She'd known how to play as soon as she saw the instrument. Sometimes, she dreamt violin music, always distant, calling. Songs she never heard before, not knowingly anyway.

The instrument was decorated with twisting vines and roses in red and white. Harper painted it as a teenager, wide awake in the early hours of the morning hidden under her bed with a torch. It was her only link to home, one tiny remembrance other than her name, and playing it sometimes soothed her. Sometimes it made the pain so great it felt as though her chest would be torn open and her heart bleed out onto the floor.

She placed the violin on her bedside table, under the lamp, in the hopes its proximity would let her dream a way home.

Harper walked through a forest of eyes. Wide globes, narrow slits, they watched from trees and vines, floating through the air around her. Blue, brown, green, and grey, each glowed with unnatural light. Warmth radiated from her own eyes as they shone with the same fire.

The path before her wended between their scrutinous looks, overshadowed by trees, which reached so high as to block out the starlight. Behind her, new eyes appeared afresh to hide the path back. There was no returning to the past. That which was, could be no more. All that remained was that which may be, which would be.

Generations before her possessed the Sight. Many after her would inherit it. It had been part of her longer than she could remember.

Like grandmama ... The words floated from her like vapour before dissipating on the air. A distant part of her recognised the dream for what it was and wondered at the knowledge. The memories were hidden from her waking mind and never lingered.

She travelled down the endlessly unchanging path until everything blurred together. Her legs were wooden, moved by invisible strings. She wanted to stop, to sit and rest, but the rolling orbs crowding behind her allowed no respite. They watched, doing nothing to guide or help.

Harper shook off the lethargy constraining her body like thick vines. Each step brought her closer. Closer to what, she did not know. Did not know if the path ever reached a destination or if it was an eternal journey in an infinite forest.

She sped up, faster and faster until she was running. Branches whipped past her, caught her hair, tore it from her head. The pain was real, making her gasp. Tears blurred her vision. Thorns scratched her skin, jagged scars burning as sweat dripped onto them. The brightness of the eyes turned her night-blind. She tried to peer beyond them, but their light obliterated everything else.

Wood splintered. Something heavy thwacked into the dirt behind her. A low, deep growl reverberated through the soles of her feet. It met with the trembling fear deep in her chest, mixing sour in her stomach. Each ragged breath dragged frigid air over the bile coating the back of her throat, sharp and foul as the taste filled her mouth.

Vines threaded through her shoes, twined around her ankles. She fell. The wind was knocked out of her to be replaced with deep lungfuls of mist as it rose to cover her. Gravel and dirt clung to her hands as she pushed herself up, kicking away tendrils and roots. The eyes closed in around her. Too bright. Harper cowered behind spread hands. Sand and grit clogged her lashes.

Even through her hands, the brilliance of the hovering orbs seared her retinas, burning, blinding. When she opened her mouth to scream, no sound came out. Harper collapsed, splayed out in the dirt as though dead. Sensing her capitulation, the lights dimmed. She looked up, lying on her back, blinking back tears as she met the critical gazes surrounding her.

"What do you want?" Her voice was barely more than a whisper.

But the disembodied orbs had no voice. They hung motionless, unblinking.

Harper scrambled to her feet, took a step forward. They crowded around her, flashes of static pushing her back. Accusatory stares bore right through her, anguish and loss reflected in hauntingly familiar irises that glistened with rivers of unshed tears.

"What do you want?" she yelled. The eyes shimmering in front of her receded. She took another step forward. "Get out of my way."

A thin passage opened between two blue eyes, one navy as midnight, the other bright as noon. Pushing past them scorched her skin like walking between walls of fire. The scream caught in her throat, refusing to be heard, refusing to die. Harper swallowed it whole and forced her weary limbs to run again.

The eyes followed. Neither fast nor slow. Watching. Waiting for her to weaken again.

The stale, salty smell of sweat filled her with each aching breath. It obscured the earthy petrichor of the forest, acrid fear dense in the air. Her lungs ached from running, the stitch in her side bursting into red blossoms of pain.

With a thud that almost knocked the breath out of her, Harper hit something solid. Liquid, warm and sticky, oozed over her hands and arms. She jerked back, but the eyes crowded in around her. Pushing. Shoving. Viscous fluid coated her, dripped in ribbons between them, dropped to the ground in thick glops so Harper slipped and slid each time they thrust her forward.

The shining globes forced back the shadows of the night to reveal a grotesque mimicry of the real world. Before her stood an old alder tree, its trunk twisted and cracked, its branches lost in the darkness above. Blood dripped from the knots and scratches in the tree's bark. Slashes rent the air, carved into the rising mist. The runes hung, black and jagged, so real against the silvery backdrop. A compulsion hooked through her chest and dragged her forward, painful, impossible to resist.

A wide rend almost cut the tree in half and Harper peered in, pressured by the weight of the eyes surrounding her. The lilac glow emanating from her eyes illuminated the body interred within.

Harper awoke with a shout. She jumped out of bed and scrambled away until she hit the far corner of the room. The tang of fear lingered in the air. The door opened with a bang a moment later and Grace rushed in, crossbow in hand.

"What is it?" she demanded as the door slammed shut behind her. She flicked on the light as she assessed the room.

"Nothing," Harper rasped, her breath still ragged. "Nothing at all."

Somewhere in the back of her mind, she noted the crossbow. It had been stored in Grace's chest for six months, gathering dust. It gleamed in the lamplight, newly polished, the sharp tip of the bolt glittering.

Grace glanced down at Harper, the crossbow still raised in readiness. "Bad dream?"

"It was so real."

Grace set the crossbow aside, clicked the safety on, and sat next to her. As Grace wrapped an arm around her sister, Harper rested her head on Grace's shoulder.

"What was it?" Grace asked as she pulled Harper's tangled hair back into some semblance of order. "What monster is hiding under the bed this time?"

"I don't know. It was … surreal. I know the dreams mean something but … but I can't always tell what. You understand?"

"Not really. You're the first unnatural thing my family has allowed to walk around unfettered in, well, ever, and that's only because no one else knows about your magic. We have a lot of experience imprisoning witches. We don't have a lot of experience comforting them after nightmares. I've got no precedent here."

"I appreciate your sacrifice," Harper said dryly. She did mean it. Even now, it was hard for Grace to go against generations of demonhunter blood.

"Then tell me what's going on. Is it related to what we were looking for earlier?"

"I don't know." Harper pulled away in frustration. "I didn't See what killed the woman in my dream. Only that she was dead. Dead and … and …" Harper swallowed hard before continuing, "and her eyes were gouged out. Someone took her eyes and left the rest of her in the nook of an old tree. I don't know who did it, or when, or if it's the future or the past or … Sometimes I really wish your father *had* 'cured' me. I don't want to experience these things, Grace."

"I know." Grace pulled her close again and stroked her hair. "You shouldn't let the lights go out. You know that."

"I know."

"Want me to stay?"

Harper nodded wordlessly.

Grace unstrung her bow before clambering into Harper's bed. She raised an eyebrow at the violin on the nightstand. Harper squirmed, but her sister said nothing about the instrument. "I'll read to you until you fall asleep."

As Harper lay awake, listening to Grace read from her antique Bible, concentrating on the steady light of the night lamp, she contemplated the house, their lives, her magic. As much as the visions terrified her, there was a sense of correctness to having them: a calling to right the evils she Saw.

Chapter Nine

The next morning, Harper was up and out before the sun, not that the sun stood much chance of penetrating the flat, grey clouds shielding earth from sky. The streets were eerily quiet as she left the residential area and crossed the Ouse, heading toward the cathedral. The last vestiges of mist still clung to the alleyways. Harper contemplated her shoes as she trudged through the city. It was a dull, depressing dawn.

The toll of Great Peter called York back to life, its unmistakable voice clear and reassuring. As the days got shorter, more people stayed in their stores overnight, so it was not long before shopkeepers emerged to slide away shutters and open their doors for business.

Harper gave one of the proprietors a small nod, covering a yawn as she peered in the window of a contorted bookstore. The shop slithered up between two taller buildings as though it had grown through the crack like a weed. Its roof was crooked, its windows mismatched and wonky, the door slanted yet snug in its surround. Thick glass distorted the scene within and gave the books grotesque proportions. The titles of those nearest the window were distinguishable, but those further within were warped beyond recognition.

Chimes jingled as Harper opened the door. She couldn't face the cathedral archives and risk tests in the dark this morning, not after the nightmares. Grace had fallen asleep quickly, her dark hair spread over

Harper's pillow like the roots of a tree. For Harper, sleep had been more elusive, coming only in dribs and drabs, neither deep nor restful.

She used makeup to cover the circles under her eyes as best she could, but no amount of concealer could lighten the weight compressing her spine or hide the twitch in her eye. Her shoulder blades itched like someone was following her. Queen's Guard. The eyes from her nightmares. The ghostwalker's spirit. Hesychia.

Harper rubbed her eyes, shook her hair loose, and rolled her shoulders in an attempt to dispel the prickly sensation.

"I need caffeine," she muttered, as she tackled the uneven stairs to the local history section. Only her familiarity with the bookstore stopped her from tripping on the loose-fitting carpet or the piles of books, which lined the sides of the staircase.

She took down a few books and inhaled the familiar scent of glue and paper before skimming the contents with the ease of a professional reader. Remembering the heat behind her eyes when she Saw the ghostwalker's death, Harper tried to bring that feeling to the fore, wondering if it would make any genuine supernatural content pop out like a magical highlighter. Nothing seemed to change.

Harper flipped back a few pages in the book she was holding: *The Scryer of Wombwell*. She was familiar with the history. William Byg was one of the first documented scryers in England. His work featured heavily in her thesis. A crystal ball was his bailiwick to search for lost or stolen belongings. By most accounts, he'd done nothing but help, yet he'd been condemned to public humiliation, his books supposedly consigned to the fire.

Very few people, then or now, were aware Byg's diaries and spell books were preserved in the cathedral archives. Even his punishment was mild compared to what would have happened to him a century later. In the mid-1400s, witchcraft was still prevalent in England—condemned certainly, but not regarded with the abject terror that would plague the land in the 1500s nor subject to the draconian enforcement measures employed now. Harper tugged at her collar, an invisible noose tight around her throat.

She read the tale aloud, following the lines with her finger, hoping for some inspiration from her magical forerunner. "And I did say unto the spirits, 'Spirits of light, reveal unto me the place where lies the jewelled Bible of Lady Latimer and reveal unto me the name of the demon most foul who didst steal it from her bower.'"

As she read the words, her eyes burned and watered. She snapped the book shut. There couldn't be power in the words. Despite the archaic terms, it was still a modern translation feigning to be an original quote.

"That was incredible."

A voice of wonder made Harper jump; she hadn't heard anyone else come in. She wiped her tears away with the sleeve of her jacket. As her eyes cleared, a deep shadow to her side coalesced into a black-clad teenager.

"You're one, too, aren't you?" There was a hopeful glimmer in the girl's wide, kohl-rimmed eyes.

Harper took a step back. "One what?"

The girl cupped a hand over her mouth and leant forward with a conspiratorial whisper, "A witch. I saw your eyes."

Harper's chest tightened. She tried to swallow, her throat dry. "You're making a very dangerous accusation." She forced the words out, her voice too high-pitched.

"It's okay." The girl gave her a wink. "I'm one too. We're the same."

Harper reviewed the girl's black lace dress and velvet cloak, then considered her own colourful patchwork jacket.

"We are *not* the same," she hissed. Fear cramped her stomach. If a stranger discovered what she was, it would mean the noose for sure. "I don't know what you thought you saw—"

"I *did* see." The girl's lips formed a petulant pout. "Your eyes were purple, and you were reading a spell."

"I was reading a passage from a history book. My eyes are *hazel*. The dust is making them water and you saw a reflection, that's it. What kind of stupid, childish game are you playing? Trust me, you won't like the attention you get if you keep this up." Harper checked herself, took a deep breath, then continued in a more measured tone. "If the Queen's Guard hear you, they won't stop to notice you're a kid playing dress up. They will *arrest* you. They will *question* you. And if you do manage to convince someone you're genuinely a witch, they will *execute* you."

Tears spilled down the girl's cheeks, black tracks of mascara streaking her artificially paled skin. "You're right, you're not like me," she stuttered. "You're mean." Clutching her books to her chest, she turned and ran out.

Harper collapsed back against the bookcase. The girl was undoubtedly one of a wave of teenagers who flouted authority and gained cheap thrills from pretending they were witches. Still, guilt gnawed at her stomach for making the girl cry. She'd lashed out in fear, exactly the same as any other human. Exactly the way she feared others would do if they knew what she was.

On the off chance the magic came from the book and not from her, Harper bought the slim volume for her personal collection. There was nothing in it that would normally warrant attention, so she had no excuse to take it to the cathedral. Although the close encounter left her terrified, there was elation in the knowledge she'd consciously invoked her Sight again. It left her physically drained but mentally buzzing.

She hurried home, her gaze dropped to the crooked paving slabs lest a violet hue give her away, but deep in the pit of her stomach, a nervous hope simmered. If she could control the magic, she could use it to find Hesychia and stop the murders. Selfish thoughts whirred through her mind. Not just Hesychia. She could use it to find her family, long lost in the mists and vanished even from her memory. A little more knowledge, a little more practice, and she could find her home, her kin, find herself.

Macabre images cluttered Harper's thoughts—the hangman's noose, a gleaming guillotine dripping viscous crimson, searing flames' frenzied dancing. Just images, they lacked the gut-wrenching terror of her visions. Fists balled into her skirt, Harper marched into the house.

"I'm home," she shouted to the empty hall. There was no reply. Grace was working a late shift at the veterinary clinic, so she was safe for a little while. She ran up the stairs to her room and tossed her satchel on her unmade bed. Its landing scattered the red, blue, and purple cushions she normally piled up to make a reading nook. The slam of the door behind her caused the scarlet curtains to flutter, gold-threaded patterns glinting despite the lack of direct sun.

Harper locked the door to their joint bathroom after checking her sister's room was empty. Then she wedged her chair under her bedroom door's handle. After switching on all four of her bedroom lamps as well as the nightlight plugged into the wall, she drew the curtains closed. Beyond the haze, the sun's vague orb seemed to give her a reproachful look, reminding her of the glowing eyes from her dream.

Using a long screwdriver, Harper pried loose a floorboard under her bed. Her stomach churned with doubt. Torch between her teeth, she rooted around in the space under the floor. The magic paraphernalia were shoved into a far corner, just in case anyone noticed the loose board.

Papers lay on top; notes too descriptive or too personal to go in her thesis. Each crinkle reverberated like a crack of thunder. Behind the documents lay her small stash of potentially magical items. A petite bronze statue tipped away from her exploring fingers. The thud as it fell was louder than the roar of blood in her ears. Harper froze, dread spreading a chill through her limbs. She slithered out from under the bed and pressed her ear to the bedroom door.

Silence.

Harper let out a long sigh and resumed her search. Laying on the floor, she pushed her arm in up to the shoulder. She scrabbled in the corners, unable to see. A sharp scratch on her finger elicited a curse through clenched teeth. She felt along the edge of the athame to find the handle. Something moved. Long fingers wrapped around her wrist, thin, furry, too many. It scuttled over her skin, leaving goosebumps in its wake. Dust broke apart under her touch and clung to her fingers.

"I know you're in there," she said. The knots in the floorboard imprinted on her cheek as she stretched as deep into the hole as she could. "Come out already."

As she spoke, her fingers brushed something solid. Her teeth rattled from the vibrations as it rolled into the wall. Reaching out again, slower this time, she encountered a smooth, curved surface. She wiggled her fingers to coax it closer, but the trail of wetness from her touch made it slick and hard to roll. Eventually, she teased it close enough to wrap her hand around it and pull it out.

The crystal ball was slightly too large to fit comfortably in her palm. A smear of blood dried on its surface. Harper sucked her scratched finger as she held the crystal ball up to the light with her other hand. It was unremarkable, a large marble no child would want. Clear, plain, boring.

She'd obtained it during a raid in Knaresborough a couple of years earlier—a group purporting to follow the prognostications of Mother Shipton, the famous prophetess of the region. Her powers were considered so great, places as far away as the Americas and Australia blamed her for tragic events; from the sinking of ships, to pandemics, to the drowning of children. Harper's research cast serious doubt over these stories, but the evidence was there—Mother Shipton's visions had been real.

The hypocrisy of being involved in the raid bothered Harper at the time. Another one of those occasions when Archbishop Marshall dragged them into his war against the supernatural. A war she wanted no part of. It felt like fighting herself. While Harper lacked the infamous witch's skill, there was no doubt their magics shared a kinship. Her stomach twisted, bile rising in her throat.

The women they'd found meeting at the Petrifying Well practiced no magic. They were ordinary humans who dabbled in mysticism for the thrill. Their collection of faux magic items had been impressive but worthless according to the senior cathedral archivists.

Harper slid the board back into place, then sat with her back against her bed to study her find. It was only glass, yet she'd never been comfortable with the idea of throwing it away. She'd found the crystal ball tucked in a corner, dusty and unused, a relic from an earlier obsession before the women focused on Mother Shipton. It probably didn't even work. She'd slipped the crystal ball into her satchel when no one was looking. Flames cleansed everything else.

She stared into its depths, unblinking, willing something, anything, to happen. Lamplight caught on its clear surface, dazzled, seared trails of colours across her vision. She twisted it counterclockwise, mesmerised by the twinkling caught within. It flickered like fire, as if something inside the crystal refracted the sparks and made them dance.

A shimmer seeped through the glass like drops of rain trickling down a window. The colourless glass darkened to the hues of stone, shining and slick with running water. The maw of a cave split the rock, a skull with long, bulging teeth. Thick saliva drooled from incisors browned with peat. The image expanded beyond the edges of the crystal ball and filled the room. Animals were stuck within the cavern's teeth, petrified to stone—bear cubs, rabbits, and pups. Underneath the yellowed bone, faces appeared, their mouths locked in frozen screams. All around, the continuous drip of water. Acting against nature, it transformed flesh into stone.

Water drenched Harper's face, thick and dark. It crystallised her eyelashes, her sight growing murky. Cloying mucus stuck to her skin. It trickled into her mouth, slick and metallic on her tongue. She gasped and the sludge drained into her lungs. Coughing and spluttering, she doubled over. The crystal fell into her lap as she clutched her chest. The maw of the cave closed, receding until it was nothing but a tiny dot. Then it was gone.

Her lungs ached as though she were deep underwater. Her eyes were dry and hot. Grit scratched her corneas as she blinked furiously to clear them of floating lights. She remembered that cave: the last of the would-be witches had fled there. They'd kept a lab there, of sorts, using the mineral-filled water to petrify common items in an attempt to look magical.

Determined not to let her visions best her, Harper opened the book she found that morning and flipped to the page titled *'Lady Latimer.'* If the crystal let her See the Petrifying Well, maybe it could show her the murderer too.

She grabbed her notebook from the desk next to her and rewrote the spell to suit her purpose, hoping the overall pattern would remain the same. Invoke spirits of light. Tell them what she was seeking. Try to sound like she was on the side of good. Between words, she worried the end of her pencil between her teeth.

Fear and hope raged in her stomach, pressed on her spine, tightened her lungs. The blood still seeping from her finger offered an opportunity. Guilt squirmed through her gut. She should try to find the murderer, but if this worked, she could do that spell as well. The temptation to reach into her past was too great.

Harper scratched out the spell and scribbled in new words, before she could change her mind. She pressed the bleeding digit against the crystal ball, a pinprick of pain. Balancing the sphere in the other hand, she held it up at eye level, peering into it intently.

The reflection of her violin, still lying on her bedside table, distorted and stretched over the crystal's surface. Both distant and deep within, Harper could hear the strains of a long-forgotten tune, melancholic, mourning. It weighed on her heart, her eyes moist. Her words were heavy as though spoken through someone else's lips. "Spirits of light, reveal unto me where lie those who share my blood and reveal unto me the name of the demon who didst separate us."

In the centre of the crystal, bands of colour pulsed like a plasma ball. A stream of brilliant white arched to the edge where Harper's blood congealed. On either side of the light, blue feline eyes hovered, staring. Then they blinked and vanished. The other lights died, leaving one strong thread pulsing. The white turned pink, then red, then black, as the blood was sucked through solid crystal.

Specks flew off like ash, clouding the ball. It was thicker than fog, blacker than midnight, grimmer than nightmares.

The air crackled with static. Harper's hair floated around her as if submerged in the sea. With a crash, the lights went out, bulbs shattered. The crystal rose, reflected her purple-eyed stare, captured her in its depths. Within the darkness, figures twisted and writhed, features barely discernible as their ghostly hands stretched out, begging, pleading.

She watched with horror as the ash buried them, pouring into screaming mouths, smothering, rising over their heads, along arms stretched out in desperation, rising, rising. Each finger was consumed, vanished, gone forever. A lump rose in her throat and tears stung her eyes. Her voice came out a hoarse whisper. "They can't be dead. They can't—"

Music swelled, discordant, too flat then too sharp. It cut off her words and set her teeth on edge. Every string on her violin snapped with a loud twang, then silence smothered the lightless room.

The darkness within the crystal split, glowing white breaking through. Pointed, sharp, mouthless teeth contorted into a cannibalistic grin.

The crystal rolled from Harper's numb fingers and shattered into bloody shards on the wooden floor. Darkness flowed out. Ash and static melded together and expanded to fill the room. A wide grin glinted like a demented Cheshire Cat. Laughter ricocheted like a bullet. Harper had no thought but to escape, but her limbs were stiff with terror and her jellied legs couldn't run.

She groped for a weapon, years of training instinctively taking over. The laugh echoed inside her, clattered through her skull. The eyes from her nightmares watched her, crowded in. And those whispers from before ... *"Never scream ... Never scream ..."* over and over and over, caught in a web of terrible laughter.

Harper clawed at her desk until she found something heavy, bound with metal. With a strangled cry, she smashed Grace's Bible down on the mocking grin.

Chapter Ten

"Ow." It was a male voice, sharp with annoyance, with a harpsichord buzz in the background. "Do you mind, young lady?"

Harper scrambled onto the bed and grabbed the matchbox she kept in her bedside cabinet. The first match sparked and died, eliciting a long, drawn-out sigh from the floor.

"You really are quite useless. Just my luck, to be summoned by an incompetent witch. At least it will be entertaining if you set yourself on fire."

The second match lit. Harper held the small flame to a candle until the light held steady. Warm, yellow light flickered around the room, and banished the darkness. It caught in the broken glass covering the floor, appearing like a sea of licking flames. In the centre of the carnage lay Grace's heirloom Bible. A roiling fog oozed out from underneath it, one tendril splitting off to wave in the air.

"If you would be so kind as to remove this onerous weight, Harper dear. I am sure you did not summon me to carry your books."

"What are …" Harper coughed, licked her lips, and tried again. "What are you? How do you know my name?"

"What am I?" The laughter returned, muffled but no less gleeful. "You summon me and you do not even know what I am?"

"I didn't summon you." *I don't think I did anyway.* She ran back over the spell in her mind trying to work out where she went wrong. If the scryer of Wombwell had summoned a demon, she was certain his punishment would've been far harsher.

"You summoned. I came. Although, you made it very difficult."

"You came from where? Through the Veil?" Harper's breath caught. Surely her magic wasn't so great as to breach the Veil. The tendril of smoke waved at her again.

"Where I came from is unimportant, but do not believe yourself so powerful as all that. I am an illusion spirit. You were doing something very dangerous, silly girl. You were about to draw attention you did not want. Do you not know that when you look for something powerful, something may also look back at you? It has been searching for you for so long. And you nearly handed yourself up to it on a platter."

"I asked the crystal to show me my family. If something wasn't holding them captive, they'd have come looking for me years ago. How do I know it isn't you?"

"I refuse to answer any further questions until you take this ludicrously heavy book off me."

Harper shook her head. "No way. Grace's Bible might be the only thing stopping you from harming me. It's going to stay there until you answer my questions and I work out a way to banish you."

The creature sighed again, its tendrils wafting around like the flap of nervous hands.

"Fine," it huffed. Then it floated up, passed through the Bible with the ease of air, and coalesced into a sooty sphere about the size of a tennis ball on top of it. A wide grin split its featureless form. "If I wanted to hurt you, dear Harper, I would have done so already." Then the grin zipped closed, and the creature settled back through the Bible onto the floor. It waved its tendrils as though trapped by the tome and cried in a plaintive voice, "Help me, Harper darling."

"Why do you …? I mean, why?" Harper rubbed her forehead. "If you can do that, why do you need me to move the Bible?"

"Because you are my mistress," the creature purred. "You summoned me, and I am bound to you. By placing this monstrosity on top of me, you gave an implied order I was to stay here. It really is quite uncomfortable."

Harper took a deep breath. "So, if I order you to stay there after I move the Bible …"

"Then stay I shall."

"Okay. You aren't allowed to do any magic and you have to stay where you are so I can see you," Harper commanded, feeling somewhat silly.

"As you say." The creature bent a tendril toward her in mimicry of a bow. Harper shoved some of the glass aside with her toe, then lifted the

Bible. The so-called spirit popped back into the spherical shape it seemed to prefer.

She picked her way over to her trunk, kicking the shards of glass into the corner as she did so. Pulling out several bundles of dried herbs, she lit the end with a match and the room was permeated with scents of sage and dill. It didn't work against witches, but she was willing to try the old superstitions; after all, she hadn't expected the crystal ball to work either. She wafted the smoke toward the spirit, whose grin only widened.

"If I called you here, I can make you go away," she said. "Umm, let's see. Creature of darkness, return to the place from whence you came, bother this realm no longer."

Nothing happened.

Harper dunked the smouldering herbs into the carafe of water on her nightstand. "Never did believe in those things anyway. Maybe ..." After a minute or so rooting through her trunk, she pulled out a bottle of clear liquid.

"Creature of evil, begone from this place. In the name of Jesus, son of God the Most High, I banish you." She sprinkled Holy Water over the spirit, then, when it had no effect, upended the bottle over him.

The creature bristled like an angry cat, but the noise coming from it was closer to a purr than a hiss. "That tickled. Are you really trying to vanquish me? You cannot succeed. Maybe this will prove to you my good intent. We are bound, you and I, bound by blood."

Harper bit her lip as she peered down at its Cheshire Cat grin. She certainly had no idea of how to get rid of the thing. The ball of black fuzz seemed to stare back up at her, despite its lack of eyes. She worried the loose ends of her plait.

"Are you the thing that took my memory and my home?" Harper asked.

"Of course not." The creature chuckled. "I do not have that kind of power. When you tried to See it, your magic called to it. It was about to See you, so I cast an illusion to keep you safe. It will not stop searching. You do not want to banish me. I can protect you."

Harper found herself nodding, then shook herself. "Why should I trust you?"

"Trust or not, I do not care. You *need* me. I need you. Simple. It is close to finding you. It has already been in your dreams."

"So, my nightmares about the murders are related to my amnesia? Hesychia is responsible for whatever happened to me too?"

"Hmm. Hesychia." The creature rolled the word around, tasting it, testing it. "I do not know what creature haunts you, but it is ancient and powerful with practice in the dreamscape. It could be a hesychia. Killing witches can be dangerous. It could be you Saw something and were banished to keep you silent."

"Something that's repeating now?"

"Lores of affinity would account for your worsening nightmares in the scenario you propose."

Harper glowered at the indistinct ball of ash. It knew more than it was letting on, of that she was sure. If it had to obey her, maybe it was the lesser evil to let it stay and to force it to tell her everything. If it had to obey her ...

"You have to do what I tell you? If I tell you not to hurt anyone ...?"

"You requested a spirit of light. I would not harm someone. You are perfectly safe with me, dear. Safer than without me."

Harper raised an eyebrow at the cloud of black fuzz. "You're a spirit of *light?*"

"I am an illusion spirit and that is what illusions are, Harper dear. Tricks of light, of sound, of perception. I can hide you from the darkness in your dreams, from this hesychia. I can hide the whole house from those hunting you, human and demon alike. I can teach you how to control your magic."

Harper could hear Father De Santos reading warnings from the Bible as the family sat in their cosy lounge by the open fire. *The serpent told the Woman, "You won't die ... You'll see what's really going on." Now compare this to Luke's Gospel, where the Devil tempts Jesus and is denied. In the first passage, the serpent brought about the fabled Fall, only a parable but teaching us the consequences of listening to demons. In Luke, the Devil retreats and is ultimately vanquished.*

"You won't die ... You'll See what's really going on."

Harper's hand moved toward the creature, almost of its own accord. It offered her a chance to catch a murderer. It offered her a chance to go home. She watched her finger, still oozing blood, touch an almost intangible tendril. Her hand itched to the bone with static charge. Electric jolts fizzed through her blood. Yet, instead of pain, energy surged through her. Images flashed before her, like she stood within another's mind:

A stage. A man in chains, locked in a tank of water. A silent audience, mouths agape. Then thunderous applause as he stood, free, before them.

A tree hovering over blue flame, fruit bursting forth, filling the air with the scent of oranges. Peel torn away, white cloth within revealed by mechanical butterflies.

A dull, grey block of metal, sitting on an intricate diagram burnt into the wooden table. Fizzling as yellowed liquid flowed over it. Lead, whitened and flaking away, bright gold revealed.

A turbaned man hovering five feet above the ground, weightless as a helium balloon.

Harper gasped and yanked her hand back. The static-filled air pricked her lungs, burnt her chest as though she inhaled hot smoke.

"Your magic?" she asked the creature, her eyes hot from the visions.

"Ours," the spirit replied. "Some things were my magic, others were theirs, tricks I taught them. They were some of the most infamous men of their times."

"I don't want to be infamous."

"You want something even harder to achieve." Its pointed grin was sharp as a knife digging into her heart. "You want to possess power and to remain *un*seen. Your magic is sloppy, obvious, indelicate. Listen to my teachings and you could become the greatest witch the world will never know."

Harper tugged her braid. All choice in the matter had been taken from her: use her abilities and risk death or bury them and remain forever lost. Magic was the only recourse left to find her home. She wasn't going to learn enough by trial and error. Not when she couldn't even banish the thing she herself summoned.

It's an illusion spirit. For reasons she couldn't explain, she believed what the creature was telling her. Whether it was some illusion it created for its own benefit or whether it was her own desperation overriding all common sense, she couldn't say.

"What do you get in return?" she asked, one last piece of sense puncturing her numb mind.

"What do I get?" The creature laughed again. Harper grit her teeth against the sound, but it didn't echo as it had before. "Why, Harper dear, I get to watch."

A chill ran down her spine as pointed teeth split the darkness.

She took a deep breath, her fingers crossed as she twisted them into her hair. She prayed it told the truth or else she was about to make the biggest mistake of her life. With no idea how to get rid of it, she couldn't think of any other options.

"You help me find this murderer, help me learn enough magic to get my family back, do nothing to harm any humans, and you can stay."

A slender tendril snaked across the floor, up the leg of the bed, and around Harper's arm. It snapped around her wrist like a manacle. When it spoke, the air rushed from the room with the percussive force of thunder. Her ringing ears could barely make out the words as the magic took effect.

"We have a deal."

Chapter Eleven

The low sun stretched the silhouette of Bishopthorpe Palace across the broad swathes of green grass running down to where the River Ouse skirted the boundaries of the archbishop's property. Usa waited beneath a weeping willow, strands of leaves flowing over her like a mermaid's hair.

Shouting echoed from within the stone edifice humans took so much pride in. As if stacking rocks in unnatural ways was somehow glorifying. Rock could be worn down by weather, water, and wind. Even those who sought refuge within it would eventually be caught.

Usa recognised the voice emanating from the building. 'Deacon' humans called him. He claimed to work for God, but the hateful bile that spewed from his mouth represented no god Usa knew, of the humans or of her kin.

Many times, he'd polluted the air of York with his admonitions and scaremongering. The twisted tales he told gave humans the beady eyes of crows and the tender noses of rats. He urged them to seek out her Folk and to kill them wherever they may be found. His hands never touched death, but for as long as his voice issued the call to arms, Usa's kin would never find peace.

The breeze ran its fingers through long strands of aromatic herbs planted in squares near the building. Usa let their savoury, wholesome scent flow through her. These plants, natural and beautiful, had been collected and restricted, made to grow in slavery to humans. Within the wind, the voices of her kith and kin begged for her help.

Usa, hide us.

Usa, protect us.

Usa, save us.

Old superstitions made humans believe these herbs kept them safe. For some, it may even have been true, offering protection against creatures of Faerie so dark and twisted Earth herself reviled them. To Usa's kin, every bit as natural to this place as the humans who claimed to own it, the herbs were cleansing and welcome. Their pleas solidified her resolve.

Let humans believe their silly superstitions kept them safe. Let them drop their guard.

In the distance, a deep bell tolled a warning, sending humans skittering for their dens. Usa waited, still and silent. He would come.

When the shouting in the hall ceased, the deacon rushed outside. The long material around his legs hampered his movements, tripped up his feet so he almost fell. Mist rolled off the river to greet him. In his arrogance, he paid it no heed. He stood on the bank of the Ouse, the water gold, pink, and blue as the sun sank. He pressed a light against his face as he spoke to the air. Usa had seen such devices before. They were a blessing to her, helping the Folk remain invisible. Humans coveted them like dragon gold and guarded them as closely. She hung back in the shadow of the willow, listening.

"The owner of this phone is currently unavailable. Please leave a message after the tone." *Beep.*

"Archbishop. I'm at Bishopthorpe. It's sunset, where are you? I've found something ... terrible. The man who was murdered, the ghostwalker ... I went to their guild. In their records ... This isn't the first death like this they've encountered. The Veil has been breached. Please, you must return quickly. It's unsafe. York isn't safe. Please hurry."

Usa, hide us.

The voices swelled, crashed through her body with the force of a storm at sea. His voice brought death. Something dark twisted through Usa's core, a weed strangling her reason, giving way to an emotion she didn't recognise.

Usa, protect us.

The willow didn't bend as she passed through the veil of its branches. The deacon paced up and down the riverbank, his eyes drawn to the water as the light faded from the sky.

Usa, save us.

Usa's hand penetrated jawbone and teeth. Her fingers closed around speckled, slimy muscle. His shout of horror became a gurgling cry as the tongue that had killed so many broke away from his body. Soft, pink lips flaked from his face as Usa wrenched her hand away from him. As soon as their connection broke, his corpse thudded to the ground. Mist rushed in. It billowed over the body like a shroud.

She looked down at the bloody flesh in her hand. He would tell tales of her people no more.

It should've brought catharsis but instead, a strange pain broke through her surety. If she didn't know better, she might have thought it was the thing humans called doubt, but such actions were not in her nature.

What am I becoming? The thought washed through her, banished almost too quickly to hear, but something of the sentiment remained in her spirit. As she vanished with the sun, the voices lingered on the air.

"Never tell…"

"Never tell…"

The whisper floated past Harper as she strived to block out the sounds around her. The creature she'd summoned insisted a state of meditative calm was best for casting magic.

"Never tell…"

"What did you say?" Harper cracked open an eye.

"I did not say anything," the bristling ball of soot replied. "You are too easily distracted. Your magic is sloppy, amateur. To think I have fallen so low as to be forced to rely on such a subpar witch."

Harper flopped back against her cushions with a sharp exhalation. She'd dragged them onto the floor along with a map and an old necklace of Whitby jet. With her crystal ball shattered into a thousand pieces, she'd thought to find the hesychia by scrying.

"None of this makes sense," she blurted out, fists thumping the floor in frustration. "Bits of stone on rope or chains, crystal balls, images in still water, there are so many descriptions, yet none of these things inherently hold magic. Why would a piece of amethyst be able to find a lost child better than a piece of peridot? It's rubbish. Or at least I thought it was."

"If I am to teach you, then you must suspend that disbelieving nature of yours," the illusion spirit admonished. "The power for some things is within you. The magic comes from you, not from the stone, yet a free object such as a pendant can be useful. If you scry with your finger on a map, then your finger will try to direct itself. A pendant will let the magic do as it must. Do you understand?"

"Kind of." Harper rolled her shoulders. "Let's try something else. When I Saw the ghostwalker die, the being that killed him was difficult to See. I think the hesychia, or whatever spirit it is, isn't entirely tangible, which means I can't kill it with a blade, and I can't trap it with chains or rope. How do I fight it?"

"I will teach you how to draw a containment circle," the creature said. "That will allow you to capture an ethereal. And we will continue to work on your visions and scrying, so you know where to capture them."

"I'm trusting you."

A low purr emanated from the static cloud. "I am so glad to hear you say so, Harper dearest. Trust is vital. Now, you will need a clear space of floor and some chalk …"

***

There were dark circles under her eyes as Harper dragged her eyelids open to give the chalk drawing on the floor a critical once over. Her furniture was arrayed against three of the bedroom walls, the fourth having the door through to Grace's room, leaving more than enough floor space for her to draw a circle a metre in diameter. The illusion spirit was making good on his promise to teach her magic. That didn't mean he wouldn't let her blow herself up if he thought it would be funny.

"What is this?" the scornful spirit asked. He was pooled in her lap, a tendril raised to peer at the circle she sketched on the bedroom floor. "And why is it pastel green?"

"Does the colour make a difference? You're lucky I had any chalk at all. Would you rather it was pink?"

"The girl asks if it makes a difference. Tch." He slipped out between her crossed legs, flowing into the circle then out again. "*This* is *not* a containment circle. *This* is a child's game. No one will ever believe you are a real witch if you cannot even make a basic circle."

"I don't want people to think I'm a real witch."

He *tsked* at her again. "Magic is about showmanship, theatre. What something is, is less important than what it seems to be."

"Well, I believe this is a containment circle." Harper crossed her arms over her chest and glared down at him.

"And I believe you have a death wish," the spirit snapped. "It does not matter if you believe it is a containment circle, what matters is if the creature you wish to trap believes it. Whatever killed this ghostwalker is more powerful than you are. Erase this nonsense and start again."

"Still only have coloured chalk," Harper muttered as she took a damp cloth to the floor. Moving to a different section of the room, she picked up her chalk and tried to summon the burning sensation behind her eyes she'd come to associate with magic.

"Air. Fire. Water. Earth. Spirit." She cited each of the elements as she sketched the corresponding symbols into her circle. It reminded her of reciting the catechism at school, the only girl in her class who didn't know it by rote. This time she lacked Grace's helpful whispering in her ear. In school, at university, in a fight, Grace always had her back. Her conscience prickled at doing something behind her sister's back now.

"How's that?" Harper asked when she finished sketching. It was almost a perfect circle, just a little wobbly on the western side.

"Better," the spirit conceded. He rolled over the diagram, which sparked like an electric wire. "Oooh, I almost felt a tingle that time. Nowhere near good enough, but definitely better. Do it again."

Harper continued to erase and resketch the circle until almost every inch of her floor was too damp to draw on. A hint of pride swelled in her chest as she closed the loop on a perfectly round circle, the first she'd managed. Some of the individual elements were a little wonky, but the core was solid. She ached like she'd gone ten rounds with Gabriel, the only one of Grace's siblings who could still decisively beat her every time. This one would work. It was almost as satisfying as the one time she managed to knock Gabriel on his butt.

She scooped her teacher up and tipped him into the circle before he could protest. There was a flash like magnesium and faint vertical bars rose from the edge of her design. He poked one of them with a slender tendril. It gleamed as he touched it and he withdrew, fluffing himself like an angry cat. Muttering in a language Harper couldn't place, he splayed out and covered the circle in ash and static. The light barrier wavered where he touched it, then dissolved.

He flowed out to reform at her feet, a ball of soot split with a crescent moon grin. "Now that, dear Harper, was *almost* a containment circle."

Harper huffed out a deeply held breath, scooped him up, and deposited him on her shoulder. They both examined the imperfect spell. Ribbons of light skittered along its edges. The spirit chuckled, a waspish buzz. Harper's lips twitched, something bubbling up in her stomach. All the stress, all the fear, burst out of her and she dissolved into giggles. She collapsed backwards onto her bed, unable to contain her mirth.

A bang on the bedroom door interrupted her laughter. She sat bolt upright, the colour draining from her face. "Who is it?"

"Grace. Who else? Why have you blocked the door?"

"Umm." The vague guilt she'd been carrying all afternoon blossomed in Harper's chest. Hiding things from Grace was wrong, but her sister would disapprove, maybe even enough to abandon her. Harper tried to tell herself it would never happen, but the fear remained, heavy in the pit of her stomach. Fear she would lose the family she had now in her attempts to find the one she'd lost.

She quickly stuffed her notes in a drawer and kicked some pillows over the almost-containment circle then shoved the chalk and her map under the bed, deliberately aiming for the chuckling creature who had slunk there when Grace knocked. She unwedged her chair and opened the door to find her sister glowering at her.

"Hey, Gray."

The bedroom door banged against the edge of the wardrobe as Grace pushed past Harper into the bedroom. She stood in the centre of the room, toes almost touching the pile of pillows as she peered around, her eyes narrow and suspicious.

"Why did you block the door?" she repeated as she tested the window locks.

"Well, you know how it is with the landlady bringing prospective renters by all the time, one can—" Harper stopped abruptly as Grace glared at her.

"Don't try that with me." Grace shook a finger at her. "Lying is a sin and you are shockingly bad at it."

"Isn't that a good thing?"

"Spill."

"Hello there, Ms. De Santos, such a pleasure to meet one of your family at last." A silky voice emanated from under the bed.

Grace's knife was drawn before she finished turning. "Stay behind me, Harper."

The creature slithered out of the shadows, his wide grin locked in place. Without hesitation, Grace threw the knife. The illusion spirit oozed around it like blood seeping from an open wound. Shoving Harper toward the door adjoining their rooms, Grace took a step back, arms raised defensively.

"Get to the locker." Grace's eyes never left the grinning apparition.

"Gray, it's okay …" Harper dodged her sister's guard to stand between Grace and the creature.

"Harper, get out of the way." Grace's eyes widened as they darted from Harper's set jaw and crossed arms to the chuckling ball of soot now clinging to her trainers.

"It's a spirit," Harper explained. "An illusion spirit and—"

"What?" Grace shrieked. Harper staggered and fell onto the bed as Grace pushed her aside. She stamped on the creature. Her heel pierced his core, but he simply flowed around her shoe and reformed a couple of feet away. "Harper, what in heaven's name have you done?"

"Gray, please—" Harper pleaded. She worried she'd gone too far, pushed Grace over the line of what she could endure.

"What is that *thing* doing here?" Grace snapped, but Harper noted with relief that she at least dropped the volume. "Why are you protecting it?"

"I kind of accidentally summoned it," Harper admitted. "Or him, I guess. I'm sorry. I never asked what pronouns—"

"Him? Him?" Grace interrupted. "That thing is not a 'him,' a 'her,' a 'ze,' or a 'them.' It's an 'it.'"

"I find that mildly insulting." The creature's grin broadened further. "I am indeed a 'him.'"

"If he thinks of himself as 'him,' what else matters?" Harper asked.

"You talk like it's human," Grace spat. "It's a demon." She grabbed the Bible and slammed it down on top of the spirit. He oozed out from underneath and reformed on top of the book. Harper swallowed a giggle.

"Now, now, Grace darling, that was very inhospitable of you."

"Harper, get rid of it," Grace demanded.

"I … can't." Harper grimaced, then continued while Grace managed a look that was both incredulous and fuming. "It was an accident, but he can hide me from the Queen's Guard. He's going to be my teacher. I'm already getting better at controlling my magic." Harper nudged a pillow aside with her toe to reveal the edge of the chalk circle.

Grace's eyes narrowed. "Harper, that thing is a heresy. It cannot stay here."

"Heresy, hmm …" The creature rolled over to Harper and bumped against her shoe. Then he slithered up her body until he rested around her neck like an overly familiar scarf. "I like 'heresy' and I would hate to argue with a De Santos. They are the foremost experts after all. If she says I am a heresy, then 'Heresy' I shall be."

"You aren't helping," Harper muttered then said louder, "I need him, Gray. I have to learn. Things are getting out of hand. I didn't mean to summon him. It's like magic is leaking out of me. If I can't control it, I'll get caught. If I don't find a way to deal with the dreams, I'll go mad. Please. Give it a week. We have a pact. He can't hurt anyone."

She found it strange to be making all the arguments she made to herself. The hypocrisy smarted, like vinegar in a wound.

"Ever heard of a monkey's paw? I'm going to get Godfather. No one will believe it if it says you summoned it. He'll vanquish it." Grace pivoted on her heel and marched to the door. A chill spread through Harper. She lunged and grabbed her sister's arm. Grace turned with a snarl. "What are you doing?"

"Grace, please." Harper stared into her sister's dark eyes, pleading. "I can't … I can't go through another exorcism. If he even suspects I did this … Grace, you can't tell. The spirit can help me find the murderer. What if this wasn't a one-off killing? Please Grace, I can do this. I swear."

Grace shook her arm free of Harper's grasp. Her glare made a thunderstorm look friendly. "You have one day to clean up this mess or I will." As she slammed the door behind her, Harper caught her final words. "You'll regret this."

Harper stared at the closed door with a dazed expression. "She needs to sleep it off. She'll come back. She always comes back." Said aloud, the truth of the words offered some reassurance, easing the pain in her heart. Grace knew what she was. She didn't like it, but she knew, and she always came back.

A tickle around her throat reminded Harper she had bigger worries than Grace's temper. She tucked her chin to glare down at the spirit around her neck. He gave her a jaunty wave then dropped onto her desk.

"Why the hell did you do that?" Harper asked. "You're supposed to hide me, not out me to my sister."

"You are a bad liar," the self-proclaimed Heresy replied. "I like that about you."

"That doesn't answer the question."

"It was funny."

"You picked a fight with Grace for your own amusement?" Harper stiffened, then turned away. She relaxed her shoulders and spread her fingers wide to siphon off the tension. "It wasn't funny. She doesn't understand."

"I think you will find it was most amusing. I needed a distraction. You are a terrible witch. You spent all afternoon scrying for your sister and could not find her when she was right outside the door."

"She wasn't outside the door this afternoon," Harper grumbled. Her jubilation with her progress drawing the containment circle vanished, a bone-deep weariness setting in. Maybe the spirit was right: she was a terrible witch.

Chapter Twelve

It was too bright. The nightlight was not this intense.

Harper wrinkled her nose as she rubbed her eyes with the back of her arm.

Far too bright.

She squinted up at the ceiling. Dark lines momentarily twisted into multi-legged creatures, which scuttled across the white stucco, then morphed into cracks in the plaster as Harper opened her eyes fully.

It was morning and she hadn't dreamt at all.

"Did you stop my nightmares?" Harper rolled over and leant on one arm to examine the black shadow splayed over her desk.

"I told you something was looking for you," the fuzzy creature replied as it quite literally pulled itself together. "I also told you I could hide you from it."

"Grace?" Harper jumped out of bed and ran across to the shared bathroom, but when she knocked on her sister's bedroom door there was no reply. "Grace, talk to me. Heresy stopped my nightmares. Even your father couldn't do that. Grace?"

When she got no response, she cracked open the door and peered in. The room was still dark; Grace's light-blocking curtains forbade the sun entry. Her room was the mirror of Harper's—desk, chair, bed, dome-lidded trunk of weapons—but her décor was reds and greys. On the wall above the bed, a smoky-furred kitten waved from a charity calendar. A silken lump huddled in the middle of the bed. Leaving the door open to let light in, Harper tiptoed across the room and poked it.

"Eurgerofeearp."

"Grace, c'mon. We've got to talk. Wake up."

A hand slunk out from under the blanket to swat Harper away. "I said, get off me, Harp."

"I didn't have a single nightmare last night. I can learn to control this, Gray, but I need the help. This is safer. I swear to you. I'll swear it on the Bible if you want."

"Swear on something you believe in, agnostic." The blanket slid back to reveal a ruffled Grace, loose hair nebulous around her shoulders.

Harper smoothed it back, leaving her hand resting on her sister's head. "I *need* to do this. It's safe. I swear on *you*."

Grace's eyes met hers, searching. "I don't like it. Are you sure you can't banish it? I can ask Gabriel. You know he'll help and he won't ask too many questions. Even if he does think you're possessed again, you know he wouldn't hurt you."

"I'm sure. Please don't tell Gabriel. I couldn't bear it if …" Harper choked. "I lost one family. I can't lose another. I can't bear to see my brother look at me with those cold, judgemental eyes. Please don't tell him. Trust me. A few days. Please."

Grace extricated an arm from the blanket to wrap around Harper. "You've got me backed into a corner here, you know."

"I know." Harper wiped her eyes. "Thank you. For trusting me."

Grace squeezed her hand, then flopped back on her bed and tugged the blanket over her head. "Three days, Harp. Now, go away. I'm on a night shift."

With a plan agreed, Harper trusted Grace to stand by her to the bitter end of it. She took the victory and left her sister in peace. Back in her own room, she dressed in a hurry, throwing on jeans and a T-shirt with a rainbow across the chest.

"You stay here," she ordered when Heresy attempted to roll into her satchel. "Who knows what alarms you'll trigger if I take you to the cathedral. Anyway, you said you could guard the house. Grace is here. I don't want anyone somehow detecting I've been doing magic and coming for her instead. Stay here and protect her. And stay out of her way. I may not be able to banish you but I guarantee she'll find a way."

Harper snatched her bag up before Heresy could argue and closed the bedroom door firmly behind her. She considered tying some of the landlady's protective herbs around the handle but quickly dismissed the idea. If they weren't effective against a witch, why should they stop a spirit? Why would a spirit who could pass through a book even need to use the door? As far as she knew, he could pass right through the wall or even the floor.

Pondering how Heresy managed to interact with solid objects and be incorporeal, Harper was lost deep in thought as she entered the cathedral.

The archbishop waited for her at the entrance to the undercroft. His skin was ashen and there were deep circles under his eyes. For once, he did not smile as he greeted her. "Good morning, child."

"What's wrong?"

"Please come with me."

He turned and headed down into the crypt. They passed the tomb of Saint William and continued until they were well past the area where tourists, or even members of the congregation, were permitted. Here, long rows of tombs stood as testament to the lives of those most important to the church, their carved effigies watching over the cathedral in death as their occupants watched over it in life. A new sculpture lay atop one of the empty tombs at the end. A darkened form stooped over it without touching. Ghoulish light emanated from somewhere behind the tomb, casting charcoal shadows over the figure's features.

"Archbishop, what …?" Cold squeezed her heart. A hand snaked into hers as the archbishop led her closer, his fingers cold and clammy.

"Paul was murdered last night." Archbishop Marshall heaved a sigh. "On my own palace grounds. I ordered his body be brought here for sanctification. I did not want the impersonal hands of the police to defile him. He wouldn't have wanted it, either."

"But they have to do an autopsy, surely." Harper was unable to pry her eyes away. She'd always been wary of the deacon's zeal for finding and persecuting anything with even a whiff of the supernatural, but he'd been a fixture of her day for years. He was always first there, opening the door to let her in, telling the world it was safe. Without him there to declare it so, who would reassure York that night had passed?

Her breath caught as she remembered the shadow following him through the cathedral as he snuffed the candles out. It had been the same day the archbishop asked her to find the ghostwalker's murderer. Harper covered her mouth and scrunched her eyes closed, willing the burning to disappear. Tears spilled over and rolled down her cheeks. *Did I See his death? Was I supposed to save him?*

"You have seen death before, child," Archbishop Marshall reminded her, his tone sorrowful.

"Not of someone I know," she whispered. "Not in real life. Just in …"

The archbishop said nothing. Father De Santos would have told his oldest friend of the demon who plagued her with visions before he performed the exorcism that freed her. It was a story everyone believed, except for Grace and Harper herself.

In her mind, images crowded together—the eyes surrounding her in the dark; the ghostwalker, illuminated in her vision until his life was stolen; people screaming in the crystal ball as ash buried them. The fluttering of the torches on the walls made it appear as if the corpse moved, but the archbishop walked on, dragging Harper with him. As they reached the end of the mausoleum, he addressed the man examining the body.

"Doctor Siddique, I believe you've met Harper Ashbury, member of the De Santos family and employee of this cathedral?"

The ebullient enthusiasm of their last meeting was gone from Saqib's face. His features were drawn, tired, and he stooped as though carrying a great weight. He nodded to the archbishop and gave Harper a sneak of a smile, which vanished immediately. "We met."

"What happened?" Harper asked, her voice shaking.

"That is what I hope you and Doctor Siddique will tell me. He didn't exsanguinate or die of shock from his wounds. The paramedics and our own examiner could find no obvious cause of death." The archbishop's lips pressed together as he regarded his friend's corpse. His hand trembled on Harper's shoulder.

As she studied the deacon's remains, bile piled in the back of her throat. His eyes were closed, his body dressed in his ceremonial robe with his hands folded over his chest, clasping a rosary. There was no obvious trauma to the body. His skin was pale and sallow, the only colour a few flecks of blood showing through a square of white cotton laid over his mouth and chin. Harper reached out without thinking and pinched the cotton between her fingers, then dropped it and jerked back. An involuntary gasp choked her on the bitter taste of myrrh.

She gazed upon jagged flesh, blood caked where once lips had been, his mouth an unlocked chest. Empty, a dark cavern of silence. In death, what was missing told a greater story than ever passed his lips when he was alive.

"Never scream ... Never tell ..."

Harper's head shot up. Her heart beat so violently she was sure it shook her bones hard enough for Archbishop Marshall to feel it. The whisper slipped away through cracks in stone and into tombs, until only the memory of the words remained. Neither the archbishop nor Saqib looked up. Their still countenances showed no signs they heard the multi-toned voices. Harper recognised them. She'd heard them before, a promise at the end of a nightmare.

She wondered what Heresy would say. He professed to know nothing about the murder of the ghostwalker, and Harper would never risk bringing him to the cathedral, but maybe if he saw this, he could tell her something.

"Did you find anything where Ghostwalker Adams was murdered?" she asked Saqib.

"At the scene, no." Saqib glanced down at Paul's body, and Harper hastily covered his mutilated mouth again as the scientist continued, "However, once the medical examiner finished her autopsy, I did find something ... unusual on the body. I was reviewing the ME's photos when I noticed some odd cuts on the inner lining of the throat. They were far too small to be seen by the naked eye; I had to use a specialist camera and magnify by a factor of over one hundred to even see a hint of it. Definitely too small to have been carved by a human hand."

"Was that how his vocal cords were removed?" Harper asked.

"Now that's the interesting bit. It wasn't. The cuts were actually tiny runes. Here." Saqib pulled a manilla folder out of his case and handed it to Harper. Inside were photos of a gelatinous, pinkish substance. Harper frowned, then blanched, when she realised it was a close up of the ghostwalker's throat. "I came by to show you yesterday, but you weren't here. I don't think they're Viking or Celtic, but I could be wrong. They don't match anything I could find at the university library anyway. I was hoping you'd recognise them."

Harper traced the emblem with one finger. She had seen it before. Or rather Seen it before. It had been stamped in the mist of her vision of the ghostwalker's death.

"This looks familiar." She offered the photo to the archbishop who perched his glasses on the end of his nose and leant closer to peer at it. "I don't know what it means though. I'll cross-reference the symbols with our artefacts, maybe speak to the Jorvik Centre to see if it's an obscure Viking dialect or something." She glanced at the corpse lying between them, the decomposing elephant in the room. "Does this lettering appear on … on Deacon Paul as well?" She forced back the lump that rose in her throat and clamped her lips closed as her stomach churned.

Saqib pointed to a lamp on the other side of the tomb, the source of the strange light Harper noticed earlier. "I have been experimenting with different light wavelengths to see if non-visible light can be used to perceive supernaturals. I should be able to get a clearer picture of the writing. I'll have to go back to the lab to develop and analyse it, but I'll send you copies of whatever I find."

Leaving Saqib fiddling with equipment, Harper turned back to the archbishop who was staring at the photo with a frown.

She thought of the translucent spirit she Saw by the river where Ghostwalker Adams died, and wondered if Saqib's light experiments would reveal the hesychia to normal human vision. Paul's missing lips fit her theory: a personification of silence muting one of York's most vocal anti-supernatural citizens. "Did anyone see anything? If this happened at Bishopthorpe, surely someone …"

"No one was home last night. We were all called away on an emergency. Unrelated, I'm certain, but poor timing for Paul."

Archbishop Marshall did not voice his disappointment at her lack of success in catching the murderer, but the thin line of his mouth and the tightening around his eyes were enough. Harper balled her fists in frustration. She'd been selfish searching for clues to her own past when she should've been concentrating on finding a murderer.

"If you were all called away on an emergency, what was he doing at Bishopthorpe?" she asked.

"Searching for me. I deeply regret the business that took me from home last night. Had I been there, maybe his death could have been prevented. When he couldn't find me, Paul called and left a message stating he found something supernatural relating to Ghostwalker Adams'a death and the Guild. They know something. Something they have hidden from the Council and the Queen's Guard. I suspect his lips and tongue were taken as a warning. This is the second such death of a member of my congregation. I do not want to see a third. Find what did this, Harper."

"I will," she promised, words whispered only to herself.

Chapter Thirteen

When she reached home that afternoon, Harper paused to pet a tabby tomcat waiting for her by the garden gate. He belonged to a neighbour but regularly visited every house on the street begging for treats. Grace was always happy to oblige with titbits from the bowl of pet snacks at the veterinary clinic.

Harper sat down on the wall, absentmindedly scratching behind the cat's ear. After the chill of the crypt, the autumn sun warmed her icy skin, and she was in no hurry to leave its beams. Tension melted as she sat in the garden. Like the déjà vu when she met Saqib, something about the house simply felt right, as though she'd seen it in a dream.

There was warmth in the red bricks, the crisp white of the bay windows inviting and homely. A small crazy-paved yard gave them some separation from the street and enough room for two chairs in which to sit and sip tea while the sun set over York's ancient wall. One of the only reasons Grace accepted Harper's insistence they live there was because the house wasn't overlooked to the front. There was a road, a steep verge, and then the wall, imbued with every trick known to humanity to keep out invaders, both natural and supernatural.

The front garden was also full of so-called protection. An assortment of cards proclaimed herbs that would grow when the weather was warmer. It never ceased to amaze Harper how people still clung to medieval superstitions to protect them from magic, although they'd never worked on her. Sage for cleansing, dill for prosperity and to ward off spirits, mint for protection or to eat with lamb.

"Haven't seen you in a couple of days." Harper patted the cat on the head, glad of his company.

The cat purred in appreciation as he rubbed his head against her fingers. "But Harper dearest, you saw me only this morning."

Harper snatched her hand back. *"Heresy?"*

The cat purred again, but this time with an unsettlingly familiar self-satisfied smirk. "I do have to get out and stretch." The buzzing voice emanated from the cat without its mouth moving. "Would you rather I travelled in my true form?"

"I ... well ... just get out of there. You'll hurt him." Harper glanced up and down the street, fearful of the twitch of lace curtains. All was still. She held out her hand with a snap of her fingers. "Come on. Grace'd kill you if she caught you messing with an animal. I've barely persuaded her you should stay as it is."

The cat sniffed Harper's outstretched fingers. It sneezed and a cloud of black dust billowed out. Once free of Heresy's possession, the tabby shook itself then started to wash. Heresy floated into Harper's hand where he collapsed in on himself until he was once again a grinning ball of soot. Harper pulled her sleeve down over him before someone could happen by. Goosebumps prickled her arm as he slid over her skin to tuck himself between her neck and the emerald bow at the top of her plait. He was almost weightless, barely more noticeable than her hair, save for a faint electrostatic buzz, which made all the follicles stand on end.

"Brrr, poor cat." Harper gave the tom one last pat before going into the house.

Once she was safely in her room and both the bedroom door and the door to the Jack-and-Jill bathroom she shared with Grace were locked, she shook her shoulders to knock Heresy loose from his perch. She glared down at his unfazed grin.

"You're supposed to be guarding my stuff, aren't you?"

"Your bedroom is so boring. I am guarding the whole house, you know."

"You can't possess whoever you feel like and sit on the front wall."

"But I *like* cats. I like them *very, very much*. It does not hurt them. It is simply that their wishes become secondary to mine."

Harper shuddered. "Leave him alone. If you want to watch the street without being seen, sit in the peephole." She sat down at her desk, pulled her laptop over, and switched it on. Heresy slunk up the desk leg to coalesce next to her hand. "There's been a second murder. Before he died, the deacon sent Archbishop Marshall a message saying he found something relating to the Ghostwalkers' Guild. So far, we've been doing all our research using physical items—books, maps, crystals. I thought there might be something electronic. Not something obvious, or it would've been banned by the Queen's Guard, but maybe something that appears innocuous. Some fantastical ghost story everyone thought was fiction but which is actually related to these deaths."

"You can read a website," Heresy answered. "What do you require my aid for?"

"If there was something on there, the Guild will have taken it down by now. Is there a way to find information that's been removed or get into their private database? I was thinking some variant on scrying might work better than a search engine and would be less traceable."

A long tendril stretched out to poke the screen. It fizzed and blipped, then Heresy's grinning face looked out at her.

"There is," he said, the buzz in his voice amplified by her speakers. "You are far too poor a student to attempt it. However, if you can get me to the computer where the data originated, I shall do it. I will also search for chatter on the internet for you."

"You know how to use a computer? How? You're, well, incorporeal, and you told me you haven't been in this realm since the nineteen-twenties."

"Dear, dear Harper." Heresy chuckled. "Who do you think *invented* the internet? It certainly was not one of your kind. Other realms have been using it for decades longer. There will be a supernatural community here."

"No," Harper whispered. "The Queen's Guard monitor everything in this country, they would've noticed."

"We are not so easily found." Heresy snorted in derision. "We keep ourselves hidden from human enforcers. Your Queen's Guard are not infallible. If I am here, why not others?"

It was as though Harper had been doused in frozen river water, as though … as though someone walked over her grave. She wrapped her arms around herself and pulled the ends of her long-sleeved top over her hands. Every scrap of oxygen was hard fought for as she dragged in each breath. Lights danced before her eyes. Dizziness rolled through her head.

His casual implication that there were supernaturals all around them was simply unbelievable. She'd escaped persecution only because Father De Santos believed he'd exorcised the demon within her and because

Grace helped her hide her magic. There were some places where there were still high concentrations of supernaturals. Japan welcomed them and then all news from that country ceased with only minimal goods being allowed in or out. Whether due to some supernatural apocalypse or heavy censorship from the Guard, Harper didn't know. Venice was infested so badly it had been wiped from the maps.

Even in the British Isles there were wild places where supes still roamed free. But not in England. Veil, Queen's Guard, and Council kept them at bay. Even if a Yōkai in Japan could access the internet there, they wouldn't be able to communicate with someone in England. It simply wasn't possible. Yet Heresy spoke as if they were right there on the doorstep. Her mind fogged, blank, as she tried to picture it.

"More?" she managed to choke out.

"Of course, Harper dear. Did you really think you were alone?"

Chapter Fourteen

Travelling uphill was wrong, unnatural. It was where Usa was compelled to go, yet every step was torturous, dragging, heavy like an anchor sinking.

Warm and sweet, a scent of human origin drifted down the hill, wanting to drag her back to the bottom with it. It would be easy to abandon the role she was forced to play, to cascade over the cobbles and forsake this aberrant duty. To forsake her tributaries and those who called to her for protection.

Usa, hide us.

Usa, protect us.

Usa, save us.

Their voices gave her no respite, no crack to seep through and escape. They wore her down with the inevitability of water flowing endlessly over rock.

She followed the scent further up the hill. Not in four hundred years had she wandered so far. Maybe not even then. It was all so different now, yet still so familiar. Her stone. Her people. Her responsibility.

This scent was here then, too. It had come on great ships over the ocean, been subdued and tamed, provided false nourishment, killed, polluted. Stories came through the sea, tales of death and deforestation. Homes lost in lands far away. Closer to home, tales of her people sculpted and sold. Secret ingredients added, stolen from her kin, to create wonder, yes, but also to create greed.

Chocolate.

She rolled the word around her being, absorbed the scent until it became part of her. Just as humans came to hear of York's ghosts, so too they came to feast on York's chocolate. It drew them like fish to wiggling worms, an illusory promise of contentment.

The mists curled around her ankles, welcome and moist, a clinging reminder of home. Usa forced herself to continue climbing. Vapours led her on, swirled ahead of her, beckoned, until she stood bathed in light at the chocolate shop window.

Inside, a woman sung an old sea shanty to herself as she worked. It was a song Usa knew well. She remembered the fisherfolk, reeking of trout and bass, who sang it in their tiny dinghies, and the sailors, coarse and rank with the stench of salt and alcohol, who sang it as they wandered along the riverbank.

Again, Usa fought the urge to leave, to return home and be herself, to forget the compulsions this body forced upon her. She didn't recognise shame or sorrow, emotions still too human for her, but pain rippled through her as the heaviness increased.

The woman approached the window, eyes sliding over Usa as if to deny her existence.

Eyes blind shut. Usa let the words join with the voices urging her on, the ritual as much a part of her now as their pleas.

The woman placed a tiny milk chocolate house on the ledge. Its roof was a white chocolate mushroom, its door etched like the bark of a tree. A slender figure made of chocolate and sugar perched on the doorstep, delicate gossamer wings so realistic Usa expected the fairy to quiver and fly away.

When the woman turned her back, Usa leaked under the door like the tide invading ever inwards at the shore. Reformed on the other side, she reached out. Her fingers brushed the edge of the woman's hijab. The chocolatier still hummed to herself, just as the ghostwalker had done. Threads of gold and blue floated within Usa's hand like silk from the east.

Must she die?

Usa cursed the thought, expelled it from her being so violently that the woman heard and spun. Her eyes widened as she gaped at a creature she never believed existed and should never have seen. It was too late now. She *had* seen. She must never be allowed to tell.

Usa reached inside the woman's head. The scream bubbled in her throat, drowned before it could pollute the air. She flailed, her arms flapping uselessly, passing through Usa like the oars of a boat, barely rippling her surface. Her whole body jerked, unable to fight or flee Usa's inescapable grip. Her eyes were wide, her silent scream reflected in them. Usa felt as though she could see right through this human woman. She could see the chocolatier's kin, those who relied on her, those who needed her. Tears leaked from her victim's eyes and Usa felt water slip down her own cheeks.

Usa, save us.

The voices clamoured through Usa, begged for attention, pleaded for their lives. She knew her duty. Her hand closed in the woman's mouth. Water bubbled through her victim's nose, dragged into her lungs with every untaken breath.

Her eyes turned misty and grey. Her body stilled, limp, lifeless. When Usa withdrew, the woman's shell dropped to the floor. All that remained in Usa's hand was a bloody muscle and a smattering of pink and white.

She let the hair-fine tastebuds dissipate in her body and the flat, smooth muscle of the tongue melt away. Then she knelt next to the corpse, arranging it as she had the others. As she worked, she sang, the sound of mermaids disappearing beneath the sea. Before she left, Usa lifted the little house off the window ledge. The chocolate fairy, with its sugar wings, gazed back at her lifelessly.

Another of those I should have protected. Another I let the humans catch. They must find us no longer.

She no more recognised anger than she recognised guilt as she dashed the figure against the floor. It shattered into a thousand glistening shards. Gathering up the pieces, Usa let them drift and melt into her body, turning her clear form muddy before they settled in her depths. She would return the little fairy to zir kin, where ze belonged.

"Never taste ..."

Chapter Fifteen

A day later and Harper's mind was still reeling from Heresy's revelation, but his internet searches were all dead ends. She tried using the map of York to scry for the hesychia but came away with nothing but a splitting headache. The only time even a tingle of magic had needled her skin, her scrying crystal dropped onto Castlegate, a small street not far from York's main square and the Shambles. There was nothing there relating to supernaturals but she walked over just in case.

When she got near, her stomach flipped at the sight of yellow-and-black police tape cordoning off the end of the narrow street.

"No ..." The whisper pushed past her lips as she attempted to squeeze by the burly police officer guarding the perimeter. She fumbled in her pockets, then waved the archbishop's pass in his face.

"Doctor? I think this lady's here to see you," the officer called over his shoulder.

When Saqib's head poked out of the chocolate shop about halfway down the street, the tension gripping Harper's chest eased until she realised what his presence meant. He waved her past the tape, his brown eyes clouded with sorrow. She hurried down the street with incongruously modern brick buildings on one side and fading wooden-fronted shops on the other. The chocolate shop was situated on the modern half of the street, the panelled-glass frontage at odds with a supernatural mystery.

"Another?" Harper asked although she already knew the answer.

There were tears in his eyes as he nodded. "Tahira. She is, was, a friend of my mum's. I went to school with her son."

Harper hugged him. It broke her heart to see the joyful man she met only a few days earlier now struck by grief. "What can I do?" she asked.

"We have to find whatever is doing this." Saqib squared his shoulders as he stepped away from Harper, his jaw tight as he glanced past her to the open door of the chocolate shop. "They took her tongue, Harper. Silencing her, like the others."

Harper guided Saqib away from the police. She couldn't see any Guard; they were probably inside. She leant closer and spoke low, "I think I know what's doing this. I don't know what those runes are yet, and I don't know why they're doing it, not exactly. There was a demon in ancient Greece, Hesychia. She was a personification of silence and she worked for the god of dreams …" Harper bit her lip, cutting off the rest of her sentence. Whatever it was in her heart that told her to trust this man couldn't be allowed to overrule common sense. She couldn't tell him why she thought the killer was connected to dreams without exposing her magic.

"Do you know how to stop her?" Saqib asked.

"Not yet. But I will. There must be something at the Ghostwalkers' Guild, something Deacon Paul saw, but they've refused to let the archbishop have access to their Guildhall. We need to retrace his steps."

Saqib's voice dropped lower. "You know a way in without their permission?"

"Grace and I will find one," Harper promised. "I'll call you tomorrow."

Harper and Grace waited until an hour after sunset before sneaking over the back fence, through the alley behind the house, and venturing onto the street. The road was a silent river of mist, which washed onto the pavement. The haze glowed in the electric light that stole out between closed curtains. It swirled around their ankles, clung to their dark clothing, crept up their legs. Grace kicked at it as she strode through. Harper hurried to keep up with her, glad the vapours were taking the brunt of her sister's irritation at having to call in sick to the clinic.

"Are you sure this is a good idea?" Grace asked for the fifth time as they approached the Guildhall. Harper glared at her; the silent rebuke lost in the darkness. While they'd made up after their fight, Grace was still prickly, upset by her refusal to stop using magic. The gruff manner she usually reserved for strangers knocked Harper's confidence. Nevertheless, her sister's presence was reassuring. Grace gave up everything to stay by her side: family, calling, friends. Her sister would not desert her now.

"Got anything better?" Harper retorted.

"If we get caught, they're going to call the police."

"Then shut up so we don't get caught. Are you ready to go in?"

Grace gave a brisk nod, then knelt at the base of the wall and offered her sister her knotted hands.

Harper slid her machete into its sheath at her waist, not wanting to risk catching herself on the sharp blade when Grace boosted her. The weapon was uncomfortable, unfamiliar after so long living peacefully in suburbia. It had saved her life many times in the Highlands of Scotland and the Amazon Rainforest.

Harper suspected she wasn't the only citizen of York to carry a weapon. The papers reported increases in people wearing silver or iron and buying angelica, mint, and basil for protection. The cathedral almost ran out of Holy Water. Attendance at Sunday morning services had gone up and Saint Peter's was seeing increased footfall during the week as well. When they spoke earlier in the day, Saqib confirmed the same was true at his mosque with people flocking there for Jummah prayers that Friday.

Weapon secured, Harper placed her foot in Grace's hands, who gave her a sharp shove upwards. Harper caught the end of the wall, using her momentum to haul herself on top. The wind rustled through the trees but other than that, Harper could hear nothing. Lights from the Ghostwalkers' Guild Headquarters barely penetrated the bushes and shrubberies ringing the garden. Beyond, York Cemetery stretched into the darkness. She shuddered and swallowed the wish to jump from the wall and run toward the light.

Seeing nobody about, Harper reached down a hand to Grace. Her sister took a run at the wall and Harper hauled her up the rest of the way. The trees grew close to the wall on the other side—a quiet descent and the opportunity for a quick escape, if needed.

Harper held tight to Grace's hand as they pushed through the undergrowth. Her breath was uneven, shallow, and she forced herself to inhale deeply, let her panic dissipate as she breathed out. The moon was a perfect semi-circle as though sliced by a knife. Its dim glow edged leaves and grass with silver. Harper said a quick prayer of thanks for the mercy of its light.

As they neared the building, the hubbub of voices reached them, paired with the clink of glasses and the scrape of cutlery on porcelain dishes. The clatter was subdued, the voices deep and heavy. Harper and Grace watched from the bushes as one man scurried in the front gate, glancing behind him as he slammed it shut. Where once the ghostwalkers trod without fear, now they knew they were not immune to what lurked in the shadows.

Keeping low, crawling under window ledges, and skirting pools of light, the two women made their way around the building. At the back, all the windows were dark. Grace motioned picking the lock and Harper shook her head. She unslung her backpack, which let out a muffled curse.

Grace's eyes narrowed, her mouth a thin, hard line as Harper opened her bag and an almost invisible shadow slunk out. Ignoring her sister's icy stare, Harper scooped Heresy up and placed him on the window ledge.

"You could phase through Grace's Bible, but you can sit on my shoulder so I know you can choose if you interact with stuff," she whispered. "Can you go through the glass and open the window from the inside?"

Dancing white teeth split the shadow, melted into the glass, distorted, widened, as Heresy passed through. There was silence for a moment, then a loud click. Harper pushed up on the windowpane. It creaked open a centimetre.

"Little help, Gray," Harper muttered to her sister who was standing with her arms crossed, glaring.

"Do you think it's wise to teach it to break into places?"

"Not now," Harper hissed. "Help me."

With a disgruntled huff, Grace grabbed the windowpane. They stole through and into the Guild. Long black cloaks hung from the walls like grim reapers. Above each hung a brass plaque bearing a name. Hudson. Grothe. Casile. Mitacek. Adams. Harper paused when she reached the dead man's name. His peg was empty, a void in the shadows, his cape still in a Guard evidence locker.

A small cough drew her attention to the door, where Grace stood, arms folded over her chest. Harper checked the schematic she'd downloaded onto her phone, the device held close to her body so no one would see the light. It had been surprisingly easy for Heresy to access the council's intranet and find the plans. She wished he could've penetrated the ghostwalkers' defences so easily and saved them a trip.

"This way." Harper gestured through the open door and down the corridor.

Floorboards creaked and groaned at every footstep. Doors moaned and squealed a protest at every inch they were opened. Harper strained her ears, listening to the muffled voices eating dinner, tensing at every pause in the conversation. But no running feet echoed through the mahogany-panelled hall and no lights or alarm blared to life.

Heresy slithered ahead of them and phased through doors to check the rooms beyond, then alerted Harper and Grace if there was anything worth exploring further. Desks only revealed neatly kept accountancy ledgers and contracts signed with dramatic flourishes. Bookshelves concealed no hidden rooms nor texts that would explain Deacon Paul's terror.

"This place is boring." Grace's whisper echoed Harper's thoughts. "No wonder they don't let people in. It's like any other office building, just a bit plusher."

Harper stifled a laugh in her sleeve. "Maybe there'll be skeletons in the closet upstairs or bodies buried in the basement. Up or down first?" She nodded toward the broad staircase at the end of the corridor; straight ahead ascending and to the left disappearing downwards.

Grace gestured toward stone steps leading down into blackness. Harper tugged her braid over her shoulder, the stray frizz smoothed by her sweaty palm. The roar of blood in her ears drowned out all other noise as she tried to step forward, only to find her feet frozen to the spot. Her breathing became ragged as she beheld the abyss and she clutched her phone so tightly her knuckles cracked.

"Harp. C'mon." Grace's insistent tone barely punctured Harper's panic. *"Harper."*

A bright light seared her vision. Harper instinctively raised her hands as light danced behind her eyelids. Despite this new danger, her panic faded to a dull ache in her chest.

"Looks like we caught ourselves a pair of thieves." A male voice came from somewhere behind the light. Harper opened her eyes, wincing, and was able to make out two blurred figures at the top of the stairs to the first floor.

"Shit," Grace muttered next to her. Harper elbowed her sharply in the ribs.

"We're not thieves," Harper said. The two men weren't carrying any weapons she could see, but their tight shirts revealed impressive muscles, which might've been attractive in other circumstances. From their casual attire, Harper guessed they worked for the Guild rather than being ghostwalkers themselves.

"We're here investigating the murders of Ghostwalker Adams and Deacon Paul," Grace added. "Paul was here right before he was killed. We know you're hiding something."

"And you think this gives you the right to break into our Guildhall?"

One of the men stepped back to mutter into a walkie-talkie. The other descended, scorn written clearly across his face as he looked the two women up and down. Even the crossbow hanging at Grace's belt gave him little pause. "Tell me why I shouldn't call the police right now."

"Because you don't want us to tell the police why we're here. And because I am the goddaughter of the Archbishop of York, and this is my sister. Believe me, you do not want to get on my godfather's bad side and, after the death of his friend, you're already skating on very thin ice."

Harper rolled her eyes at Grace's arrogant tone, but it worked. The man paused on the bottom step and looked back toward his companion. While he was distracted, she cast a surreptitious glance toward the basement stairs, but Heresy was nowhere to be seen.

"*He* wants to talk to them." The second man joined his partner. He clipped the walkie-talkie to his belt and gestured down the hall behind them with a nightstick. "That way. Come quietly and no one gets hurt and no one has to call the police."

"I demand to know where we're going." Grace's fingers twitched toward her weapon.

The man holding the nightstick chuckled, a grating, mirthless sound. "You've earned the interest of the Master Undertaker. A rare thing indeed. You can walk to his mausoleum, or we can knock you over the head and drag you. Your choice."

"Gray, we should go." Harper placed a hand on her sister's arm. "We have to see this through. We can't fight our way out and run away."

"A De Santos does not run away."

"But they do strategically retreat." Harper pursed her lips firmly closed as Grace's eyes narrowed. When her sister's glare returned to the goons accompanying them, she added louder, "Maybe we can persuade the Master Undertaker to work with us. Afterall, he must want to know who murdered his man as much as we want to know who murdered ours."

Grace gave a curt nod. She stepped to the side of the hall and gestured with a sweep of her arm. "Lead the way."

They were led out through the kitchen door at the back of the building. The gravelled car park beyond was lit by spot lamps, which pooled light around cars like personal shielding. When they reached the cemetery gate, even Grace's haughty façade cracked. Her sister's trepidation sent a cold shiver trickling down Harper's spine as the man opened the gate and ushered them through.

The cemetery was pitch-black but for the wavering light of the guard's torch. Even that thin beam of brightness didn't reassure Harper, rather it created more darkness, throwing long shadows behind each blade of grass. Darkness piled upon darkness, pressing in, consuming, suffocating. Clouds overpowered the moonlight as the stars twinkled out, handful by handful.

Panic welled inside Harper, the sense of disconnect and loss the dark always summoned. Wary of what could lurk between the gravestones, frozen, pretending to be stone, hiding behind edifices of death. It didn't matter that she didn't believe in ghosts. What mattered more was whether they believed in her.

Grace took her hand, their fingers linked as they picked their way between tombstones. The guard prodded Harper with his baton.

"Don't tell us the archbishop's lackeys are afraid of some wee ghosties. I thought you lot didn't believe in the undead." One of the men laughed, pushing Harper forward. Grace knocked his baton away with her free hand. Her knuckledusters rung like a funeral bell as metal struck metal.

Harper fingered the hilt of the machete at her hip, not wanting to draw it on another human. It was likely she and Grace would win in a fight, even without weapons, yet she didn't want to fight her own kind. *I'm a witch who hunts supernaturals. Which side should I be on?*

Grace went ahead of her, arm reached back, fingers still entwined. She trod carefully, her usual swagger gone. Torchlight caught her spiked stilettos. Practicality was not a De Santos watchword. *We've been doing this too long, gotten too confident.* Grace's heels sank into the grass, mud glistening as they ripped free. Focusing on the sparkle of light against patent leather, Harper tried to forget the crushing black above and the rotting dead below.

Near the centre of the cemetery, the guard in front held up a hand. Harper's heart thudded in her chest, her breath heavy as though she'd run for miles. The man pointed to a white marble mausoleum, lit by floodlights to catch every intricately sculpted face and flower that adorned it.

"That's where we're going, ladies," he said. "A pretty tomb for two pretty girls if the Master Undertaker isn't satisfied with your story."

Harper wasn't sure if the shiver down her back was her own or a judder escaping from Grace's body into hers.

"You're a creep." Grace may have been trembling, but her voice was strong. Never show fear. That's what Gabriel, Grace's oldest brother, always said to them, *'Never show fear, no matter how dark it is, no matter how strong your enemy. Never show fear.'*

'But feel fear.' Miguel, the next oldest, would chime in. *'Feel fear. It's God's warning. It keeps you alive.'*

The guards should have felt more fear. When Grace gave Harper's hand a morse code squeeze, she spun into action. Grabbing the end of the nightstick, Harper used the momentum of the man's swing to pull him off balance and topple him over her hip. A whimper came from behind her as Grace's knuckledusters impacted vulnerable flesh. When Harper's rival tried to stand, she knocked him back with a swift kick to the solar plexus, leaving him gasping for breath on the ground.

Grace's opponent lay curled into a foetal position, clutching his groin, emitting a high-pitched moan. The victor dusted off her hands with a self-satisfied smirk. Her family fought more than animalistic supes, they fought the humanoid ones too. The ones hiding in plain sight, who were as susceptible as anyone else to a swift kick between the legs.

"Hurt them. Disable them. Live to fight another day," Father De Santos had said as they drilled in the garden. "This is no honourable fight between gentlefolk. This is a fight for survival. Your survival and the survival of the innocents who depend on you. Fight dirty. Fight to win."

Harper picked up the fallen torch, her palms so slick she almost dropped it. Despite Father's words, violence made her uneasy. Thank heaven for Grace who wasn't scared of the dark and who had no inhibitions about using whatever means necessary to get her own way.

Grace casually poked one of the guards with the pointed toe of her shoe. He contorted his body away from her with a groan but stayed down. "Thank you *so* much for escorting us," she said. "Such a polite introduction to your Master Undertaker. You've been such gentlemen. If either of you ever dares hit my sister again, you won't get away with a simple bruising. I'll break your sorry—"

"Good evening, ladies."

A disembodied voice interrupted Grace's tirade. It rolled through the air, mellow yet commanding, quiet yet overpowering. Both women instinctively turned to it. Harper swung the torch around, catching an apparition in its beam.

It appeared as a man, black cloth against black night so it was hard to judge his size or era. His feet did not deign to touch the ground. His black cloak billowed in an unfelt breeze. A stovepipe hat disappeared up into the darkness. Vapours clung to him with the desperate fingers of a jilted lover, grasping yet sliding off. Only his face was clearly visible, hanging suspended in the air like the man in the moon come down to earth. His skin was wrinkled yet timeless, creasing around his frown as though it knew no other expression. His eyes were black as his garments. Dilated pupils mocked the torchlight, irises expanded resentfully into white. Inhuman. Ghostly. Deadly.

Harper's breath caught in her throat. Her eyes burned with Sight as spirits escaped from the graves to stretch pleading hands toward him. Translucent and white, they thronged around him, some scornful, some fawning. Their whispers carried on the winds, too many to count, too many to hear their words, a susurration building to the crescendo of a waterfall, plummeting, falling …

Harper heard one voice through the crowd, one far-off person calling her name, then there was nothing but darkness.

Chapter Sixteen

When the torches' beams hit Harper and Grace, Heresy had flattened himself against the floor, nothing more than a shadow. As Harper was led away, the deception demon hoped her interview with the Master Undertaker would not be fatal for her; he would hate for the fun to end so soon. Although he would barely admit it to himself, he kind of liked her. It was like wanting to scold a puppy for making a mess yet being unable to stop laughing at how proudly it presented it.

Following was pointless, he could not conceal her now. Instead, he rolled down the stairs with a small giggle as he bounced in the dark. The low hum of electronics and the buzz of fans floated up to meet him. A faint smell of paper and ink hung in the air. Jackpot.

No one was in the library, which stretched out on either side of him at least as long as the house above. Heresy slunk past the computers and the first few bookshelves. The door above had not been concealed; there would be nothing here the Guild wanted to keep secret. This place was for show, for the Guard and for low-ranking members. As a cat was drawn to shining lights, Heresy could not ignore the fluttering sense of his magic indicating a hidden area.

He squeezed between books, in and out of pages, gathering puffs of dust and ink residue into his body. Within a few minutes, he found a book out of place. Rather than wood beneath it, he sensed the sharp tang of metal. Flowing freely through the back of the shelf, he entered the narrow passageway hidden behind. He allowed himself a quiet cackle as he drifted to the ground.

The surface beneath him was rough and unpaved. At the other end of the passage, light leaked around a door. Voices, muted and vague, drifted through the air. Dirt and cobwebs littered the tunnel. Heresy rolled up to one of the spiders; a large, hairy creature, tormenting a fly trapped within its web.

"Pray excuse me," Heresy said, his grin broad. His mouth opened wide, white teeth glimmering. The spider scuttled away, not fast enough. Heresy enveloped it. Black particles twisted and spun, sucked into the spider's body like a vacuum until nothing of Heresy's body remained.

The spider twitched a leg experimentally. He wiggled the new body to the left, then did a little jig to the right. He crawled back up its web, all eight beady eyes on the juicy, black body of the fly. It burst in his mouth like an overripe grape, blood and protein glooping together, filling him. Heresy laughed, a tiny, tinny sound coming from the usually silent spider.

He scurried up the wall with ease, exhilarated to have a physical form again. Not his favourite form but, alas, there were no cats nearby. Squeezing by the door was a tight fit. He wiggled through at the top then ascended to perch on the frame and look around. Two people sat at the sole computer, their backs to him, both leant over it and blocked his view. The walls were lined with bookcases and cubby holes, along with several cabinets dotted around the floor, made up of long, thin drawers.

One of the drawers was open, a portrait of a woman laid out in it. She had thick, black hair and striking green eyes, her nose slightly turned up at the end, her ears almost pointed. Heresy didn't recognise her. She could have been human, maybe with elfin blood way back, or she may have been a fellow supernatural, he was not sure. Around the portrait, someone had sketched each of her features larger than life—one bright eye, the outline of a nose, elegant and fine fingers. Heresy darted along the wall, down a bookcase, then over to the cabinet for a better look.

Next to each diagram was a rune. Although he could not read them, he had seen their like before from older members of the supernatural community who had yet to catch up to modern writing and letters. Each also had a short text in English.

'Vision of long-lost child,' by the eye.

'Spell scroll,' by the fingers.

'Candle of sleep,' by the nose.

It was nonsensical. Making a candle out of a nose was a ridiculous proposition. Heresy turned his attention to the two people at the computer.

"There. This is it." The taller one pointed at something on the screen.

"Don't be daft," the other replied. "That's a tourist story made up by Ghostwalker Hudson back in 1834."

"But based on a real sighting."

"There's no such thing as a 'real sighting.'" The shorter person sighed. "We have both been in the Guild long enough to know there're no such things as ghosts."

"It could have been based on a real supe though. Maybe a Japanese mokumokuren or something else that travelled over here."

"Even if it was, that creature only took eyes. Not like Adams and that priest who broke in. Whatever is killing people now is taking voices."

"Fine then, we'll keep looking, but if what the Master Undertaker suspects is true, we won't find anything."

"They only took one file. There must be a reference somewhere else to what's going on."

At the mention of a missing file, a shiver of anticipation ran through Heresy. All the hairs on the spider's body stood on end. Heresy struggled to keep possession; the less in tune he was with the spider's nature, the harder it was not to revert to his natural form. The spider skittered back and forth, then calmed as Heresy regained control.

He found an empty corner and amused himself by creating cobwebs in geometric patterns until the two ghostwalkers abandoned their search and retired for the night. They switched the computer off and turned out the light as they went, plunging the room into darkness.

Heresy drifted out of the spider's body, ignoring the now useless creature as it collapsed in exhaustion. He phased through the computer tower and joined the flow of electricity as power returned to it.

It was not long before Heresy was skimming through the lines of data representing the supernaturals' own secret internet. It was freeing to be out from Harper's critical gaze. The dark net was full of obscure rituals, runes and circles, and spell poems as well as code humans would have recognised. There was a lot of chatter. More than he would have expected in England. He had not been in Europe for a couple of hundred years, his last stint in the mortal realm having been in the Americas, but England had long been both a hotspot and a danger zone for magic users.

He vaguely remembered he had been tasked with exploring some human computer, but the supernatural community was far more interesting. Something was changing, yet no one directly referred to what, and Heresy had been out of the loop for too long to make sense of their oblique references. He found several mentions of a 'Magician,' but speculation about this being did not seem related to York or the murders. He did find an increase in the number of protection and concealment spells being sold.

He eventually made his way back to the ghostwalkers' network. The files saved locally on the computer were easy to access. Scanned copies of old documents. Fabrications about so-called 'ghosts.' Boring. To Heresy's mind, there was nothing worth removing a life over, but then, humans killed each other for the oddest reasons. It was simply in their nature, he supposed.

At first look, he discovered nothing unusual or that might relate to the deaths Harper told him about. Based on the discussion of the two people earlier, he had not really expected to find anything. Instead, he looked for signs of something being removed. Deep in the memory, through layers of backups and heavy encryption, he finally caught a whiff of magic. Elusive as a dream, tenuous as mist, yet unmistakable—evidence someone used magic to remove something from the ghostwalkers' network.

He followed the spell out of the network and back into the endless electronic world. The trail was difficult to follow, even more ethereal than Heresy himself. Sometimes it became so weak he could no longer sense it, only to find tendrils of it nearby. It was recent; at the rate of decay there would not be a trail for much longer.

The trail ended abruptly in a particularly intricate firewall rune. It was a thing of beauty, drawn specifically to stop other supernaturals from entering the caster's server. Heresy grinned to himself—he liked a challenge.

He also liked something he could pilfer. If he found out more, he could use it on Harper's laptop to keep other supernaturals away from her. It would not do for the one who wanted to find her to succeed. It would end all his fun if he had to give her up.

It was harder than he would have liked to trick the rune into letting him pass. He eventually succeeded in making it think he was part of the information it was designed to protect. He squeezed himself through the electronic gap caused by its momentary confusion. Soon he was lost in exploring, his original purpose in infiltrating completely forgotten.

Another strong rune attracted him, a data cleaner of some sort flying through the network. He followed it, eager to see what the user was trying to hide. When he thought he almost caught up, the rune disappeared, leaving him at a dead end.

Disappointed, Heresy turned back down the path, only to find the way blocked by another rune. This one was even stronger than the one protecting the server and so bright it mentally burned. For hours, Heresy tried to trick his way past it, but nothing worked. Even a spirit could tire and he was running out of ideas. Panic was not an emotion he was capable of. Irritation most certainly was.

He made himself as tiny as he could but found no gaps in the magic.

He made himself huge but could not break past it.

He tried to match the magic but it was too clever for him.

Heresy was trapped.

There was a ringing in the distance, and a green circle appeared between him and the offending rune. It was similar to a summoning circle but contained a symbol the demon had never seen before. He tentatively poked it with an elongated tendril.

"Tired of fighting me?" a calm voice asked. It was male and young, although not a child. It was also human.

"You have passed my tests and been found adept enough to have my attention," Heresy replied haughtily.

"Then perhaps you can tell me how you got into my computer and who sent you."

"I would rather not."

"Then you will stay in my cage forever," the man threatened.

That sounded exceedingly tiresome to Heresy. "You should let me go. I have very important work to do. I am looking for a murderer who could expose our whole community."

"Who sent you?"

"A witch. She will be angry if you do not let me go and will cast the most terrible spells on you." That was sort of true. Heresy sniggered to himself.

"I'm not in the habit of letting demons wander loose," the man said. "Lead me to your witch and I'll consider a deal."

Heresy weighed up his options. If he led this man to Harper, she could get hurt and he could get banished again. On the other hand, staying was no good if he remained trapped and bored. Maybe if he played along, he would find a chance to escape and give both humans an amusing fright in the process.

"Her name is Harper ..."

Chapter Seventeen

Harper opened her eyes to endless trees.

"Harp? Harper? Wake up." Grace's voice was distant, lost in the woods, echoing, fading. Her sister had vanished, along with the graveyard. A dense forest surrounded Harper, a memory of a dream.

"Grace!" Harper tried to shout back. The word echoed until it was consumed by the trees. Scuttling feet replaced it, almost hidden by the patter of rain. Pinpricks of footsteps scurried over her skin. Hairy feet caressed her lips as they leapt between them to weave silken threads of silence. Sticky cords stretched across her mouth and snapped her lips closed. She clawed at her face, unable to breathe. When she wrenched the seal off her mouth, the spiderweb caught at her fingers, trying to bind her once again. She screamed, the sound a muffled whine in her chest. White filled her vision. Arachnid feet tickling her eyelids and crawled through her lashes.

She shook her head, body writhing, contorting as she tore them off her face. Over and over, spinning and falling, always more dropped from the forest canopy. Harper tumbled down an embankment. Roots bruised her ribs. Rocks clawed her skin. Webs caught on tree branches, but they barely slowed her descent as they snapped. When she hit the bottom, water closed over her head, freezing cold, and spiders fell from her like leeches burned by a cigarette's embers. She slipped and slid, unable to gain purchase on lichen-slicked stones.

Water broke over her head and cascaded down her as she orientated herself. Ripping the remaining spider's webs from her mouth and nose, Harper doubled over in the icy stream, gasping for breath as she splashed water on her face to banish the lingering sensation of skittering feet.

When her extremities started to numb, she dragged herself out of the river and up the opposite bank. Her legs still shook, but she managed to scale the embankment to lean against a nearby pine.

There was something familiar in the way the moss clung to the trees, in the weak light trickling through the canopy, in the calls of birds and rustle of squirrels. Hidden from sight, the brook babbled like a fairy tale, belying its deadly cold. Strains of music, almost too high to hear, blended with the tinkling of water against stone.

A prickling on back of her neck made her turn. Cold sweat trickled down her spine. Eyes, watching, waiting, but where? She turned again.

"I've been waiting for you, Seer."

A voice, welcoming, soft as a lullaby, drifted around her. She yawned and covered her mouth. Her eyelids were heavy, and she blinked slowly. A single violin played low music, soothing, a half-forgotten sign of security, promising it was safe to sleep. Maybe lacking it was why she slept so badly. Maybe here she could find rest. The moss on the ground invited her down with its softness.

"Sleep, precious one. Sleep and come to me."

"Who are you?" Harper's lips formed the words, but her voice died in her throat. Talking was too much effort. She needed to lie down.

Without realising it, she was kneeling on the floor, patting the moss as she searched for the best place to lay her head. She shivered, freezing, but her mind ignored the caution of her body. Like Grace's fearful calling, the warning was distant and surreal.

Pain, sharp and burning, broke through her lethargy. She jumped to her feet. Blood welled in three fresh stripes on the back of her hand.

"Run, Harper. Run." A new voice, familiar yet alien, inhuman yet trusted. She ran.

"Harper Ashbury, you wake up right this moment."

Grace's voice, sharp, commanding, the general always to be obeyed. Harper tripped and fell again. Ice cracked as she stumbled into the brook.

Her eyes opened wide as she spluttered and gasped. Cold, marble faces glowered back at her, flickering, moving in the candlelight. Skulls leered from the walls. Cherubs judged from the ceiling. Something hard and unyielding lay beneath her, cold as the stones of the stream. Then a warm hand on her shoulder.

"Hey, take it easy."

Harper brushed dripping hair out of her eyes to reveal Grace frowning at her, an empty memorial vase in her hand.

"Sorry. You passed out." Grace slipped out of her sweater and handed it to Harper to dry her face. "This was the only way I could wake you up."

"Where are we?" Harper sat up, dangling her legs over the side of her impromptu bed. "Grace, would I perchance be lying on someone's tomb right now?"

"Given we're in a mausoleum, I'd say there's a very strong likelihood." Grace smirked as Harper leapt to her feet to put some distance between herself and the marble coffin. When she pushed wet hair out of her eyes, the back of her hand smarted. A graze of three stripes, like in her dream.

"You caught your hand on a tombstone when you fell," Grace said, catching her looking. "You're lucky it wasn't your head."

"Welcome back to the living, Ms. Ashbury." A man's voice behind her. Harper spun around.

At one end of the mausoleum was a raised dais with a throne, the man in the stovepipe hat poised elegantly upon it. He peered over steepled fingers, his brow furrowed in thought. Harper twirled the ends of her hair around her finger.

"Thank you." She glanced over at her sister. "What's going to happen to us now?"

"Ms. De Santos and I spoke while you dreamt," he said. "I cannot tolerate trespass upon our grounds. However, I believe in this case at least, we have a shared goal: to find the being responsible for the death of Ghostwalker Adams and to ensure no more people are needlessly killed."

Harper wondered if there were people, like trespassers, whom the Master Undertaker thought could be needfully killed.

"Who do you think killed him?" she asked.

His brow furrowed further, scoring deep lines across his face. "If we knew that, there would only be one more death. Without this knowledge, there will be many."

Harper shuddered but stood her ground under his unblinking gaze. "Yesterday, the deacon of Saint Peter's Cathedral was here. Do you know—?"

"That he was here? Yes." A smile played on the Master Undertaker's lips, sharp as a knife. "No one sets foot on Guild land without my knowledge. That he died soon after? Yes. There are no deaths in York of which I am unaware."

Harper hoped 'set foot' could be taken literally. If he discovered Heresy, she would have bigger problems than an accusation of trespassing. She twisted the end of her braid around her fingers as she tried to think of a way to retrieve the spirit from wherever he'd vanished to.

"Paul said you knew something." Grace squeezed Harper's arm as she stepped forward to stand directly before the Master Undertaker. "He told Godfather this isn't the first time the ghostwalkers have encountered this. What happened before? Who did it?"

The Master Undertaker inhaled sharply, his nostrils flared. He straightened, towering over Grace. "How did he come by this knowledge?"

"According to the message he left Godfather before he was killed, Paul found out you're hiding something from us and from the Queen's Guard. If you want to stop more people dying, you'll tell us what it is. Don't tell us, and their blood is on your hands too."

Bones creaked within the Master Undertaker's floating robes as he descended from the dais. He seized Grace's chin, skeletal fingers gouging into her cheeks. Bone cracked like thunder in the marble crypt as Grace's brass knuckles hit his jaw.

"Touch me again and you lose the hand," Grace warned, her fist still raised.

"We gave the priest no knowledge." The Master Undertaker glowered at her as he spoke through gritted teeth. "The knowledge of that death is forbidden to all but the highest ranking of our members, and I would go to my own grave swearing none of them would disclose it."

"Then you aren't as omniscient as you like to make out," Grace said. "Either he got the information from your guild or someone else knows. You've already admitted he was here. Either your faith in your people is misplaced or he snuck in without you knowing and read your histories."

The Master Undertaker resumed his seat. He regarded the two women for a long minute. "I ... do not know how he came by the knowledge but it is no longer here to be read. After his trespass, our computers were hacked, our firewalls breached. They left behind a virus that corrupted many of our files. Only a few hours ago were we able to ascertain that a document was missing. Only one. A letter written by one of our brethren a hundred and fifty years ago. I went to our archives to find the original letter, to see why the correspondence would be of interest to anyone outside our guild. The letter was gone. When I opened the folder in which it was kept, there was a burnt circle with a line through it and nothing else."

"You suspect witchcraft." Grace crossed her arms over her chest. "Did you report it?"

"Do *you* tell the Queen's Guard all the goings-on inside Saint Peter's?" The Master Undertaker's sunken eyes held Grace's, who stared back without blinking. When he failed to get a response from her, he continued. "We prefer to manage our internal matters ourselves. Our chief librarian remembered something of the letter. Not much, simply that it spoke of the murder of a woman who was found with no scars. Her eyes, ears and tongue were removed, her bones broken. I have a strong suspicion it is related to Ghostwalker Adams' departure from this life. To use our archives, one must sign in. It is rare these days, since all the documents are accessible by computer. I checked the last signature on the log. It was Adams. Now I have told you all I know."

"Like hell you have," Grace muttered.

The Master Undertaker bowed his head. "I do not know why Ghostwalker Adams was chosen as the target of this crime. Maybe any of us could have been the victim and it was a whim of fate that cut the thread of his life. Maybe there was some reason, some story of his that touched upon a truth best left lost."

"Fat lot of help you've been," Grace spat. "Come on, Harper. Let's get out of this sham drama. He's not going to tell us anything."

"Wait. He wants to know who killed Adams as much as we do." Harper glared up into his hollow eyes. "Don't you have to protect your guild members? Don't you want to protect your customers? If the city loses night-safe status, the ghostwalkers' business will suffer. You know something else. I know you do."

The Master Undertaker shook his head, the ghost of a smile returning. Darkness closed in around him as candles extinguished in small puffs of smoke. "I have told you all I can. Look to history, Ms. Ashbury. See what occurred one hundred and fifty years ago." Darkness flooded the dais and Harper instinctively retreated.

"Let's go." Grace dragged her back through the tomb, up the stairs, and out into the night as the last of the candles guttered out. "What a load of tourist-crap hooey."

Picking up the torch from where it still lay on the ground, Grace guided Harper through the graveyard to the far gate, one for ordinary people, which didn't back onto ghostwalker grounds.

"What about Heresy?" Harper glanced back toward the pricks of light which were the Guild headquarter windows.

"I told you that thing was trouble," Grace replied. "We'll have to leave it and good riddance. I don't think it can actually do much, thank God. I should've vanquished it when I had the chance. We can't go back in

without risking implicating you in its summoning. C'mon. We're leaving."
Harper nodded and crossed her fingers behind her back. She hoped he would follow her commands and search the ghostwalkers' electronic database before heading home. Maybe he would find the story the Master Undertaker referenced.

Tripping along behind Grace, Harper barely noticed the dark as they left the graveyard. The Master Undertaker's words filled her mind. *Look to history ...*

Chapter Eighteen

Harper hardly slept. Heresy's warnings were reinforced by the return of her nightmares. Words whispered over and over by so many voices she couldn't make them out. Every sleeping moment was tormented by hovering eyes watching her. Every waking moment, she waited with shallow breath, anticipating a tap on the shoulder, a shout, a bag over her head. Every creak of the old house, every footstep in the corridor, caused her to start, terrified the Queen's Guard had come to take her away.

She couldn't even play her violin, afraid the music from her dreams would manifest and lure the one Heresy claimed was seeking her. Every time she looked at the instrument, anxiety ran through her nerves like lightning. Her only link to home was, perhaps, not the lifeline she'd believed but the last vestige of memory of a creature who hunted her and may have killed her family.

Only in the depths of the cathedral did she feel safe.

"Let's see." Harper sucked thoughtfully on the end of her pencil, muttering to herself, " 'Medicine murder,' 'red trade,' divination, 'anatomy murder,' blood magic of various kinds, representative substitution, food, ritual, potions. There sure are a lot of different uses for a human corpse, or bits of one. What is wrong with the world? Half of these aren't even supernatural."

Although she still thought a hesychia was the most likely suspect, the Master Undertaker's revelation didn't tally, with more than the victim's voice being taken. Unwilling to block off any avenue of investigation, Harper was looking up historical accounts that matched the Industrial Revolution murder he mentioned.

She tried to focus on the book in front of her, the leatherbound diary of an explorer from a dark time when the British Empire dominated the seas. It described the rituals of peoples the explorer witnessed on his travels, including one sect who believed wealth could be gained by harvesting human organs. Different organs granted different types of wealth. They'd captured the explorer who managed to escape with his life by convincing them of his poverty and joining in their greedy ritual. It had done him little good. Harper cross-referenced with other history books and found Queen Mary II had executed him less than a month after his return to England on suspicion of witchcraft.

"I see your research has taken an interesting turn." Alfred's voice made Harper jump. She slammed her book shut, though it was far too late. While Alfred knew one of her areas of study was visions, what she was researching now was far too visceral for passive sight. *Unless you're reading entrails, I suppose.* She ignored the churning in her stomach. A sandwich sat at the bottom of her bag, untouched. Grace would scold if she found out, but the graphic descriptions of some of the texts entirely put Harper off her food.

"I know this looks weird," she said.

"With all that has happened in this city recently, I would be surprised if the archbishop did not ask you to investigate."

"Oh." Harper tugged her braid, scanning the stack of books she'd been reading. Alfred peered at the titles over her shoulder. "Look, you know more about this stuff than I do. Why would you think the archbishop would ask me? I'm still a junior."

Alfred regarded her over the rim of his glasses with a look that quite plainly said 'don't be an idiot.'

"Fine." Harper grimaced. "But he told me not to tell anyone, okay?"

"Of course. I would never betray a secret."

As Alfred sat down next to her, Harper thought she caught the vanishing ghost of a smile on his lips. "Is there something you're not telling me, Alfred?"

"Harper dearest, if I were to tell you all the things I am not telling you now, we would be here until the sun grows cold."

For a moment, he sounded like Heresy. She was certain the spirit had been caught, just as they caught her and Grace. She didn't know who to feel sorrier for.

"May I?" Alfred gestured to her notes, and she slid them across the table to him. He tweaked the collar of his shirt and pushed his glasses up his nose. "Have you considered blood magic? There are many spells that could be created or strengthened by using human tongues and lips. Especially those of a talented storyteller or preacher. Siren Song, Banshee's Wail, Lullaby, to name but a few. The 'story' element may also be significant, perhaps a deception of some kind. They usually involve elemancy but could be done with blood magic too."

"I didn't know you studied blood magic." Harper skimmed through her list again. Alfred's clearance obviously went much higher than hers. She wondered if he was also tasked with investigating. "Am I even allowed to know about those spells?"

"I have studied many things," he replied. When she looked up, he added, "There are more things in heaven and earth, Harper, than are dreamt of in our philosophy."

"What's that supposed to mean?" Harper frowned.

"It means—" His voice choked and cut off. He stared at her sketch of the rune-like symbol she'd Seen hovering in the mist in her vision. "This is dangerous, Harper. This is something in which you should not meddle. How did you find …? No, I don't want to know." The shadows under his eyes darkened and his voice dropped. "We don't have to go through this again. There are other ways."

"Other ways to what?" Harper asked.

He peered at her for a long moment, his amber eyes glittered and warped. Harper squirmed in her seat.

"I don't agree with this." He spoke abruptly, rigid in his chair as an inner battle waged. "The archbishop set you this task. I must trust him."

"Alfred, what do you mean 'go through this again'?" Harper asked. "The Master Undertaker of the ghostwalkers told us this isn't the first time these murders have occurred. What do you know?"

"I can't say." Alfred's eyes slid over the desk and away, as though it were made of ice. "It's a betrayal to even say this much. Yet you are my friend and following this path puts you in danger. It would be a betrayal to say nothing."

The law dictated Harper should report his strange behaviour, he clearly knew more than he was letting on, but he was a friend and a high-level archivist, he may well have legitimate reasons to know of this magic and Harper was the last person to start a witch hunt.

"You should not investigate further." Alfred's green eyes were dark as he met her gaze. "You of all people should not be involved in this, Harper."

"Why not?" she asked, startled.

"Because if you look too hard for someone who wishes to remain hidden, you become the victim of their desire to disappear."

"You think the killer will target me to keep their secret? Like they did with Paul?" A remnant memory of spidery feet tiptoed down her spine and goosed her skin. Her eyes burned and she blinked rapidly, hoping their colour didn't change.

"All I know is this: You should not involve yourself in this. There are forces at play beyond your ken."

"Alfred, what—"

"You cannot stop this. Protect yourself." His chair squealed against the tiled floor as he pushed it back. Before Harper could question him further, he scanned his credentials and disappeared into the Sixth Vault, slamming the door behind him.

Looking down at her scattered notes, Harper's shoulders slumped, and she let out a sigh. Every time she found something new, it set her back even further, put her in more danger. She rubbed her eyes. The lack of sleep wasn't helping her concentration. She covered her mouth out of habit as she yawned, although no one else was around. 'The devil makes work for idle hands.' 'A yawn is an invite to possession.' Harper didn't believe these kinds of common superstitions, but the older members of staff would cluck and frown, then watch her with beady eyes for the rest of the day.

Maybe a quick nap wouldn't hurt. Fresh eyes and all that. If God was real, the heart of the cathedral was the safest place in the world to sleep. She lay her head on her arms, the book her pillow, and drifted off.

It was dark. The darkness of light banished and forbidden. The darkness of a Godless world.

Harper was alone. No land beneath her feet. No breath on the air. She could see nothing, hear nothing, feel nothing.

This was her worst nightmare, hopeless darkness, yet her heart did not pound, and no sour gall rose in her throat. Her eyes were dry and no tremors shook her body. She stretched her arms, fingers extended into the nothingness.

Something light and feathery brushed against her skin. Rather than jumping back, she reached for it and found something soft, warm, the touch of a human hand. She grasped it tightly and it squeezed her fingers in return. Then it was gone.

Run, Harper. A voice she'd heard before whispered in her mind, urgent and breathless.

"Are you looking for me, Seer?" A different voice rolled through the darkness, arid and crackling like summer lightning rending the sky over the Yorkshire Moors. "You should know better than to venture into the darkness. You should come home. To your family. Where are you hiding, Seer?"

She wanted to run toward the voice, if only she could find its source. It knew her family. She would beg it for answers. But her feet wouldn't move and her mouth was too parched to speak.

"I have almost found you, Seer. I made you perfect. You are mine. There are others, but none are you, my precious Seer. Come home."

Run, Harper. Run fast and don't look back. Never look back.

The words unbound her feet. Solid rock pressed against her soles. Obeying the whisper from the darkness, Harper ran blindly. She didn't look back.

Keep running, Harper. I'll protect you.

When the first light came, she stumbled, disorientated by its sudden brightness.

A single, wide eye hung before her, a glowing purple iris and a pinprick of a pupil watching.

Her shadow sprang to life in front of her as a second eye opened behind her. Soon they were everywhere. Large, small, all unblinking as they watched her.

The fear she missed in the dark came crashing back at these strange lights. It welled in her stomach, both freezing and boiling. It settled hot in the back of her throat, acerbic and metallic. Cold, gelatinous orbs pressed against her, trying to restrain her. She broke through the circle and fled.

The darkness faded into the familiar streets of York. To her right, a river of black ink. To her left, buildings of brick and stone gave way to grass and trees.

His final path. The thought flashed across her mind as she ran. *Look to history.*

A vision. Would she now be able to See what happened to the ghostwalker when he was killed, here in the heart of the city?

No. This wasn't the same place.

She was further upstream than the murder. Tower Street Gardens. The park by Skeldergate Bridge, the last bridge over the Ouse within the safety of York's wall.

She stopped running. There were no stars, no moon to light the way, but the glow of the streetlamps reduced it from panic-inducing blackness to mere breath-stealing night.

Pressing her bare feet into the ground, the mud shifted and squelched between her toes. Scents of sour urine and stale beer wafted from under the bridge. Goosebumps prickled her arms where the bitter autumn air scraped over her skin.

Naked branches groaned overhead, like joints stretching and popping into place. Their long-fingered shadows gouged the earth, beckoned Harper on. The ground clung to her feet, sucked at her toes. Her muscles ached with the exertion of dragging herself free.

Harper blinked and found herself facing an old alder in the centre of the park. She hopped from root to root as she circled it, avoiding the mud roiling beneath, bloated like methane-bubbled peat. Spritely violin music danced her like a puppet as it filtered through the mist.

As her hand trailed over the trunk of the tree, bark tore at her fingers, drew blood. Flecks of bark contaminated her, a thousand needles through her veins. Spiked fingernails of wood pierced her clothes. Her hair snagged on jagged branches, yanked from her scalp. She had no breath, no scream, the only sound the mad jig of the violin. The tree grasped at her, ripped her apart, claimed her. Bark split open like a sharp-toothed maw as the tree dragged her into its depths, devouring her.

One last, drawn-out note hung in the air like a noose.

The bark snapped shut, cutting out the wavering light of the streetlamps. Two eyes hung before her, bright violet and shot through by blood.

A voice whispered in her soul, *"Eyes blind shut ..."*

Harper was running before she was completely awake, books left lying on her desk, jacket and bag forgotten.

As she sped out of the cathedral, she barely noticed the sun had set. Mists caught at her feet as she sprinted in short bursts, pausing occasionally to lean against a wall and catch her breath before running again. Droplets of rain splatted against the tarmac of the deserted streets. Wind whined, driven through crooked ginnels and whipped through naked tree branches. Harper kept running.

When she reached Tower Street Gardens, caution outweighed her fear and she lingered in the last pool of light at the top of the path. The land dropped away in front of her, a steep hillock of grass down into the park. She was stiff, heavy, barely able to breathe. All she could see were those lilac eyes.

"I can do this." The darkness swallowed her hollow words. The tree at the centre was nothing more than a silhouette against the glittering backdrop of the Ouse. From the edge of the park, Harper couldn't see if the bark split open or not. It could have been a figment of her imagination, nothing more than a dream. She didn't recall a gaping hole in the tree.

"A dream, Harper," she whispered to herself, a quiver in her voice. "Just a dream. There's nothing there."

Every step was a battle: her body wanted to flee, but her mind drove it forward, slow step by slow step. Darkness closed in around her and a single tear escaped and slid down her cheek. It dripped onto her collarbone, cold. The air before her rippled, catching the streetlamp's glow and scattering it. It wavered like a mirage, barely there. Harper raised a hand toward it, entranced by the glittering lights. The mirage mirrored her, a barely visible humanoid form with a featureless face. As their fingers touched, the sensation of ice spread through Harper's body and froze her in place. It weighed down on her and stilled the rise and fall of her chest.

"Go back." A feminine voice to match the feminine curves glimmering in the uncertain light. It didn't mean the creature was female, whatever it was might not even have a concept of gender, but it fit with her hesychia theory. A shallow dip appeared where a mouth might have been as the apparition spoke again, slowly, as though forming words for the first time. "Only death awaits you."

When Harper blinked, crystals of snow fell from her lashes to dissolve against her burning cheeks. No one was there. In the space of a heartbeat, the spirit had appeared and vanished again. The chill of her presence remained, if it was indeed a hesychia and thus a 'she,' as though she still watched from some hidden place.

"It's going to take more than that to stop me, Hesychia, or whoever you are." Harper's voice rang clear in the empty park. The hesychia's spell broke, her limbs free to move again. She jogged the last few metres to the tree.

Harper took a deep breath as she reached the alder, regretting it immediately as her stomach heaved. It smelled like her dream, caustic and acrid, but entwined with the stench she remembered, there was something else. Something rotten. Something dead.

Trembling fingers caught on rough bark as she stumbled over roots, circling the tree. A hard lump rose in her throat, and her stomach rolled as the smell strengthened. Then her hand met nothing.

The tree had been wrenched open. It was pitch black inside, exactly like in her vision.

"Please, no," she whispered. "Please God, don't have given me this vision only to be too late to save her."

Harper leant into the tear and stared down into the dark well within it. The smell was overpowering. Harper pinched her nose, but the air stung her eyes, seemed to leak in through her skin. Her stomach heaved, bile filled her mouth. Gritting her teeth, Harper stretched her other hand into the darkness. Soft hair flowed over her fingers, then she touched something cold, clammy. The darkness glowed violet and Harper's eyes burned with Sight.

"God …"

Harper's legs collapsed beneath her. She clutched her stomach as her last meal splattered across the ground. The voices clamoured in her head, screaming, splitting her like rusty nails hammered into her brain. As the burning faded from her eyes, she could only see one image against the black backdrop of the park.

Blank, bloody eye sockets and a face frozen forever in a silent scream.

Usa watched, concealed by the shadows of trees and soft, silvery vapours. It had been a quiet night, the mist high, her friend. When the Seer arrived, ripples of her disquiet cut deep waves through the air like she was a rock smashed into the surface of a still pool.

Usa wasn't used to seeing humans at night. For reasons she couldn't comprehend, they feared God's moon and stars, hiding away in their unnatural structures as soon as the sun set.

A tightness filled Usa and her eyes dropped from the human to her own hands, humanesque but not of their flesh and blood. They had been coated in human blood, though. Those humans were part of her now. This woman was not one fated to die. She was almost one of the Folk. Usa had tried to warn her of the danger. When they touched, it was like a winter's morning when no sun appeared to warm her.

A strangled cry drew Usa's attention back to the human. She lay upon the ground, her skin sallow and glistening, short puffs of breath hanging in the air. Usa cocked her head to one side. She couldn't understand the human female's reaction. Humans lived for death, took each other's lives without care.

The water running down the human's face stirred a strange sensation in Usa's depths. It was not unlike a prayer, but it was a feeling Usa had never experienced in all her hundreds of years. Ignoring the painful affliction, Usa focused on the woman again.

She thrashed her arms until she found what she sought and pulled a bright light from somewhere in her coverings. She spoke into the light just as the deacon had, her voice high and fast, her words indiscernible. Maybe humans heard the voices of their kith and kin through these lights, just as she heard the call of hers.

Usa, protect us.

Usa, save us.

Their pleas were unrelenting, within her day and night. Pain welled in her chest again and Usa turned away, unable to watch any longer.

Another human arrived, a male, but he made no attempt to speak to the Seer. Instead, he lurked in the shadows under the bridge, hidden to all but Usa. Even she couldn't perceive him clearly, tall but otherwise nondescript. He wore a long covering that obscured his build. His eyes were locked on the female.

"Is that her?" he muttered into a light in his hand.

The answer must've satisfied him, as he nodded decisively and strode away.

As the world filled with flashing blue lights and excited chatter, Usa, too, slipped away into the darkness.

Chapter Nineteen

Scales glimmering in a mob's torchlight, El Culebrón's plaintive moan rises as its eyes roll back and close forever.

A lost jumbee, hair plastered to its body, wet with river water not its own, killing, drowning, dead.

The kelpie's wild ride, tail crashing like thunder as it dives into water. Grasping the bridle, the beast tamed, safe, harmless, red blood flowing with the river, throat cut.

All with human victims, too many to count, never seen. Buried or entrusted to flame before she arrived for the hunt. A death sentence. It is their nature, nothing more. And so, they are condemned.

Are they monsters?

Am I?

The homey scent of tea and the warmth of a woollen blanket brought Harper back from the edge. Neon lights blinded her after the darkness of her thoughts.

"Please state your full name and date of birth for the record." An unknown voice, lost somewhere in the brightness.

"Who's there?" Harper rubbed her eyes and squinted toward the speaker. "Where am I?"

"Please state your full name and date of birth for the record."

As her eyes adjusted, a grey man formed. He was unremarkable. His suit plain, inexpensive. No ring adorned his hands, which clasped clipboard and pen. Average build. Average height. Bland expression. A man no one would look twice at if they passed him in the street. Harper squinted at him again, trying to commit his face to memory, but as soon as she glanced away his features swam and disappeared.

The room was also grey and plain. Metal table, metal chairs, concrete walls. A floor-to-ceiling mirror ran the length of one wall. A solid door with no window broke up another. Harper's stomach still roiled at the memory of what she saw in the tree, the acid reflux sour on her tongue. She couldn't remember anything after that, couldn't remember coming here. She glanced at the mirror, half-expecting to see violet eyes.

"Where am I?" Harper inspected the man in front of her again. "What's going on?"

"Please state your full name and date of birth for the record." The man repeated himself like a stuck record. No more emphasis in his question on his third asking than the first. Unchanging, but unrelenting.

Harper rubbed her wrists in her lap, imagining the cold snap of the metal handcuffs affixed to a bar on the table before her. A cup of tea sat next to them in a porcelain cup and saucer. Harper bit her lip, glanced up at the man again, but he appeared uninterested in anything but his clipboard.

"Har …" She took a deep breath and licked her dry lips before she tried again. "Harper Ashbury, no middle name, my date of birth is January seventeenth." She was careful to give no more information than she was asked for. She bit her lip to hold back a giggle as Heresy's words came back to her—*you did not ask.*

"Place of birth?" the man intoned.

"Why do you need to know?"

"It's part of the background checks we must complete. Place of birth."

"Yorkshire," Harper said.

"Yorkshire is a large county, Ms. Ashbury. Be precise."

"Unknown." Harper scowled. Her name she knew, but the date was a guess based on her apparent age and the cold winter day on which she was found. Her place of birth was a supposition. The documents the Church made for her simply stated 'Yorkshire.' If it was where she came from, no one ever stepped forward to claim their lost child.

"Family?"

"Unknown." She glared at him. She'd been through this line of questioning too many times. Teachers asking for family histories. Official forms she had to leave blank. The reopening of the old wound made her defensive, channelling some of Grace's haughty arrogance as a shield.

"But as we're being 'precise,' until I was eighteen, I was a ward of Danilo and Maria De Santos of Canterbury."

"Is it true that you basically appeared in this world twelve years ago without any documentation or records whatsoever?" The man finally met her gaze. His opaque grey eyes bored into her brown ones.

Harper bristled. "It's a little fanciful to put it that way. I was found. I had amnesia. I still don't remember anything before that day. It's somewhat of a sore topic. If it's relevant, I'm sure my foster family will provide you with whatever documentation you require." She folded her arms across her chest and leant back in her chair.

"I'm sure they will, but I am asking *you*." Harper flinched at the sudden emphasis in his voice.

"Then ask me a question I might know the answer to." Harper dragged in a deep breath, resisting the urge to push her chair back and away from him. The empty handcuffs gleamed with an unspoken promise.

"You have very few associates, Ms. Ashbury. You rarely attend social events at your church or with your co-workers and you have not kept in contact with any classmates from university. Indeed, they report you have always been aloof, preferring to stay home and study than to go to parties or events."

"Is there a question in there?" Her solitude had never been by choice and even years later loneliness tore a jagged hole in her chest. At least one of those university classmates had joined the Guard. "Is it a crime to study while at university? Or to want to go home and rest after a hard day's work?"

"What are you hiding from your peers?"

"I ... nothing." Harper stiffened, her throat dry.

"Why were you trespassing at the location of Ghostwalker Adams' murder?"

Harper looked up at him sharply, the last of the fogginess clearing from her mind.

"Who are you?" she asked again. "Where am I?"

"That is not something you need be concerned with," the man replied. "If you do not answer the question, then I will assume you are hiding something and shall employ other methods."

Harper's pulse quickened. Her nails dug crescents into her arm as she clung to herself, her breath fast and uneven as panic swelled. Only one organisation would respond like that. The archbishop's words floated back to her from what now felt like an age ago. *Already, people are disappearing. The Guard show no mercy. Most never return.*

"I wasn't trespassing. I was asked to investigate by the archbishop on behalf of the Church and the Council of Faiths. You're the one who was with Doctor Siddique that night, right?" Harper squinted at him, the flickering neon lights made him hard to place and he had kept his face in the shadows when they met at the river, yet she was almost certain it was the same man.

"What has this investigation uncovered?"

"Nothing." Harper tugged on her braid. "Nothing at all."

"Are you still investigating?"

"I've been doing some historical research. That's all. Like I said, I haven't found anything."

"We shall see." The man made a note on his clipboard, stabbing the pen into the paper. "Where were you two weeks ago last Friday?"

"Let me check my phone." Harper reached into the pocket of her jeans but it was not there. She swallowed hard, trying to keep her hands from shaking as she patted down her pockets, her thoughts snarled and panicked. *What do they think I did? Do they know about the summoning? About the visions? Did they already have a file on me? Do they suspect? No.* She forced herself to take a breath and check her pockets again, slower. *If they knew, they'd have come for me before this.*

The man spoke again. "We have confiscated your gear. Please answer the question."

Harper tried to still the shuddering that seized her whole body. A vision of the dead girl's face appeared in her mind. She hadn't looked like she died over two weeks ago, but then again, Harper wasn't sure what a corpse should look like at that stage of decomposition. She certainly hadn't smelled fresh.

"I was at work. I work at the cathedral as a junior archivist and collector. If you speak to the head librarian, they should be able to pull the records showing when I logged in and out." Her voice was thin and high-pitched. *I sound guilty.*

"What time did you arrive and leave work that day?"

Harper hesitated, her work times would imply she played a little fast and loose with the curfew. Still, it was a recommendation, not an actual law, and she would rather confess to a small misdemeanour than be accused of a larger crime.

"I arrived at about eight that morning, not long after the bells rang." It was a relief that her voice maintained an even tone as she settled into her story. "I left about one and had lunch at the restaurant owned by the Japanese refugees. It was busy, but I go there a lot, so the staff can probably verify it. I returned to work via a couple of antique bookshops. Part of my job is to keep an eye on new stock that might be of interest to the Church."

Harper paused as the man made a few notes. She hoped she hadn't accidentally caused trouble for the archive or the cathedral.

"These texts of interest to the Church," he said. "What are they regarding?"

"Things the Church believes might be detrimental to the souls of its parishioners." Harper twisted her fingers in her hair. Her heart thudded painfully against her ribs, surely audible to her interrogator in the quiet room. "Theories they find blasphemous or heretical. Incorrect theology. That kind of thing."

As a low-ranking employee, she wasn't sure how much information the church and the Queen's Guard shared. She doubted their goals were the same. Whatever their relationship, the man nodded at her cagey answer as if her words meant something more.

"Did you stop anywhere else on your way back from lunch?"

Harper suppressed a sigh of relief, then tensed at the implication. "No, just those two shops. I returned to the cathedral at approximately half two. Again, the head librarian can verify my location. At half four, I joined some colleagues who required help with a musical text. As I play an instrument, they asked me to look over the book they were studying to see if the musical annotation in the borders was decorative or actually meant something. I worked with them until a little after six. Because it was already dark, one of them drove me home."

The man slid a piece of paper and a pencil across the table. "I need names of the shops and your co-workers."

Harper hastily scrawled them down with a silent prayer her alibi would absolve her of whatever crime had been committed and didn't implicate another innocent.

"What am I being accused of?" Her legs trembled, hidden beneath the table. "I've answered your questions, it's only fair you answer mine."

"You are not being accused of anything, Ms. Ashbury." His grey eyes pierced her, the colour of mist and hiding as much. "I am merely establishing a few facts to confirm your innocence."

Harper ground her teeth. Definitely the Guard. Protect the masses even if it means persecuting the individual. Guilty until proven innocent.

"I will return shortly." The man folded her paper and tucked it into the pocket of his suit jacket. As he stood, Harper flinched back, but he made no move toward her. He turned to leave, then paused to look back at her.

"The music," he said. "Was it significant?"

"Is that relevant?" Harper challenged. She wasn't willing to tell him the notes were the key to a code within the text. The writings were old, the hideout it described unlikely to still exist, but someone would've been sent to check it out anyway. If they found anything, she hadn't heard.

"We shall see," the man promised ambiguously. He left without asking further questions.

Harper lifted the teacup to her lips. Her hand shook, splashing the now cold tea on her jeans. She sniffed the liquid, then sat the cup down again without taking a sip. Who knew what might be in it? Some cleverly disguised truth serum or something. If anyone was going to develop one, it would be the Guard, and they'd make it so people didn't know it existed too. Her research suggested truth spells were real, so it was possible, she supposed.

She avoided looking at the mirror, afraid whoever was staring back from the other side would see her eyes flash purple. Ever since Grace pointed it out, she felt as though she had to hide all the time. She would have bought sunglasses, if anywhere in York sold them in October.

Her mind rambled in the suffocating silence. Even the pounding of her heart was distant and unreal. The bright neon glow of the flickering light overhead was almost worse than darkness. Almost.

Harper rested her elbows on the table. As she breathed in, she counted to seven, held, then released slowly the way she'd been taught. Calm coated the panic in her core and stilled her shivering limbs. She closed her eyes, trying to ignore the itching of raised hairs on the back of her neck.

It seemed like hours before the door opened again. Harper hadn't slept, for fear of dreaming. Her head lay on her folded arms, too heavy to lift, as though the whole world sat upon her shoulders while she waited.

"Harper!"

Her neck cracked as she looked up. "Grace?"

The weights fell away and Harper jumped up, throwing her arms around the taller woman's neck. Grace stroked her hair as she returned her embrace. Harper was relieved that the last of Grace's irritation had vanished in her fears for her sister's safety.

"It's okay, Harp," Grace promised. "I've come to take you home."

The tight knot in Harper's stomach eased as she looked into Grace's stormy eyes. "What's going on?"

"They were concerned you murdered the girl you found."

"Why were they asking me about two weeks ago? Has she been dead that long?"

"No. She ..." Grace took Harper's hands and gripped them tightly. "According to Godfather's sources, she was seen alive less than two hours before you found her."

The room swam and only Grace's strength kept her from falling. Harper wrapped an arm around her stomach as Grace steered her back to the hard metal chair.

"I ..."

Grace leant over, her breath tickly in Harper's ear. "Save it for home." She squatted down in front of her sister and patted Harper's hand until the dancing lights faded from her vision.

"If you're feeling better, we can get out of here. They're reluctant, but your alibi checked out and Godfather has been raising hell on the phone, so to speak."

"He called them himself?" Harper raised an eyebrow.

"You're family," Grace replied. "Of course, Godfather called on your behalf. The police have no right to question an agent of the Church. We're at the Fulford Road police station, so it is the police. Anyway, they had your permission slip for being out after dark. They found it at the scene. You dropped it." Grace held out the familiar slip of paper, smeared with mud but with the archbishop's signature still legible.

"It is the police's duty to protect the citizens of England." A deep voice spoke from the doorway behind Grace. A stranger stood there, the grey man hovering behind him. The newcomer was tall and broad-shouldered, wearing a tan trench coat, the shield of the North Yorkshire Police pinned to the breast pocket. He held out a clear bag with Harper's phone and keys.

"Of course it is." Grace snatched the bag from his hands and Harper had to stop herself from wincing. She wished Grace had a little less self-confidence sometimes. Maybe it would stop her from insulting the man with the key to the cell in which they stood. He looked like he would beat both of them in a fight without even breaking a sweat.

"On Archbishop Marshall's assurances of your innocence and the strength of your family name, I would ask for your assistance in this investigation." Even though he addressed Harper, the man's eyes stayed on Grace.

Grace's eyes narrowed. "Next time you want a favour, try dinner and flowers, not a prison cell and cold tea. Move out of the way. We're leaving." Harper poked her in the back.

The man didn't move save his eyes, which he dragged away from Grace to look Harper up and down the way he might have looked at dirt on his shoes. "Ms. Ashbury, the archbishop has informed me you are something of a specialist in the field of supernatural history."

It was an unusual area of study and special permits were required to research it. The Guard were undoubtedly aware of it before their questioner ever set foot in the cell. They might be in the normal police station, but it was attached to the army garrison only a few steps down the road. Harper nodded cautiously. "Eleventh through seventeenth centuries. You believe this murder is not of human origin?"

"What do you think?" the man replied. "While it is something we try to keep from the common citizens, we both know the dangers of the occasional jailbreak."

"You think something slipped past the Veil and is killing people?" Grace arched an eyebrow at the openness of the man's statements.

"Possibly." He shrugged noncommittally. "We would not be doing our job if we discounted the possibility of a witch or demon. Nor would we be doing our duty by turning a blind eye to such an abomination living in our world."

The look he gave her was cold, and Harper was reminded of the icy stare from her dream.

"If I come across anything useful, I'll let you know," Harper lied.

"My card."

The man handed a small square of paper to Grace. Harper peeked over her shoulder and caught a glimpse of the North Yorkshire Police Department's emblem and the name 'Chief Constable Bradford' before Grace tucked the card into her pocket.

"Follow me." The man turned and strode down the corridor, with a sharp gesture for them to accompany him. Grace glanced at Harper, who nodded.

"I'm getting tired of men expecting us to follow them without explanation," Grace muttered as she linked her arm through Harper's. "I swear, the next one who tries it is going to get kicked in the balls."

"The last one did." Harper hid her smile. With Grace at her side everything would be okay, no matter who this man was. He wouldn't be the first person Grace had taken down a notch or two for bullying her.

Despite Harper's fears, the chief constable led them into a gleaming white vestibule where a uniformed officer sat reading with his feet up on his desk. Bradford gestured toward a door marked 'exit' and gave them a small nod. "Goodnight, ladies. Or good morning, I suppose. The sun's coming up so the bus will go by soon. We'll be speaking again."

He turned on his heel and left before Grace could argue. Harper dragged her sister toward the door. She had no energy for another fight.

"Can we go?" Harper begged. "It's been a really, *really* long night."

Grace paused, then relaxed, giving Harper's arm a quick squeeze. "You're right. Let's get home."

Harper let out a deep breath. When the bus pulled in, she tugged Grace up the step and flashed their passes at the driver. Before they were even halfway home, her head drooped onto Grace's shoulder, and she fell fast asleep.

Chapter Twenty

Harper entered the Shambles with trepidation. She hadn't returned since the day she met Theo and experienced the ghostwalker's death. Her eyes were cast down as she hurried past the Guard, but as soon as they were behind her, she peered down the row in hopes of spying green eyes and a messy thatch of hair. Harper gave herself a shake. Even if she did run into the cute nurse again, he certainly wouldn't be interested in talking to her after their last encounter.

She resisted the urge to turn and look back at the Guard instead. The corpse in the tree haunted her and she couldn't escape the feeling of being watched since her interrogation at the police station. If they were observing her, looking back would only add to their suspicion.

To keep her mind off both Theo and the Guard, Harper concentrated on her footing, not wishing to take another tumble. The fine vapour of evening and dawn never quite vanished from the cobbled road, and the street curved, one end hidden from the other, with the old buildings looming and cutting off almost all sunlight. Harper hurried through the crowd, wondering at so many people thronging to a place representing everything they feared.

Most people might say they didn't believe ghosts or supernaturals still walked the streets of England, but deep down, they were never sure. With its range of arcane-esque stores, from the glitteringly enticing sweet shop to the alchemists' society to the deeply suspicious Witches' Tearoom, people came to the Shambles for the same reason they went on rollercoasters. The audacious nature of the businesses and the presence of the Guard made it the last place anyone with sense would expect to find real magic, yet it still gave the illusion that fae might be hiding in the gloaming mists.

Harper broke from her reverie as she reached her destination, the boutique paper shop where she bought her art supplies. Normally, it was Grace who was the snob. She was the one who wore clothes with labels and designer shoes. Harper usually couldn't care less, but she reserved the right to be elitist about her paper.

She preferred a linen or laid texture, something she could run her fingers over and recognise even in the dark. A quality that travelled through her pen to her fingers. The scratching of carbon over a rough surface. Real ink glistening as it sunk into a sheet, two perpetually merged into one. The dry, earthy smell of paper complementing the wooden scent of pencil. It was a comforting reality when she was trying to banish her nightmares. Setting pen to paper helped keep her centred. Helped keep her sane.

Transferring her visions to paper was cleansing. It allowed the dream to pass from her, its warning accomplished. Many times she'd been plagued with nightmares, the same, night after night, until she wrote them down in spidery writing, trembling, words not worthy of the paper they were written on. Then, sometimes, the nightmare would vanish, burned away as the paper blackened and curled over a candle, the threat of discovery gone in a puff of smoke. Sometimes. Not always.

Since Heresy's disappearance, Harper's dreams had grown worse. She'd written reams of notes, yet every night the forest from her nightmare grew back, undaunted. Last night she found herself there again. A thousand eyes watching. A violin wailing in a minor key. And sometimes, just sometimes, the feeling of déjà vu, like a deeply buried memory struggling to awaken.

She glanced over her shoulder as she reached the store. The eyes were always there, in the back of her mind if not in reality, watching, judging, unrelenting, unblinking. And the girl. Even in daylight, Harper could not escape her ghost. Empty sockets stared at her accusingly from an alder tree coffin. Too late, too blind. Harper pulled her coat tighter around her shoulders. *It's only the cold giving me shivers, only the cold.*

It was a chill that had lingered ever since she touched the spirit in the park. As often as Harper replayed the incident in her mind, she could make no sense of it. The killer would surely have tried to kill her too. If the creature she met was not the killer, what part did she play?

Harper tripped up the stairs of the store, grasped the cold, metal handle, yanked the door open, and let light flood out into the monochrome street. She dived into the sanctuary it offered. A little bell shook as the door banged shut behind her.

"Good morning."

The storekeeper sat knitting in a corner, a long ball of yarn winding around her ankles like an attention-seeking pet. Harper returned the woman's greeting before heading into the backroom where her paper was stored.

A few minutes later she was leaving again. No one in the street stood out as being particularly suspicious, Harper reprimanded herself as she pulled the door closed. A flash of colour in the glass caught her eye, a red smear behind the shopkeeper as if blood splattered across the wall.

Harper cracked the door open again until she could clearly see the reflection of the shopkeeper. She sat in the corner, apparently unperturbed, her red yarn spilling out across the floor. The wall behind her held rainbow shelves of ink. *The next victim? A vision like the shadow following Deacon Paul?* Maybe the hesychia was moving beyond silencing voices. Maybe she would also silence written words.

Harper flipped open her phone and dialled Saqib's number as she hurried toward the cathedral. "Hi. No time to talk. Think you can get your equipment over to the Shambles and see if you detect anything near the paper shop? Don't ask, I don't have anything concrete, just a hunch. If it's right, maybe we can catch the killer before someone else dies."

When Harper disappeared around the corner, a lanky man looked up from the shop window he was browsing. His long, brown jacket was cinched closed against the wind and a cap shielded his face from the cold.

"Jumpy, isn't she?" he muttered into his phone.

"She is on the boundary," Heresy replied. "I have shown you who summoned me. May I leave now?"

The man shook his head. "Not yet. I need to see her magic with my own eyes."

"She is not a threat," Heresy protested. "Her magic is awful."

"Any untamed witch is a threat. We'll watch and see."

He stuffed his hands in his pockets and wandered off in the direction of the cathedral, whistling a jaunty tune to himself.

The archbishop was waiting for Harper at the entrance to the cathedral crypt. She shivered at the memory of their last meeting like this. "There's not another …"

Her heart sank at his heavy silence.

"I wished to check on you after your ordeal with the murdered woman," he said eventually.

Harper tensed. "Thank you, Archbishop. I'm okay. I think. I … that poor girl. I feel like I'm not getting any closer to finding what killed them. And now another? The killer is speeding up."

"Come with me." The archbishop's robe billowed as he turned and headed toward the crypt.

When they reached the entrance to the Hall of Testing, the archbishop slipped his key card into the slot to access the archives. It was more ornate than Harper's and longer, seeming to contain more information.

When they passed through the door, they did not stand in the Hall of Testing as Harper had grown to expect. Instead of a vaulted room, they stood in a curving corridor. A gentle fountain resided in a niche in one wall, a metallic cup hanging next to it. There was nothing else save a wooden door, barely visible before the wall arched away. It seemed too easy to simply walk down the corridor. There had to be a trap. She gasped, spinning around, her heart thrumming, expecting danger. Yet, no voice echoed giving instructions and nothing attacked them.

"Where are we?" Harper frowned as she examined the water fountain. It looked familiar. Like the one beyond the Hall of Testing.

"This is my cathedral." Archbishop Marshall rested a hand on the stone wall. "There is nowhere I may not tread. Nowhere I will not be recognised. As you are with me, you too are allowed passage."

Harper reached out to the fountain. Cool water splashed over her fingertips. She filled the cup and took a small sip, expecting the bitter taste of some poison. Clean, pure water washed over her tongue and dripped down her throat.

"We skipped the Hall of Testing?" she asked dubiously before taking another sip of water.

"This cathedral is part of me and I of it." The archbishop patted her shoulder. "Those same rites that bind us also allow me passage."

"But what if someone forced you to unlock the door?" Harper pointed out. "I didn't even see it scan biometrics."

"Harper. Have faith." The archbishop's voice brooked no argument. Harper pressed her lips closed, swallowing her questions.

As she followed the archbishop down the long, curved passageway, she counted the doors. There were thirty in total, each leading to a research room or library, save the seventeenth, which led to the First Vault, and the thirteenth, which lead to the break room. The archbishop went through door thirty-one. Harper turned back to count again, but he took her by the arm and propelled her through. His grip encircled her bicep like iron.

The door led onto the middle of a spiralling stone staircase. To the left, it descended into the depths of the earth. To the right, it ascended … where? Harper was only aware of one entrance to the archives, yet the only thing above them was the cathedral proper and the streets of York. The archbishop released her arm and set off up the stairs. Harper closed the anomalous door behind her and stepped onto the stairway when his feet turned the corner and vanished.

She kept her eyes glued on the stairs, each sneakered step squeaking as she followed the archbishop. Worn slabs bowed under the weight of a thousand footsteps, smooth and slippery, the shape of crescent moons. Harper kept one hand to the wall as they ascended. Fiery torches heated her face but she was glad of their presence. Shadows slithered up and down the stairs, writhing in the inconsistent light. Although Harper was certain they were above ground level, no windows slit the stone to let sunlight flow through.

The world became an eternal spiral, the only sound the creak of her shoes and her laboured breath. Archbishop Marshall, though stouter and older, had long since disappeared above.

One … two … three … one hundred … one hundred and one … two hundred …

The endless turning left Harper dizzy and she lost count. She leant her forehead against the cool wall as she rubbed her temples. Her toes twitched as they sought safe purchase on the narrow steps. If she fell now, she might roll forever, a bloody slinky caught in an infinite tumble. Still dizzy, she continued upwards, one hand on the stairs in front of her, vertical but on all fours as she continued the climb.

When daylight finally came, Harper stumbled across the room without looking to clutch the window ledge and peer out at the autumn silhouettes of the trees of Dean's Park.

"What is this place?" When she caught her breath, she turned to find the archbishop reposing on an oak and velvet throne. It was so unlike his plain, practical style that she rubbed her eyes to make sure she wasn't seeing things.

"See for yourself." He waved his hand, encompassing the small room.

Stone walls hemmed them in on all four sides. Out of the opposite window, Harper could see the southwestern tower of the cathedral. She had climbed both towers many times, right to the top and out onto the roof. She'd never seen this room before. Moreover, there was no way past it. The stairs ended here. Rushing around the room, she leant out of the windows at a precarious angle, not heeding the bitter wind nor the uncompromising drop. There were no other rooms, no stairs, the walls not thick enough to be concealing anything. The tower opposite didn't have any corresponding windows.

Harper's heart thudded a painful beat against her sternum. *This room should not exist.* She had stood on the roof. Stood above a room from which there were no stairs, no ladders, no door leading onwards. She shook her head, scrunched up her eyes, then looked again. Nothing changed. She still stood in an impossible room.

She looked back toward the archbishop. His dark eyes hadn't wavered, his pose so relaxed it must be deliberate. A slight smile quirked his lips, gone in a second. *Is he laughing at me? This must be a joke of some kind.*

Digging her fingers into the gaps between the stones, Harper hoisted herself up to sit on the window ledge. She leant out so far, the wind grabbed her shirt and flattened it against her skin. Her hair streamed out behind her, raven black against the clear blue sky. She stretched out her other hand, her fingers taut and straining, certain if she reached far enough, she would encounter the edge of the illusion, that maybe the park and the other tower were merely a painted backdrop, and she wasn't in the northwest tower at all.

Thunder shattered the air and reverberated through the walls of the cathedral. Her fingers slipped, nails scratching painfully on stone, heart in her throat as gravity yanked her downwards. The wind stole her scream. Her hair snarled across her face, blinding, gagging. Her knees locked around the ledge, then slipped. The world tipped and rushed closer. Wind screeched a banshee's call. Bile, sharp and bitter, coated her tongue.

Fragile flesh hit immovable stone. Blood squelched as it splattered against the feet of the saints. Sight faded as they watched her, the condemnation in their eyes burning hotter than the crack in her skull. Each breath laboured, stolen by crushing rocks that shattered her ribs and flattened her lungs. The ground shook beneath her as heaven thundered its condemnation. Sunlight dying. Fire beckoning. Hell's black maw opened beneath her.

Sharp claws dug into her wrist, barely sensed over the terror of death. The earth disappeared and she tumbled into the fiery pit, scorching, her eyes red-hot.

"Harper."

The devil called her name and she trembled, on all fours on the floor, scrambling, grovelling.

"Harper."

Harper let out a deep, shuddering breath and opened her eyes. A hand rested on her head, cool after the scorching heat.

"Never do that again. You could've been killed."

The crackle of flames faded. The gravelly voices of demons scattered into nothingness. The burning sensation behind her eyes dissipated, leaving a pounding headache. Still shaking, Harper placed her hand in the steady one held out to her, and the archbishop pulled her to her feet.

Great Peter's third toll sent tremors through the room. Harper glanced out of the window at the clear autumn sky. No thunder, just the cathedral bells proclaiming the hour. The archbishop watched her, his face creased with worry.

"Has anyone ever … has anyone ever fallen from up here?" *What did I See? Who were they?*

"Some," he answered. "Accidents, mostly. I am glad we do not have to add you to their number."

"Accidents *mostly?*"

"Even the cathedral has ghost stories, Harper." The archbishop rubbed his forehead with one hand, not meeting her eyes. "We try to keep them from the public. I don't want this place of peace and worship tainted by fear. Why and how those people died is not what we came here to discuss."

"What is this place?" Harper asked again. "How come I've never seen it before?"

"When was the last time you climbed the northwest tower?"

Harper tugged on her hair, leaning against a reassuringly solid stone wall. The fall was like a dream, details slipping from her memory. She tried to hold onto them, to the terror, the anguish, but it was gone, like mist under the scorching sun. "About three or four years ago."

"That explains it then. The tower renovations were only finished two years ago."

"Oh." Harper felt a little stupid for leaning so far out the window. Scaffolding had obscured the tower for over a year. Of course, it was explainable. The Church would never use magic. Even if they found a way to use it that was theologically acceptable, it would mean war with the Queen's Guard, the archives ransacked, their books fuel for the pyres. At least as far as York was concerned, it would be an apocalyptic event. There could be no winners in a war between faith and state. It was why the delicate balance of ignorance was preserved by both. The Guard didn't demand to see the archives or meddle in Church-led hunts. The Council of Faiths didn't demand access to the Guard's strongholds or publicly condemn them. Harper recalled the archbishop mentioning the Council petitioned for details on those unfortunates taken for questioning. It was an unusually bold move.

"Did anything ever come of your request to the Queen's Guard?" Harper asked. "There's been nothing in the papers about the missing people. Did you get them back?"

The archbishop took a deep breath, his gaze out the window on a flock of birds wheeling over the park. His knuckles whitened as he gripped the stone ledge. "Some few returned. For others, they invoked the Anti-Supernatural Security Act of 1734. A handful remain completely unaccounted for. The Queen's Guard say they know nothing, that these disappearances are of supernatural origin. I do not know that I believe them. However, we have no evidence to say otherwise, and the Queen has cautioned the Council against pursuing the matter further. We don't abandon our parishioners so easily, but we've had to take a subtler approach. Finding this murderer will help. The public will calm, and the Guard will no longer need to act with such brutality. I pray this ends when the killer is brought to justice."

Harper bit her lip, her fingernails digging into her palms as she balled her fists. She was failing. Not only the women who were the most recent victims, but the people of York who lived in fear and those taken by the Guard.

"Why did you bring me here?" she asked. "Is there something here that will help?"

"You believe the killer may be a demon from ancient Greece, but you don't know how to catch them or why the murders are happening. Many rituals are triggered by celestial occurrences and the Greeks have a particularly strong connection to the stars. The contents of the astronomy tower may be useful to you. If you can find an example of when this happened before, you may find the culprit or a way to stop them."

Harper scolded herself for being so obsessed with the room itself that she ignored its contents. A desk stained dark as coffee took up most of the centre of the room. It was covered in leather-bound books and coiled scrolls. Feather quills sat snug with ballpoint pens placed in a pot. One piece lay unfurled, its corners pinned down by small metal globes and glass paperweights filled with twirling galaxies.

The archbishop rested his elbows on the table as he watched Harper over steepled fingers. His eyes measured every move she took as she walked around the room, fingers trailing over an angled torquetum and a brass sextant, two of the few items she recognised. She twitched her shoulder blades. The heat of his gaze bore through her, physical, like two hot pokers driving her forward. The last lingering sensation of descending into hell left her skin raw, sensitive to every puff of air, every look.

She paused by a modern telescope, jarringly out of place in this renaissance science festival. Next to it was a device she'd never seen before: Two smaller telescopes bound together by a brass wheel that rested flat between them. It turned as though oiled and she swung it this way and that. The light caught on it, trails like comets soaring down its length.

"It's a repeating circle." The archbishop's voice was cool, factual, at odds with the emotional heat of his stare.

Harper tugged her collar, a drip of sweat rolling down her spine. Lightheaded, she leant against the wall and rested her cheek against the cool stone. Her hand tightened around the repeating circle of its own accord. Lights flashed behind her closed eyes. *A repeating circle, like the murders, happening again and again.*

Her stinging eyes were drawn to the cobalt-blue ceiling panels with shining, golden stars, and thin trails of silver that marked the constellations. A prickle of static flashed across her skin as a comet streaked across the depiction of the night sky. When she was certain her eyes were brown again, she turned to the archbishop. "May I stay here and study? Do I have clearance?"

"These murders must be stopped," he said, his tone grave. "For that, I will give you any clearance you require. I shall leave you to study. Stay away from the windows."

Having dispensed his warning, Archbishop Marshall left, the flap of his sandaled feet soon fading. Harper pulled a pen and notebook out of her bag and unrolled a moon chart to study, pinning its corners with pen pots and glass galaxies.

She remained absorbed in star charts and planetary movements for several hours until the harsh vibration of her phone cut her concentration. A quick glance at the screen showed a message from Grace:

Godfather wants to see you. That so-called scientist is here.

CHAPTER TWENTY-ONE

When Harper reached the public areas of the cathedral, Grace and Saqib were sat talking at the side of the nave. The cathedral was busy, filled with the susurration of prayer and glowing in the light of hundreds of votive candles. Pillars stretched almost to the heavens, painted royal blue and blood red. They arched to form a vaulted ceiling, golden knots joining them at the apex of the nave. In between, rainbows of coloured glass cast spotlights on dancing dust motes, twinkling like fairies.

Though she couldn't hear the discussion, Harper recognised the taken-aback expression on Saqib's face. It was a common look from people who weren't accustomed to Grace's somewhat astringent conversation style. Seeing how Saqib kept opening his mouth then closing it immediately, it appeared to be less a conversation and more a lecture. Harper wiped the smile from her face as she joined them, but Grace's scowl showed she noticed the laughter in her sister's eyes.

"What's up?" Harper asked as she scooted in next to Grace.

"I checked out that shop in the Shambles like you asked." Saqib glanced at Grace in case she was going to interrupt. When she remained silent, he continued, "I didn't detect anything, but that could be because nothing was happening. I've found the runes are most discernible under shorter wavelengths on the border between ultraviolet and x-ray. Now, I can't flood the area with x-rays and leave it monitoring, there's too many people, but there's almost an active element to these runes. It's hard to explain, but it's like they were carved *by* light and there's a lingering energy. I'm hoping that means whatever carved them will be detectable by my equipment. I've been developing something similar to a Geiger counter. I hid the prototype in the shop. It's linked to my phone, so if it does find anything, I'll get an alert."

Harper made a mental note to avoid x-rays if she was at Grace's clinic or the hospital. Broken bones came with the territory for a De Santos, but Harper didn't remember her eyes burning with magic when she had x-rays before. But then, her magic hadn't been fizzling beneath her skin, barely contained.

"What makes you think the killer will target the paper store?" Saqib asked. "If the hesychia wants to silence people telling stories about supes, why not one of the bookstores?"

Harper twisted her fingers into the ends of her hair, her eyes automatically sliding away from Grace's hard stare. "She's targeting the storytellers, not the stories themselves. Adams. Paul. Even Tahira told stories through chocolate. If she's silencing people who spread word of supes, not only spoken word, it makes sense to go after writers. And the paper shop in the Shambles is the most well-known stationers in York."

Saqib rubbed his chin thoughtfully. "What about the girl in the tree? We haven't managed to identify her, but she had the same runes around her eyes."

Darkness poured in and clouded Harper's vision. She fell into empty sockets, a void where there should have been sight. Eyes crowded in around her. Gelatinous orbs glooped against her skin. Her own eyes were speared with pain as though claws dug in and ripped them out.

She clapped her hands over her face lest Saqib see the telltale lilac glow. Before he or Grace could ask what was wrong, she fled the cathedral, guided by years of familiarity, not caring who she bumped into. She ran from the darkness, into the light.

Harper collapsed onto the grass of Dean's Park, which bordered the cathedral to the north. Cool earth, still wet from the morning's rain, soothed the heat in her skin. She pressed her forehead into it and gulped down moist air. Gentle fingers brushed loose strands of hair back from her face.

"What did you See?" Grace asked softly in Harper's ear. The mist damped her voice, the day too gloomy for many people to be abroad. "Your eyes flickered purple for a millisecond. I don't think Saqib noticed, it was too fast. A logical mind would dismiss it as a reflection."

"I don't think he'd turn me in," Harper said weakly. Something in her trusted him. Something felt right. Like Heresy. Like the too-big-for-two house. Her reservation was less around him handing her over to the Queen's Guard and more around how many hours she'd have to spend as a science experiment. She sat up, tucked her knees up to her chin, and rested against Grace's side.

"He works with the police," Grace remonstrated. "Maybe even the Guard. If he catches you, then you'll go to jail, at best. Just because it's been sixty years since they last hanged a witch, doesn't mean they'll mind breaking their streak if they catch you. They already suspect you might be the murderer."

"But I'm not."

"They won't care about facts. They'll pin every unexplained happening of the last decade on you, then set up some gallows in the middle of town and give everyone a half day holiday to come watch."

"Grace, calm down." Harper glanced around but no one was within earshot of her sister's hushed tirade.

"I don't really think—" Grace started hotly, but Harper interrupted.

"They're back to normal now. Right?"

Grace peered deeply into Harper's eyes then nodded her satisfaction. "Nice and brown. But be careful. I told Saqib you'd been feeling ill since finding the body and needed some air. He'll be expecting you back in soon. Don't let him trigger you like that again."

"I'll try not to. It's not like I have much control over it."

"I thought that ridiculous demon was supposed to be teaching you," Grace said. "Not that I trust it to do it properly, but it's the *only* reason it was worth keeping it around. I assume it never came back."

Harper worried the end of her braid. "I haven't seen him since the Guildhall. I need him, Grace. Without him, the nightmares are back. What if my magic gets out of control?"

A rare flash of panic tightened Grace's eyes and twitched her cheek, then she covered it with the usual De Santos bluster. "Good riddance to him. We don't need a demon's help to control your magic, we've always kept it hidden before. He's too small to do any real harm. Let the Queen's Guard deal with him. They have a cyber division. They've probably already caught him. Oh." Grace's face fell at the implication.

"He wouldn't talk," Harper reassured her sister. "Well, he'll probably talk a lot, but I doubt he'll tell them the truth about anything."

Grace threw her arms around Harper and gave her a tight hug. "I wish you wouldn't take these risks."

"I know. But, Gray, it's who I am. You're going to have to accept that one day. C'mon. We still have a murderer to catch, remember? I'm going to hang around the Shambles for a while. Maybe I can save a life. You go home, I know you've got a date to prep for. I'll call if anything happens."

"And if the hesychia does show up, what then? Do you have any plan at all on how to stop it? You said you could barely See it. If you can't see it or See it, how can we fight it?"

Harper whispered, her lips barely moving, "Magic."

A young man on the opposite side of the park watched as the two women returned to the cathedral. He hunched on a bench, shuffling the toe of his boot against the grass as though it was a new and suspicious material. He held his phone to his ear and muttered, "She has a lot of faith in you, doesn't she?"

"She is bound to me." Heresy's sullen voice crackled from the phone imprisoning him. "If she gets hurt, I get hurt. If she dies, I get sent back."

"I almost feel bad for making you talk," the man replied. "She would be terribly disappointed if she knew, but I have my orders."

"You sound almost resentful. Starting to regret this job now you have seen her?"

"No. I just hate fieldwork." He closed the phone with a click before Heresy could protest further. "I hate fieldwork, but I have to find the rest of your coven before I report in," he said to himself, eyes locked on the doorway where Harper disappeared. "Then they will be dealt with."

Harper yawned and stretched, her entwined fingers pushed out so hard they almost popped. She'd stopped for tea at every tearoom and window shopped past the point of reasonableness for even the most materialistic soul. She'd run out of excuses to hang around the Shambles and she was bored.

She knew what she must do. Grace would no doubt call it an unacceptable risk, but Harper was out of options. It was selfish to keep putting her own wellbeing over that of the victims and those who disappeared. If she caught the killer, no one else needed to die. Maybe then those arrested by the Queen's Guard could come home.

"Come on," she spurred herself on. Closing her eyes, she concentrated on the sensation of her eyelids pressing against the cornea, the strain of ligaments as her eyes moved, the almost unnoticed fizz in her retinas. She pictured her own hazel eyes gleaming bright purple.

Opening her eyes, Harper glanced at her reflection in a bottle-glass window. Still brown.

She contemplated her image without blinking, trying to bring the burning sensation to the fore. Something scratched her eyeballs. Flickers of static sparked on the back of her eyelids. It was like trying to pick up a shard of ice. It hurt and slid away from her, melted as she clutched at it. Tears of pain and frustration welled. With a shudder that was almost a sob, she paced back and forth. Other shoppers skirted around her, but she only had eyes for her own watery likeness. Still brown. Then something in the reflections behind her caught her attention.

It wasn't the bright red of the shopkeeper's knitting nor the rainbow display of the paper shop's window. She Saw a village hut with a man stood outside, leaning on some sort of farming tool as he spoke to his wife in the doorway. Their whispers filled the air, although Harper couldn't make out the words. The stench of dung and rotten vegetables obliterated everything else. Her eyes watered, obscuring the vision.

"No, I need to See. I need to know," Harper pleaded, but by the time her eyesight cleared, the village had faded, and her eyes were brown again.

She trembled from the force of the vision, so much more than Sight, the lingering stench enough to make her gag. The image she'd Seen was alien, yet familiar, like a drawing from a museum or a costumed mannequin. Maybe another iteration of this gruesome cycle back in the days of Viking settlements in York. She wished she could have Seen the sky. Archbishop Marshall's hunch about the deaths being triggered by some star pattern or moon phase was logical, but the information she had was too sparse to pinpoint. If she could find out exactly when the Master Undertaker referenced and when it happened in this Viking village, she might be able to use the three points to discern a pattern.

Harper pulled out her mobile. "Please have your phone on. Damnit, Gray." Harper wanted to slam her handset down in frustration when the familiar voicemail message started. Instead, she tried to channel whatever magic might be out there down the line. "Hey, Gray. I need you to get this message. Pick up. I'm heading to the Jorvik Centre. I think there's a Viking connection to whatever's happening. The Master Undertaker said to look to history." Harper glanced over her shoulder. "I think we can check out the museum and still be back here before curfew. All the murders have been around sunset, so the shopkeeper's safe enough for now. Meet me at Jorvik as soon as you get this."

'As soon as you get this' turned out to be almost an hour later when the Centre was near closing. Harper hung around the gift store waiting for her sister, but none of the facsimiles triggered another vision. Once Grace arrived, Harper purchased them tickets to the museum itself. She dismissed the recreation area hoping actual Viking artefacts would contain some hint.

"This stinks," Grace pointed out unnecessarily.

The two women picked their way across the exhibition, trying not to trip over excited schoolchildren and tourists. Harper's stomach clenched, as it did every time she set foot on the see-through floor. It revealed an old archaeological dig of Viking York, or Jorvik as it was known then. Despite having been to the Centre several times, Harper could never quite overcome the fear that her next step would send her tumbling into the dirt below. The curators had certainly done everything they could to provide an immersive experience.

"It's amazingly authentic," Harper said. "It smells exactly like the old settlement in my—"

"Imagination." Grace cast a meaningful glance at an older couple behind them examining one of the glass display cases dotted around the room. "Of course, it does. You've been here before. Every person living in the north of England has been here. They all remember this smell."

"I suppose." Harper's shoulders slumped. It was possible her memory was playing tricks on her, simply supplying a suitable scent.

"What are we looking for, exactly?" Grace asked while she perused a display of Viking artefacts along the far wall.

"Anything with those runes," Harper said. "Or referring to a wave of strange murders."

"Wouldn't anything like that already be in the cathedral archives?" Grace asked as they moved on.

"Well, Alfred has seen something like that writing before, so there's a good chance, but I don't know how to start looking. When I searched the archives, I got nothing. That means it's probably higher than my clearance."

"Godfather can fix that. This is a waste of time. If there were anything even potentially supernatural here, it wouldn't be on display."

"Well, I am rather hoping this smell or being near the artefacts would trigger another ... imagining," Harper admitted. "Or there'll be something everyone else missed."

Grace gave her a look of pure exasperation. "You're here trying to See something?"

"I Saw hints of the girl in the tree before she was killed," Harper whispered. "If I get a vision of what happened before, then that's more useful right now than spending hours in the archives or wandering around the Shambles."

With a quiet harrumph, Grace turned her back to resume her silent interrogation of the information boards.

Harper wandered around the room, pausing occasionally to flick through one of the interactive screens.

"Hey, Gray, look at this," Harper called her sister over.

Grace strolled over, linking arms as they stood side by side. "What am I looking at?"

"Are you sure you're a De Santos?" Harper asked jokingly.

Grace pursed her lips and nodded toward the display. "Get on with it, Harp. This is not how I planned to spend my evening. I'm supposed to be on a date in an hour, remember? I already cancelled on Antoinette for your stupid ghost walk. I'm not doing it again."

"Sorry." Harper grimaced thinking of the reaction of the young man who helped her when she twisted her ankle in the Shambles. Maybe if he hadn't seen her books, they could have gone for tea. She bit her lip to hold back a wistful smile. *I have more important things to do than date.* She swallowed a sigh, then pointed to one of the urns. A close-up photo of it was displayed on the information screen in front of her. "That symbol is similar to one Saqib found. It might indicate something like this happened back then too."

"Or it might be a common Viking word," Grace said. "For all we know, it simply says, 'Mine'. That would be normal and possibly part of ... of this thing."

"Grace."

"I know, lives are at stake, but this isn't helping. If we want to help, we need to ..." Grace glanced around then leant over to whisper in Harper's ear. "We need to get out there, track this thing down, and kill it. Quickly. Visions, light wavelengths, this stuff isn't helping."

"What if the answer on how to kill it is here?" Harper asked.

"Then I can't see it." Grace pulled her arm back and stepped away from Harper. "I'm going home to change. If you find something *useful*, let me know and I'll hunt. *This* is pointless. This is not the De Santos way."

Grace turned on her heel and marched off. Ever since Harper summoned Heresy, Grace had been short-tempered. *More short-tempered,*

Harper amended. The illusion spirit had been gone far too long for a simple reconnaissance mission. The only thing that made her think he was simply out there having fun was the fact the Queen's Guard hadn't come knocking.

As she continued to browse the exhibition and make notes, Harper noticed a man pretending to read an info poster. He studied her with darting eyes, his face twisted in disgust. She balled her sleeves in her fists and tucked them under her arms. She was being paranoid. The whole place stank of stale urine and dead fish, *everyone* looked disgusted. It wasn't personal. She shook her head, letting strands of escaped hair fall across her face. When she darted a glance toward the man, he was gone.

CHAPTER TWENTY-TWO

That evening, Harper waited until the paper shop closed and Saqib arrived to relieve her vigil. The lights above the shop came on after it was locked up for the night, the proprietor staying overnight to maximise her business hours in the diminishing October days. Yawning and drained, Harper drifted home when the lights went out.

When she reached their terraced house, Heresy still hadn't returned. She didn't know why she expected anything different. Maybe it was her paranoia, but something seemed off in the house. The feeling of being watched tickled her back. The house was silent save for the creak of floorboards under her feet, like it too was watching.

When she got upstairs, she found her bedroom window open. She stared hard at it, trying to remember if she opened it that morning when she was getting ready for work. Her bed was scruffy, but then it always was. Her desk was neat as she left it, down to the pencil with the snapped tip, graphite sprinkled across the page. A vague uneasiness slithered through her gut, but there was no indication of anything amiss.

Before going to bed, Harper placed a souvenir from the Jorvik gift shop under her pillow and left the light on. After half an hour of trying to sleep, she pulled the trefoil necklace out from under her pillow and placed it next to her instead. Sleeping on top of an object may have been documented as an effective way to direct dreams but it certainly wasn't a comfortable way to do it. She was sceptical about it working anyway. It wasn't like she could get a real Viking artefact. The archives had several of them, but she couldn't think of a plausible excuse for taking them out of the cathedral. She hoped the process was more of a subliminal direction than actual magic, in which case the Jorvik replica should work as well.

Although she wished to avoid nightmares, her need to find the murderer outweighed Heresy's warning that something was hunting her through her dreams. As she drifted off, she focussed on the image of the village from her earlier vision.

Harper gazed out over the twinkling Ouse as it wended through the grounds of Bishopthorpe Palace, high against the banks where Grace fished with her brothers in the summer.

Her breath floated in the air, following the sway of the river flowing to the east. A willow tree wept into the water, long hair washed in its flood. Where ground and water met, a person lay. No breath rose from his body, and it held no heat to ward off the morning frost. Harper's footsteps crunched as icy tendrils of grass broke beneath her boots. She knew who he was, who he had been, yet she still needed to see for herself even through the dream-lens of detached emotion.

Deacon Paul lay as he did in the crypt, arms crossed over his chest, rosary clutched in his hand, eyes closed as if in prayer yet crinkled as if smiling. Harper hoped it was a sign the deacon had found peace with God. She recalled his long speeches denouncing evil, which he saw as anything even slightly deviating from the norm. To her, that made him a threat, but she never hated him for it, would never have wished him dead.

Sight blazing, she knelt by the body, ignoring the moisture seeping into her knees. His mouth was parted, ripped open, lipless. Within, nothing but darkness. His soul escaped his mutilated earthly shell. Then, glowing to her Sight, runes appeared one by one, so familiar now yet still meaningless.

Harper bit back a curse of frustration, her anger hot even in the dream. This was telling her nothing. She wanted to See the murder. See the killer. Or See the next victim so she could save them. She stood, staring down at the body, challenging it, but nothing changed.

When she stepped back, the branches of the willow tree floated on the wind, caressing, covering the body, creeping gradually closer until Harper could see him no more and she stood alone on the riverbank.

Bishopthorpe Palace faded into the fog and the sparkling river dimmed. The grass grew whiter as frost blossomed and spread. On the wind, sheep called to each other through the mist. Her breath hung close, curled through her hair as she walked down a rough, dirt path.

I know this place. A thought came from far away and she nodded to herself. This was where her life began. Not in Bishopthorpe by the Ouse, but fifty miles away in the Dales.

Harper had meandered alongside the River Swale that frostbitten morning, not knowing where she was going or where she came from.

"What are you?" A voice broke through her reverie, and she blinked. The stupor lifted as though she stepped out of a dream.

"I'm a … I'm Harper." The words were heavy, foreign on her tongue. She didn't know where they came from.

A man stood before her. His long, dark coat settled around him, held the silvery mists at bay. Aside from a white collar around his neck, he was garbed entirely in black. Even his eyes were black. He was too defined, too solid, too dark. Harper looked down at the white skirt covering her feet and the white sleeves settled over her hands. It was wrong. This monochrome world was not real, not her.

"Where have you come from?" The man's voice cut through the air like an ice pick.

Harper wordlessly pointed behind her. The man's eyes never left hers. Her hand fell to her side.

"I don't know," she said through cracked lips. "I don't know."

The words released something within her. A bone-deep ache spread from her bare feet and up her legs. Sharp lines scored her skin. She pushed her sleeves back and found colour, oozing and cracking, her knuckles red and brown. Her chest throbbed with pain, prickly, heavy as though she had run a great distance.

"Child, look at me." The man's voice was nearer, less sharp, as he brushed her hair back from her face. His tone expected compliance without question, and she obeyed. He examined her thoughtfully, then pulled a chain out from under his collar. He lifted it over his head and settled it around her neck. It was heavy, a large gold cross now hanging against her chest. She raised a cautious finger to touch it. A flash of a vision—*a boy, kneeling by stone, dark red in a cup, heady and burning down his throat, an oath spoken in a language she didn't know.* She blinked and the vision disappeared.

"I understand now."

Harper didn't, but the man's tone was confident, soothing. She followed him as he took her hand and led her away from the Swale without looking back.

A voice lingered in the mists, barely a whisper, hardly more than the susurration of wind through leaves.

"I will find you, my Seer. I will bring you home."

Harper awoke the next morning to sunlight blazing through her window.

"Urgh." She rolled over, wrapping her blanket around her head to cushion herself against the pounding headache.

"I thought you were never going to wake up."

Something cool and effervescent brushed Harper's cheek.

"Heresy?" Rubbing her forehead, she peered into the heaped blanket through blurry eyes. "Where the hell have you been?"

"Looking for the information you requested," Heresy said haughtily, then added, "Mostly."

Harper glared down at him with narrowed eyes. He was impossible to read, his only feature his ever-present grin. No eyes. No body. Just ash, teeth, and tendrils.

"You've been gone for days," she accused. "How do I know you weren't getting up to some mischief?"

"I do not deny I found mischief." Heresy's grin widened. Harper wanted to smack him. She was still torn between fear of what he was and hope for what he could teach her. "You also found mischief while I was away. You invited it in. I felt it here, past the wards I left. Of what did you dream, Harper dear?"

Harper's breath caught in her throat, her chest tight. Her vision flickered and she leant back against the headboard. "I Saw Deacon Paul at Bishopthorpe, straight after he died. Then I Saw … It was a memory, not a vision. My first memory. Being lost by the river. Meeting Father De Santos. He led me out of the mist." Harper hugged her knees to her chest and Heresy wrapped himself around her ankles in what she hoped was supposed to be a comforting fashion. Aside from the static buzz, all the hairs on her legs standing on end, she did find it comforting.

"It was here," Heresy said. "Only for a moment. I told you something was searching for you. It found your dream. You must be more careful or it will find you too."

"I heard it," Harper said. "There was a voice in my dream. One that wasn't there that day."

"Or one you did not hear at the time."

"What is it?" Harper asked.

"Something old. Something powerful. As long as it searches blind, I can cause it to overlook this place. When you call out to it, it comes. There are many who seek a witch, from them I can hide you. This being searches for you, Harper, and only you."

Harper shivered and pulled the blanket up around her. "Why were you gone so long? Our deal was that you protect me."

"And that is why I have returned," Heresy said. "Our bond is strong. When you were in danger, it summoned me back here. You are a terrifying person, Harper Ashbury. You have more power than you know, but you have no talent to wield it. To summon me from where I was—"

"Where the hell were you, Heresy?" Harper pushed the blankets aside, the fear she'd been carrying now a simmering anger tight in her chest. The ball of fuzz around her ankles shrank in on itself.

"I was captured." Heresy dragged each word out as though he found it impossible to believe. "There was a man. He trapped me. Traced you through me. Followed you. We were there when you found the girl in the tree. And at the paper store, outside the cathedral, at the Viking recreation. He said you were a threat. I told him you were not, of course. If you are imprisoned or killed, my adventure here ends."

"Your concern is so touching." So that's why the Queen's Guard were involved so quickly. They'd already been following her, tipped off by Heresy. Grace had been right all along. "I'm sending you back."

"What about our deal?" Heresy protested, one thin appendage stretching out to poke her in the forehead. She batted him away but her hand passed through the static cloud, which immediately reformed.

"What about our deal?" Harper hissed. "You admitted you told someone about me, that they've been following me because of you."

"They already knew about you. They sensed your magic before I came to hide it. The stakes have not changed. You want to catch this murderer. You want to learn how to use your magic. You want to stay safe from that which hunts you. You need me. They have nothing. If they believed you to be a threat, do you think you would still be here? You found a body; they cannot prove you killed her. They cannot prove you summoned me. I am hardly a reliable witness for your courts. And I do not return empty-handed. I have the information you wanted."

Harper pinched the bridge of her nose. The splitting headache from her dream prevented her from thinking clearly. If they did arrest her, there would be no court, no trial. Just a cold room and a colder questioner. Like the grey man at the police station. Yet if they were sure, they wouldn't have let her leave. They would've disappeared her already.

"Tell me what you found out. All of it. If you found something useful, and you keep teaching me, I'll let you stay. I'm trusting you, Heresy."

A low purr emanated from the static cloud. "Your trust is very important to me, Harper dearest. I will tell you what I found. A file erased from the ghostwalkers' computer, expertly done. There was no way to retrieve it."

"That's not helpful."

"I am not done," Heresy replied delicately. "I followed the trail of the person who erased it. That was how I was captured, helping you. While he held me captive in his technology, I was able to explore it and I found a copy of the file. It spoke of a time, not long after the Veil was raised, when the city of Chester awoke one morning beset by ghouls and spirits. You may have heard of the event."

Harper nodded. "Chester was quarantined for years. To this day, it's deserted."

"What was of interest were two events the writer mentioned in conjunction with the mass haunting, or whatever the event was. He was a ghostwalker of York, sent to investigate by the guild. He breached the quarantine and found a corpse lying in the centre of the roman amphitheatre–a woman with no eyes, no nose, no ears, her hands both cut off, her throat ripped out. The second event was an auction, hosted by a humanesque creature, yet too tall and too slender to be a man. For sale, the pieces of the dead woman, advertised as useful in blood magic, accumulation of wealth, concealment spells, and much more. His conclusion was that her gruesome death tore a hole in the Veil. He escaped the auction but never spoke again, his larynx and tongue simply gone. He ended his life soon after his return to York. Jumped from the top of the cathedral."

Harper remembered the terrifying plunge her magic had forced her to endure. She clutched a trembling hand over her roiling stomach, thrusting down bile. Her head pounded, the sensation of a stone-cracked skull.

"Why Harper dear, you have gone the most magnificent shade of green." Heresy chortled.

Harper squeezed her eyes shut. Her stomach settled as she rubbed her temples. The suicide wasn't important now, Heresy's information about what happened in Chester was.

"The stolen organs are going to be auctioned off? I was on the wrong track all along thinking it was a demon of silence and dreams. This makes sense though. It explains the girl with no eyes, if she was particularly perceptive. It could have been me." Harper clenched her teeth so hard her jaw ached. A chill prickled her spine. She shook herself and continued. "A ghostwalker is a master storyteller, his voice might be more valuable at auction than a regular person's. A chocolatier will have superior taste buds. And Deacon Paul's sermons were legendary for their fire and brimstone. Were they the best people for those senses? At least within the radius of York?"

"It would be logical," Heresy acknowledged. "I also discovered an auction is coming. I do not know where or when this one will be yet. I will need further access to your computer to ascertain this information."

"Before you do, there's something else." Harper crawled out of bed, unlocked her desk drawer, and took out the notebook she used for work. She opened it to the page where she'd sketched the symbols from Saqib's photographs and quickly filled Heresy in on what she learnt during his absence. "Do you know what these mean?"

She placed the open book on the bed and Heresy flowed onto it; dark particles swirling over cream pages.

"This is old," he said.

"So are you, right?"

"This is older, much older. I have seen similar to this before, but I cannot read it. I first came to your realm only three or four hundred years ago. These are part of an ancient magic. I will research it when I am on the internet."

"Why should I let you back on the internet after you got caught last time?" Harper challenged. "If it was there, surely the police, or Saqib, would've found it."

"That will not happen again," Heresy said in his usual, haughty tone. "Your people are exceedingly blind. Everything is on the internet. If you know where to look."

Chapter Twenty-Three

Despite her misgivings about the spirit accessing the internet again, Harper left Heresy at the house while she returned to the cathedral to continue her research. Saqib texted her first thing saying he would watch over the paper shop with some new equipment he wanted to try out, so at least Harper didn't need to worry about the shopkeeper.

Ever since the archbishop took her to the astronomy tower, the thirty-first door was always there. The climb was arduous, but either repetition was making her fitter, or familiarity made it seem shorter.

Harper took the last few steps two at a time, grateful to reach the top. There was no sunlight today. A storm riding in from the North Sea smothered the area in angry thunder and broad sheets of rain. There was a little bit of Harper that had to admit one of the reasons she chose to study up in the tower was to see how the glassless room fared against the squall.

Dark wood shutters closed the windows off, shutters which she would have sworn were not there on her previous visit. She eyed them suspiciously but no visions of labourers installing them were forthcoming. Harper opened the one at the top of the stairs, the one farthest from any antiques or paper. Water streamed past either side of the window, regurgitated through the mouths of gawking gargoyles. Lightning crashed overhead. Metal rods on the cathedral roof protected it from harm.

A flutter of excitement fizzled in her stomach. Fire ran through her veins like electric current through wires. She wanted to reach out and touch that power, like Adam touching the finger of God. All the hairs on the back of her neck stood on end as a static chill goosed her flesh.

She slammed the shutter closed.

Finding the book she'd been reading on her last visit safely tucked on the shelf where she left it, Harper curled up in the velvet throne and resumed her studying with occasional pauses to scribble in her notebook. Heresy may have a good lead with his auction, but they still didn't know where or when it would occur, and Harper hadn't entirely given up on her hesychia theory either. If there was an auction, Heresy agreed it could be timed with a celestial event to make the pieces on sale more potent. Above her head, the constellations on the ceiling turned, almost imperceptibly, in time with the earth.

After she finished the book, Harper took her notes to the desk. She spun a gold-and-cobalt cardboard planisphere between her fingers. If it was a hesychia, with so many constellations named after Greek myths, there could be a link.

In one corner of the tower hung a multilayered brass disk, similar to the simple planisphere, but far more ornate. The surface was stencilled like the gears of a pocket watch. The disk beneath was etched with myriad crisscrossing lines. Harper took down the astrolabe and carried it over to the desk. She twisted it around in her hands. It would've been nice if this antique equipment came with user manuals.

She flicked through the contacts in her phone until she reached Saqib's name.

"Hey, Harper. You found something?" His cheery voice broke through the gloom of the day and brought a smile to her face.

She fiddled with the astrolabe again. "Maybe. I need some science-y help. You ever used an astrolabe? Or some more modern equivalent?"

"Never used one myself," he said. "Not really my area of expertise. I know they have been used in the past to determine prayer times, dates for Ramadan, stuff like that. Now we use more modern tech. It's unlikely that someone at the mosque might know, but I can ask."

"Not yet. It's only a hunch at the moment. Don't want to get anyone's hopes up. Even if I find out what triggers the murders, I still don't know who's doing it or how to stop them. Could the timing be celestial? A planetary alignment or something like that?"

"Well, there's no purely scientific reason," Saqib said. "Planetary alignments have a negligible effect on Earth. However, there could be a spiritual reasoning, not that this murderer could possibly be following any faith I know of. Still, a lot of religions use celestial timings."

"There's negligible *physical* effect," Harper amended. "Has it ever been proven if there's a magical effect? Hang on a sec. Grace is calling." Harper put him on hold to answer the incoming call. "Hey, Gray. Can I call you back?"

"Harper dear, what could possibly be more important than talking to me?"

Harper glared at her phone. "Heresy. You best get out of Grace's phone before she notices, or she's going to banish you herself."

"As if she could." Heresy chuckled. "She would not notice if a host of demons took up residence in her phone. I feel quite safe. You, however, should not. I have found the auction. It is tonight."

"I'll be home within the hour." Harper hung up and retrieved her original call with Saqib. "I'll have to call you back, something's come up."

She took a deep breath as she glanced at the covered windows. The stomach-lurching sensation of falling was still there in the back of her mind. Harper bit her lip as she opened a shutter and leant over the ledge, rain threading into her hair and running down her face. There would be worse tonight if Heresy's information turned out to be accurate. Another fight. Another death.

Harper squared her shoulders, closed the shutters, and packed away her notes. The more she practiced magic, the harder it was to stomach the idea of fighting supernaturals, but if Heresy found the one responsible for murdering the deacon and all those other people, she would steel herself to do whatever she had to.

The De Santos family weren't wrong about supernaturals killing humans. There was plenty of evidence to back up their firm belief that magic was evil. Yet despite her 'possession,' they had never shown Harper anything but love. They protected and nurtured her when others would've handed her over to the Queen's Guard. Betraying the trust of the parents who raised her hurt Harper, yet she couldn't stop magic leaking into her dreams and didn't want to if it meant saving someone's life. Her foster parents would respect that decision at least.

She briefly toyed with the idea of asking the archbishop for backup but abandoned the notion before she reached the bottom of the tower stairs. If she and Grace went alone, they risked injury or failure. If others came with them and she used magic, she would be hanged for sure.

By the time she got home, the rain had all but vanished. A glimmering rainbow looped the horizon. Hope.

Grace was at the front door, waving goodbye to their landlady and another prospective housemate.

"Any good?" Harper gave her sister a hug as she entered. She manoeuvred her back into the house and nudged the door closed with her foot before their landlady noted how Grace somehow managed to wave sarcastically.

"Worse than the last one. Looked like a ghost as soon as I introduced myself." Grace smirked.

"You do this on purpose," Harper accused. "You manage to get dates just fine. How did it go with Antoinette? I almost forgot you—"

"I don't want to talk about it." Grace folded her arms tight across her chest. "Don't you have some emergency to sort out?"

Harper opened her mouth to question further but the scowl on Grace's face made her think better of it. "You're right. We don't have time for that now. We've got a lead." Harper dashed up to her room to look for Heresy, dragging her sister behind her. "We have to talk—"

"Hi, Harper."

She slammed the door with a yelp. "Saqib? What are you doing here? Grace, what is he doing here? Why is he sitting on my bed?"

"The chair's taken," Grace said with a grin as she dropped into it.

"Why are you here, Saqib?" Harper asked again. She wasn't used to anyone being in her room. She felt exposed. Yet, deep in her stomach, a small fizzle of hope sparked. Maybe it didn't always have to be just her and Grace against the world.

"Because he has a car," Grace said before Saqib had a chance to speak.

"That's it?" he asked. "I thought you asked me here for my scientific expertise."

"That too," Grace said. "I thought it might be useful to have backup for this. We don't know what we're running into and, quite frankly, we're rusty, Harp. I can't explain to Godfather what's going on, can I? You were the best meat shield I could find, Saqib."

"You're okay with this?" Harper looked at him incredulously.

"I'd rather not go," Grace said, before he could reply, "but I will not allow people to be auctioned off like cattle. A De Santos does not ignore the pleas of an innocent."

Saqib rolled his eyes. "She's been talking about what a De Santos does and does not do since I got here. I've got a friend watching the shop, by the way. It's probably safe enough if the auction is tonight, but my mate'll keep an eye out in case. Don't worry, he's not in law enforcement. He's my tech guy, does troubleshooting for me."

"Wonderful. Our backup is IT support." Grace flipped her hair back. She rolled her eyes. "'Have you tried turning the killer off and on again?'"

Harper glared at her sister as she took a seat next to Saqib, who scooted over to give her space. Trying to be surreptitious, Harper leant over to tie her shoelace and peeked under the bed to see if Heresy was hiding there.

"What's going on, Grace?" Harper shot her sister a questioning look as she sat up.

Grace's smile cracked, her eyes flicking to the open laptop. The impression of teeth flashed across its black screen.

"He ... um ... we ..." Grace coughed. A shudder ran through her, but her voice steadied as she looked up, the regal De Santos tone once again coming through. "The auction is happening tonight. At midnight to be precise. I'm supposed to be on the night shift at the clinic, but I've already called in sick."

"How did you ...? Never mind." Harper cut herself off. Grace couldn't explain the information without mentioning Heresy. That her sister deigned to speak to the spirit at all showed how on edge she was about the murders. "Where is it?"

"How Stean Gorge. I checked the map, it'll take us about an hour, hour and a half to get there. Then we need to break in and find the auction site. I've already packed our weapons, torches, and some snacks. It's a bit inconvenient it's at midnight. It's not like we've got loads of time to prepare, or like it would be easy getting there on public transport."

Harper kicked Grace in the shins. "Will you shut up for a minute?" she hissed, then turned to Saqib and asked, "Are you okay with coming? It's a big place and dangerous in the dark, even without the possibility of supes running around. But Grace has a point about the car thing. It'll take forever to get there by bus and they frown on crossbows. It's up to you. It's a risk, but we could really do with your help. It's a good chance for you to test your theories on detecting magic too."

Saqib traced his foot around the edge of a floorboard "I'll do it," he said, looking up to meet her eyes. "It's too good an opportunity to miss, scientifically, and I can't sit by and let more people be hurt. I don't know how to fight like you two, but if there's something I can do to help, I'll do it, may Allah (swt[1]) protect us. Wish it were happening during the day. I don't usually have to leave the lab, so I rarely go out at night."

"Midnight makes sense," Harper said. She squashed her worries about him detecting her magic. Now she was over the surprise at an outsider sitting on her bed, the sensation of rightness was dominant again. "From a superstitious viewpoint anyway. Aside from the fact that doing it during

---

[1] swt – Subhanahu wa ta'ala. Arabic for 'Glory to Him, the Exalted' or 'Glorious and Exalted is He.'

daylight hours would expose them, legend says the Veil is thinner at midnight, the 'tween of one day and the next. Any kind of liminal space makes magic stronger. There's no science to back that up, as far as I know, but it doesn't mean it's not true. Sorry, Saqib."

"I think of it as science that hasn't been discovered yet," Saqib said.

"We best get going." Grace glanced out of the window, then over at Saqib. "It'll be dark soon and he doesn't have a pass."

Saqib pulled a slip of paper out of his pocket and waved it under her nose. "Do too. You think my imam is any less devoted to finding this murderer than your archbishop?"

Grace blushed. "Sorry." She offered Saqib her hand. He shook it as though it were a viper poised to bite him at any second. Grace gave him a tentative smile. "I'm worried, I didn't mean to be rude. I know everyone on the Council is dedicated to protecting people. It was thoughtless of me not to ask if you already arranged something."

"I forgive you." Saqib bowed his head slightly toward her. "Don't suppose you packed anything I can use? Some kind of big shield maybe?"

Grace laughed and Harper's shoulders drooped in relief. "If you aren't proficient with a weapon, I'm sure I can sort you out with something. I've got some incense vials, if you don't object, as well as some herbal pouches, which can be quite effective. Of course, that's more from the pepper than any supposed protection properties, but I find it works the same. Come with me, you can check my stash for something that might suit you."

As Grace led Saqib out of the room, Harper snuck over and poked her blank laptop screen. "Psst, Heresy, you in there?"

The screen cracked in a familiar crescent of teeth and his sly voice came through the speakers. "You are welcome, my dear. Do try not to get killed. I am having so much fun."

"You're not coming?" Harper tugged on her braid.

"I will come if you wish. However, I do not want the demonhunter to get confused and mistake me for her target or the scientist to poke me full of pins in his lab."

"Come," Harper said, before she could change her mind. "But if you let Saqib see you, I'll do something nastier than banishing you. I'll make you a guinea pig for *my* magic experiments."

Chapter Twenty-Four

Mist swirled around the car and danced in the fog lamps. The light scraped across black tarmac. Cat's eyes gleamed, waiting to pounce, razor claws swiping at tires. The moon hovered behind naked silhouettes of trees and stars twinkled through their branches like an adornment of fairy lights. Frolicking stars, fallen from the sky, flickered around the trunk of an old oak, illuminating a skirt of long grasses. Then the tree was gone, consumed by the unending darkness. Harper clutched her shawl closer around her shoulders and settled back in her seat.

She kept her eyes on the broad beams from the headlamps. Suffocating night hemmed them in on all sides. Seatbelt, too tight across her chest, squashed her sternum into her pounding heart. Lungs compressed against her spine, breathing too shallow. Her breath hung in the air in front of her, a reflection of the rolling mists beyond the window.

The trees, before so distant, closed in to line the road like spectators, arms waving in silent cheers. They cut sharp shapes through the white vapours skulking around the base of their trunks. Out of the corner of her eyes, Harper caught glimpses of movement and a pair of bright amber eyes.

When she looked again there was nothing but darkness. She gripped the handle of her knife tighter.

It's nothing. There's nothing there. There's nothing there.

A shadow flashed across the beams. Saqib slammed on the brakes. Blunt pain across her chest took Harper's breath away.

"What was that?" she gasped.

"Deer." Grace, sitting in the front passenger seat, twisted her neck so she could look at Harper in the back. "You okay?"

Harper gave a small shrug. "I hate to be the whiny child, but are we nearly there?"

Saqib leant forward on the steering wheel as he peered into the dark. "Almost. We're running a little late since the Guard at the checkpoint insisted on phoning the Council for confirmation of our passes. Let's hope they remember for our way back. I need you to watch out for the turning. It'll come up fast."

"Fast? You drive like my grandmother." Grace propped her feet up on the dashboard.

"I would like to reach our destination intact," Saqib replied testily. "I don't drive at night, pass or not. I'm not insane."

"You could let me drive," Grace said.

"That would be more insane," Harper warned. "If you like your car, don't let Grace drive it."

Saqib sniggered. Grace crossed her arms and stared out the passenger side window.

Harper glanced up at the night sky, clear for once, the stars glimmering. Sometimes it was hypnotic. Sometimes it terrified her. She wished she could remember why.

A ten-minute eternity later the slick tarmac was replaced by crackling gravel as Saqib turned off the main road and onto the track leading to the gorge. When he cut off the engine, silence swallowed the car whole.

"So, er, this is as far as we go." Saqib gave the steering wheel a shaky pat.

"Never been out in the wilds at night before?" Grace asked with a grin.

"I grew up in a good, God-fearing household," Saqib said indignantly.

"So did I." Grace opened the door and got out of the car. Leaning on the roof, she stooped and beckoned Saqib with her free hand. "God will protect the righteous who act in His name."

"You sound like a zealot, Grace." Harper hopped out of the car to join her sister. She kept one hand on the vehicle, fearful it might vanish into the fog if she let go. The moon gave the mist a pearly luminescence. It wasn't much better than pure darkness but it was better.

"I wanted him to feel safe." Grace pouted but she couldn't hide the slight smirk in the corners of her eyes. "Plus, it is true, you know."

"I know it a lot better in the daytime when I'm not hunting a murderer."

Saqib opened his door and slowly put his feet on the ground, but he didn't get up. He slid his fingers in and out of a set of knuckledusters in his lap. "I came here once as a kid. It was nice. In daylight. Lots of thin bridges and sharp drops, though."

"Torches will help." Harper tightened a strap around her head. When she flicked the light on, it cut through the darkness in front of her. She let out a shaky sigh. She wanted to be strong, to help Saqib believe she and Grace knew what they were doing.

"We'll each have a headlamp." Grace tossed one to Saqib, then straightened as she slipped into General De Santos mode. "Everyone is to carry a light at their belt as well. Saqib, if something jumps out at you, hit it with the torch, they're heavy. Harper, you take the rear. Watch out for ambushes. Saqib, you have the least combat experience, so you go in the middle—"

"I have *no* combat experience," Saqib protested but Grace could not be so easily stopped.

"As the only ranged combatant, I will go first." She notched her crossbow and slid in a hand-length bolt.

"Maybe I should wait in the car." Saqib's eyes darted to the dark woods and back to the relative safety of his vehicle. Grace pressed a leather belt holding a dozen glass vials into his hand.

"Olive tree incense from the Holy Land," she explained. "If something attacks you, throw this at its feet. Best case, the ungodly creature will scarper. Worst case, it has to walk over broken glass to get to you."

"I'm still not sure …"

"It's incense, it's prayed over, the same God is listening and that's all that matters," Grace said firmly. Saqib still looked dubious, but he stood up and pushed the car door closed behind him. All three jumped as the lights flashed, the click of the door ringing in the emptiness.

"Let's get this over with," Harper snapped. Grace raised an eyebrow. Harper shook her head and gestured down the muddy path to the gorge.

It was slow going. Grace swept the twisted path ahead with dimmed torchlight while Harper peered into the grey silhouettes around them.

The banks of the path inclined steeply on both sides as they headed deeper and deeper into the gorge. Dense foliage and tall trees quickly blocked out any signs of stars or moon. Mist rolled down the hills like a silver waterfall, cascading over their feet, leading the way deeper into the ravine.

Harper soon gave up on watching for ambushes from the sides. All her torch did was make grotesque mockeries of the swaying trees and glimmering vapours. Every twisted branch was a creature, teeth sharp and claws outstretched. Each root was a devil slithering down the hill to bury its fangs in their flesh. Deep in her mind, a violin sang a melody that had long haunted her nightmares.

"Harper?"

The hoarse whisper brought her back as Saqib's pale face peered at her.

"There's nothing there," she whispered back. "Keep going."

He nodded and scurried to catch up with Grace who hadn't slowed, always one to confront her fears head on.

"We're nearly there." A smoother whisper. Heresy. He'd stayed quiet in the car lest Saqib hear him, but outside, with the wind's sombre whistle, he could speak quietly. Cool vapour tickled her neck as he uncoiled from under her hair and stretched to hiss directly in her ear. "I can sense them nearby."

The trees became sparse, replaced by craggy rock and stone slippery from the light dusting of rain in the air. Forced inwards on the narrowing path, the mist rose almost to waist height, the ground lost in its depths. The fog muffled each footfall into the unknown. It tumbled over the edge of the ravine, like an Amazonian waterfall, to churn in the depths below. Harper tested each step before trusting her weight to it. Stone cut her arm as she hugged the wall on her right, afraid a misstep would plunge her into the void on her left.

The light around Grace's silhouette flashed twice, then swept in an arch through the air. It caught on a metal frame, little taller than a human. Then Grace stepped out over the gorge. Harper's breath caught in her throat, a lump forming in her chest as she held back a cry.

Grace seemed to levitate as she marched over some invisible path. A bridge. Saqib mentioned bridges. Harper released her breath.

"Go on," she encouraged Saqib, who was standing at the foot of the bridge, gripping the railing but not moving forward. This close, Harper could see 'bridge' was a generous description. 'Board' was closer to the mark, barely wide enough for one person. She gave Saqib an awkward pat on the shoulder. "It's got to be safe, right? The people who run this place would've taped it off or something if it wasn't."

"Yeah. Sure," Saqib said, his voice hoarse. As he took the first step, his shaking arm rattled the railing. He ran his hand forward, never letting go. As he took his second step, the bridge creaked and swayed. He wrapped his arms around one of the side struts.

"That's it, I'm going back. You don't need me for this." Saqib edged back toward Harper, but she placed one foot on the end of the plank, blocking his path.

"We do need you." She hoped he couldn't hear the thunderous staccato of her heart roaring blood through her ears. "You're one of the team now. You aren't the only one doing something they're scared of. If you want to get your breakthrough, you need to go where the supes are. Tonight, that means crossing this sorry excuse for a bridge. Believe me, it's less scary than telling Grace you wussed out."

"You and Grace are scared?" Saqib asked.

"The blusterier she gets, the more upset she is. But don't tell her I told you. As for me …" She swallowed hard, the lump in her throat stuck and nauseating. "I'm scared every time the sun goes down."

"A demonhunter scared of the dark?" Saqib's grip loosened as they talked.

"Just cross the bridge already." Harper gestured to the other side. "I want to get this over with, too."

"InshAllah (swt), I can do this." Saqib turned back with a firm nod. The only sounds were the scuff of his feet on the wooden board, the scrape of metal as his hand grasped the railing. Grace turned back to watch. She jerked her head toward Saqib, her hands raised in a question. Harper waited until Saqib's feet were on firm ground again, then flashed her torch once. Grace returned the signal, then turned, the air behind her dark as her headlamp once again illuminated the path ahead.

Harper had never been afraid of heights, but she couldn't deny the shake in her legs as she took the first step out over the black abyss. Solid wood beneath her feet quelled her nerves and she was soon on the other side. The metal and wood construction settled behind her with a groan.

Saqib gave her a reassuring squeeze on the shoulder, before silently heading after Grace. The path twisted around the side of the gorge—narrow, slippery, finite. Harper concentrated on Saqib's back a metre or so ahead of her.

"Left," Heresy whispered. Harper flicked her torch on and off twice to get Grace's attention, then pointed the beam toward the narrow slit of a cave ahead.

Stone scraped Harper's back as she squeezed through the slender passageway. Saqib's grumble was a distant, foreign noise ahead, the man barely a shadow in the ever-rising mist. He moved faster than her, stepped out of her torchlight, turned the corner, and disappeared. She was alone. Underground. No moon, no stars, torch only revealing close, endless stone. No sound, no footsteps. Alone.

"I am here," Heresy whispered in her ear.

Harper suppressed a shudder. She'd almost convinced herself he was harmless but now, following his directions into blank nothingness, her doubts flooded back.

The mist abruptly dropped away, the passage widening fast. Grace grabbed Harper's arm and pulled her to the side. Moonlight flooded the broad ledge on which they stood. A few metres away, stone gave way to a curtain of stars, as though they stood at the end of the world. Fine mists roiled like a witch's cauldron, the dark ground visible underneath. Saqib was standing on the other side of the exit, reading something in the stone with fascination. He held his torch close to the wall as he muttered rapidly under his breath.

"What is it?" Harper asked uneasily. "Where are we?"

"On the other side," Heresy said.

"The other side of what?" Grace asked. While Saqib was distracted by the stone, she looked up at the sky, a slight frown creasing her forehead.

"The other side of the mist," Heresy said.

"We crossed the Veil? Into another realm?" Harper asked breathlessly.

"Nothing so extravagant," Heresy said. "This is still your world. It is simply not *only* your world."

"Whose world is it?" Harper asked.

"Ours."

CHAPTER TWENTY-FIVE

The answering voice was deeper than Heresy's and devoid of any charm or welcome. Harper and Grace's torches blinked out, leaving them with nothing but the moonlight. Harper unsheathed her machete and held it in front of her like a shield. When she stepped forward, the warmth of Grace's body moved with her. They stood back-to-back, eyes unable to pierce the darkness around them. Harper glanced over at Saqib. He was still studying the stone. Although his lips moved, she could no longer hear his muttering as though she watched him on a muted screen. She turned back toward the voice.

"Who are you?" Harper kept her voice steady by sheer effort of will.

"I am the Auctioneer." The voice crashed through their skulls like the clank of metal coins falling and falling. A golden gavel flashed in the darkness.

She and Grace had fought the supernatural together before, but not like this, not against something so old and so sure of itself. They'd never fought something incorporeal, creatures that shouldn't exist on this side of the Veil. Hopelessness sank heavy into the pit of her stomach. Harper gripped her machete tighter. *Can our weapons even hurt this demon?* She pointed her blade toward it, feigning confidence. "What have you done to Saqib?"

"He has no value. I appear only to you who may yet participate in the auction. The human male remains unaware of us."

"Show yourself," Harper demanded.

"Why? Can't you See me, witchling?" the voice mocked.

"A trap," Heresy said quietly, tucked away hidden under Harper's hair. "Do not try to See him, he will take your eyes and sell them."

"Like that poor girl's." Fire burned in Harper's stomach, anger searing away the hopelessness.

"If you speak of the sightless one in Eboracum, alas her eyes are not ours to sell. Such a valuable child. Whole, I would have had a hundred bidders. Even alone, her eyes would have fetched a pretty price. Be careful that what stole her Sight doesn't also take yours."

"What of the others?" Harper asked. "The ghostwalker, the deacon, and the chocolatier? Do their senses form part of your macabre sale?"

"Once upon a time, wares of all origins, exotic and domestic, graced my domain. You speak of that which I am no longer permitted to touch. It is a lucrative business, for the soul traders and black marketeers. Those you speak of were not killed for profit. Seek not to defy the ancient of Albion. Your power is great, but not great enough. Stay here, and marvel at the mysteries of the auction. When midnight tolls, it will begin. The buyers will soon be gathered. Here you will find great wonders, if you wish to bid."

To the left, the mists churned violently, frothed up to head height, and then dropped away. A young woman stood there, her head lowered, dark hair obscuring her face. A diamond twinkled at each pointed tip where her ears poked through her hair. Around her neck, a twisted rope hung, red as blood. A light emanated from within the vapours but it illuminated nothing but her. Long fingers held a ream of embroidery showing a timeline of scenes from the last hundred years. Too many fingers, too thin, too pointed. Harper gawked at her, momentarily forgetting the danger around them.

"A weaver. A long tale affixed in thread, a banner of human life," the Auctioneer said. "She will sew a wondrous story for her owner or they may cut her life like the finest of threads and enjoy a brief respite from the weariness of history."

The mists rose and covered her again, then fell away to nothing.

"Her life is not yours to play with," Grace growled, but she got no further as the mist spun and rose again.

This time it dropped to reveal the crouched figure of a man. He uncoiled with the grace of a ballerino, reaching up to the dark sky as if searching for a lifeline home. His dance twisted and soured as he turned and spun. Inhuman, his limbs moved as if boneless. A noose-like collar whipped across his shoulders as he twirled. His body warped and distorted as his dance accelerated to a frenzy—a butterfly caught in a net. A crack of lightning spiked through the clear sky, its source unknown. It struck his outstretched finger and he collapsed.

He raised his head, crumpled and kneeling on the ground. When his eyes met Harper's, they were pitch black. They cleared gradually, turning brown, dark rings surrounding irises flecked with green. She had seen them before, in the mirror. Harper closed her eyes and turned her face away, knuckles white around her weapon.

"A beautiful manipulation of the human form," the Auctioneer said. "For those who require their own puppet, their avatar in the world, or their control over it. You will note the eyes can still show the true nature of the owner, but otherwise a perfect vessel."

"Let him go," Harper shouted. She dived toward the dancer, but the mists covered him, and he was gone before she could reach him.

"Maybe you wish to bid on something more exotic," the Auctioneer said.

This time the mists barely reached Harper's knee before they dropped away to reveal a small humanoid. Neither male nor female, him nor her, zir skin was pale blue, zir eyes incandescent as if all the stars had been drawn into them. On zir back, diaphanous wings fluttered wearily, zir feet caught in the mist like quicksand, keeping zir from flying away. Red rope, tight around zir neck, looked like a slit throat. Ze looked up at Harper plaintively, rose-pink lips forming a silent plea.

"Do not touch it," Heresy said, too late.

When their fingers met, a fiery jolt streaked up Harper's arm. The force of it knocked her back, almost wrenching her shoulder from its socket. She dropped her machete. The metal tip glowed brilliant as a ruby against the deep brown stone. Harper contemplated the fae creature who mirrored her as she rubbed her aching shoulder. The creature lowered zir eyes. A sob wracked zir chest as the mists rose and drew the fae into their depths. Harper spun to face the floating gavel, the only clue she had as to the Auctioneer's whereabouts. Grabbing her still-hot weapon, she strode through the mist until her foot bumped into something solid.

"Let them go," she repeated, a sob caught in her throat. *Just because they aren't human, doesn't mean they aren't innocent. Nobody deserves this.* Anger boiled through her, hotter than the fae's touch, bright enough to overcome her fear of the dark.

"I intend to," the Auctioneer said. "Once I receive payment. You could free them all if you wished, witchling. Your eyes for their lives. The Sight of one of your lineage is invaluable."

Harper's chest tightened, caught somewhere between panic and guilt. Before she could find the air to speak, Grace stepped in front of her. "Stay away from my sister. Harp, don't listen to him. He doesn't know anything. He wants to ensnare you."

"You could also be very valuable," the Auctioneer said. "Your blood alone would draw many bids. Your life to play with, almost priceless to those harmed by your family. There are many who wish pain upon your house, demonhunter."

"They can wish all they want. I will vanquish them before they lay so much as a finger on me or mine."

"He is stalling you," Heresy said. "Midnight nears and the auction will begin. You must be either buyer or belonging then, else you will be fair game to any who can capture you."

"You can't sell us if you don't appear," Harper said. "You have to catch us first and your mist isn't strong enough to do so, or it would've already. We won't give in to you."

"Then leave, witchling." The Auctioneer's laugh clattered off the stone. "Leave behind those you saw, leave them to their doom. Leave, if you can find the exit."

Harper looked back toward the crack they entered by. She could see the bob of Saqib's torch, weak through the misty haze. The exit would be nearby. It must be. Yet solid stone towered above them with no hint of a crack.

"It is an illusion," Heresy whispered in her ear. "Not a very good one. I can guide you out, as could your Sight if it were safe to use."

"I won't leave them behind," Harper said through gritted teeth. She lowered her machete and said loudly, "I wish to bid."

"Harper, no." Grace grabbed Harper's shoulder and dragged her away from the Auctioneer's voice. "What the hell do you think you're—"

"Trust me." As Harper turned to look at Grace, heat seared her retinas, the mist between them reflecting a lilac glow. "Trust me."

"Very well," the Auctioneer intoned. "Let the auction begin."

Zir golden gavel flashed like lightning through the darkness and the thunderclap reverberated through the stone underfoot.

Shapes coalesced in the mist. Vague, indistinct, some humanoid, some outlines only seen in a book of fairy tales. They appeared in rows, as if already seated. Their forms grew more distinct as darkness and mist ebbed away to reveal skin of all colours—blood red, mucus green, pustule yellow. It reminded Harper of an image online of a Japanese marketplace; a fleeting glimpse of the outside world that had been replaced by the Guard's golden crown and red crossed halberds only an hour later.

All eyes turned on her—slits knifed through the air; wide wells threatened to drown any caught in their gaze; eyes of moss and earth, eyes of fire and ether, the eyes of Harper's nightmare. She thought she'd come to terms with Heresy's warning that supernatural creatures existed all around. The vast and growing crowd took her breath away. She squeezed her eyes shut, sure it was another vision. Not real. Not possible. Buzzing vibrations drilled through her ears.

She retreated, machete raised in front of her. Something gelatinous collided with her back. The sharp scent of decay filled her nose and mouth. It threatened to suck her in, only Grace's strong hand gripping her shoulder dragged her loose. Bands of viscous liquid clung to her back and hair as she pulled away, the *gloop*, *hiss* of heavy fluids, dropping and burning, acidic, on the ground.

Bile rising in her throat, Harper shook herself. Thick globs of goo flew off her and splattered the other bidders. As repulsed as she was, they withdrew, too many arms retreating to their bodies, spidery fingers scuttling back into dark recesses. Harper looked up at the creature she'd run into, a plague-ridden blancmange. A hundred eyes floated through its body, blue and green like spots of mould.

"Ssssoooorrrrrrrrrrryyyy." Zir voice oozed from a crevice near the centre of zir body. Ze squelched aside with a wobbly bow.

"Erm, sorry." Harper pinched her arm, certain she'd awaken any moment. Despite its monstrous appearance, the creature didn't threaten her. It merely apologised again, unbent from its bow, and glooped away.

Gripping Grace's hand, Harper steered them to the edge of the emerging throng. As she wove between the grotesque and the fanciful, the sensation of being watched faded. Most of the auction's patrons paid her no heed. She was one of the crowd. One of …

"Harper?" Grace's fingers digging into her palm stalled Harper's train of thought.

"Wait," she cautioned. "I don't think they mean us any harm. They'd bid on us but they won't attack us and we can't take them all on anyway. We need the Auctioneer to appear." Something heavy materialised in her hand; a disk with the number '94' inscribed on it.

"Is that how many are here?" Grace asked in a low whisper.

"Maybe some are online," Harper answered. "If there's that many here, we have no chance."

"Harper, you must leave them. We've got to get out of here. Come back with reinforcements. I brought Saqib into this. He'll be killed if they turn on us."

"If you leave, you will not be able to re-enter," Heresy warned.

"I won't leave them, Grace. Whether or not this is related to the murders in York, these people are being kept in slavery. I'm not ... I'm not so different from them. You heard the Auctioneer. I won't abandon them." Harper's voice dropped so only Grace would hear. "The Auctioneer *will* appear. How else can ze run this abomination of a sale? Ze must become corporeal. And when ze does, we take zir out. That's how the stories always work, isn't it? Take out the jailer, open the jail? We neutralise zir, they all go free. Us too. It's the only way we get out of here without one of those damned ropes around our necks. Wait ..."

A hush fell. The eyes of every creature turned to a single point in the darkness. Above them, one by one, the stars winked out.

"Welcome and good evening, fellow gentlesen." The Auctioneer's voice bounced off the stone, surrounded them. Harper's eyes watered with the strain of not blinking.

"Soon," she whispered. "Be ready, Grace."

"Always."

"Our first lot is one I know is hotly anticipated. An early example of the Magician's signature pieces, do not be fooled by its animalistic appearance ..." As the Auctioneer continued his sales pitch, Harper watched the gavel. The mist swirled, and another soul appeared for sale.

She shifted her grip on her machete and balanced her weight on the balls of her feet. "If you need to, grab Saqib and run."

"Like I'd leave you," Grace said. "One sister over a dozen strangers, remember?"

"I ... now, Grace."

The gavel flashed again. The faint outline of a hand emerged. Dark material wafted in the breeze, defined only by where the vapours were not. She threw her machete as hard as she could toward the blank spot, a cry of victory on her lips as it hung, quivering, several feet above the ground. Screams ripped the air, jagged slices of sound through the mist. They cut Harper's ears and blood dripped down her neck.

A thunk as Grace's crossbow bolt hammered home above Harper's blade. The click as her sister reset the weapon, yanking another bolt from her belt. The bidders scattered in all directions like debris from a shipwreck; some sinking, some flying, some fleeing around them. Chaos. Grace fired again.

The bolt hung in midair, silent, only half the distance the other travelled. It spun, lazily, almost bored, then plunged back through the air toward them. The two women dived out of the way. The bolt embedded itself in the stone where Grace had stood as if rock were nothing more than soft clay.

Laughter filled the air. Ear-splitting. Gleeful. Insane.

"You think you can harm me with your childish toys?" the Auctioneer mocked. Zir voice swarmed around them. "If you kill me, what then? Would you kill all my patrons? Would you kill my wares? Or rescue them from a place you can neither enter nor See only to bring them to a world that condemns them?"

"I hate to agree, but if you have any other bright ideas, now would be a good time," Grace shouted.

"I thought if we killed zir, the auction would end," Harper shouted back. Something burned her skin, tightened around her neck. She touched her throat and encountered something slick with blood, coagulating, almost rough. Like rope.

A flash of silver tore toward her. Harper dived aside. Her own machete sliced her bicep as it flew through the air. She bit back a curse. Heresy flowed down her arm, cool against the blazing wound. Harper had a fleeting worry about what giving him more of her blood would do, before her blade banked, turned in the air, and plunged toward her chest.

"Grace!" she screamed. Too late to dodge. Pain, scorching like lightning, tore through her, an electric jolt across her heart. Then the blade pierced her skin. It tore along her clavicle as she threw herself to the side. She couldn't breathe, all oxygen gone. A garotte, tight and coarse, her own blood turned on her, captured her for the Auctioneer. Mist thundered over her, sucked her into a vortex of swirling colour, a galaxy against the black night.

Glass shattered, pinpricks of pain barely noticed as consciousness ebbed. An earthy, woody scent filled Harper's nose. A long moan hung in the air, rising in pitch until it passed from human hearing.

The garotte vanished. Air rushed back in to fill the void, and Harper writhed on the ground, gasping. The pain in her shoulder made her want to scream. She clenched her teeth, breath in short, sharp pants whistled between them. When she gingerly touched her collarbone, her hand came away sticky with blood. It gleamed bright in the sunlight.

Wait.

Sunlight?

Harper looked up at Grace. Her sister's face was pale, her eyes wide as they flitted around trying to make sense of the scene. Harper was sure she looked equally spooked.

"Where did …?" Grace spun, searching around them, but they appeared to be alone. "What's happened? I … where'd they all go?"

"Alhamdulillah, it worked." A triumphant shout made them both turn to see Saqib jumping up and down, a grin as wide as Heresy's on his face. "I can't believe that actually worked."

"What worked?" Harper scrambled to her feet, spinning in the sunny clearing. "Where are they? The prisoners. Where are they? What happened?"

"I saw your knife attack you, so I figured if I threw one of these nearby, it would probably hit whatever was holding it." Saqib held up one of the vials of incense. "I heard murmurs, but I couldn't move, not at first. Then the pressure eased and when I looked around all I could see was you two fighting the air. I was desperate, so I figured, same God, said a prayer and lobbed it. Incense is supposed to purify the air and it worked. We've been teleported or something. I've got to document this." Saqib plopped down to the ground and pulled a pen and pad out of his pocket.

Grace collapsed at Harper's feet. She put her head between her knees, her hands dangling limp over her legs. Saqib talked to himself as he scribbled in his notebook. To Harper, his scientific exclamations may as well have been a foreign language.

"What an odd man," Grace muttered. "Remind me why we brought him?"

"Because, apparently, he saved the day. Also, he has a car." Still unable to believe her eyes, Harper pointed behind him. "That car."

Saqib turned to look as well, scrambled to his feet, and ran to it.

"It's my car." He walked around it, running his hands over it, practically hugging the vehicle. "How did we get back here?"

"How did we get *now*?" Harper asked too quietly for Saqib to hear. She clutched her shoulder as fresh waves of pain almost overwhelmed her. She sank to the ground and leant her head against Grace's shoulder. "It was midnight five minutes ago. The Auctioneer …"

"It was almost midnight *there*, it is dawn here," Heresy said, calm as ever.

"Harp, are you bleeding?" Grace's dark eyes clouded in concern.

"I'm okay." Harper took a deep breath. Lights of green and gold swarmed her vision.

"We need to get you to a hospital." Grace's voice was distant, almost drowned out by the buzzing in Harper's ears.

"There are people to save." Harper tried to get to her feet, but her legs wobbled and gave way beneath her. She winced as the jolt snapped up her spine.

"No. I don't think there are."

Grace's melancholy tone was so unusual, Harper stopped fighting to stand and laid down on the pathway. She rubbed her eyes, willing the dancing lights to fade. A shadow passed over her and something soft pressed against her bleeding collarbone. As her vision cleared, Grace's frowning face swam into focus, hair a dark halo, and the sky above her, warm with the colours of dawn.

A second shadow blotted out the rest of the sky as Saqib's curly-haired head came into view.

"Do you need help?" he asked.

"I think it's okay," Grace said. "We should take her to A&E. It's not too deep, just bloody, but they'll check it isn't contaminated. Go finish your notes, I'll sort her."

"What about the bidders? What about the prisoners?" Harper asked when Saqib was once again engrossed in writing. "We have to go back. We have to help them."

"It is too late," Heresy said. "The auction is over. There is nothing you can do. They are lost."

The last of Harper's strength drained out of her. Tears spilled down her cheeks.

"No," she whispered. "We found them before, we can find them again."

"It is dawn here," Heresy said. "There it is still midnight. By the time their 'now' becomes our 'now', those for sale will have been sold and will either be with their new owners, or they will be dead. It is too late for them. You cannot save everyone."

"Why not?" Harper shouted, balled fists thudding into the dirt. Her head spun like a ship in a whirlpool but anger kept her conscious. Saqib looked over, eyes wide. "I can help people. I *can*. I won't be some damsel in distress saved from wandering in the mists. I was a teenager then. I couldn't help them. Now … now …" She wasn't even sure what her words meant, they burst out of her from some subconscious place. She remembered the blood on her hands and bare feet when Father De Santos found her in the mist. Her first memory. Had she been fighting to save someone then too? Had she failed them just as she failed the poor creatures trapped by the Auctioneer?

"We can't save the people trapped there." Grace's mouth twisted like agreeing with the spirit was sourer than eating pickled lemons. "But we did learn something important."

"Really? What?" Whatever it was, it couldn't be worth the lives lost.

"That we can find these auctions. Next time, we'll be better prepared. Next time, we'll win. A De Santos doesn't stand by while innocents are hurt." There was a steely determination to Grace's voice and the watery sunlight glistened in the corners of her eyes. She wrapped an arm around Harper. "Now, however, the only thing we can do is get you stitched up." As they limped toward the car, Grace added, "We learned something else as well. Your hesychia theory and the Master Undertaker's repeating history theory are both wrong. The killer is something from Britain, probably something local, and this isn't like Chester."

"So, all our leads are wrong," Harper said through clenched teeth. Her feet scuffed the ground, too heavy to lift, and she leant heavily on Grace.

"In science, disproving a theory is often as important as proving one," Saqib interjected. "We're closer than we were and we're not following a false lead anymore. This wasn't for nothing."

Anger drained away leaving only regret and despair. Darkness edged Harper's vision without adrenaline to sustain her and her head dropped onto Grace's shoulder. Her sister bundled her into the car, grabbed the first aid kit from the back, then clambered in next to her. Consciousness flickered as Grace dressed Harper's wound.

"But those people …" Harper's tongue was woollen as she tried and failed to summon the last remnants of a fight.

"MashAllah (swt)," Saqib said as Grace made the sign of the cross over her chest. "We will pray for them. It is all we can do. Next time, we will do more."

Chapter Twenty-Six

Darkness. Warmth. Something digging into her shoulder, pulling at her torn flesh. Grace's soft humming, barely audible over the throaty engine growl.

Flashing lights, sirens wailing. Then bright white. People talking, shouting. Running footsteps. Agitation and impatience straining Grace's voice. A few minutes later, Saqib's calmer voice, talking sense. Heresy nowhere to be heard.

Gentle hands touching her shoulder, examining her wound. A training accident, Grace explained. The nurse's voice was calm, familiar. Not a bad cut, just needed dressing and a bandage. Harper rested her head on her sister's shoulder and closed her eyes.

Once again, she stood in an ancient village. Flaxen-haired people huddled talking in small clumps, their whispered voices speaking an unknown tongue. As Harper walked among them, they turned their heads to track her passage with wide eyes.

A woman slumped against a fence. Her faint weeping pattered against the wood like rain. She raised her head as Harper passed, her eyes and cheeks drenched.

Muddy lanes led to fishermen mending their nets while the day's catch writhed in barrels next to them.

A pair of ravens mocked her from a rooftop with their haughty cawing.

In the corner of a hut, a *nisse* sat hunched over a pile of clothes. The Nordic gnome tipped its bright red hat, a splash of colour in an otherwise muted picture, then the wizened little man faded from view.

Harper wandered in and out of their houses, through their market, past families and merchants. They all watched her, whispering to each other as she went by, an unintelligible susurration.

A woman cradling a baby locked eyes with her, her expression serene, emotionless. The child lay quietly in her arms and Harper couldn't tell if it was alive or dead.

In another hut, a man sat staring into a fire. As he spoke, the flames soared and formed images of heroes and monsters upon his wall. An ancient magic beyond Harper's understanding.

The dream was so vivid, even the smells—putrid and rotten mixed with smoke and charred meat. Harper's stomach twisted and she looked away as a rat glared at her over its meal of torn offal.

Bloody entrails dripped down the side of the barrel where the rat sat, its ruby eyes sanguine. Harper followed the blood smeared across the floor. It led her back the way she came, and she wondered how she could have missed the crimson tracks.

The trail came to an end at the base of a wooden table where a man lay, unmoving. His face was in shadow, turned away from the door. Another man sat in the corner, crying quietly, while a tonsured monk prayed over the lifeless body.

Blood slithered down the table leg to pool on the floor. Harper took a step closer, almost close enough to touch the monk, yet he did not stir from his prayers. She may as well have been a ghost, unnoticed, incorporeal. She drifted closer to the dead man, his sunken cheeks and sallow skin gradually revealed. Blood painted his lips black as tar.

Harper clapped a hand over her mouth as acid surged up her oesophagus. Where his nose once lay, now a great, dark hole wept blood over his face and shoulders. It stained his shirt, soaking in and sticking to his ribs. Even his trousers were slick with it, as though he was standing as it cascaded over him, then fell back upon the table in death. Harper couldn't tear her eyes from his shoes, unable to look at his face or motionless body any longer. The blood even soaked the laces of his trainers.

Trainers?

Harper awoke, the bright sun through the window doing little to banish the dark atmosphere of her dreams. She tried to scramble out of bed only to bash into unyielding metal bars.

"What the …?" A white-curtained booth swam into focus. To her left was a tall metal pole with a bag of clear liquid attached. Tubes dangled from it, slithering across her blanket to embed themselves in the flesh of her arm. Harper pressed her fingers to her temples and scrunched up her face as she tried to remember how she got there.

"Shhh." Grace stroked her hair, as she had since they were young. "We're at the hospital. You were a bit out of it, so they decided to keep you for observation. Saqib went home, but they let me stay since we're family. Now you're awake, we can probably go. You didn't actually lose much blood; the cut wasn't deep. I reckon the shock caught up with you. Shame you weren't paying attention, the nurse was cute."

"Grace, is this really the time?" Harper's racing pulse threatened to break through thin skin. "There's … I Saw …"

"Another nightmare," Grace said, her voice flat.

"No." Harper shook her hair out of her face. "The village I Saw before, it wasn't the past, Grace. It wasn't the past. I know. I Saw it. I know where the next murder will be. We can stop this one."

The curtain surrounding the bed swung back, forestalling Grace's response.

"Welcome back to the land of the living, Ms. Ashbury."

"Theo? I mean, Nurse Edwards, I guess." Harper gawked at the nurse, the same man who helped her in the Shambles back before these nightmare-esque murders began. She swallowed the lump rising in her throat. The same one who'd seen her research books and looked at her dumbstruck and fearful.

His smile was pleasantly asymmetrical, his hair still ruffled even though he was on duty. Although it was still fresh in Harper's mind, the fear and anxiety from their last meeting was nowhere to be seen on his face. "Theo is fine, if I can call you 'Harper.'"

"I … yes … of course." A blush stained her cheeks, not helped by the mirth in Grace's eyes nor the thumbs up she gave Harper behind Theo's back.

"How are you feeling?" His fingers lingered on her wrist as he checked her pulse. Harper hoped he would attribute her quickened heartbeat to her injury.

"I'm okay," she replied. "Bit sore, but nothing major."

"Is this, um, related to the subject of our last conversation?" Theo glanced at Grace.

"Uh. Yeah. I guess so," Harper said. "Theo Edwards, he/him, meet my foster sister, Grace De Santos, she/her. Theo sorted my ankle the day I tripped going into work."

Grace eyed him up a little too eagerly in Harper's opinion, blatant eyes flicking up and down as they shook hands.

"Anyway, if you could get the doctor to discharge us," Harper continued, "we really need to be going. Important stuff to do."

He seemed to catch her meaning, but his knowing wink only deepened her blush.

"We'll have you out of here in no time. I apologise for my reaction at our last meeting. You took me by surprise, that's all. Thought about it a lot afterwards and I kept coming back to, 'I wish I'd asked her to grab a coffee.'" He gave a half-hearted shrug. "But now you're my patient, so that's all water under the bridge. Ethics and that."

Harper's heart ached and tears formed under her eyelids. She took a deep breath, willed them not to fall. It was only because she was tired and injured. Not because she hadn't been on a date in months.

Theo scribbled something on her chart, the click of the pen sounding so final. "I'll get the doctor so you can be on your way. I hope next time we meet, it will be under better circumstances."

"Me too." Harper gave him a wan smile as he left then shot the openly giggling Grace a glare. Theo gave a wave as he left the room, accompanied by a smile that made her stomach flip. Maybe if they met again, it would be third time lucky.

Sitting at home in her own kitchen, a mug of strong tea clasped in her hands, Harper finally started to feel better. Her shoulder still ached, and she thought longingly of the painkiller prescribed by the doctor, but her head was clear and the strain of tension in her back and neck had eased.

Grace and Saqib sat at the table with her, each lost in their own tea, expressions glum.

Harper opened her mouth to speak, but the words wouldn't come, and she dropped her head with a sigh. She knew what they were thinking. Now the heat of the moment passed, they were thinking they shouldn't be there. They were thinking about the ones who weren't—the ones they couldn't save. Even Grace, the lifelong demonhunter, felt guilt. Grace, the one who picked up other people's rubbish so some animal wouldn't get stuck in it and fed the pigeons when she thought no one was looking. Human or not, those beings at the auction had been innocents and it hurt her sister to abandon them.

Grace clicked her tongue in annoyance. "This is ridiculous. This is no way to win a war. When you lose a battle, you don't give up. You fight even harder in the next one."

"Yes, general." Harper forced a small smile. Saqib nodded.

"We know the auction isn't the answer," Grace said. "Which means there's still a killer out there. Assuming the Auctioneer told the truth, buying and selling body parts is illegal for supernaturals, so whoever is doing this must be taking them for another reason. We know this is unrelated to the incident in Chester, despite what the Ghostwalkers' Guild thought."

"And you said it's something British," Saqib said. "At least my mate said nothing happened at the Shambles, so we didn't go chasing some shadow at the expense of another life. Nothing last night made sense. I still don't understand how it happened, or why the Auctioneer decided to talk to you two and not to me."

Harper tugged on her braid as she sent her sister a pleading look. Grace gave a small shake of her head and Harper's shoulders slumped. She winced as pain sliced across her collarbone.

"As the ladies are suspiciously silent, I will answer." A smooth voice came from under the table.

Grace's eyes narrowed and her fingers stiffened around her cup. Harper froze, tea half swallowed. While she might have almost made up her mind to tell Saqib about her visions, she certainly wasn't prepared to tell him about Heresy. At least not until she'd convinced him she wasn't evil.

"What the …?" Saqib pushed his chair back and ducked his head to look for the speaker.

"I can explain," Harper said, wishing she could. "It's … um …" She jumped up to shield Heresy from Saqib's view but it was too late.

"Hello." Heresy slithered out and waved a tentacle of dust motes. He peered around her ankles, his Cheshire Cat grin ever present. Saqib scrambled away from the table. His chair clattered to the floor as he backed away until he hit the wall. Blood drained from his face, his chest rising and falling rapidly.

"Harper, what do you think you're doing?" Grace hissed.

"Saqib, this is Heresy, he/him. He's a friend." Harper glared down at the spirit. "Despite the moniker he's chosen for himself, he's not evil, just a bit mischievous sometimes. He's been helping us. He was the one who found out about the auction."

"That's a jinn." Saqib's too-wide eyes darted from Harper to Heresy and back again.

"No, he's … well I don't know what he is exactly."

"Illusion spirit," Heresy supplied, his grin broadening.

"He's a creation of God like we are," Harper said. Grace gave a small snort but didn't contradict her.

"It is a pleasure to meet you." Heresy elongated and doubled over himself in what could have been a bow. Then he stretched out a tendril toward the quaking Saqib who shrank away. "I do so hope we can be friends."

"I …" Saqib licked his lips and tried again. "It's, um, nice to meet you too." He circled the table until he was standing behind Grace. His eyes never left Heresy and his ever-widening grin.

"In answer to your questions," Heresy said, "you escaped because you had faith. Faith that Grace wouldn't have given you something to defend yourself with if it was useless and faith that the blessing of your god was with you. It only worked because the Auctioneer was in a hurry. You did not vanquish him. He decided it was not worth the fight. As to why he wanted to talk to Harper and not you, well, to a supernatural, you simply are not interesting."

"Which is a good thing," Grace added. She was still glaring at Heresy and her hand twitched with the instinct to go on guard. She looked over her shoulder at Saqib, her eyes narrow. "If you tell anyone about this, I'll—"

"I won't." Saqib raised his hands in surrender. "Good jinn can't be seen and I can definitely see *that*." His eyes darted to Heresy then back to Grace. "But I do believe you and Harper aren't evil."

"I control him," Harper said. "Please, Saqib. Trust me."

"If you say you can control this, um, spirit, I believe you." He still looked dubious, a hand resting on the back of Grace's chair to support his quaking legs. He shot Harper a weak smile. "Maybe it's even an advantage. If I have someone to test my equipment on, we might be able to find a way to detect the killer."

Heresy chuckled. "My dear boy, as if you could even come close to finding me with your toys of metal and light."

"I know where the killer will be next," Harper cut in, before a debate started. Grace stamped on her foot. But like the house, like Heresy, Harper knew this was right. Things were falling into place now, like someone assembled a puzzle in the back of her mind.

"He found something else?" Saqib gestured toward Heresy.

"I …" Despite that sense which told her this was safe, despite Saqib's trust in her, Harper still found it difficult to force out the words. Her throat tightened, lights sparkled before her eyes, the air too thick to breathe, a buffer against the pain of rejection. "I Saw it in a vision. I'm a … I'm a … a witch."

Her confession was met with silence. Then Heresy sniggered. "Why Harper dear, I never expected you to be so bold."

"Shut up," Harper snapped. Saqib gaped at her like he'd seen a ghost. His shoulders were taut, his knuckles white on the back of Grace's chair. Harper's stomach churned, tossed between hope and doubt. "It's okay. I'm not going to hurt anyone. I don't get power from a demon or devil or some other ungodly place. I was born with it, as far as I know. It's part of me, like some people can paint and others can't. I See things, I have dreams. Heresy's been teaching me spells."

Her eyes brimmed with tears at Saqib's horrified stare. He was the first person Harper had ever told. Grace didn't count; she found out on her own. Having him look at her like that cut into her heart. They'd gotten on so well, so fast. A shared love of knowledge and joy in discovery. She'd hoped so hard she could trust him.

Grace turned to face Saqib. She bent her head to look him in the eyes and placed a hand on his shoulder. "Harper isn't evil. You know who I am, who my family are. Do you think I'd be here if her powers came from somewhere dark and unnatural? Do you think I'd call a devil-worshipper my sister? You trusted me with your life before. Trust me now. Harper isn't evil. And if her magic … if her magic can help us stop a killer, then doesn't that prove it's good?"

Harper swallowed the lump forming in her throat, tears spilling over at Grace's words. She reached out wordlessly to take her sister's free hand and squeeze it tightly.

"If it is any consolation," Heresy added, "she is also not a very good witch. Quite sloppy really. She could not hurt someone if she tried."

"Not that she would," Grace added, glaring at him. "But Heresy's right. Harper's really new at most of this. She barely even counts as a witch."

"So, let me get this straight." Saqib took a step back and held up his hands, preventing any further explanation. He was shaking, his voice uncomfortably loud. "You're telling me that Harper is a witch? That she's going to use magic to stop this killer? That someone's life, our lives, might depend on her magic and *she's not very good at it?*"

Harper and Grace exchanged a glance. Saqib jabbed an accusatory finger at Harper who flinched.

"You better get good at it quickly," he said.

CHAPTER TWENTY-SEVEN

Later that night, after Grace picked the lock, she, Harper, Saqib, and Heresy entered the Jorvik Viking Centre. Freed from milling crowds and chattering children, the deserted museum was eerily still. More than that. It was dead, a mausoleum of unburied artefacts.

Flickering safety lights alleviated the darkness, but shadows jumped and danced between each strobe. Something was there, in the corner of Harper's vision, but every time she turned it was only a mannequin or a poster. It was like a cheap movie jump scare designed to make her immune to the horror so she would be caught unawares when the real demon came. She twitched at each illusion of movement, heart in her throat. Another shadow wavered and Harper spun. Nothing.

Obscured between green lights and grey shadows, anything could've been hiding behind the display cases. The handle of a curved knife fit comfortably in her sweaty palm, but she missed the familiar weight and balance of her machete, now lost in some shadow realm in How Stean Gorge. Not that she thought a blade would do much good tonight. This killer was someone she couldn't See. What was to say a blade would do any more harm to them than it had to the Auctioneer? "This place stinks," Grace muttered, mouth twisted in disgust. Echoes skittered off the glass cases and floor.

Saqib took a deep sniff, then wrinkled his nose as the acrid scent of tallow, fish, rot, and dung assaulted him. It was a familiar smell for Harper, almost comforting despite its putrid nature. They'd come here every summer holiday when she and Grace were teens, although her sister only went under protest.

Harper shrugged in response to the other two's scowls. She regretted it as the stitches in her shoulder stretched and tugged at her skin. Her grunt of pain was soft, but Grace gave her a hard look and her eyes flicked to Harper's wound. Harper gave her a wan smile, mouthing 'I'm okay.' Grace's frown deepened; her lips pursed. She gripped her crossbow so hard it creaked under her gloved hand.

Turning back, Grace took point. Despite her sister's misgivings about Saqib, Grace walked in front of him, one hand stretched back toward him as she made sure to keep her body between a civilian and danger. He was less sure-footed as he trailed after her, weighed down by bags of scientific equipment Harper couldn't even begin to understand.

Before she dropped too far behind, Harper took a step to follow her sister, when something flashed out the corner of her eye. A chill trickled down her spine, as if someone had doused her in icy water. The hair on her arms stood on end. Her breath hung frosty in the air. Light vapours obscured the see-through floor and the archaeological dig underneath.

Suppressing a shiver, Harper scanned the empty room. As quickly as it appeared, the mist was gone, the air warm again. She took one last look around, then ran after Grace and Saqib.

Ice stabbed through Usa's torso as the girl ran off. She didn't care about the life of one human. In her ageless existence, hundreds had died within her grasp. Some fell into it, others were driven, and some were merely caught in an unlucky storm. Some she saved. Those to whom she owed a debt or who were lucky enough to catch the favour of her capricious whims. Most died. She did not regret their deaths. She did not regret. Regret was human, unnatural for her.

Somehow this was different. Usa looked down at her hands. Human-shaped hands. Hands she never had before. It was a form of respect. She killed so others might live, but she didn't kill as herself. She came ashore and took lives to which she had no right. This was not the lore of nature. It was a reaction of fear.

Inhabiting the form humans took seemed appropriate. Yet strange thoughts and feelings battled within this new body, alien and uncomfortable. It recalled to her an ashrai she had once met, far from home, become human in search of a human soul. She had a soul, one in concert with her nature, and she hadn't understood his strange desires nor how taking on human flesh had changed him so. She wouldn't wish this form on anyone, for the feelings battling within her made no sense. If she had spoken longer with the ashrai, not dismissed him as a traitor to her people, maybe she would've understood her own soul better now.

She stood for a long time—her limited body constraining her as unfathomable feelings of guilt warred within.

But the voices still called.

Usa, hide us.

Usa, protect us.

She had a duty. To her kindred. To this land. The lot had fallen to her, oldest of the spirits of this region. Humans were getting too close. They had to be stopped. She had to do this.

Usa, save us.

She would be as untameable as the sea. And as unfeeling.

Harper leant against the wall, watching in fascination as Saqib set up his equipment. It all looked very technical to her, but he handled the multitude of wires with ease, a modern-day snake charmer. She still couldn't believe he knew what she was and didn't hate her. The relief of it made her buoyant. Careless. She needed to concentrate.

"There, all set up." Saqib dusted off his hands as he surveyed his work with satisfaction. He'd positioned various lamps and machines around the room, disguised behind the existing light fittings. "I can access the programming through my laptop," he explained, "and I set up a couple of cameras so I can see what I'm doing."

"Sounds good." Harper rolled a piece of white chalk between her fingers. Grace had dropped them off in the recreation of the Viking village, before slinking off to check they were alone. When she returned, she confirmed the museum was empty, then took up a sentry position at the only way in or out of the village.

The plan was simple. Set up surveillance equipment, draw the containment circle near where the body would be as if it was part of the magic of the display. Then they could retreat to a safe distance from the museum and wait to see what they caught. With no one in the museum now, the killer would hopefully arrive before their victim to get into position. Even if not, the autopsy report showed the bodies hadn't been moved after death, so Harper was confident the killer would have to step into her containment circle before anyone got hurt.

"What'cha doing?" Saqib asked Harper. Her hand twitched as she resisted the urge to hide the chalk behind her back.

"Come stand with me," Grace said. Harper hid a smile at the half-offer, half-command of her tone. Saqib inched past an animatronic fisherman, frozen part way through gutting a fish, and tucked in behind Grace at the sole entrance.

"What's Harper doing?" he asked.

Grace waved a hand toward Harper and gave her a tight nod. "A containment circle, apparently. Now be quiet and stay out of the way."

Grace's voice faded as Harper headed deeper into the village. Its denizens seemed to watch her, their heads turning as she passed them. They reminded her of the forest of eyes she kept dreaming of and she shuddered.

It was like her dream, the figures still moving, whispering, despite the museum being closed. The *nisse* sorting clothes, the ravens perched on the rooftop, the marketplace ...

Although none of it was real, Harper stopped in the market to scrutinise the woman holding the baby. Her fingers brushed the cold, hard skin of the child's cheek. Glassy eyes examined her. The mother rocked it back and forth in her arms singing a soft lullaby, but the child never moved, never whimpered, never blinked. A shiver ran through Harper and she hurried on. The mother watched her go, still crooning a song to the corpse of the baby in her arms.

Harper didn't look back when she reached the corner. Even the beady eyes of the rat were less terrifying than the empty gazes of the woman and child. The encounter had left her shaking, her knuckles white around the hilt of her blade. The scene before her was almost exactly as it had been in her dream as well, with the old man summoning images from the flames.

"It's not real," Harper muttered. "It's a projector hidden inside one of the props. It's all fake."

She moved on, concentrating solely on her objective. She couldn't be too late. Not again. Steeling herself, she entered the hut where she Saw the body laid out in her dream. The monk was there, bent over in prayer, but the bed lay empty. The door to this hut was the one place the killer would have to step. Harper slid her knife back into its sheath and knelt to sketch.

"Harper, someone's coming."

Grace's terse warning sent Harper scurrying behind the monk. When no one immediately appeared, she darted out and closed the containment circle. Keeping to a crouch, she scampered over to where Grace and Saqib waited near the door.

"Saqib, take Heresy and hide over there somewhere," Harper instructed. She scooped Heresy up off the floor and dumped him onto Saqib's shoulder, then gave them a shove toward the nearest hut.

"Move, idiot," Heresy hissed in Saqib's ear. "Unless you want to become animatronic fish food."

Saqib ducked into the dubious shelter of a replica hut and peered nervously around the hunter in the doorway.

Harper and Grace retreated into the shadows, crouched, and waited. Harper held her breath as the tap of footsteps drifted down the corridor.

They all ducked when the janitor came into the room, his mop and bucket on a cart behind him. He sat his phone down on the edge of one of the displays, removed his headphones, and cranked up the volume as he dusted.

Harper stared at the mop. They arrived late enough that the cleaning should've finished for the night. The circle she drew so carefully would be washed away. It was intended to look like part of the display to a casual observer, but it didn't mean he wouldn't accidentally erase it while washing the floor. Panic rose in Harper's throat. Fear the janitor might recognise it wasn't part of the usual display. Fear he'd call the police.

Grace and Harper's hiding place was little more than shadow. If the janitor didn't find them, the police definitely would. Harper had no idea how they would explain being in the museum, armed and after hours, with an occult symbol sketched on the floor. This was not going to plan.

The janitor dusted the tops of the fences, his cloth flicking over the head of the mourning woman. He sang along to his music with gusto. Harper hoped the music would mask the sounds of her footsteps as she crept closer. Theoretically, she knew how to do a choke hold from her self-defence training, but she'd never used it on a human before.

Before she could reach him, the janitor froze. Harper's stomach sank. He'd seen them. But he didn't say anything or move toward her.

Harper caught a ripple in the air, then Grace's crossbow bolt thudded into the wall next to her, missing both Harper and the janitor by inches.

"It's here." Grace fired again but Harper still couldn't see anything. Then she caught a faint undulation, like a mirage on a hot day.

"Saqib, the lights," she yelled as she dashed toward her sister. "It's in front of you, Gray. Move."

Grace rolled to the side. A wet splash hit the wall where she'd crouched. She grabbed the dumbstruck janitor and dragged him to the side then shoved him into the relative safety of the hut sheltering Saqib.

Ultraviolet lights came on. Anything white flared into eye-watering brilliance. To Harper, it was as if the world turned violet. She could clearly See the outline of a woman standing where Grace had been. It was the same figure she glimpsed where the ghostwalker died and in the park by Skeldergate Bridge, the one who tried to warn her away from the girl in the tree.

"What is it?" Grace shouted.

Seeing hadn't given Harper the answer. She stood between the spirit and the others, their eyes locked. They were the cold eyes of a killer, hard as ice and deep as death. Harper stood transfixed as the image reached out to her.

"I do not want to harm you, Seer," the vision said, "but I will protect my people."

"I'm not threatening them." Harper backed away from the apparition. "Why do you call me 'Seer'?"

"Do you deny who you are?"

Harper edged through the village toward her circle. "If you know I have magic, then you know we can be on the same side."

The spirit followed, hesitant footsteps that squelched like blood splatter, her hand stretched out toward Harper. "We could be, but we are not. I do not wish to harm you, but I know with whom you ally yourself."

Something flew past Harper and splashed into the woman. As if black soot particles had been mixed into a pool, Heresy's darkness spread through her, turning her watery features into a silhouette. Now able to see their assailant, Grace fired again, but the second bolt passed through the woman as harmlessly as the first.

"You, I shall not mind killing." The woman aimed the void of her gaze at Grace. "Your line is soaked in the blood of my kin."

"Hey," Harper shouted, and the spirit turned back to her once again.

"I ... regret? Is that your human word?" The woman paused, a faint frown on her glass face as she tilted her head. "I have never ... regretted ... before. Your death I shall, I think."

"Then walk away and stop killing people," Harper said.

"I … cannot." The woman spoke slowly, as if forming the words, or the thoughts, for the first time. "I tried to save you before. You did not listen. My people cry ever louder. Your sacrifice will give them safety."

"If your people are in danger, maybe I can help them," Harper offered to keep her talking.

"No." The woman's gaze turned hard again. "Your folk would destroy my folk. We are at war. A concept you taught us."

She lashed out. Harper dodged too late. The air was knocked from her at the ice-cold impact. She staggered backwards, doubled over and gasping. The woman followed her. Pretending to fall, using her momentum, Harper stumbled, narrowly missing smudging the circle she'd sketched upon the floor.

The spirit's body shimmered, delicate, deadly. She took a step toward Harper. Then another.

An eerie green glow clashed with Saqib's ultraviolet lamps as the circle activated and beams of light shot up to make a barred prison. The spirit stood within, trapped. She ran a finger across the bars.

"A magic dam." She cocked her head to the side, her eyes distant. "They still call me. They still need me." The bars fizzled like water dripped on an electric hob. Steam rose from her hand as magic sparked.

"You don't have to kill anyone," Harper said. "Please. Let us help you. You're silencing those who threaten supernaturals, aren't you? There must be a better way. Don't make me vanquish you."

The woman's soft smile was at odds with her blackened eyes. "Supernatural? I am as much a part of this ancient place you call York as the dirt beneath your feet or the trees growing on the riverbanks. Vanquish me and your city will lose its soul." She looked down at her hands, stained black by Heresy's presence within her body. "I cannot take you with me, school of matter swimming within me. When my task is completed, I hope it may help you escape."

"What are you talking about?" Harper asked. Too late.

The spirit disintegrated, collapsing in a wave of water which washed away Harper's chalk circle. Grace's yelp drew Harper's gaze as the woman reformed on the far side of the room. She leant over, barely humanoid. The janitor and Saqib scrabbled to get out of her way. The janitor tripped over an earthenware pot and fell hard with a cry of pain. Grace sprinted toward him, grabbed the spirit's upraised arm, but her hands clasped nothing but water. The woman swiped at the fallen janitor. Water drops flew from his face and struck the wall as his head snapped back.

Grace screamed and the woman disappeared in a splash.

"Harper. Harper." Grace hadn't stopped screaming as she knelt over the janitor who lay unmoving on the ground. Harper ran over, but it was too late. As Grace frantically tried to administer first aid, Harper knew.

He was already dead.

There was a gaping hole on his face where his nose had once been. A faint voice lingered on the air. It was the sparkle of sun on a fish's scales, the lapping of water against stone, the cry of gulls. Harper was the only one who heard it.

"Never smell ..."

"We should go." Harper knelt next to Grace. "She got what she came for. She won't come back."

"No," Grace said stubbornly. "I can save him. I know how to save countless different kinds of animals. A person can't be that different."

Harper clasped her sister's hands. "He's already gone, Grace. He wasn't injured by any method our medicine can heal."

"I don't accept that." Grace ripped her hands away.

Harper wrapped an arm around her sister's shoulder, fighting back her own tears. "We have to leave." She grabbed one of Grace's arms and Saqib seized the other. Between them, they pulled her to her feet. Her high heels scratched the floor as they dragged her away from the body.

"Not like this," Grace protested. "We can't leave him here like this. We should call the police. Saqib knows people there. They'll buy it from him. He can tell them–"

"Tell them what?" Harper shoved Grace against a wall. When Grace seized Harper's shoulders to push her aside, Harper pinned her sister with an arm thrust across her chest. Fire spread along her collarbone, but she didn't loosen her hold. She looked Grace straight in the eye. "What would you tell them? That a woman made of water stole his nose and he spontaneously dropped dead? How are you going to explain why we're here?"

Grace's sharp nails dug into Harper's flesh. They glared at each other; a battle of wills re-enacted so many times. Grace's mouth twisted in a thin line, the colour drained. She clenched her jaw and shoved at Harper again but it was weaker, the fight gone.

"He's dead, Gray. We failed."

Harper loosened her grip as Grace's hands dropped. "You're right, Harp. I know. It's just ... it feels so wrong."

"We should've saved him. First the auction, now this ... None of it is right." Harper hugged her sister, her face buried in Grace's shoulder as the tears she tried so hard to repress flowed freely. Grace returned her embrace, too tight, but Harper didn't care. They anchored each other against a sea of grief and guilt.

"There was ... there was nothing else we could've done."

Harper had almost forgotten Saqib was there; she was so used to it being just her and Grace. His hands were shaking, his eyes darting back and forth.

"There's one thing we can do for him." Grace wiped her eyes. Harper let her go warily as Grace returned to kneel next to the corpse. She closed the dead man's eyes then rested her hand on his forehead as she prayed. When she finished, she made the sign of the cross over him.

"Amen. I will tell Godfather how you died. He will make sure you are cleansed and buried in the holy ground of whatever faith you followed," she promised at the end.

"May Allah (swt) replace your hardships with blessings." After a moment of silence, Saqib shook himself. "Let me gather up my stuff and we'll get out of here. I'm sorry it didn't work. I ... I did doubt you, Harper. I was afraid of your magic. But ... Science did nothing. Only your magic affected her at all."

"No, I could See her when you switched your lamps on," Harper said. "Then something made her visible to the rest of you."

"That would be me," a voice squelched from their feet. "Not that anyone is thanking me."

"I kinda threw him in the direction you were looking." Saqib's skin was still clammy, his hands shaky, but a little of his normal, upbeat tone returned. "I think I'm getting good at that."

Harper gave him a slanted smile. "If you keep saving the day, we'll make you a permanent member of our party."

"We should go," Grace said softly. She'd finished laying out the body and Harper didn't have the heart to stop her. From the photos she'd seen of the other victims, their bodies had been laid out almost identically, so it wouldn't draw suspicion. Grace looped a trembling arm through Harper's uninjured one. "What did she say to you, Harp? I couldn't hear. Why did she kill him?"

"I don't think she wants to kill them," Harper said. "Whatever she is, I don't think she understood what she was doing until now."

"'Whatever she is.'" Heresy snorted derisively. "You have lived in York this many years and you cannot even recognise the River Ouse?"

Chapter Twenty-Eight

The next morning a heavy fog draped over York. It settled on the walls like drifts of snow and tumbled downhill to the river, undisturbed by human presence. No one wanted to take the risk. No one wanted to come home changed. Before, Harper would've laughed at such silly superstition, but now she looked out into the blank nothingness and a frisson of fear sparked in her chest.

The mists seemed to have a life of their own. Dark figures danced within them, reminiscent of the tortured souls in the crystal ball. It was a writhing, frenzied dance. Broken, twisted, grotesquely contorted. At the same time seductive, sensual, a hedonistic perversion. A silent plea to join their torment of pleasure. The figures merged and broke apart, melded in ecstasy, fled in agony, forever trapped in a Tartarian cycle.

Maybe they were prisoners. No one knew where the mists came from, why the sun couldn't burn them away as science dictated it ought. The people who disappeared could be there, incorporeal yet alive, waiting to possess the next unwary trespasser, to return that person as a husk of who they were.

"Hello?" Harper's voice was flat, muffled, as she stood on the banks of the Ouse. The crenellated peak of Lendal Tower was hidden by the mist. The bridge was merely a suggestion through the haze, its colours muted and dead.

The Ouse rippled velveteen under the fog, but otherwise did not respond.

"I don't think she wants to talk." Grace crouched a short distance away, barely a smudge of shadow herself, as she watched Saqib take samples of the water. "And she might not like you stealing bits of her."

"But this is a river," Saqib protested. "Heresy can't be right. That woman can't be the river. People boat on this river, even swim in it."

"And how many has she drowned over the years?" Grace asked coldly. "It wouldn't take much for it to look like an accident if you slipped in."

"No," Harper said quietly. "We're safe. She's the spirit of the river, its soul. I don't think she's used to acting independently of normal water physics. The Ouse isn't suddenly going to lash out and murder you. Being a river is simple, unemotional, but now she's become human to kill. It's different."

"What are we supposed to do?" Saqib asked. "If we kill the human version, does the river version remain or would the Ouse disappear? That would cause a lot of problems."

"Without her, the water would still be here, I think. Like the dryad in your grandfather's story, Gray. When he killed her, the apple tree didn't disappear, but its apples were never as sweet or as plentiful afterwards. I think if we imprison or … or if we have to kill her … we'd still have water. Maybe another spirit would reform here, or maybe the bit of her that's the river would remain without a soul."

Harper contemplated the lapping water of the Ouse, centre of York for centuries. There was an ache deep in her chest at the thought of harming it. She squared her shoulders: if the Ouse kept killing, she'd have no choice. There had been no further word on the missing people either, disappeared into some Guard black hole. If she couldn't stop the Ouse, those people might never be seen again.

Harper walked over to stand next to Grace, linking her arm through her sister's and leaning her head on her shoulder. "How many times have we walked by this river, Gray? How many summer evenings sat sipping cocktails on this shore? How many commutes to work over these bridges? Yet we never suspected there was a water spirit living here."

"Why would there be a spirit living here?" Grace said. "It shouldn't be possible. She's within the walls. The stones were imbued with God's power by Saint William. The Queen's Guard make very public displays of strengthening those wards. They used to *execute* supes by forcing them to try and cross it. The barrier on the walls should make it impossible for anything supernatural to be in the city centre."

"I'm here," Harper pointed out.

Grace's brow furrowed in thought. "But to become one of the largest rivers in the country, she must be, well, pretty powerful."

Harper bristled at the unsaid, 'unlike you.'

"What if she was here all along?" Harper asked.

"What do you mean?"

"What if they lied, Gray? The queen, the Church, the Council, everyone. What if the Purge didn't work? Heresy has said there are supes in England, and she's a river, as much a part of this world as we are. More even. She's been here longer than humans."

"If there's been a river spirit in York all along, then what else is there?" Grace paled. "This isn't some small-scale incursion like Father taught us to fight against. This isn't a tiny tear in the Veil. How many others did they miss in the Purge? What if this *is* Chester? Or worse, Venice?"

"This is their home," Harper said. "She feels threatened. Not by us specifically. By humans. She spoke as if she was protecting someone. She's the river, the lifeblood of this land. What if she's protecting all those who rely on her for water? Fish, animals, other spirits, the ecosystem of the land itself. You go with Saqib, make sure he gets safely to his lab."

Grace cast a glance at Saqib who was packing the vials of Ouse water into a box. "Should he really be taking that back to the lab? If the police find out it'll be bad enough, but if the Guard—"

"I won't tell them." Saqib joined them, his sample box slung over one shoulder. "I know some of my funding comes from the Guard, but I'm not employed by them or the police. My actual wages come from York University and the Council. I would never work for people like the Guard. Having some communication with them is useful, though. They know things. I might learn something."

"Sounds dangerous," Grace said.

Saqib's mouth quirked in a smile. "Been spying for the Council for five years now. It's nothing new. You coming back to the lab with us, Harper?"

"There's something I have to do here," Harper replied.

Grace's nails dug into Harper's arm as sisterly intuition finished Harper's earlier deductions. "You're trying to find a supernatural? Are you crazy? You're going to play the witch card?"

"I think I know where I can find someone who might be able to help. If I'm right, then they won't hurt me. They've been living here for years."

"And you're about to blow their cover. Plus, we don't know if the Queen's Guard are following you." Grace yanked Harper's arm.

Harper winced, her hand flying to her injured shoulder. Grace's grip loosened, but she didn't let go.

"I have to agree with Grace on this one," Saqib said, his mouth drawn down, an uncharacteristically solemn expression on his face.

"That's why I'm playing the witch card." Harper wrenched herself free with another grimace. "I'm one of them. Maybe they'll talk to me. The Ouse didn't trust me because I was with Grace. Maybe alone I can convince someone we want to help."

"Harp—"

"Gray. I'm doing this." Harper stared hard at her sister. "You've trusted me so far."

"I better not have to avenge you or anything," Grace griped.

"You won't." Harper hid her smile as she gave Grace a quick kiss on the cheek. "I'll go straight to the cathedral afterwards. It'll be fine. I know what I'm doing."

"Humph."

It was the closest to permission Harper was going to get. With a wave to Saqib, she took the stairs up to the street two at a time before Grace could change her mind.

Once she was far enough away that Lendal Tower and Bridge were completely lost in the fog, Harper sank down on a bench. She rested her head on her hands. The throbbing in her shoulder grounded her. Grace wasn't wrong. If the Queen's Guard were still on her trail, they could disappear her and no one would ever know.

The supernaturals might get rid of her themselves in order to stop the Guard following her to them. If she found them, what then? Would they help her stop a killer who was trying to protect them? They might, if it meant the Guards' scrutiny of the area lessened. Harper couldn't breathe, trapped. A butterfly in a net, a rat in a maze. No way to turn where someone wouldn't die.

Gulping down cold, moist air, Harper wiped her hand across her forehead. The cool caress of vapours against her skin soothed her.

"Don't give up," she said to herself, the words weak and faint. She said it louder as she ground her heels into the pavement and forced her aching body to stand. "Don't give up."

She rolled her shoulders, sucked a short gasp through gritted teeth, and drew a curved knife from her satchel. She strapped the weapon around her waist, one hand rested on the hilt. Harper knew York city centre well, she'd lived in the city for years, but she walked slowly and kept her eyes on the ground in front of her. Her fingers brushed over brick walls. Her ears strained for any small sound—the scuff of feet on pavement, the purr of a vehicle, the metallic ring of a weapon. Nothing but the creak of her own shoes and the faint panting of her breath. Beyond that, silence.

No one comes out when it's like this, she reminded herself, but it was a hollow comfort. No one *human* would be out. Everyone knew someone who had a friend whose cousin, or sibling, or child had been lost in the mist. Logic said they fell in the river and drowned, or met some unsavoury human, a quick knife between the ribs. Whispers said something *inhuman* lurked in the mists and stole souls away to another land. Then there were the people who came back changed, their eyes hollow, jerky movements like marionettes, a dark edge to their looks, hard and uncaring.

The mist lessened as Harper headed deeper into the city, the density of buildings preventing it from flowing so freely. It still came up to her knees as she wended her way through familiar alleys and ginnels, then through the open space of the Shambles Market. The stalls emerged from the churning vapours, eerily empty and quiet. The swirling haze washed out colour, as though she walked through a ghost town.

Piles of white built up like snow, stinging her eyes. They coalesced into human forms and reached to each other in an uncanny parody of shoppers and sellers. Harper waved a hand straight through a figure in front of her. It neither turned nor acknowledged her presence. *Is this where people vanish to, or is my Sight showing me effigies of those the mists consume?* Whatever they were, they prowled with the grace of a lioness stalking her prey. Dark holes gaped where mouths should be, their mocking laughter almost higher than audible range.

One spun to face Harper, its bright white eyes reflecting her violet ones. As it reached toward her, its mouth formed words she couldn't decipher. Tendrils of mist flowed from its hand to brush her hair back from her face. Its cold touch lingered on her neck, over her thudding pulse.

Harper sprang back and the world turned pure white. She choked in a breath of freezing vapours. Within the white, silvery grey shadows danced like dark flames. She flailed wildly, trying to clear the air around her. The laughter increased; high-pitched, grating like nails on a blackboard. Stumbling forward, she broke out of the mist, doubled over and wheezing. When she looked back over her shoulder, a humanoid form stood behind her, blank and featureless, waiting for the sculptor's blade. It raised its arms, as if offering a hug to a friend. Harper ran.

She dodged through the stalls and zigzagged between bodies, which grew out of nothing in front of her, and dissolved back into nothing behind her. She plunged into the relative safety of the ginnel on the other side and emerged breathless onto the Shambles itself. The figures crowded at the other end of the alley but did not enter, held at bay by some invisible barrier.

The windows of the glass shop next to her were lined with delicate, multi-coloured cats. Their heads turned toward the mist people, eyes glowing, tails twitching. The mist retreated from their pointed stares. Figures blurred and pooled into an inanimate haze once again.

The cats turned their eyes on Harper. Sparks crackled within her sockets as their gaze collided with her Sight. Then the light faded from the cats' eyes and they became nothing more than glass. She breathed a deep sigh of relief and turned to examine her surroundings.

Thin mist groped at the first-floor windows. Patches of artificial light twinkled through the vaporous curtain. Excitement rose in her chest, or maybe adrenaline, she couldn't tell. Someone was in the Shambles, on a day when no human would venture forth. She wasn't wrong about the people who worked there, if the term 'people' could be applied.

Her goal was the paper shop near the end of the street. Any shop would do, but she hoped to fare better speaking to a supe she was already on good terms with. As she was a loyal customer, she hoped the proprietor would listen to her, help her, despite the bloody glimpse she Saw on her last visit.

Harper curled her sneakered toes over the uneven cobbles to keep her footing on the slick path. Each window she passed glowed more vibrantly than ever before. Smells of tea, flowers, and fudge hung in the air, enticing.

When she reached one teashop, she took an involuntary step toward it. Her hand rested on the handle as she peered through the window. The proprietor, a wizened lady with a grandmotherly smile, beckoned her in. Steam rose from the indigo end of the rainbow of kettles behind her. Harper turned the handle and cracked the door open. Light spilled out into the street, carving through the mist and releasing the tempting aroma of freshly baked cookies. Tea leaves tumbling into the pot sounded like the light patter of rain, a sound of anticipation, the promise of a deluge to come.

"Enter, child."

The woman's voice was deep and rich; the honeyed overtones of golden Assam, the delicacy of Darjeeling, the homely comfort of English Breakfast.

Harper's Sight blazed. Feverish heat consumed her head and drowned out the woman's voice. Taking a hasty step back, then another, Harper slammed the door closed. She ran the rest of the way to the paper shop, slipping and sliding over the wet cobbles, and scrambled up the steps to the bright red door. She wanted to meet a supe, but she was going to do it on her own terms with one she already knew, not whatever lurked in the tearoom, inviting as it might seem.

Harper stiffened her spine and squared her shoulders, then darted through the door and shoved it closed behind her before the mists could seep through. Tendrils of silver and shadow clung to her legs and clustered against the window. They watched. And waited.

"Stop it," Harper scolded them, then winced at the inadequacy. Nevertheless, the mist retreated and its fingerprints faded from her clothes. *Did it listen to me or dissipate naturally?*

"I was not expecting any customers today." The woman behind the till broke Harper's rumination.

If Grace were there, she would've pointed out the lunacy of opening the shop, but Harper stayed quiet.

"Paper-based emergency?" the lady asked. Harper shook her head. She examined the woman. The flash of vision she had at the paper shop before wasn't a warning of murder. Heavy in her gut, Harper knew it had been something else.

She could see nothing unusual about the proprietor who sat, as she always did, knitting in the corner, so she turned her attention to the wares by the till, trying to See out of the corners of her eyes. A faint red glow surrounded the woman. The yarn in her hand transformed to liquid blood as the needles clicked. As soon as Harper looked directly at the proprietor, the vision vanished.

"What is it you want?" the woman asked bluntly.

"I want to know what you are."

The woman's eyes narrowed, a flash of red that could've been a reflection of the yarn. "I am the owner of this shop."

Harper shook her head. "You're not human. Don't worry, I'm not going to hurt you and I won't tell anyone. I'm a supernatural too."

The woman's eyes bulged in shock. She froze, a momentary indecision on whether to continue the façade and scream or to reveal herself.

"That's a bold statement," she said in a low voice. "Prove it."

Harper had been afraid of this. Violet eyes only proved an ability to put in contact lenses and the magic she did with Heresy wasn't the showy kind. Scrying and containment circles wouldn't help her here.

"I can See things others can't. What you're knitting isn't yarn." Harper gambled what little she'd Seen would be enough. "It's a liquid. I don't know what. You glow too and there's something slightly off, but I can't quite put my finger on it. You don't look human."

"All that proves is that you have stumbled into places humans should not tread." The yarn tumbled to the floor as the proprietor stood. When she flicked her fingers, sharp scarlet nails caught the light, and tendrils of liquid crimson flew through the air to snake around Harper's arms and legs. The red glow consumed the store like fire. One of the knitting needles, sharp and glistening, lifted from the floor to grind its point against Harper's neck.

Harper resisted the urge to swallow; any slight movement would cause the needle to cut her.

The woman stepped closer, a knowing smile on her lips. She was shorter than Harper, even in her natural form. The heat from her flame-red hair scorched Harper's cheeks. Her ears were sharp enough to slice skin from bone. Poppy red eyes, black pupils and no whites, drilled into Harper's soul. Then the woman nodded sharply. Harper blinked and everything returned to being as it was. The proprietor was once again entirely human, sat in the corner knitting an ordinary ball of yarn.

"I always thought you had the potential," she said, not looking up from her work, "but most humans who do never realise it. You are different. Your power used to be free. Now it is locked inside you. As the protection nears an end and weakens, your perceptions are sharpened, your power no longer suppressed and dormant."

"What protection?" Harper asked. "Is that what the Ouse is doing? Silencing threats?"

"We will be concealed again soon," the woman said nonchalantly.

"If that happens, will my magic weaken?"

The woman considered the question for a moment then nodded. "Probably. You are human, no matter your gifts. When the time comes, your power will fade."

"When will that be?"

"When a royal dies and the moon is hidden, so too will we be."

Poetic, but not terribly practical.

"Magic does not have to be practical by scientific terms," the woman said. "Magic, like science, has rules, but those rules are not the same."

"You can read my mind?"

"I offer you this advice freely, witchling. Do not try to make deals with the fae. You are too easy to read. You will lose."

"I need answers and no one human can give them to me. I have no choice but to seek out the fae. I need to know what's happening. I need to know where I came from. I need to know what I am. If the Ouse's magic will take away mine, I need to know now, before it's gone again. If she's silencing people who stir up hatred, why should my magic be affected?" Selfish desire and guilt burned acidic in Harper's stomach.

"Shadows follow in your wake. One of your kind and one of ours. One is bonded to you. He knows more than he has told. Deception spirits always do."

"How can I make him tell me?" Harper's brow furrowed. The woman had confirmed her fears about Heresy, yet he was helping her. In a way. For now.

"He won't hurt anything. Much." A slight smile played on crimson lips. "He is only a minor spirit. Too small to cross from another realm by his own power."

"But there are things that can cross over on their own?"

"Some, not many here in Albion. The humans erected a mighty magic to keep our kind out, but they failed to exile all of us before they raised it."

"The Veil is magic?" Harper swayed, lightheaded. The strongest anti-magic shield in the world couldn't possibly be made of magic. It was insane.

"The Veil simply is. It has always separated the realms. Before, one could see, communicate, through it. Now, it is almost impenetrable. Those here are just as trapped as those outside the barrier, however we are trapped in. It was a necessary sacrifice."

"Why? Why didn't you all choose to leave knowing you would have to spend the rest of your lives in hiding?"

The woman's eyes flashed, and Harper took an involuntary step back. "You have lost your land. I have not lost mine and nor would I for any reason. There are those who cannot leave—rivers, trees, mountains—and there are those who could but chose not to. This is our home. We have not given up on it because it is infested by humans."

Harper was shocked at the vehemence in the woman's voice.

"You intend to fight humans?" she asked, her grip tight around the knife hilt.

"In our own way." The woman looked down again and Harper let the blade slide back into its sheath. "Some of us are patient. We wait. Tend the land. Others take a more direct approach. Some of us disagree with this. It is such as these who made the humans fear us. They only see the small number whose nature it is to destroy, and they believe it is the same for all of us. We are not the same."

"I'm sorry." The guilty knot tightened further in Harper's stomach. She had allied herself with the people responsible. *Whose side should I be on?*

"Leave this world and forget about it," the woman said sharply. "Forget your past and be who you are, not who you were."

"I can't. Who I was *is* who I am. The person I don't remember. You said I used to have power, that I lost my land. I don't remember it. I have to know. Can't you understand? You who remained here under threat of death to preserve who you are?"

The click of knitting needles stopped.

"You cannot stop fate," the woman said. "The oldest and greatest of Eboracum shall complete her duty. I sympathise with you, but you are a threat to those of us who dwell here peacefully. I will not help you. Seek out the Magician before the ritual is complete and ze may grant your wish to remember, but be careful what you promise zir in return. Nothing is free."

"Who—" Dizziness swept over Harper. The shop tipped, warped, elongated, shrank. She stumbled into a shelf, which twisted away from her hand. Inkwells fell and shattered, the sound high and sharp against the deep roar in her ears. She hit the corner of a table and pain shot up her leg as it crumpled under her. Glass bit her knees and palms as she hit the floor. The air was hot. The smell of burning paper and leather choked her. Her eyes smarted from smoke she couldn't see. The shopkeeper's red yarn unspooled over the floor, rivulets of blood dying it darker.

The shopkeeper's voice was deep and distant. "Leave now, witchling, and the next time you pass my threshold, come as a human customer or be prepared to stay for a very, very long time."

The door swung open. Mist poured in, tugged on Harper's clothes, and dragged her out into the cold. She tumbled down the stone steps as the door slammed behind her. Her head struck stone. Hot coals blazed in her skull. Curled up, the cobbles poking and prodding her, Harper clutched her stomach, fighting nausea. She panted, air too thin, as she waited for the final blow.

Cool vapours stroked her cheek. The burning faded, leaving only the scent of citrus and bergamot. Fog melded with the sky in an endless, flat grey. Harper took a deep breath and held it, then blew out a long stream that entwined with tendrils of mist before her eyes.

The pain in her knees and hands dulled to a distant throb. There were no cuts, no blood, not even redness to mark her injury. Her head still pulsed, bright lights behind her eyes, but the cold mist soothed it, drew out the fire, and left only a memory.

Harper pulled herself up on the fudge shop's window ledge. Inside was dark and lifeless. Although only a few feet away, the paper shop was invisible in the fog; not even a glow from its window pierced the gloom. She took half a step forward, then stopped, rubbing her cold fingers together. *She could, will, kill me.* The meeting hadn't ended with the triumphant partnership she'd hoped for. *But I've learned a lot.* With a shake of her head, she proceeded instead toward the near end of the Shambles.

Unobserved, a tall shadow separated itself from the mist and followed her.

Chapter Twenty-Nine

Sitting at a broad oak desk in the Third Vault, Harper flicked through the glossy, high-resolution photos from Saqib. She tried not to think about what they were. The thought of what she was actually looking at made her stomach roll and someone with an alarming lack of foresight failed to install plumbing this far into the archives.

She laid out the images from the first victim; a glistening throat into which runes were carved. Beneath them she laid the pictures from the other victims. The dark staring eye sockets of the girl who could've been her; the empty mouth of the chocolatier; the gaping hole in Paul's face, and now the dark abyss of the janitor's stolen nose. Harper swallowed the bile rising in her throat and forced herself to keep analysing the photos.

She'd been unable to enter the Fifth Vault that morning, usually a sign someone else was using the index card room. Instead, she'd found an out of the way corner in the Third Vault, dedicated to supernatural creatures and non-redacted magical history, as far away from the tap of others' footsteps as she could. The labyrinthine layout of the mahogany bookcases afforded a lot of privacy, although they also made it easier to sneak up on someone if one knew where they were. No one else appeared to be in; each of her footsteps echoing into the silence. No one else had braved the mists, save whoever barred her from the Fifth Vault.

Despite reassuring herself, Harper still peered around the corner to make sure no one was approaching before settling back in her chair, spindles digging into her spine. The desk she chose was surrounded on three-and-a-half sides by bookcases that towered to the ceiling. They housed newer books, which most archivists therefore found less interesting. Their spines were vivid and cheerful, belying the bloody tales enclosed within. If Harper ignored the difficulty of accessing the vault in the first place, she could've been in the children's section at the public library.

She grabbed one of Saqib's photos at random and stared at it without blinking, trying to summon the burning sensation of her Sight. This close, she could pretend she wasn't looking at a corpse, the shot magnified so all features save the writing were outside the frame.

The runes still meant nothing to her or to Heresy, who had examined the text again the night before. They could be nothing more than the residue of the Ouse's method of killing, like bullet fragments or rope fibres. Or understanding them could unlock the mystery. She tossed the picture back on to the table. It floated gently down. Harper wished she had something heavier to slam.

How do these specific deaths keep supernaturals safe? The deacon and the ghostwalker, I get, but the janitor? Why will my magic be repressed if the Ouse continues? There's something more here I'm not seeing.

Rubbing her eyes, she returned to the books she'd been perusing.

'*The spirits of lakes and rivers often appear to be a negative influence on society.*'

'*It was the choice of the river spirit whether or not to release the body of a drowned person.*'

'*Contemporary writings evidence the water spirits' regular demand for human sacrifices. In the north, the Trent, Ure, and Ribble all required periodic sacrifices: the Ribble every seventh year, the Trent every third year, and the Ure, the most bloodthirsty, required annual sacrifices.*'

'*Ashrai originated in Wales but have been known to contaminate English waters, penetrating as far as Yorkshire and the Humber. They fear God's sunlight and rarely emerge from the depths. Despite their supernatural origins, there are few accounts of them harming humans.*'

'*The river Foss has long been associated with the Norse Fossegrim, the Vikings' equivalent of an English Nixie, a supernatural being thought to inhabit the site of the old watermill. Appearing as a beautiful young man, he required a sacrifice of goats. If the sacrifice was sufficient, it was believed the Foss could grant the petitioner the ability to play ethereal music. When discontent, the river spirit would lure women and children to their death with his haunting tunes. Some think the Viking settlers also brought a nøkk with them, a similar undine who inhabits rivers.*'

York was the most haunted city in England and proud of it, but there was no mention of sacrifices required by the Ouse. The book described how water spirits often took the guise of women in white or fair folk, but none depicted exactly the form Harper had seen. The description of pale ashrai was closer or the idea that the Vikings brought spirits that later came to inhabit the twin rivers of York: the Foss and the Ouse.

She wondered if that meant the books, and thus the folklore, were simply incorrect, influenced more by people's paranoid imaginations than by fact, or if the lore had been changed to throw people off the truth. One of the reasons the archivists existed was to find the facts within the fiction. There was always a lot of 'work in progress' and 'to the best of our knowledge.'

Harper was relieved to find very little lore conclusively linking witches with water cults, although one book did go on for several pages about how a witch's bubbling cauldron could symbolise a sacred well. The closest Harper had ever been to a bubbling cauldron was a boiling saucepan.

A large cauldron, almost as tall as she was, its base blackened by the fire, contents bubbling and spitting, a spoon in her hand, poised over the luminescent green liquid.

Harper blinked away the strange vision. She didn't have time to be distracted by irrelevant Sight brought on from her reading material. She closed the book and placed it back on her stack of research.

Older writings on the Ouse were mostly favourable; the river provided water to the surrounding countryside, fish to local fisherman, and was no more temperamental than any other large river. Around York, the Ouse was generally perceived as serene and steady. In fact, the river was even viewed as blessed, for it parted at the command of Saint William to save many lives when the Ouse Bridge collapsed a thousand years ago. There was no recent history of supernatural occurrences nor anything matching the mutilated corpses. Despite the ghost stories, York centre was counted as safe.

What could induce an apparently peaceful river spirit to act so aggressively now? The river was acting contrary to her nature. Everything Harper knew about spirits indicated they were bound by a strict set of rules and behaviours—they did not have the same free will as humans.

Therefore, maybe what was happening had nothing to do with the river itself, merely that the Ouse was conducting the ritual, not that the ritual was related to water. The river was ancient, its spirit probably one of the most powerful supernaturals in England.

"I thought you stopped investigating this."

Harper's heart leapt to her throat at the voice behind her. She clutched her chest and took a deep breath. "Alfred. Will you stop sneaking up on me, please? I've not seen you in days. Where have you been?"

"Thinking." He sat down next to her, his eyes unfocused as he looked at the photos.

"About what?" Harper prompted.

"About you. About these murders."

"Care to be more specific?"

He pinched the bridge of his nose and scrunched his eyes closed. When he opened them, they were tight with worry. "You're in danger, Harper. Whatever is killing these people wants to silence humans, wants to hide. The closer you come to discovering them, the closer they come to killing you."

"Alfred, what do you know? If you can't tell me, tell Archbishop Marshall."

"Know? Nothing, except you don't have the power to stop this. There is only one life you can save, Harper. Your own. Please do so."

"Alfred—"

He strode away, long legs swiftly taking him around the corner and out of sight. Harper tugged her braid, anger spiky in her chest. His obvious unshared knowledge was a betrayal. They were co-workers, friends. How could he believe she was in danger but not share it with her?

Harper shoved her belongings into her satchel, not even noticing how the photos crinkled and tore. Leaving her research books in a messy stack, she followed Alfred.

He navigated the vault with the ease of long familiarity. The twists and turns in the rows of bookcases made it easy for Harper to sneak and dodge out of sight when he paused to examine a dusty tome or to tidy someone's abandoned documents. He worked on autopilot, brow furrowed in thought. He barely paused at the checkpoint into the Fourth Vault, and Harper followed moments later.

When he reached the iron-bound door to the Fifth Vault, Alfred withdrew a key card from his blazer pocket, similar to Harper's but more ornate. He slid it into a slot next to the door and bent over to let the door scan his iris. Harper expected to hear the buzzing electronic voice that granted admittance. Instead, Alfred took a step back and glanced over his shoulder.

Harper ducked behind a bookshelf, heart pounding. At the dull scrape of metal against wood, she risked a peek between the open shelves. Her eyes itched from dust and magic as the burning sensation of Sight blossomed with little resistance.

The door glimmered with black light broken by pinpricks of white, like a cloudless night sky. The iron bars gleamed, slick, almost viscous. Where two bars crossed, the metal glowed violet. Harper couldn't tell if it was a trick of her Sight or a visual representation of the anti-magic wards placed on the door.

Alfred pressed one of the iron pegs that ran through the door. The cylinder of metal receded into the wood at the slightest pressure, emanating an amethyst light. He repeated this several times on at different pegs. There was a mechanical whirr deep in the wall. It rumbled through the stone-slabbed floor to vibrate against Harper's soles.

Access granted, Twelfth Vault, Alfred Eldrædson.

Harper checked the Dewey Decimal number of the nearest book to make sure she was in the right section. She knew the door to the Fifth Vault like the back of her hand. It was her destination almost every time she came to the cathedral. She knew, beyond any doubt, where that door led.

As Alfred creaked it open, Harper peeked past him. From this angle, the door that led onwards to the Sixth Vault should've been obvious, as well as the mosaiced floor of the Fifth. Instead, indigo-and-iris satin draped over ebony book stands and a thick crimson carpet. She rubbed her eyes and looked again but, Sight or no Sight, the image didn't change. The door clicked closed behind Alfred, leaving Harper with more questions than she started with.

She leant back against the bookcase, gold-trimmed corners of books sharp between her vertebrae. The pain in her shoulder threatened to scatter her thoughts while at the same time reassuring her she was not asleep. Tricks of light and mirrors. Clever technology. That's all it was, it had to be. She'd seen it in the Hall of Testing before. Mirrors and spinning floors like a sideshow horror house making the room appear endless when on other days it was no bigger than her lounge. Spinning floors. Her mind grabbed the image like a lifeline. The rooms beyond must rotate, despite their solid stone appearance.

With her skirt bunched in trembling hands, Harper approached the door. "God, if you're listening, help me," she whispered. "I have faith in Grace, and she has faith in you. Prove to me my magic isn't evil." Heresy had only shown her a couple of incantations, tricks to help her hide from whoever captured him and followed her. Harper hoped a door was easier to fool than a person. Her fingertips burned. Flashes of lilac reflected in the gold as she slid her filigree pass card into the slot by the door. "I am stone. I am wood. I am the cathedral, house of God. I am one who belongs, meant to be here, let me pass unseen."

She continued to repeat the phrase as a panel slid aside and she let it scan her iris. Then she pressed the same places that glowed purple when

Alfred touched them. The iron bars receded into the wood as easily for her as they had for him.

Access granted, Twelfth Vault, Archbishop Simon Marshall.

Harper blinked in surprise, then she remembered the archbishop's words the day he showed her the astronomy tower. *"This cathedral is part of me and I of it."* A rush of adrenaline flooded through her. It might not have been how she intended the spell to work, but it *had* worked. She bit her lip to hold back a grin and eased the door open.

The room on the other side was vast, far larger than any of the other vaults. The walls were lost in darkness. The only light came from crystal chandeliers hanging in a row down the centre of the hall. Fire flickered within the crystals, forbidden everywhere else in the archives. The cut glass refracted and reflected. Shimmering multi-coloured flames frolicked across the floor and ceiling. They pierced the darkness like will-o'-the-wisps guiding the unwary to death.

To Harper's left and right, rows of satin-clad book stands stretched out like grasping fingers wrapped in funeral cloth. The books, chained and padlocked closed, rustled as she walked past. Static zipped through the air and tingled against her bare skin. When she reached out to touch one of the books, all the hairs on her arms stood on end. Strands escaped from her braid rising as though she touched a Van de Graaff generator. She sucked on her stinging fingers as she headed deeper into the vault.

Mint and basil cut through air heavy with the scents of glue, paper, and ozone. Whispers echoed off the curved stone ceiling, their source hidden. The susurration trickled chills down her spine. Where the earlier vaults were paved with unyielding stone and tile, her feet sank deep into the carpeted floor of the Twelfth Vault.

The chandelier's light exposed her, but Harper made no move to leave the crimson path or to hide. Darkness hemmed her in. Nyctophobia roared to life. Old fears tore at her heart. Her staccato breath dragged lukewarm, dry air over her tongue, thick with the taste of books and dust, but also something new that burned with chilli heat. She twisted her fingers into her hair. It took all her concentration to goad one foot in front of the other. The rainbow lights thrust through the darkness, blue, green, grey, like eyes staring out of a dark forest, like a nightmare come to life.

Harper fumbled in her bag, until her fingers closed on something hard and heavy. She thrust it toward the darkness like a sword as she flicked a switch.

A beam of lilac cut through the black and scattered the hovering lights. The visible light was only there to reassure her that the device was on, according to Saqib's explanation. As his UV lights had helped Harper see the Ouse at the Jorvik Centre, he'd given her a smaller, portable lamp to carry.

The light bolstered her courage. She squared her shoulders and took a firm step forward. With her panic lessened, the roar in her ears receded allowing other sounds through. Keeping her torch low, Harper crept toward the scuffling of shoes and the swish of pages farther into the vault.

The stands of books spiralled out from the centre of the vault. As Harper delved deeper into the vault, they strained at bindings of iron and silver, moved by a force even her Sight couldn't perceive. She tucked her elbows in, wary of touching the frenzied tomes. Where pages cracked open, they glowed iridescent violet to her Sight.

Magic. Bound and contained deep within the cathedral. An electric thrill built in her core, fear and excitement bubbling together. She wanted to stop and think, work through the implications, but she didn't have time. She had to find out what Alfred knew. Let him berate her for being in this forbidden place. She'd been lied to, everyone had been lied to, and she wanted answers.

She wandered deeper into the vault, in hopes an answer lay at the source of indistinct echoes. Darkness closed in behind her, pushed her onwards. Her feet ached and her shoulder throbbed as though she'd walked for miles. Then Alfred's familiar tones reached her accompanied by the rustle of frantically rifled pages. She still couldn't see him, the darkness veiling anything more than a few metres ahead, but she stumbled towards his voice. He warbled, as though uncertain or afraid of the words he read, speech hushed to a reverent whisper.

"Never scream, never tell, never taste, never smell."

A susurration came with it. The voices from her dreams. A dissonant cacophony filling the vault. More and more voices joining, out of sync, some whispering, some wailing. Harper fell to her knees. The torch thudded to the floor and its light flickered out. The voices yanked at Harper's hair, scratched against her skin, punctured her ribs and thudded with her heart. They stole the air from her lungs and froze her blood in her veins. A scream died in her throat, her tongue glued to the roof of her mouth. Her nose clogged and she couldn't breathe. The taste of iron welled on her lips, slithered down her face, viscous as it slid onto her tongue.

She pushed her fingers into her ears and squeezed her eyes shut, curling into a ball, as small as she could be. She didn't know how long she lay there, assaulted by the whispers. When they faded, she remained lying on the floor, a hiccoughing sob the only sound she could make. A dark red halo stained the tear-soaked carpet beneath her head. Her eyelashes stuck, then ripped, as she opened her eyes.

Despite the broken torch, the purplish light remained like dim moonlight. Unable to stand, Harper crawled onward. As her eyes adjusted, she was able to make out the rows of books. They lay quietly now as though they too had been cowed by the onslaught of voices. When she turned the corner, one book glowed brighter than the rest, a few metres away in the direction Alfred's voice had come from. Alfred himself was nowhere to be seen.

The book lay open, a snapped length of chain jangling beneath it. Harper approached it cautiously, but it didn't try to shock her as the others had. Its pages were warm to the touch, the linen texture reassuring. In the vague light, she could barely make out a spell of runes on the page. A tingle zinged through her bones as she traced one symbol with her fingernail. It was the one repeated on each of the victims.

"Never." Harper breathed the word, remembering the lines Alfred had read. If he knew about the spell, did other archivists? Did the archbishop? If Alfred believed this was what the Ouse was doing, surely he must have reported it.

Like you reported knowing it was the Ouse?

Harper closed the book. It was bound in dark leather, the colour of which was indeterminate in the half-light. Its cover shone with silver-tipped runes that writhed and wriggled. The burning in Harper's eyes grew so hot it brought tears to them. Gradually, the shapes formed familiar patterns until English words were etched across the cover:

The Hiding

Chapter Thirty

By the time Harper left the Twelfth Vault, Alfred was nowhere to be found. She wasn't sure whether to be relieved or annoyed. Part of her wanted to confront her friend, to demand he tell her what was happening, but part of her feared seeing the betrayal in his eyes. *Which side should I be on? Which side should I be on? Which side am I on?* The question spun in her mind, never giving her peace.

She wandered through the vaulted nave caught in a haze of breathy murmurs.

"Never scream…"

"Never tell…"

"Never taste…"

"Never smell…"

All whispers that haunted her visions, all runes carved into the Ouse's victims, all words of the spell in *The Hiding*.

Her feet took her first to the archbishop's study, an autopilot search for safety, for someone to take the decision away from her. Her hand trembled in doubt as it hovered centimetres from the oaken door. If the archbishop discovered her magic, would he try to save her or would he hand her over to the Guard, eyes heavy with disappointment? Harper's chest was tight with fear and uncertainty. Her braid was puffy, hair pulled loose by worrying fingers. She paced back and forth outside his office door.

"Harper? I didn't expect to see anyone here today what with the heavy mists and curfew imminent."

She jerked away from the door at the archbishop's greeting as he came up behind her. "I ... um ... there was ..."

He wrapped an arm around her, opened the door, and guided her into his study. Mist piled against the window, as though the world outside had ceased to exist. A chill hung in the air with no fire to ward it off. Slight pressure on her shoulders lowered Harper into a chair beside the cold grate.

"There is no harm in you being here," the archbishop said as he took the chair opposite. "I am merely surprised. What can I do for you, child?"

His warm, calm tone soothed Harper's nerves. Archbishop Marshall had been a steadfast figure in her life for over a decade. The thought of him betraying her made her nauseous. Not sharing the secret of her magic was one thing, normal in her life, but to find out that life was a lie ... She couldn't even contemplate it.

"I know about the Twelfth Vault." The words slipped past her lips of their own accord.

Instead of the shock or anger Harper expected, the archbishop merely nodded. "I know. I'm glad you came to me. I feared you might stew in your own thoughts as you are wont to do."

Harper's mouth opened then closed again. She was as voiceless as the dead ghostwalker. Eventually she squeaked out, "You ... you know?"

"This is my cathedral. Nothing takes place here without me being aware of it."

"You're not angry? Or ..." Harper chewed her lip. 'Or going to kill me' sounded ridiculous even in her head.

"I am impressed with your resourcefulness in gaining access to the vault." The archbishop leant back in his chair, folding elegant fingers over the gold crucifix resting on his chest. "For your sake, I wish you hadn't seen it. I fear, with your history, this knowledge may harm you. That is why it was kept from you."

"There was a book about these murders. If I'd seen that, I could've known what was going on sooner."

"Explain."

"I think all the body parts are being taken in order to complete a ritual that will hide supernaturals from humans."

"Allowing them to return unopposed. Can you stop it?"

Harper took a deep breath then nodded. "I think I can." She crossed her fingers tucked under her legs as she watched his face for any sign of anger or fear, hoping he'd trust her and not probe further. The only way she could think of to stop the Ouse was with magic.

The archbishop bowed his head. "I pray once this threat is ended, our missing people may return home. I shall leave the matter in your capable hands and, no doubt, those of my godchild."

"Aren't you going to say anything about what's in the Twelfth Vault?" Harper blurted out.

"You knew there were classified materials to which you had not been granted access."

"But those books don't simply describe magic. They moved. They are magic."

"Not all magic must be destroyed to be made safe, child. I knew this would be hard for you, after the trials you went through. I admit, I was unsure if you could be trusted with the knowledge of the higher vaults. What we do is illegal in England, immoral by the standards of most of her citizens."

"It's forbidden by Church doctrine."

"Is it?" There was a glint in the archbishop's eyes, a star glimmering in the depth of night. He walked over to the bookcase by the cold grate and took down a battered paperback Bible with bent corners and well-thumbed pages. He placed it on Harper's knee. "Show me where in the Gospels it says this."

"I ... I don't know ..." Harper tried to remember but she'd never had the knack of quoting chapter and verse save a couple of the most well-known.

The archbishop tapped the book. "This is where our faith starts, Harper, but it is only the beginning. Ours is a living religion, a living relationship. We worship a servant God and, as long as I am archbishop, this cathedral will be a servant to the people of York. We risk the magic in the vaults to protect them. It is not at odds with our beliefs, but it is something most of our parishioners would struggle to accept. We are commanded to love our neighbours. You must decide who your neighbour is, child. Now, I believe you have your own service to perform in protecting York. How is a choice only you can make. When it is done, come speak to me again."

The archbishop plucked his Bible from Harper's numb fingers then guided her out of his office as the curfew bells rang. She stumbled away, her mind reeling with the implications of his revelation. She wished there was more time to ponder it, to decide the right course of action.

As she passed through the nave of the cathedral, her eyes were drawn to the great east window. The darkness of night robbed the normally vibrant figures of life. The figure of God stared down at her. *Ego sum*

Alpha et Omega.' I am the Beginning and the End. Grace and Saqib would tell her to trust God. That humans could fail but God is eternal.

"What should I do?" Her shout reverberated through the empty cathedral. Myriad versions of her voice bounced back to her, tinny from metal, cold from stone. "Who am I?"

"Who do you want to be?"

Harper spun around, her hand flying to the knife sheathed at her belt. She hadn't heard anyone approach.

A young man stood between her and the main altar, a stranger. He wore a long coat, covering scruffy jeans and sneakers. Even slouching, he was taller than she was. His hands were empty. Harper relaxed her shoulders and released the handle of her blade.

He shook his head, a rueful smile on his angular face. "You won't survive long if you think I'm unarmed."

Harper gripped the knife again, drawing it slowly. "Who are you? If you want to kill me, why speak?"

"Well, I *am* supposed to be killing you." He shrugged apologetically. Harper's heart thudded in her throat. "But I'm not going to."

"You're Queen's Guard," Harper accused.

"Them?" The man's face twisted in disgust. "Those morons?"

Harper's eyes bulged. She'd never heard anyone describe them with such contempt. Fear, yes, but he acted as though they were nothing. On instinct, she checked for eavesdroppers, but the cathedral remained empty.

"The Queen's Guard are dogs," he spat. "They do as they're told. They bark and scare people, but they are no real threat. Not to us."

"Who are you?" Harper pointed the knife at him, balancing on the balls of her feet. "How can you be so blasé about the Guard? What if someone hears you?"

"They won't." His lips curled in a half-smile. "I've seen to that. I'm like you. Well, not exactly like you. I'm what they call a techno-witch, although I'm not a fan of the term myself. That's how I caught your little demon. He made the mistake of trying to take information from my computer, so I trapped him and questioned him."

"You're the ones who took the information from the Ghostwalkers' Guild?"

"Yes. If people found the auction, like you did, and realised it was a normal occurrence, it would jeopardise all of us. We can't let them know there is so much magic on this side of the Veil."

"You know about those auctions and you let them happen?" All of Harper's bitter frustration poured into the words. "You let people be sold and you come to kill me? You're right, you aren't like me."

"An unknown witch who cannot control her powers is also a threat to us. If you slip up, you could begin a new era of witch hunts. None of us would be safe."

"You followed me to see if I was going to slip up?"

He shrugged again. "And now you have. They noticed that little exhibition in the Shambles, and whatever you did here lit up like a Guy Fawkes Night display."

"The Queen's Guard?"

"No, my coven, but if they noticed, others will have noticed too."

"If there are other witches out there, can't they teach me to control my magic?" The mere thought of joining people who turned a blind eye to others' suffering made Harper sick to her stomach.

He tilted his head to one side, misty blue eyes narrowed.

"Did it never occur to your coven to teach a new witch rather than kill her? If I'm like you, you should protect me."

"We protect coven and clan. We don't bring in outsiders." He spoke the words as if by rote, and Harper realised his confidence was a sham, a shield learnt from his coven the same way she hid behind a pretence of Grace's authoritative arrogance.

"So, you kill them," Harper accused.

He squirmed, dusty brown hair falling across his face as he shook his head. "I didn't want this job. I was simply the closest. I won't hurt you. I'm warning you now so you can hide because I can't speak for the others."

"Is that why you're here, to warn me?"

"You need the demon." He avoided the question with a grimace. "He'll help, I think. If you die, he goes back to where he came from, so he'll protect you."

"But that's not all," Harper prodded. "Why did you reveal yourself to me?"

"What do you intend to do about the Hiding?"

After searching for meaning for so long, his casual naming of the ritual sent anger racing through Harper. "I intend to stop it before more people are killed."

The words hung in the air between them.

"How?"

"Well ... I don't know." The book she found hinted at how to do the ritual but made no mention of stopping it that she could decipher, her Sight doing little more than translating the title. "Can you help?"

He hesitated, looked down as he shuffled his feet. Harper relaxed her stance, but held the knife ready.

"I shouldn't," he said at last.

"You bound Heresy. He's made of smoke, and you bound him. Can you bind something made of water? I tried, but my magic wasn't good enough. If I can bind her, she won't be able to kill anyone else."

"You know who's doing the ritual?" he asked.

"Don't you?"

"No. We're not part of their society. We're human, albeit fae-touched humans. They mistrust us and we them. They'd never tell us about something like this. The Hiding is a mixed blessing to magic users as it hides everything supernatural, regardless of whether you want to be concealed by it or not. And by hiding all magic, it weakens us spellcasters. It's like magic becomes diluted or really far away. There is debate among the clan elders as to whether we should try and stop it ourselves. They won't do anything, though. They'll argue until it becomes moot. We hide in the shadows as much as any inhuman supe."

"We should work together," Harper said. "If your coven won't act, you're no better than the killer. Teach me how you trapped Heresy. Please. Before she kills again."

Silence stretched between them. Harper held her breath.

"I can't," he bowed his head, "but I do not wish you ill. Be careful, Harper Ashbury. Win or lose, you'll still be in danger."

He turned on his heel and walked away as silently as he had arrived.

Chapter Thirty-One

Harper sat in the quire for a long time, lost in thought, praying for a plan that could save everyone. By the time she left the cathedral the fog had lifted, revealing a blanket of twinkling stars. The cold breeze was calming as Harper sat on the front wall of her house, oddly reluctant to go in and face Storm Grace. Her sister wouldn't react well to confirmation they were surrounded by supernaturals, nor to Harper's decision to protect them, despite her mixed feelings on the auction.

Harper gazed up into the sky. The waxing moon cast an eerie glow over the street and banished her fear of the dark. A galaxy of stars glinted like sunlight scattered over the river. *I miss the stars.* Harper twisted her hair around her fingers, wondering at the unbidden thought. When she did go out at night, rare as it was, she always concentrated on the stars and moon, often the only light.

Back when she first came to live with Grace's family, Mama Maria taught her to face the darkness within and without. Curfews were for ordinary people, she said, a De Santos was not scared of the dark. A De Santos was one with the dark. She always spoke of the family like this, as if Harper were one of them despite not sharing the name.

A deep ache settled in her chest—grief, nostalgia, and longing. She clutched her shirt over her heart. The pain of loss knotted her stomach and balled in her throat. She clung to it, desperate to trace its source.

The lights dimmed. Blood dripped from her fingertips, surreal against the grey of the night. A lone star peeked through a blanket of clouds. It glinted through the branches of a canopy of firs. A child, sneaking out, afraid of being caught by …

Harper jumped, almost falling off the wall. She cursed at the sudden pain in her hand where three thin, red streaks of blood welled. They criss-crossed the faint marks from the graveyard, which hadn't yet fully faded.

"Meow."

A white cat sat on the wall next to her. Its feather-duster tail was bristling, its fur all on end as it hissed. Its blue eyes caught hers.

"Heresy?"

The cat hissed again. A shiver rippled through its fur like a winter breeze through long grass, then it hopped down and trotted away.

"Thanks for nothing, cat." Harper pressed her handkerchief against her hand. She'd been about to remember something, something important, but it was gone now. Something to do with the sky. Try as she might, Harper couldn't bring back the memory.

All around her, source-less and ethereal, music drifted through the night. Voices, rich and lilting, airy and weighty, male and female twisted through the unknown melody of a violin. Harper closed her eyes and listened, unsure if the music was real or a figment of her magic.

The language was not one commonly spoken on her shores, but Usa knew the music in her soul. Written in honour of a distant sister, it resonated within her waters and rippled her surface as the breeze undulated with the power of human voices. They sang tales of passion, of love and hate, of death and mourning, of humanity and of fantasy.

Once the ritual was complete, those voices would lose their power, lose their threat. The Hiding would smother them, keep them prisoner, and release her kin from the captivity of fear. With the ritual came sacrifice. Hers. Theirs. Her victims'. The victims of others let loose to roam by the very spell she cast to protect her tributaries.

The next sacrifice inexorably called as the moon waxed toward full. There wasn't much time left. Usa stilled downwind of the song. She must have patience. He would come. He always did. This need for rushing didn't suit her, not here in Eboracum where she was patient, steady, calm.

Here she was not the rapids, nor was she meeting the rolling sea. She would wait, until the time was right, until the victim was ready.

This one she knew well. As a child, he splashed his feet in her, tried to catch her fish, the twinkle of childish laughter on the wind. Many evenings he stood on the bridges that girdered her and crooned tales of her people. He sang with the elegance of a gull; his voice was no threat. Yet he listened. He heard and stored within him all their secrets.

Usa closed her eyes and let the music flow around her like streams of water around rocks. Words telling a story of the Rusalka. Words exposing the secrets of the water.

Usa, hide us.

Usa, protect us.

Their voices wove through the song, soaring where it whispered, hissing where it crescendoed. She couldn't stop now. If she did, then those she killed would've died in vain. If she did, her kith and kin would be slaughtered.

Usa, save us.

They needed her. Their lives, their very souls, were within her power to hide or expose, to save or to watch die when the last Hiding ended. Death was demanded. She would make sure it was not theirs.

The silence following the music was light as mist. Then the clatter of feet and the chatter of tongues, as the listening humans left. They flowed past her, never seeing her through the driving rain. He came last. Lingering on her namesake bridge as ever, ignoring the rain to sing to her. She would miss his song, his tribute. He didn't deserve death. Had he fallen into her, she may even have saved him. He was invisible to the humans, like she was, and spoke to her in a way he could never speak to his own kind. An affinity resonated between them.

Usa, save us.

She willed herself to ice within; she had a greater, an older obligation. He listened. He remembered. He was the one chosen for the Hiding. She could no more ignore the compulsion of her duty than she could flow backwards.

Her hands covered his head and slid through his soaking hair, one with the rain. His voice choked off, gurgling, spluttering as he fought her hold. He was weak, alone. He dropped to his knees, fingers stretched heavenwards. Gnarled and clawed, they begged for mercy where none existed. If there was mercy, her kind wouldn't need the Hiding.

Ripples ran through the false body Usa had given herself. He should be dead now, his part in the tale over. No more to hear. No more to sing. Pain blossomed in her chest like a drop of black dye spread through her, polluting her. Head clutched in his hands, he wrenched from her grasp. Tears and rain mingled in his eyes, the whites scored by rivulets of red.

As he scrambled away from her, he tripped on the uneven paving. Rain slicked his clothes to him, sucked them to his ribs just as his skin sucked into his gaunt cheeks. The darkness welled within Usa as she looked into eyes that so recently gazed at her in adoration. She wavered, emotion rolling and crashing through her.

Usa, save us.

"God save me," he whispered.

She drew herself up, taller, stronger, hardened her being for what she must do.

Her hands crashed through his skull like a tsunami. He fell, his dying breath silent, and his shell collapsed over the rail and tumbled into her depths, leaving nothing but broken conches of flesh in her hands.

She received him. That distant part of her that was her, the real her, wrapped him in herself and submerged him deeper in her darkness.

The part of her that was now separate felt the splash of his body, the bite of blood flowing, the breath of soul extinguishing. From each of her hands dripped human blood. It flowed into her and tainted the rain. She raised her face to the sky, inviting its water to replenish her as it had through the ages. Then she walked down to her shore and released the last of his body into her body. Three more pieces to go.

"Ears stone deaf …"

Chapter Thirty-Two

"Hey, Heresy, I have a question." Harper cringed at talking to her cornflower-blue front door even from inside where no one would spy her. As per Harper's order not to possess the neighbours' cats, Heresy had taken to concealing himself in the peephole when he wasn't teaching.

"I am hardly surprised," Heresy answered in a bored tone.

"Do you think the guy who captured you is dangerous? He confronted me at the cathedral today. He's been ordered to kill me, but he didn't. I don't think he wants to, either."

"The boy has no spine." Heresy waved a tendril out of the peephole.

"What do you think he'll do? Do I need to watch my back?"

"No." Heresy chuckled. "He is too scared to kill you, too scared to help you. He will go and hide in a cupboard and wait for it all to pass. He was terribly boring. Except his magic. His magic was interesting. I might have stayed for that had he been the one to summon me."

"You almost sound like you want him to kill me," Harper said dryly.

"Of course not, Harper dearest." Heresy chortled. "If you die, my fun ends. Besides, you are much more entertaining."

"Yeah, I thought as much." Harper flicked his tendril. "Do you know what he did to trap you? Can you teach me?"

"I do not," Heresy said delicately. "I do not think it is good knowledge for you to have."

"I'm not going to trap you," Harper said in exasperation. "I'm going to trap the Ouse. Clearly the circle you taught me before was not good enough."

"Or you were not strong enough," Heresy replied. "Or maybe trapping water in a circle made of chalk was impractical."

"I didn't miss you when you were gone," Harper snapped.

Heresy chuckled. "You missed the good night's sleep. You do not need to be afraid of the boy. He will not harm you. If he wanted to, he would have done so by now."

"That's not comforting," Harper grumbled. "If he keeps following me, you warn me, okay?"

"Absolutely," Heresy replied. "Your safety is of paramount importance to me."

"Sure. I'm going to go talk to someone who actually cares about what happens to me."

When she burst into the kitchen, Grace was sat at the table, reading a book with her feet up on the opposite chair, a cup of coffee cooling beside her.

"I'm really glad our landlady hasn't found anyone else to live here yet." Harper dumped her bag at the bottom of the stairs then joined her sister at the table. "Gray, this is so much bigger than we thought—"

"Saqib's in the attic praying." Grace didn't look up from her book.

"Why is he in the attic?"

"To pray."

"I meant … never mind. Is there anything left in the coffee pot?"

"Check for yourself."

"Gray, this is important. Stop being annoyed with me, put down the book, and talk to me."

Grace lay her book face-down on the table. "I'm studying," she protested.

"You're reading a cheesy romance and hiding behind a textbook because you don't want anyone else to know." Harper gave her sister a hard stare. Grace stared back, but the corners of her mouth twitched.

"Maybe," she conceded as she got up to grab another mug. "What did you find out today?"

"That this is much bigger than we thought." Harper quickly filled Grace in on the details of the day, including her encounter in the Shambles, the book in the mysterious vault, and the vague threats from the techno-witch.

Grace refilled their drinks while they talked, then sat opposite Harper at the pine dining table. "Do you think Alfred is working with the Ouse?"

Harper quickly shook her head. Despite her pain that the Church kept secrets from her, in her heart of hearts, she couldn't believe evil of those she'd trusted all these years. "Definitely not. He was trying to protect me.

This book was in the Twelfth Vault. I didn't even know there was a Twelfth Vault until today. It's way over my clearance. He probably recognised the symbols but didn't know what was safe to tell me."

"Did that book teach you anything other than more damned spells? Who the next victim is? When or why?"

"From what I could gather from the illustrations, there are various types of Hiding spells designed to conceal particular items or stop things being perceived by specific senses. Take lips to stop someone speaking and spreading the word, take a nose to stop people smelling whatever you want to hide. Most of the spells used one sense but across the centre pages was a circle, much more complex than the ones Heresy is teaching me. All the senses were represented, everything we've seen stolen: vocal cords, lips, tongue, eyes, nose, and more. There were fingers, a heart, ears. The Ouse is not done killing, but when she is, she's going to complete that ritual, not to hide something small or from a few people. She's hiding everything magical in the whole county, maybe the whole country."

Grace's fingers tightened around her mug. She was lost in thought and the swirling depths of too-sweet coffee as she stirred. Her spoon clattered onto the table, leaving dark splotches of liquid. "What do we do?"

A voice came from the stairs. "It seems pretty obvious to me."

"Pull up a seat, Saqib." Grace nudged one out with her foot. "Decided it's safe to be around me again?"

"That's why you were in the attic?" Harper hazarded. "To avoid Grace? Did you hear everything?"

"Yes and yes, and in case the landlady did one of her surprise visits." Saqib poured himself a coffee before joining them. "The river took body parts from people strongly associated with that sense: the voice of a ghostwalker who makes a living describing the supernatural; the lips of a man known for his sermons against supe influence; the taste buds of a chocolatier who makes 'magical' chocolates, and the nose of a man who cares for the smelliest place in York, a place designed to take you back in history to a time when supernaturals still roamed the land freely. We haven't identified the girl in the tree yet, but she is probably unusually perceptive in some way. That or she can do what Harper does."

Harper shuddered, and Grace reached across the table to pat her hand. Her sister's fingers were ice cold despite the steam rising from her mug.

"You're right." Harper nodded toward Saqib, then looked straight into her sister's dark brown eyes. "*We* can stop her, Gray. You, me, Saqib, and Heresy. She doesn't *want* to kill people. We can persuade her to stop, convince her there's another way to hide the supernaturals."

"Talk to it? You *cannot* be serious." Grace thumped the table with her fist and Harper jumped. Everything magic was evil to Grace's family. She knew the history, the harm supernaturals had done to humans. She also knew the harm humans could do to a supernatural. The pain of the exorcism haunted her, even now, deep down inside her bones. Cold plunged through her like she was freezing from the inside out. Light poured from her, her soul broken open …

"Enough."

Harper looked up as Saqib leapt to his feet, leaning over the table toward Grace, whose eyes narrowed dangerously. Saqib ploughed on. "Are you forgetting your own sister is a supernatural? What if this ritual is the only thing that's been hiding Harper? I'm not fully convinced magic can be a good thing, and I'm terrified if there really are supernaturals all around us, but I don't think Harper is evil. If she's not, maybe there are others like her who simply want to be left alone. In the Quran, al-Baqarah 102, it states magic was taught by devils, but some scholars have argued that there may also be 'natural' magic. I'm not a mufti or an imam, I don't have the answers, but maybe there are questions to be asked, and maybe there are others who are creations of Allah (swt), just as we are. Maybe, some things we deem as 'magic' are just a science we don't know yet. What I do know, is that I don't want anyone else to die, no matter who they are."

Grace's eyes widened, her hand unclenching. "I'm sorry, Harp, but we're talking about something out there killing people. We're talking about all those unsolved murders and disappearances. We're talking about the people who go out one evening and come back different the next day. We can't let the Ouse complete this ritual and we absolutely cannot help her find another way to hide."

"I agree with Saqib." Harper studied her fingers, unable to look up at Grace. "They can't all be bad. Sure, there are types of fae that are inherently incompatible with humans, but they aren't deliberately evil. Remember the wolf you treated? When we were camping with your family? Most people would have shot it, they steal sheep, they can hurt people, but you wouldn't allow it."

"Harper, this is different—" Grace protested but Harper cut her off.

"No, it isn't. They have a right to exist. You're *demon*hunters. These aren't demons."

"Like the one you've got hanging around all the time," Grace said. "That thing is a bad influence."

"He's protecting me. He helped us, with the auction and at Jorvik." Harper took her sister's hands, as she thrust as much conviction into her voice as she could muster. "I need him. The dreams I've been having aren't all about these murders. There's something out there, something worse than the Ouse. It's looking for me. Heresy can keep me hidden."

Grace's eyes narrowed. "If there's something hunting you, then I say we kill it too. Have you considered that maybe your dreams have been getting worse *because* of Heresy? How do you know it isn't lying to you? It's a *deception* demon."

"The dreams were worse before he got here," Harper said. "I think this Hiding was protecting me as well as the other supes. Now it's wearing off, my magic is getting stronger, or at least becoming more noticeable. Maybe the Hiding even hid it from me. If we can stop the Ouse from killing again, from completing the ritual, I'm going to need help in taming this power, in staying hidden. I *need* Heresy."

Anger simmered in Grace's eyes, but her sister pursed her lips and didn't argue further. She tugged her hands out of Harper's and crossed her arms with a defiant look.

"So, what do we do?" Saqib broke the tense silence of the glaring match between the two women. "If we do nothing, the supernaturals stay hidden, Harper included, but more people die."

"I won't have anyone die to keep me safe," Harper interjected. "You can agree with that much at least, can't you, Grace? Your family has always put their lives on the line to protect others. You can't ask me to let someone else die to protect me now."

Grace stalked across the room to grab the kettle and yank the faucet over to fill it. As enraged steam whistled, her shoulders slumped. "No, I can't," she whispered, her voice almost lost.

Harper hugged her from behind. "Thank you."

When Harper sat down again, Saqib continued, "As Harper said, the rhyme wasn't complete, so either there are more victims we haven't found yet or the Ouse isn't done killing. You said you thought there might be a celestial pattern, Harper. Could it be moon phases, or planetary alignments, or something to do with constellations? Has the Ouse been doing this ritual on a cycle?"

"I don't think she's ever done this," Harper said, "but I am certain it's happened before. I think—"

A crash cut her off and a siren blared through the house.

"What the ...?" Grace snatched up a kitchen knife as she spun.

A cloud of black particles burst through the kitchen door and the siren grew louder as Heresy spun around Harper's head.

"Intruder. Intruder." His warning ricocheted off the glass cabinet doors, loud enough to make the crockery within rattle.

"Where? Who?" Harper tried to catch the buzzing demon, but her hand passed right through him.

"Hi, umm, Heresy let me in," a polite voice said from the doorway. Heresy's alarm shut off as he settled on Harper's head like a burnt halo.

"Who are you?" Grace growled.

"He's my tech guy." Saqib's brow furrowed. "The one who watched the paper shop for us. What are you doing—"

"He's the guy who confronted me in the cathedral this afternoon." Harper finally managed to swat Heresy away. "You're supposed to guard the door, not let intruders in."

"I guard the door from magical attacks," Heresy said primly. "Not people who walk in because *someone* forgot to lock it behind her."

Harper sighed and gestured the bemused newcomer to a seat. "You may as well sit down and explain yourself. Unless you've changed your mind and decided to kill me after all."

Chapter Thirty-Three

"He would have to kill me first," Grace glowered. The self-proclaimed techno-witch gulped and took a chair next to Saqib. Heresy floated to the floor and slithered under the table to lurk in its shadow.

"Harper?" Grace asked, the edge to her voice sharper than a knife.

"I don't think he's going to hurt us," Harper said. "If he was going to, he would have done it when I was alone."

"You could've taken him, Harp." Grace smirked as her gaze roved over the man's thin frame. Her lip curled in contempt.

"I'm not so stupid as to attack her head on," the stranger replied. "I don't do fieldwork. I definitely don't do fighting. That's not why I'm here."

He was meant to be there, in their kitchen, in their house. Almost like déjà vu, it was the same as the feeling she got when they first came to the house and when they met Saqib. It hadn't been there in the cathedral, but it was present now, stronger than ever before.

"What's your name?" she asked.

"AJ," Saqib said before the intruder could answer. His arms were crossed over his chest, and he leant away from the other man as he glared at him. "He/him. Assuming you gave me your real name."

Heresy snickered and AJ tried to stomp on him. "His name," Heresy chuckled, "is Alastair Jeremiah Maximillian Kingston Taylor the Third." Grace snorted.

"AJ it is then," Harper said, before Grace could recover enough to give a more candid response.

"Who are you really?" Saqib asked.

"And why are you here?" Harper added.

"I really am a tech guy. Sorry, Saqib, my coven asked me to keep an eye on you to make sure your research didn't become a threat. So, I found an IT request you raised and pretended I was a contractor for the police. As to why I'm here, after I left Harper this afternoon, I kept thinking about what she said. How we're responsible because we know what's going on and aren't doing anything. I've walked down the Shambles a hundred times. I've been to that chocolate shop. They were normal people and they died to keep us safe. That's not right."

"What about the rest of this coven?" Grace asked suspiciously.

"They're on the fence," AJ admitted. "Some want to stop it. Others think we benefit more than we lose out. They're being selfish. Our coven has survived for five hundred years by only looking out for ourselves. We can't do that. Even when we passively let things happen, blood is on our hands."

"I don't trust you," Grace said, unnecessarily, in Harper's opinion.

"From what Harper said, we might need him," Saqib pointed out, and Harper said a prayer of thanks for cooler heads. Saqib jabbed a finger at AJ's chest. "Although, at some point, you and I are having a chat about how you've screwed up my equipment to stop me detecting your magic."

AJ raised an eyebrow. "I did nothing of the sort. You're miles off."

Saqib's face fell, and Harper gave him a pat on the shoulder. "You found the runes on the bodies. None of us would be here if you hadn't worked that out."

He gave her a thin smile. "So, my science isn't good enough, yet, and Harper's magic failed to trap it before. What do we do? We need to find the Ouse if we're going to talk her down and we need an alternative to offer her."

"You will need a way to lure her out," AJ said. "Then you need to trap her long enough to listen. She's powerful. She could kill all of us if she wanted to."

"How did you trap Heresy?" Harper asked.

"It's not like a net you can throw over her, she has to step in the circle. A physical circle will work differently to what I do, but the theory should be the same."

"'*Should* be the same'?" Grace said.

"Hey, I'm trying to help here," AJ protested. "I don't deal with physical magics. Tech only. If you've got a better option, go ask them."

Grace glared at him and Saqib kicked her under the table.

"We'll take any help we can get," he said.

"If you can show me what you did to Heresy, maybe he and I can work out how to make it work in the physical world," Harper added. "There might be something else you can help with too."

"What's that?"

"Have you ever heard of 'the Magician'?"

"Only enough to know you should avoid zir at all costs," AJ answered. "You have reason to think ze might interfere?"

"I don't know," Harper said. "It was implied ze could hide my magic. I thought maybe ze could help to protect the innocent supernaturals without the Hiding."

"I don't think so," Grace said. "If ze was willing to do that, ze would've stopped things like that auction." A shadow flitted across her face. Harper knew her sister well enough to see the pain behind her tightened jaw and unblinking stare.

She placed a hand on Grace's arm. "We know how to find those now. Next time, *we'll* be there to stop it. If I can learn more magic, then surely between us all we can find a way." She turned back to AJ. "How do you hide your magic?"

"By being careful," AJ said. "Everything comes at a price. With the Magician that price can be steep. I don't know if ze's involved in the Hiding. Who does it, and where, changes every time. The Magician might be in favour. Ze might be against it. I don't recommend asking."

"What do you know about the ritual?" Saqib asked.

"Not much. We know it needs topping up every so often, but we don't know what triggers it or how they decide who does it. There are very few known occurrences. The only reason we know this is a Hiding is because of chatter on the dark net. We didn't have that until the 1980s, and it took a while for us to be good at using it."

"It's something to do with a new moon and a member of the royal family dying." Harper said.

"That doesn't make sense. How could they predict ..." AJ frowned. He extracted a thin laptop from his rucksack. It came to life instantly when he opened it. He typed furiously while Harper, Grace, and Saqib looked at each other, bewildered.

"Care to explain, mate?" Saqib asked casually, after no sound but the click of keys for five minutes.

"Using royalty to provide body parts would make sense," AJ said. His typing didn't slow. "They do represent the country and lores of affinity means what happens to them can affect everyone."

"Whoa, whoa," Saqib interrupted. "You're losing us. What 'laws of affinity.' Does it work like—"

"Lores," AJ corrected. "But that's not what's happening. It isn't people with royal blood being killed, unless it's extraordinarily thin royal blood. Royals rarely come to York. None are expected to visit this year, let alone this month. With everything going on, there's no way a member of the royal family will set foot within a hundred miles of York. Also, the murders don't coincide with the new moon, it's still over two weeks away."

"I don't think she lied to me," Harper said. "Everything I've read says they rarely lie."

AJ snorted. "Everything you've *read*? Anyway. It's not important. Here." He turned the computer screen around so the other three could see to show them a complex web of interlocking circles and lines over a map of England.

"Ley lines?" Saqib asked. "I've tried to use my detection equipment at places reported to be on ley lines and never found anything."

"You won't," AJ said.

"Because my equipment is bad or—"

"Not now," Harper interrupted. "What are we looking at, AJ?"

"This is the map of England after the Hiding 126 years ago. As you can see, the perception filter from the Hiding has overwhelmed almost all other magic. It took us a decade to recover even half of our strength. Now, we always thought they left it a bit late at the time, some of the coven's best casting happened in the year or so leading up to that Hiding. There was another one around fifty years ago. Magic this strong should last at least a century, if not more."

"That means they're getting closer together," Saqib said. "Maybe the magic isn't as strong as it used to be."

"Or the fae woman lied to Harper about the timing," Grace said crossly. "Or Harper misinterpreted it. Or this coven missed more than they thought. Maybe they're the ones weakening it with their outside magic. It could even be the ritual can be performed at any time, but some situations make it stronger, like the auction being at midnight. You are meddling in things that defy logic and science, things that are dangerous. You don't know what you're doing."

"We're trying to learn, Gray." Harper laid a hand on her sister's arm.

"This is pointless." Grace threw her off and stalked over to the back window. As she looked out over the still misty garden she added, "We know who it is. We stop them. You can waste time on academic questions like why it's happening afterwards."

"She has a point," Harper conceded. "Finding out there might be a flaw with the magic is interesting but it doesn't help us stop the Ouse from killing anyone else. AJ, can you show me how you trapped Heresy? Heresy, you'll help AJ and me with the magic. You hide me and this house, try and think about how to scale that up a lot. Saqib, your lights helped me See her before, you'll need to make sure your equipment is ready. Grace, you're in charge of armoury in case anything goes wrong. I don't want to kill her, but I won't let her kill any of you.

"If I can persuade her that we can help the supernaturals, maybe she'll realise she doesn't need to kill. She didn't believe me before. If I can contain her, I'll have time to convince her. But even if she doesn't believe me, we can imprison her and stop the killing. We can help those hunted by humans and those hunted by their own kind, like at the auction. We can still help humans hunted by supes, it's in Grace's DNA after all. We won't let York become like Chester. No matter what happens, we vanquish the evil and help the innocent. And we will be the ones to decide which is which. Not the Council. Not the Queen's Guard. Us."

Outside, a crystalline form huddled under the window ledge out of sight. The wetness of the mist had helped Usa travel this far from herself. It was uncomfortable to be so far away. Only when she flooded did she venture so far off course.

She should take the girl's eyes. The voice of her people, always surging through her, urged her to do it. She would not fail them. She must protect them. She should kill the others as well, witnesses who would try to break the Hiding. Witnesses who threatened her kin.

She only needed three more pieces before All Hallows Eve. So little time left. She'd procrastinated too long, telling herself she was selecting the most effective victims for the ritual. Now, as she crouched in waiting, she allowed herself to think the truth. She hadn't wanted them to die.

She'd arrogantly thought she could be like the Ocean. In her long existence, Usa had taken many lives; terrified servants herded into her depths, ships from across the sea full of metal and noise, fishermen, washerwomen, children. But she had never gone to them. They always came to her. They came to her in summer for life and for fun. They sang songs of her, blessed her, and sacrificed to her. Death was as natural as life.

But not this. Now thought shaped unnatural death. Usa looked down at her hands, so like theirs. She'd done it in honour of the lives she took, but with each person she reached inside, something of them had become her.

She did not want to kill the girl.

Let the human fall into her depths and she would be nothing but a witness to death. She was not a killer. She couldn't do this. It was unnatural. It was … wrong.

Usa had never known 'wrong' before. She had never known regret. Human emotions and values she didn't understand, but which flowed from her soul, nonetheless.

"If we layered it like so, it could work." The Seer's voice. Usa knew it well. This one had bathed her feet in Usa's waters, crossed her bridges and spoken to air and water, shared Usa's delight in the rising of the sun. Usa had recognised her voice in the place that looked and smelled as Eboracum had centuries before.

"Why don't we try it on Heresy?"

The male voice that had been in the effigy of the Viking village. He boated on her when he was smaller, with a gruff human male. They'd taken sustenance from her fish. They'd killed her fish. Usa tried to want him dead, but she'd never wanted to kill anyone. Animals eating other animals was natural. There was no violation in humans eating her fish.

"I think not." A haughty voice she also recognised. One of the Folk. She hadn't known him before and she knew all who dwelt along her banks. This one arrived recently from another realm. He had been immersed in her by the human male, a strange sensation. She'd wished to take him with her, but he was bound to the Seer.

"C'mon Heresy, we need to try it on someone. We'll let you straight out." The Seer again.

"We still need a way to lure the Ouse into it, unless you're going to draw circles all the way down the riverbank." The other female. The one who would have killed Usa before. She was only defending her own. Defending one whose life it was unnatural for Usa to take.

"If we can get her on the wall, that would be best." A new male voice. She hadn't recognised him when she spied him under the bridge, but she recalled him now. He'd never entered her, running close to her edge when small, then being herded away by women with high-pitched voices. As he grew older, she saw him less and less, until one day he left and never returned.

"Why is the wall best?" the first male asked.

"There are already bindings on the wall to keep supernaturals from passing them. It's similar to how the Veil was strengthened."

"They don't seem to work," the second female said.

Usa knew of what they spoke. The wards were stronger at night, she could sense them where she flowed near the city wall. Many of the Folk slipped in and out of the city via her waters to avoid those wards after dark. There was power there still. Maybe even enough to stop her.

"They work, just not as effectively as they once did." The second male again. "It should amplify Harper's spell, at least as I understand these things."

"I feel so comforted."

"We have to try, Gray. The river can't be happy we know what she's doing. She'll come after us at some point, probably a little after sunset, judging by her previous behaviour. If we pick a bit of wall near the water, maybe we can lure her there. Especially if it looks like I'm alone."

"Harper, that's a terrible idea."

"You can't do that. She broke out of your circle at the Jorvik Centre."

"This is stronger. This might work." The Seer, Harper, sounded so sure.

Usa could not stop the Hiding ritual. She was compelled to complete it. The others wouldn't let her withdraw. Her oath to them was like a dam holding her captive. Ripples ran across her surface. The voices of her folk still called to her, but the death pleas of her victims sang within her too.

With a splash, Usa disintegrated into water, sunk into the ground, and wended her way back to her true self.

Chapter Thirty-Four

Overhead, the waxing gibbous moon swam in a sea of sparkling stars. Around it, wisps of cirrostratus clouds draped across the sky like hair floating through water. The mouth of the moon formed an 'O,' singing a song not meant for human ears. The sun had long since set, stealing the colour from the sky, leaving only an inky blackness.

Standing on the ancient wall protecting York, Harper felt at peace. The light of the moon and stars alleviated her fears. In her mind, the image of snow-laden conifers overlaid the cityscape before her, yet there was none of the terror she'd come to associate with the scene. She accepted it. It was an unexplained part of herself, but these last few weeks, she was getting closer to an answer. To find the truth, she would need to face the darkness.

Mist tumbled over the wall and cascaded down to the riverbank. It floated, ethereal, over the water. Twinkling lights danced within it, and one solitary orb, immobile, hovered above the surface of the river. The dull, yellowed streetlights were dim in comparison. It was a false path, a masquerading lighthouse to lure the unwary. A will-o'-the-wisp maybe, or her fear making her see fae where none existed.

The scuff of boots on stone filtered through the night. Two lights bobbed atop Lendal Tower, scarcely visible on the other side of the river through the haze. Harper held her breath. For her, this was the most dangerous part of the plan, not confronting the Ouse. Although she couldn't see her sister, Grace would be at the base of the tower by now.

It had taken a great deal of arguing before Grace had consented to sneak into Lendal Tower with Heresy so the spirit could cast an illusion over the people standing guard. He'd promised it was a simple spell to trick their senses into perceiving nothing, like looping a CCTV tape. The only problem was, he had to be close to do it, so someone had to take him, someone who could defend herself if she got caught. Allowing a 'demon' to cast a spell on other humans, even Queen's Guard, had left Grace bitter and irritated.

Harper watched the tower, praying the Guard wouldn't turn at the last minute and see her sister's approach. As always, Harper had given her undefeatable argument and Grace had acquiesced: cursing the Guard kept Harper safe. It would allow her to confront the Ouse without fear of the Guard killing them both, and maybe even allow her to persuade the river to stop slaughtering innocents.

"They're down." Saqib's machines picked up Grace's flash of ultraviolet, invisible light to signify she and Heresy had nullified the Guards. All four of the humans had left their phones at the house to avoid being traced or pinpointed at the location, so they would hear nothing more from Grace until she rejoined them. Harper hoped it would all be over by then.

"I'll go wait." Saqib reached over and squeezed Harper's shoulder, before heading back toward the house. He hopped down from the wall and walked along its base, concealed in shadows.

Harper had braved the water's edge an hour previously to toss a note in. She hoped the river wouldn't see it as littering and hold it against her. Or maybe she should hope the river was annoyed and would come after her. She fidgeted with the end of her hair, rolling it between her fingers, and shifted her weight from foot to foot.

The scene had a macabre symmetry. On the other side of Lendal Bridge was the last place the ghostwalker was seen alive. To catch his murderer here seemed appropriate, like a story. Harper had seen it countless times in books, factual ones in the archives describing supernatural events. They twisted reality, made everyday occurrences more surreal and implausible by turning them into a story despite logic or intention. She wondered whose story this was: hers or the Ouse's.

"You are a long way from home, Seer. Why do you summon me?"

Harper spun around at the voice, heart in her throat. Behind her stood the translucent woman from the park. Her form was vague, barely discernible in the night, but the weight of her presence almost smothered Harper. It was a powerful aura she didn't sense from the river itself, as though somehow the spirit had separated herself from its flow.

Taking a deep breath, Harper replied, "I have come to talk to you."

As she spoke, she raised a hand to touch the corner of her eye as though wiping away a tear. At Harper's signal, Saqib's lights flooded the area. The ultraviolet refracted within the Ouse's watery form. The others would not be able to see the undine, but to Harper's Sight she shone brighter than the moon. They studied each other in silence, neither moving.

The Ouse wore no clothes or coverings of any kind, her body smooth as a doll's. Water rippled within her body. Her fingers were small and delicate. She stood slightly raised on her toes, each digit barely marked from the next. Only her face was clear, so detailed Harper could see eyelashes framing unblinking eyes. Her lips were the same murky blue as the rest of her body. Her hair, motionless like marble, clung to her head in a pixie cut. The Ouse tilted her head to the side, her lack of irises making it impossible to tell where she looked.

"What is it you wish to say?" The river's voice crashed and flowed, water rapids tumbling over rocks. It sparkled with captured sunlight, strong and steady as the broad expanse of water behind them. It took Harper's breath away. The Ouse spoke again, her voice calmer, less wild. "Speak, Seer. You are not one of us, but you are not one of them. I would hear your words."

"I'm a supernatural. Like you."

Ripples ran across the woman's surface. "I am as natural as any human. Born of this earth and this sky. I was here before your people came to this land and I will remain long after their songs are nothing but whispers on the wind."

"I'm sorry, I didn't mean to offend you." Harper grimaced. This was not going as she planned. "What do you call yourselves? What should I call you?"

"We call ourselves 'the Folk,' for there are many kindreds among us," the Ouse replied. "My name has changed much over time. My kith and kin call me 'Usa.' Why did you summon me, human?"

"I know you don't want to kill people. I've been reading about you; you aren't a murderer. You've nurtured and protected the people of York and those who live alongside you. There are other ways to protect the supe ... the Folk who live here. I've come to offer an alliance. If we work together, we can help everyone; human, spirit, and fae. Please."

The undine turned her head, seeming to gaze upstream. She was perfectly motionless. No rise and fall of her chest, no twitch or fidget, weight balanced evenly. When she turned back to Harper, her eyes were darker, as though a shadow rested behind them.

"The Hiding is the only way," Usa said. "I have existed since a time beyond your ken. Humans have come and gone. But one thing is always constant: you murder. Humans from the south of Albion slaughter humans from the north. Humans in ships come across Morimaru, sailing up me with iron and anger. Metal boats glide through the heavens, spilling fire and terror. The only time you form allegiances is to destroy my kith and kin. You took our homes and exiled us, bathed us in fire and buried us in earth. The Folk do not wish to war, to kill as wantonly as humans do. We act within our nature, but you kill with evil, with malice. I thought if I killed to protect, it would be different. All we require are a few lives sacrificed to save thousands. Is that not a mercy, in the end?"

"Not all humans are like that," Harper said.

"If they caught you, they would kill you too."

"Then let us work together," Harper pleaded. "Please, Usa. We both want to protect. We don't need to sacrifice any lives."

The Ouse laughed, the spray of a water fountain as it drops into a pool. "And you believe your army of five can do this? Two witchlings, a demonhunter, a deception demon, and an ordinary human? You believe you can protect all of Albion."

"With your help and the help of other Folk. We'll find more humans too, others out there who are like us. We can be on the same side."

"And if I say 'no'?"

"Then we'll stop you and do it anyway." Harper balled her fists in the ends of her sleeves to keep them from shaking. *What something is, is less important than what it seems to be.* Heresy's words echoed in her mind. No matter what she felt inside, she must appear resolute, undaunted. She must appear powerful. Harper squared her shoulders and took a step forward as she held one hand out to Usa. "This is your last chance. Take my hand in friendship or be destroyed."

A smile cracked the undine's lips like fractured ice. "It is not your hand I need, Seer."

The river lunged forward. Harper ducked under the Ouse's outstretched hand, grazing her arm on the rough stone wall. She gasped in pain, eyes watering, as her movement tore the wound on her shoulder. Hugging the wall, she stumbled to a run. The slap of water pursued her as the river gave chase. She raced up the slope, ultraviolet lamps flashing past, until she reached an area where the wall was no longer surrounded by roads and grassy slopes stretched on either side.

Harper skidded to a halt and turned to face her pursuer. She clutched her shoulder, bent over as she struggled for breath through heavy lungs. The river stood before her, serene as though she had simply appeared there.

"If you want to kill me, you'll have to be faster than that," Harper taunted.

The undine cocked her head, the shadows in her eyes dark as the depths of the sea. "If you want to protect people, then aid me. Give me your eyes, Seer. It is the best defence you can give the Folk, both here in the place your people name York and throughout this land."

The river took a step forward. Gritting her teeth, Harper drew her athame from her belt and sliced the cold steel across the pad of her finger in one fluid motion. When Usa took another step closer, Harper knelt and dragged the bleeding digit across the uneven stone walkway of the wall. Her other fingers smarted from where she cut them to start the circle earlier. All that remained now was to close it.

Her eyes burned hotter than the hell from her vision. Lights danced around her, blue and silver, water and moon. Energy and air were ripped from her body as she completed the containment circle with her blood.

Light flared, brighter than the circle in the Jorvik Centre. Harper fell back, shielding her eyes behind her arm, but her Sight Saw through her flesh. The Ouse stopped, caught in the trap. Her eyes were wide, her lips parted. Ice blossomed across her torso. Tendrils stretched over her shoulders and stomach, mirroring the freeze the Ouse had put on Harper in the Tower Street Gardens, the first time they'd met. Harper hadn't intended the spell to freeze the spirit so literally. *I hope my words aren't as clumsy as my magic. I hope I can follow through on my promise to protect people.* She swallowed hard, steeled herself. *Grace will succeed even if I fail.*

As the light lessened, Harper inched closer to the edge of the circle, eye to eye with the Ouse again. In the distance, the main body of water flowed, unaffected by Harper's magic or the turmoil of the spirit bound to it.

The undine raised a hand toward Harper, palm up. Swirling pools of crimson on her fingertips spiralled outwards until her whole hand was stained.

"Blood has always been within me." Usa spoke so softly Harper could barely hear her. "It washes up on the shore or out to sea. Not this blood. This blood stays within me. It stains me."

"You don't have to kill anyone else." Harper wanted to take the woman's hand, to comfort her. Instead, she took a step back and clasped her hands safely behind her back. She must not breach the circle, no matter what the Ouse said or did. No matter how sorry she was for her.

"I do." The river's voice rose with the wind. The ripples across her surface crashed together like waves in a storm. With every second she looked less human but sounded so much more human.

"It's not too late," Harper said. "We can still help you."

"You? You cannot help me." There was derision in the river's tone, but also a twinge of hope.

"I swear to you, I will do everything in my power to keep your Folk safe so long as they threaten no more lives." No sooner had the promise left her lips then something snapped around Harper's neck, her wrists, her ankles, heavy, dragging her down. She doubled over as the air was wrenched from her lungs, then dropped to her knees, bone cracking against cold stone.

The undine's hand pressed against the barrier of light, bending it, but unable to break it. Her movements were slower now, jolting and stiff. The ice patterns stretched down over her breast and almost to her elbows.

"I accept your oath, Seer of the Dales, Seer of York."

"Why do you call me that?" Harper clutched her throbbing chest as she gazed up at the Ouse.

"Your people travelled along my banks until the place where my sister merges with me, the one you call Swale. Your people were one with the Folk and we marked where they trod. They lived on her banks, ate her fish, and sang merry tunes to her. Sometimes they would vanish for a time, but they always returned. Until the time of blood. That time humans call the Purge. Then your kin, the Sighted ones, disappeared from my ken. An ancient one came from across the sea and swathed them in shadow. Until you, we only encountered your kin twice more. I heard one cry as she flew from the stone pinnacle and Eboracum was bathed in her blood. I heard a second sing as his fingers danced on the strings, then he vanished in the mists.

"Then you appeared. You played on Swale's banks as a child." An almost nostalgic smile touched the Ouse's cold lips. "You and your brother built dams in her tributaries where they cascade down the Dales. By the light of the moon you came, when the nights were long. When she was calm, you cast magic on her surface and watched distant lands. Then winter came and you did not. She knew then that the ancient one who polluted the dreams of my folk had taken you, as he took your mother, your grandmother, and all the she-folk of your blood since he came to our shores."

"What ancient one? Came from where?" Harper staggered to her feet.

The ice reached the Ouse's hands. The blood within them paled to the soft pink of roses. Harper stood, her toes millimetres from the edge of the blood circle. She stared, mesmerised, into the river's eyes. The ice consumed the river's legs, jagged scars like icicles.

"Please, we can stop this. Let me help you," Harper begged. "I will protect your folk. If you show me how to reach my family, I will confront this creature who threatens them and you. Please, at least tell me where to go and what it is."

"Her tributaries there are like the veins of a leaf. I do not know from which you came, only that it was to her south, where the land is broad and sweeps to great heights. It is a place you should not go. Your blood is there, but he is stronger. Even the Magician does not tread his domain. You cannot overcome the son of a god, not even one of dreams."

Ice clawed up the undine's throat, hardening, taking her voice as she had stolen the ghostwalker's. It glistened, razor sharp as it consumed her chin, snaked toward her lips.

"Please." Harper's voice came out a whisper. "Help me."

The Ouse's lips moved one last time, barely disturbing the air. No sound escaped, but Harper heard the voice of the river deep in her soul, cascading and magnificent.

"Protect my folk, Seer of York."

The undine's face was frozen, an ice sculpture. The water within her stilled, yet deep within her eyes, a last glimmer of movement flickered.

As the ice devoured the last of the river's body, a deep rumble started beneath their feet, a living roar coming through the stone of the wall itself. As the ground quaked, the light from Harper's circle grew brighter. It seared her eyes closed. Blinded, she lost her footing on the shuddering stone, and fell.

The impact on the turf below knocked the air from her. She instinctively curled away from the brilliant light, her arms tight around her head as she lay on the grass. She could hear seagulls squalling, the screams of children, a mournful tune with no words. Everything hurt, sharp pain in her hand and shoulder, deep aching in every muscle and bone. Grief consumed her, stronger than anything she had ever experienced. It was a sorrow of ages. It broke her into thousands of pieces.

Harper was dimly aware of the warmth of Grace's hand on her shoulder. She could barely make out her sister's voice calling her name.

A loud crack rent the air, flashing through Harper's body like a lightning strike. She leapt to her feet and dashed up the bank to the wall.

Grace tackled her, her arms around Harper's waist as they tumbled to the ground. Harper kicked and flailed but Grace's grip was unrelenting.

"Harper, stop." Another pair of hands seized Harper's shoulders as Saqib also tried to hold her back.

"She's not evil, Gray. My spell is killing her," Harper gasped. "I have to save her."

Another spear of pain took the last of Harper's strength, and all three of them tumbled to the grass. The light on the wall faded and the overwhelming grief receded, leaving cold numbness in Harper's chest.

The frozen statue of the river gleamed under Saqib's lights. The Ouse was covered in tiny fissures. One arm had already fallen away. A large fracture split one leg.

"She's cracking," Saqib said in amazement. "Like some old Greek statue unable to support the weight of its own limbs."

"We have to do something," Harper said. "The circle was supposed to trap her, not freeze her."

"It is too late." Heresy's smooth voice was too calm. He flowed off Saqib's shoulder to settle around Harper's neck.

Grace squeezed Harper's hand. "You offered her a chance of redemption. She spurned it. She could've stopped killing. Instead, she tried to kill you, too. *You* had no choice."

"There's always a choice," Harper whispered.

"Yeah, you could've chosen to let her kill you." Grace's voice took on a hard edge. "Believe me, that wasn't going to happen."

Another loud snap yanked their attention back to the wall. A large split appeared in the river's torso. This time Grace didn't stop her as Harper scrambled up the hill and dragged herself up onto the wall. She looked into the river's eyes. There was sadness there, but also acceptance.

With a final crack, the river broke in two. Pieces of her shattered as they hit the solid stone of York's wall. Soon Usa was nothing more than a pile of ice chips.

"May God grant you peace." Harper waved a hand over the circle to break the spell. She held her breath, waiting for the water spirit to reform, but the ice merely tumbled out of the circle, glittering like broken glass. Harper picked up a piece. It didn't melt, cool rather than cold, more like stone than ice. The chunk in her palm was stained pink with blood. Tears flowed freely as she stared at the fragment, her chest prickly with tight, hot guilt. It didn't feel like victory.

While Saqib dismantled his equipment, Harper and Grace carefully collected all the pieces of the Ouse in a sealed jar Saqib brought from the lab in the hopes of containing her liquid form. A version of Harper's circle was etched into the glass.

"I'll take her with me and see what I can find out." Saqib delicately stored the container in his rucksack. "Don't worry, I'll be careful. Whatever else she was, she was sentient and that deserves respect."

"Are you not forgetting something, Harper dear?" Heresy asked sweetly as they turned to leave.

Harper leant on Grace as she staggered, exhaustion crushing, from the magic and from the weight of the Ouse's death. "I don't think I'll forget this for a very long time, Heresy. I didn't want to kill her, but ... I did." The late October air made each tear cold as an icicle on her cheek. She made no move to brush them away, her arms leaden.

"The circle, Harper dearest. Or do you wish someone else to be caught in your web?"

"I'll deal with it." Saqib grabbed a bag out of Grace's rucksack and ran back to the containment circle. Pulling on a pair of rubber gloves, he poured a bleach solution over Harper's blood and scrubbed.

Harper dragged her eyes away from his bowed figure. From this distance, he looked like he was genuflecting in prayer. She wanted to pray too, to beg forgiveness, to feel justified in what she'd done. It saved lives. Even the river said it. A few lives sacrificed to save thousands. If that was okay, surely one life to save a handful was equally justifiable?

The moonlight caught the silver cross hanging around Grace's neck. Harper couldn't look at it, the guilt sour in her stomach. It reminded her that she wasn't the first one to have to choose between sacrificing one life or allowing many others to come to harm. The difference was, He sacrificed Himself. She'd killed the Ouse, although her spell hadn't been intended to. Yet, at the end, there was something in the Ouse's eyes, and Harper wondered if perhaps the river had also made the ultimate sacrifice to save those who should have been her enemies.

The moon drifted higher in the sky than Harper had seen it in a long time. Every part of her ached. An incurable, bottomless trench ruptured her chest. Was the riverbed as empty as her heart, or did water, spiritless, still flow? She couldn't face it in the darkness. Tomorrow, she would see.

"Let's get home," she said, as Saqib made his way back to them.

'You are a long way from home, Seer.' The river's words came back to her. By killing the river, she'd sacrificed a piece of herself. The Ouse had known her, known her family. Whatever had them must be the same

threat Heresy warned her of, the hunter who stalked her dreams. Her brain was sluggish and every part of her hurt. She tucked the information away, safe, to ruminate on later.

As they trudged toward their house, none of them, not even Heresy, noticed a figure, shrouded in many layers of black cloth and a deep hood. A dark hole open in the air at the bottom of the wall. Ze brushed ice crystals off zir hands and turned to the portal.

"Let's go," ze said, zir harmonic voice male and female, young and old.

Ze stepped through the portal and vanished. With a glance back over its shoulder, zir companion, a white cat, followed.

Chapter Thirty-Five

A few days later, hours after the sun had set, a light still blazed in the top windows of the cathedral's northwest belltower. Shadows flickered across the open slits as people moved within. The moan of the wind covered the sound of voices.

"You got all your stuff moved in, AJ?" Harper asked. He looked up from his laptop with a slightly dazed expression. "Your stuff? You've got everything from home and set up in the downstairs bedroom?"

"Oh yeah, sorted," AJ said. "Thanks again for giving me a place to stay. My coven wasn't exactly thrilled I helped you, although now it's happened, they aren't too torn up about the Hiding not going ahead. Apparently, once it's disrupted like this, it can't be picked up by someone else. There's some kind of tear or something."

"We didn't 'give you a place to stay.' You're paying rent. As is Saqib." Grace threw Harper a dirty look. "Can't believe I'm living with two boys. How did you square it with your coven, anyway? Didn't they object to you moving in with us?"

"Nah, I told them I could keep an eye on you better this way."

Before Grace could form a retort, Harper cut in, sorry she brought up the subject. "Are you nearly set up, Saqib?"

He scuttled around the belltower to give his equipment one last check over, then nodded. "The stuff here is great, Harper. Thanks for persuading the archbishop to let us in. If this is all equipment used to predict astronomical events, then I might be able to cross-reference and get some info on how to detect related supernatural events."

"Like tonight," Harper said. It was Hallowe'en and the second full moon of the month. Saqib had begged to be allowed to bring some equipment to the astronomy tower to observe the blue moon and see how the cathedral's equipment compared to modern day tech. He persuaded AJ to join them by asking him to compile and monitor data on his laptop. Harper joined them out of academic curiosity and the archbishop's insistence they be supervised. Heresy stayed home to guard the house, and Grace … well, Harper wasn't quite sure why her sister was there.

Grace gazed out the window at the square in front of the cathedral. It was the same window from which Harper had almost fallen. While Saqib and AJ put the finishing touches on their setup, Harper joined her sister. Her stomach flipped as she leant over the ledge. "What'cha lookin' at?"

"Nothing," Grace said. "Absolutely nothing. It's been almost a week and nothing's changed. I know AJ said it wouldn't happen overnight, that the last Hiding would slowly wear off over a few months, but I expected something … more. Tomorrow, Godfather and the Council will sanctify the river and then it will be like none of this ever happened. He didn't even believe us about the Ouse hiding other supes, said it was impossible." Grace's knuckles were white against the sandstone window ledge she gripped.

"He knows something." Harper placed a hand over her sister's. "Those people the Guard took still haven't been returned. I know your godfather is working around the clock to get them back. If they accepted the Council's explanation for what happened, shouldn't those people have been released? And the things I saw in the Twelfth Vault. Gray, there's magic there. Everybody is keeping secrets; the Church and Council, the Guard, us. There must be a way to create trust. They can't all be evil, right?"

Harper waved out the window. Below, notable only by the disturbance their passing left in the mist, two people in tan trench coats marched in sync. They strode down the road opposite the cathedral and disappeared into the night as their rounds took them toward the Ouse. "Some must have gotten into it for the same reasons your family did; to protect people. It's their paranoia that makes them see everything even slightly otherworldly as irredeemably tainted."

"I don't know, Harp. Anyone who takes people from their beds and bundles them into unmarked vans with a sack over their head has crossed a line."

"It's not going to happen overnight," Harper said. "We start closer to home. Find out what the Church really knows. You work on your godfather, express an interest in the family business, see what he tells you. Write to Gabriel and Miguel as well, especially with Gabriel being in Venice. I'll work on Alfred. He almost told me about the Hiding before. If I'm obviously more involved with De Santos stuff, I can use that to get more hints from him."

"Will they buy it?" Grace studied Harper in the half light of the moon. "If they get even a little suspicious of you—"

"They won't." Harper's heart thrummed with fear, with hope. They didn't destroy all magic. She didn't want to be chained deep in the archives like the book about the Hiding, but its existence gave a glimmer of possibility. For over a decade, Grace's kin had been her kin. She'd been cared for and employed by the archbishop and the Church. Whatever else she believed, they were family. "They'll be happy we're joining them and we have more reason to than ever after an incursion right on our doorstep."

"And fears of more to come." Grace sighed, her shoulders slumping. "I expected supernaturals to be pouring through the streets by now, causing havoc, people dying, but nothing's changed."

"Maybe they aren't as evil as people think. Remember those poor souls at the auction. They were as much a victim as anyone else. We're fighting for them, too. Maybe most supernaturals are just scared."

"More scared of us than we are of them?"

"I think we're all terrified of each other. People on both sides die because we don't understand and we don't try. It happens time and time again. Humans destroy that which they perceive as 'different.' The Ouse was right. Her people aren't *super*natural. They're as natural as I am. As you are, or Saqib, or your father. They come from this side of the Veil. There isn't an 'us' and a 'them.' We don't have to let fear win. That's what we used to do; your family, Archbishop Marshall, and me too. I won't do it anymore. I'll fight, yes, but I'm fighting fear."

"I'm fighting for life," Grace said, her eyes tight with determination.

"For life," Harper echoed. It was a promise to the city spread out before them. A promise to God.

"We're ready," Saqib called across the room.

Harper nodded in his direction, her mouth quirking into a smile as Grace sighed.

The full moon hung heavy in a sky half obscured by cloud. A faint orangey-red tinge dyed its surface.

"Why is it like that?" Harper asked. "I've seen it before, on rare occasions, but I always forget to look it up later."

"It's caused by a lunar eclipse," Saqib answered. He twiddled a dial on some kind of telescope to adjust the angle. "The earth is currently between the sun and the moon, so it absorbs most of the light. Because of the colour, it's sometimes called a blood …"

He stared at the sky, mouth agape.

"A blood?" Harper asked.

Saqib slapped his forehead. "We're idiots. The moon being hidden didn't mean a new moon; it meant a lunar eclipse. The moon is hidden from the sun. It's called a blood moon. 'A royal dies.' What do we call royalty?"

"Er, your majesty?" Harper guessed.

"Waste of perfectly good oxygen," Grace suggested.

"Blue bloods," AJ said, without looking up from his computer.

"Exactly." Saqib snapped his fingers. "'When a royal dies and the moon is hidden …'"

"A blue blood moon," Harper exclaimed. "This is the second full moon of October and a lunar eclipse."

"And Hallowe'en," Grace added.

"It must be the most powerful night of the year," Saqib said excitedly. "I've *got* to record this."

"You know, if you do get some good data tonight, it will be our first positive act to protect people; human and supes." Saying it eased Harper's heartache. It was good to have a group to belong to. Friends to watch each other's backs.

"Two witches, a demonhunter, a demon, and a scientist walk into a kitchen. Wow we sound like a joke," Saqib said.

"Good," Grace said. "It will keep us safe."

"And we, in turn, can keep everyone else safe," Harper added.

She watched her three friends, two new and one who had always been at her side. The two men excitedly jabbered in tech talk with their heads bent over the laptop. Grace eyed the telescope in what she probably thought was a nonchalant manner, but Harper knew her better.

I'll keep them safe, too. More supernaturals will come out of hiding. There will be danger, on both sides, because of us. I gave the Ouse my word. I will protect them. And I'll find my family. The Swale knows where they are. Without the Hiding, my magic might be strong enough to find the way home.

Outside, the blood moon floated over York, bathing its ginnels and snickelways in rusty light. It hung as a warning to those living below and a beacon for creatures lurking in the shadows. It could see what the humans in the belltower could not. The mists were rising, and with them came death.

Acknowledgements

My most heartfelt thanks to my husband, Chris. You read this story from its earliest draft, and walked the streets of York with me while I chattered endlessly about Harper and the gang. You believed in me when I couldn't. This story wouldn't exist without you. Thank you. I love you.

To Marmee and Dad, I am eternally grateful for all you've done for me. You taught me the joy of books. Thank you for your belief, your pride, and your encouragement. Thank you for all the stories you gifted me. I am honoured to be the child of such creative people.

Also thanks to my sister, Chloe, who always supports me, in all parts of my life.

This book would not be what it is today without the input of my beta readers, friends, and writing support groups. First and foremost, I want to thank my Writing Coven, a group of amazingly accomplished writers who I am blessed to count as friends—Taylor Grothe, Amanda Casile, Jessica Mitacek, Rae Knowles, and Tanya Pell. This book and my life would be poorer without your critiquing and cheerleading. Thanks also to Team Tea and Books, the Spaghetti Throwers, Shereen, Nemo, J. Palmer, Keira, J. Patricia Anderson, Helen, Laura, Ed Crocker, Inez Rodk, Treena McCabe, and many others.

Many thanks to my publishers, Heather and Steve, for loving my book enough to put it out there in the world. Likewise thank you to MJ Pankey, my editor, Stephanie Ellis, for proofreading and formatting, and Mire Marke, my sensitivity reader. All your inputs have been invaluable. Thanks to Elizabeth Leggett for the gorgeous cover that brings The Shambles of Harper's York to life. Also to Sarah Fletcher who provided photos of York when I discovered my computer had deleted a few of mine.

And finally, thanks to my son, Sprite, for napping consistently enough for me to finish this book. Your smile is my joy.

About the Author

Alethea (she/ze) writes various forms of SFF, with a particular love for science-fantasy, dark fantasy, dystopias, and folklore. Many of her works take place at the intersection between technology and magic. She enjoys writing stories with subtle political and philosophical messages, but primarily wants her stories to be great tales with characters readers will love. She also has soft spots for found family, hopeless romances, and non-human characters. Her short stories can be found in a variety of publications, and links for these are on her website.

Alethea lives in Manchester, UK with her husband, little Sprite, a cacophony of stringed instruments, and more tea than she can drink in a lifetime.

Bonus content for *The Hiding* & other works can be found on her website: https://alethealyons.wixsite.com/stories/seerofyork

Social media: https://linktr.ee/alethearlyons

Content Warnings

Blood (minor)
Bodies/corpses
Death/dying
Hospitalisation
Murder
Needles
Spiders
Violence
Weapons
An animatronic mother & baby are described as though the child is dead
Religion
Sentient non-humans captured for sale
Memories/dreams of a child stolen from her home

MORE FROM BRIGIDS GATE PRESS

If you enjoyed this novel, watch for *Reawakening* in September 2024, and *The Somnia* in March of 2025

The Wolf and the Favour

By Catherine McCarthy

Ten-year-old Hannah has Down syndrome and oodles of courage, but should she trust the alluring tree creature who smells of Mamma's perfume or the blue-eyed wolf who warns her not to enter the woods under any circumstance?

The Wolf and the Favour is a tale of love, trust, and courage. A tale that champions the neurodivergent voice and proves the true power of a person's strength lies within themselves.

SHADOW OF THE HIDDEN

By Kev Harrison

It's Seb's last day working in Turkey, but his friend Oz has been cursed. Superstition turns to terror as the effects of the ancient malediction spill over and the lives of Oz and his family hang in the balance. Can Seb find the answers to remove the hex before it's too late?

From Kev Harrison, author of *The Balance* and *Below*, journey with Seb, Oz and Deniz across ancient North African cities as they seek to banish the *Shadow of the Hidden*.

MELINDA WEST: MONSTER GUNSLINGER

By KC Grifant

KC Grifant comes out guns blazing with *Melinda West: Monster Gunslinger*—a devious action-packed adventure set in a very weird version of the Old West. Fast, furious, and a hell of a lot of fun!"—Jonathan Maberry, NY Times bestselling author of *Son of the Poison Rose* and *Relentless*

In an Old West overrun by monsters, a stoic gunslinger must embark on a dangerous quest to save her friends and stop a supernatural war.

Sharpshooter Melinda West, 29, has encountered more than her share of supernatural creatures after a monster infection killed her mother. Now, Melinda and her charismatic partner, Lance, offer their exterminating services to desperate towns, fighting everything from giant flying scorpions to psychic bugs. But when they accidentally release a demon, they must track a dangerous outlaw across treacherous lands and battle a menagerie of creatures—all before an army of soul-devouring monsters descend on Earth.

Supernatural meets *Bonnie and Clyde* in a re-imagined Old West full of diverse characters, desolate landscapes, and fast-paced adventure.

SEERS AND SIBYLS

Ed. MJ Pankey

Oracles.
Prophets.
Sibyls.
Seers.
Fortune tellers.

These, and many other names were given to those who had the sight, who could look into the future and see what awaits us. Sometimes, those glimpses come unbidden and unasked for. Sometimes they are given for a fee. Sometimes they drive the recipient mad with the knowledge of what the future holds.

Others view those so gifted with suspicion, doubt, envy, and occasionally anger. Rarely are prophets thanked for their predictions. They bear the curse of knowing what's coming along with the scorn and fear shown them by the rest of society.

Seers and Sibyls is a collection of 30 stories and poems about those who have the power to see the future. Will you open the book and read their prophecies?

More From Brigids Gate Press

Featuring the stories and poems of: David Marino, Beth O'Brien, Victoria Brun, Rose Strickman, Zachary Rosenberg, Erin L. Swann, Nico Penaranda, A.L. Munson, Caroline Johnson, Marshall John Moore, N.R. Lambert, Susan Jordan, Jeremy Megargee, Nwejesu Ekpenisi, Jennifer Bushroe, Laura Marden, Joseph Mathias, Stephanie Ellis, Bettina Theissen, Misty Urban, Gerri Leen, Kayla Whittle, Ivy L. James, Matthew Yap, Cormack Baldwin, Shannon Connor Winward, Jacqueline Kate Goldblatt, Devan Barlow, Jay McKenzie, Sam Muller.

Visit our website at: www.brigidsgatepress.com

Made in the USA
Monee, IL
22 March 2025